To

From

The Bond Woman

An Amish Woman's Love for a Man on "The Outside"

You are going to love them. JD.

A Novel

♥

Janice Dembosky

Janice Dembosky

The characters and events portrayed in this book are fictitious. Any similarity in names or in any other way to real persons, living or dead, is coincidental and not intended by the author. Though Amish customs have been researched for this project, the Amish community depicted in this novel is fictitious, an invention of the author's imagination.

Dedication

This book is dedicated to my mother,
Anna R. Socol Bonacci
who was my first encourager and editor.

"Wherefore she said unto Abraham, 'Cast out this bondwoman and her son . . . .'" – Genesis 21:1

BOOK ONE

THE BOND WOMAN

PROLOGUE

Hannah stood motionless beside the kneeling boy. In the stifling heat of the crowded room, she would not move to wipe the perspiration tickling her upper lip, lest they think she wept like the boy who sobbed beside her. She could feel the weight of her parents' eyes on her rigid back, silently willing her, beseeching her, to kneel and confess her sin. The piercing black eyes of the Amish bishop penetrated to her soul as he waited for her to bend.

The only other sound in the white-washed room was the flies, droning their mourning song above a long, sticky, curling trap. Held fast, the black bodies of those who had not escaped struggled and died. Hannah wanted to lift her eyes and her voice to warn the blue-black flies bumping against the sunny white ceiling, but she could not, would not, let go of her stony stare into the sunken black pits that were the eyes of the bishop.

She heard the piteous weeping of the women on the benches behind her and to her left, her mother's wailing voice among them. "Weep not for me, daughters of Jerusalem . . . ." Hannah repeated the verse over and over in her mind.

Chapter One

On the day of her undoing, Hannah Miller saw no warning sign as she stood at her bedroom window watching the break of day. No red banner of foreboding streaked the whitening morning sky as it silently spread over the stirring Amish settlement in the farmlands of Pennsylvania. There was no danger note in the chorus of the roosters or in the lowing of the cattle moving restlessly in their stalls. No whip-poor-will prophesied Hannah's fall from grace.

At four o'clock, long before the uppermost branches of tall pines had begun to reveal the new day like pale skin through black lace, she had awakened and lay listening to her father and brother plod down the narrow staircase as they made their way by lantern-light to the barn for early-morning milking.

Though seventeen-year-old Hannah had an hour more to sleep, she was wakeful, sensing that there was something special about this day. She lay searching her mind until she remembered, and then she smiled.

She had flung aside the crumpled bed clothes and felt the chill of the unheated room wash over her. Pulling the violet-and-white quilt from her bed, she wrapped it around herself and went to her window to watch the dawning of this special May Saturday, the first Saturday she had ever been asked to go to the Goodman house where she cooked and kept house on weekdays. Clutching her quilt around her shoulders, Hannah quietly descended the stairs, tip-toed barefoot through the dimly lit downstairs hallway and ran to the outhouse on a path of smooth, gray stepping stones.

On her way back to the house, she hoped she wouldn't encounter her mother. Running around in your *unnergleeder* was unacceptable, but she knew that even her mother's reprimand wouldn't dampen the joy she felt in anticipation of this day. She bounded up the stairs two at a time and closed the door to her room.

Flopping breathlessly into the soft down mattress that covered her bed, she laughed aloud and huffed out a little prayer. "Dear God, please don't let *Datt* be mad at me."

It wasn't that she feared her father. Joseph Miller was gentle with his children, especially with his daughters. Hannah didn't want to displease him who had taken her side against the bishop, two years ago, when she wanted this job on the Outside.

Hannah caught herself chewing her lip as joyful anticipation turned to apprehension at the thought of telling her father that she would not be staying at home today to help with preparations for the church meeting her family would host tomorrow. She rose from her bed to check her mouth in a small mirror propped on her dresser, to make sure that she had not drawn blood.

Surely, Datt will understand. I gave my word. I have to go, she thought as she poured water from a plain white ceramic pitcher into a matching basin to cleanse herself. She had washed her long, blonde hair the night before, so she had only to brush it and wind it into a knot that would be hidden by her prayer cap.

From her closet she pulled a starched, royal blue dress and pulled it over the soft undergarments she had slept in. She sat to tug on her long, black cotton stockings and padded downstairs to retrieve her shoes from the mud-room, but not before smoothing over her bed the diamond-patterned patchwork quilt made by her mother's hands.

Following the aroma of perking chicory coffee to the chilly, lantern-lit kitchen, Hannah joined the other white-capped women of the Miller household—her mother and her younger sister Fannie. Ham already sizzled in a skillet, and her mother cracked eggs into another, a hearty breakfast for the men who had been on the milking stools since four a.m.

"Sleepy-head, what took you so long?" Fannie teased.

Hannah ignored her sister and tied on a white apron before using a fork to lift pink ham slices from the big black iron skillet while Fannie buttered and stacked thick slices of home-made bread and placed them near a blue bowl filled with ruby-red strawberry preserves. By now Hannah could hear the men talking as they washed up at the yard pump; then came the clunk of barn shoes being dropped on the porch.

"Benjamin! Zach!" Hannah's mother, Rebecca, called her five-year-old twin sons to the table, scooped six-month-old Aaron out of his kitchen crib and placed him in a wooden high-chair next to the big rectangular oak table where the men were now seating themselves on high-backed chairs.

Joseph and Rebecca Miller took their places at each end of the gleaming oak table that Joseph had built. Along the sides of the table sat their children—Samuel, Hannah, Fannie, Benjamin, Zach and Baby Aaron in the high-chair pulled up close.

Only Hannah's oldest sister, Mary, was missing. Mary was now a wife with her own house and family and lived in her husband's church district, too far away for her mother's liking, Hannah knew.

Fannie leaned over to Hannah to whisper. "*Mamm* told *Datt* and he's not happy about you going today. I heard him say so to *Mamm.*"

Though the flush she felt belied her words, Hannah said, "I'm not afraid. I have to go."

At the table, Joseph Miller's mouth moved over a skimpy brown beard as he led his family in thanks for the Lord's bounty and then lifted his fork to signal that they could begin. The family ate heartily and chatted easily in the German dialect their "English" neighbors had long ago misnamed "Pennsylvania Dutch."

"*Fer was machst so wiescht*—why do you make so ugly?" Hannah's mother asked occasionally, correcting the table manners of her hungry sons who ate greedily.

Hannah hurried through her own breakfast and waited for the chewing and slurping of her father and brothers to slow down before she got up the nerve to speak.

"May I be excused, *Datt?*" Hannah asked, rising half-way from her chair.

"And why is it," her father asked, setting down his big white coffee mug, "that you have to go to Goodman's house to work on a Saturday? The agreement was for five days a week, not six."

Hannah obediently sat again. "He asked me to, *Datt.* He's having a guest for lunch today, and he asked me if I would fix it for them."

"You should've told him that we're hosting the church meeting here tomorrow and that you're needed at home to get ready for it."

Keeping her voice soft, so that her father would not think she was arguing with him, Hannah said, "I guess I should have, but now I have to go. I said I would, and he's expecting me. I'm sure he'll pay me for the extra day . . . ."

"It's not about money, Hannah. It's about doing your part here at home and not leaving all the extra work to your mother and Fannie."

Hannah's fair-haired mother placed a slender hand on her husband's arm and spoke. "Fannie and I will be fine, Joe. Hannah always does her part, more than her part, when she's not at the Goodman house. She said she would be there today, so she has to go."

"I sure wish *I* could get out of setting up for church," Fannie mumbled and earned a sharp look from their mother. Fourteen-year-old Fannie lowered her eyes—the only brown ones in the family—smart enough not to return her mother's stare.

"Go then," Hannah's father relented, "but, next time, you ask your mother if it's all right with her."

"Thank you, *Datt*. I'm sorry I didn't ask. I will . . . if it ever happens again. This is the first Saturday I've ever been asked to work. But I have time to collect the eggs before I go."

To thank *Mamm* for intervening for her, Hannah shot her a quick smile as she pushed open the wood-framed door and stepped to the porch of the white, two-story farm house that was her home. She paused to sniff the dewy morning air and crossed the dirt road that lay between the silvery, weathered barn and the house. Before ducking her white-capped head to enter the low-roofed chicken coop that stood alongside the barn, she took a deep breath and tried not to breathe the ammonia-laced stench within the shallow structure.

Clucking sympathetically back at the red hens that scolded and pecked at her hands as she deftly stole the still warm fruit of their labors, Hannah quickly filled a wire basket with large brown eggs and stepped outside, glad to be back in the fresh air. From beneath the porch steps, she grabbed a rag and tin bucket that she carried to the yard pump. She filled the bucket with water and settled on the bottom step of the porch with the bucket between her thighs and the egg-basket beside her. As she straddled the bucket, she thought of the lewd gaze her Uncle Jacob-the-bishop had laid on her when he had seen her sitting in this fashion on this very step two years ago.

~ ~ ~

"Have you no shame?" he had asked, even as he shamelessly stared at his niece's crotch, though her ample skirt completely covered her.

"Uncle?" She lifted her eyes from the egg she was washing, not understanding that it was the bucket clamped between her thighs that offended him.

"I will speak to your mother about teaching you modesty," he said, his scowl apparent even with the bushy beard that covered his chops. As he stomped up the stairs past her, the water in the bucket between her legs sloshed over its rim. At the wet stain that formed on her skirt, the bishop laughed crudely. "Ah, now you've gone and pissed yourself."

Though she was only fifteen at the time, Hannah knew that it was not she who had behaved shamefully, but her uncle, the holy bishop. Her face grew hot and she choked back an angry retort.

Jerking open the door to his sister's house, the bishop entered the Millers' kitchen without so much as a *Guten Morgen* to her parents inside.

Hannah didn't have to guess what had brought her uncle here so early in the morning at barely six a.m.; she suspected that she was the reason for his visit and his fury. She and her sisters had predicted as much.

A hot exchange between her uncle and her mother began almost immediately, and Hannah listened intently. Her mother's brother was formidable in his role as bishop of their Old Order Amish church district, but Hannah was proud of the way her mother stood up to him. He had come to protest what had come to him by means of gossip his wife had picked up at the last quilting: Joe and Rebecca Miller were, once again, about to send a daughter to work "on the Outside."

Without initial pleasantries, the bishop launched his harangue. "This fraternizing with the Yankees will come to no good, Rebecca! I forbid you to do so."

As she eavesdropped from the porch, Hannah imagined him sending out flecks of spit and waving his skinny arms the way he did in church. Her mother, she knew, would appear calm but be trembling inside.

"Ja, Bruder, you said the same about Mary, but it did no harm. That was two years ago. Mary's married now and upholds the old ways better than most. Besides, the money came in handy when Joe was laid up. Did you offer to help? No, it was chust Mary's little bit that got us by . . . ."

Hannah knew that Bishop Jacob Stuckmann could make any member of his church quake with fear, but not his stubborn younger sister. Her mother would hold her own.

"I had my own troubles then," he defended himself before turning on his brother-in-law. "What's wrong with you, Joe, you let your wife put your girls out for hire?"

Hannah heard her father speak in mild but firm tones. "I trust Rebecca's judgment, Bishop. She wasn't wrong about Mary, and she won't be wrong about Hannah. I'll be getting back to work now, if you'll excuse me." With Samuel following him, Joe Miller walked outside, grunted as he sat to put on his work shoes, and paused to pat the head of Hannah who still sat on the porch step washing eggs.

At her father's rare, affectionate touch, Hannah felt her face grow hot, and she kept her head bowed over the smooth brown egg she was scrubbing. Her father disappeared into the buggy house while gangly young Samuel fetched a horse. They would be off helping at a neighboring farm and would not return home for hours, until *Middaagessee*—the noon meal.

Hannah heard the argument from inside the house resume. Her mother now adopted a reasonable tone. "The Yankees was good neighbors to us, Jacob. I don't forget all that Mrs. Goodman did for me . . . drivin' us to the store, the hospital, or wherever we needed to go. When Ida and her husband died in that big car, and their boy asked me for help, how could I say no? I sent Mary to work for him, and now I'm sending Hannah, whether you approve or not."

"Bah! What's the use? You'll live to regret this, Sister. That Hannah, she's a strange one. She don't say much, but she got them dreamin' eyes. You got to watch them dreamin' eyes!" He started for the door but turned back, growling out an after-thought: "And she sits with her legs spread like a boy."

~ ~ ~

Though even now, two years later, she still bristled at the memory of his words, Hannah laughed aloud at his description of her wool-gathering. She knew that her uncle had referred to the distracted look he said she wore under his most fiery of sermons. He had complained about it to her parents more than once. Other youngsters shook with fear, he said, but his own niece stared past him, with a dreamy look on her face. Hannah had to admit that he was right. She had always had the knack of taking her mind out of the stuffy church meeting and sending it soaring into the woods and meadows outside. There was more of God there, she secretly believed, than in her uncle's terrifying sermons.

Two years older now, she better understood the bishop's objections to her mother's decision to send first Mary, and now her, out to work "in the world." To hire one's children out to work for "worldly English" people or "Yankees," that is, non-Amish people, was generally frowned upon by the church hierarchy of the Old Order Amish community; but her mother had done it anyway, first sending her daughter Mary, not so much out of a desire to defy her brother, but, rather, out of loyalty to her deceased Yankee friend and neighbor, Ida Goodman.

Her mother's friendship with Ida had not gone unnoticed by Hannah's Uncle Jacob either. This, too, he had disdained as "fraternizing with the world," but, challenged by his sister, he had admitted that he did not see a flagrant breach of the *Regel und Ordnung,* the Rules and Order of the community. He said he would wait to see if any of the members of the church called it to his attention. Though Hannah knew that whispers were carried from house to house on the invisible wires of gossip in her Amish community, no one had apparently approached the bishop, for he said no more about his sister's friendship with her English neighbor.

As Hannah dumped the filthy water from the bucket, she thought of the prophecy the bishop had uttered that day two years ago.

~ ~ ~

"You will live to regret this, Sister," he had said. "Your daughter will bring shame to this house." He punctuated his words with a slam of the door.

Hannah felt the porch shudder as her uncle thundered past her, and she heard him mutter to himself before he, Bishop Jacob Stuckmann, climbed into his buggy. Hunched like a vulture, he shot her a disgusted look, stung his nervous horse with the whip and rattled away.

She watched the dust cloud rise behind his departing buggy and said softly, "I know you're hoping for the worst, Holy Man, but you're going to be disappointed."

~ ~ ~

Shaking the painful memory of that first day from her mind, Hannah worked the pump handle and washed her hands with strong lemon-scented soap before carrying the eggs inside. She wondered if her mother would end up being the one disappointed after all. After the bishop had left, her mother, too, had given her own warning as Hannah brought the eggs to the kitchen.

~ ~ ~

"You know the bishop fears for you, Hannah. You do know that?" Her mother had sighed deeply, as though exhausted from her confrontation with her brother, and dropped into a chair at the table.

Hannah sat, too. "What is he afraid of, *Mamm*?"

"That the fancy ways of the English will rub off on you, that you will leave the church." She met her fifteen-year-old daughter's gaze and held it.

As she listened, Hannah noticed how the morning sun coming through the window lit up her mother's face, giving her the glow of holiness. "My own father isn't worried about that, so why should the bishop worry?" she said.

"Your father and I see that Mary wasn't tempted by the English lifestyle, and we expect the same of you, Hannah. Besides, the money you bring home will be put back into the land. It won't be used to buy fancy things."

"I have everything I need here, *Mamm.*" Hannah rose and carried the eggs to the ice-box.

Her mother wasn't done yet. "Yes, but you must realize, Hannah, that you will be among *amner Satt Leit*—other sorts of people, not our sort of people, the Chosen People of God. You must never forget that you are one of the Chosen."

Hannah came back to the table and put a reassuring hand on her mother's. "I better go now, *Mamm.* It's a three-mile walk to the Goodman farm, and I should be there on time, especially on my first day as housekeeper."

~ ~ ~

Two years later, Hannah again laid her hand on her mother's hand, before leaving for the Goodman farm, saying, "Anything you can't get to today, *Mamm,* leave for me. I'll do it when I get back from Mr. Goodman's house. I shouldn't be too late. It's just lunch I'll be fixing."

She descended the gray-painted porch and briskly strode the quarter-mile long, dirt driveway that met up with the dusty, unpaved road that would take her to the Goodman dairy farm. As she followed the road to where it wound its way through a stand of maples and wild cherry trees, Hannah realized that the eagerness with which she had greeted this day was now gone.

The morning sun passed behind a cloud and she wished she had worn her cape. She wondered why the memory of the bishop's visit that morning two years ago had left her with a feeling of unease.

What is tormenting me? she asked herself.

With a twinge of guilt, she admitted that she knew the answer to her own question. The bishop's fears had turned out to be half-true. But it was not the worldly ways of the English that she wanted.

It was Abram Goodman himself.

Chapter Two

Season in and season out, Hannah trod the familiar dirt road through three miles of woods that lay between her parents' farm and the Goodman dairy farm, but she never thought of the path as monotonous. With her senses alert to the sights and sounds around her, she cherished the change that each season brought to the hills and forests of Pennsylvania. She often thought that she'd never want to live anywhere else—or work for anybody besides Abram Goodman.

By now, the spring-green canopy of leaves above her had thickened, and she paused reverently at the entrance to the woods, as though entering a church crisscrossed by sunbeams. Gilded with gold as she moved through them, she had to force herself to keep up her pace, lest she be beguiled by the choir of yellow finches who sang from branches of white dogwood blossoms. Their joyous melodies matched what she felt in her heart; yet it was not spring or summer that were her favorite seasons, nor the blazing reds and golds of autumn.

Especially in winter when the glory of earlier seasons had faded, leaving the bare tree limbs graced with shimmering coatings of ice or veils of white snow, Hannah loved her church. On snowy days, she'd lift her face to be kissed by gauzy flakes falling from a deepening gray sky even as she stepped briskly to stay warm and wished that she didn't have to be the one to sully the snow. But she was always the first.

At the end of the winter days, when darkness fell early, her parents sent her bundled-up brother to pick her up in her father's black canvas-covered buggy; but when the wind turned harsh or the snow especially deep, they allowed Abram Goodman to drive her home in his rumbling four-wheel drive truck. Those cherished rides were what made winter special. Enclosed with him in the coziness of the vehicle, Hannah enjoyed the intimacy of sharing the same warm space with Abram, as though they shared a blanket in a buggy. Secretly, she disagreed when the Amish folk around her spoke of dreading frigid buggy rides and the coming winter. She was not unaware that, on the worst days, her experience would be different from theirs.

Neither was she oblivious to the difference between her parents' unadorned farm house and the grand three-story house Abram Goodman had inherited from his parents, but she was not impressed by it, though she kept the big house clean and polished. It was the mannerly ways and after-shave freshness of her handsome employer that she found in sharp contrast to boorish Amish boys who always carried a faint smell of manure and barn, even after washing.

Mr. Goodman always treated her kindly and voiced his thanks when her paycheck would have been thanks enough. Once, when she had first come to work for him when he was twenty-eight and she, fifteen, he had caught her mesmerized by a steamy soap opera while she dreamily dusted the den.

Hannah had flinched at his appearance, but Goodman winked and said, "Don't worry, Hannah. What happens in this house stays in this house. Feel free."

Feel free? She had repeated the words like a mantra all that day. Had she ever thought, before coming here to work as Goodman's housekeeper, that she had not been "free"?

Timidly, Hannah had begun to explore the world of *der Englishcher.* She listened to the worldly tunes on the kitchen radio as she went about her work. Without guilt, she used the electric gadgets—from the vegetable chopper to the vacuum cleaner—left behind by Abram Goodman's deceased mother. She marveled that they made her work so much easier, even fun. She wondered if her older sister Mary had done the same.

Hannah lived for noon mealtimes when Goodman showed up at the house, usually with his four hired men who worked the dairy farm with him. He never failed to enjoy the thick ham or beef sandwiches she made with home-made bread. He especially loved her steaming hot, savory vegetable soup on cold days. She loved the way his smile reached his gray eyes when he thanked her, and she thrilled at the nickname he had given her.

"Sure looks good, Punkin," he'd say and tuck into whatever it was she had prepared for lunch with his men or for his dinner that he typically ate alone. Remembering his easy smile and his gentle words, Hannah wore her own smile all the way home as she relived each day.

For Hannah, working on an unprecedented Saturday was one more day when she could bask in Mr. Goodman's smile. With everything ready and in the refrigerator for lunch, Hannah now took herself to the small, white springhouse for butter-churning while she awaited her employer and his guest.

Hannah liked the way her throaty, alto voice echoed off the whitewashed, cement-block walls of the springhouse as she sang, accompanied by the sound of cold water that gurgled from an underground spring and pooled in a deep trough that held sweating milk cans. She loved, too, the aroma of potatoes and sweet red apples stored in bins along the walls of the little white building across from the main house.

Standing on the dry cement floor with her legs apart, Hannah raised her strong, firm arms again and again as she rhythmically plunged the handle of the butter churn into the orifice of the wooden bucket that formed its base. She smiled as she sang a favorite church hymn in German, not because of the sacred words, but because she was remembering, as she always did when she churned the creamy yellow butter, the look of concern on Mr. Goodman's face when he realized that she had lugged the heavy churn the three miles from her home to his.

~ ~ ~

"Punkin! You look exhausted! You could have called me," he had said, as he bent to take the heavy churn from her arms.

She stopped herself from brushing his sun-streaked brown hair out of his eyes and laughed. "I have a strong voice, Mr. Goodman, but I doubt if you'd have heard me," she said, running her handkerchief across her sweating brow.

"Oh, right, no phone. But, yesterday, you could have asked me to drive over to pick it up instead of hauling it here on foot."

"I wanted to surprise you with some fresh butter. I know you really liked my *mamm's.*"

"Well, thank you, Punkin, but you don't have to work that hard for me," he said, as he carried the heavy churn to the springhouse.

~ ~ ~

Hannah broke from her reverie at the sound of Mr. Goodman's mellow voice calling her name. Pausing only long enough to wipe her hands on her apron and to pat back into place the blonde hair that had escaped from her cap, Hannah threw open the wooden springhouse door and emerged, surprised and blinking, into the late morning sunlight.

"Yes?" she spoke without trying to hide her delight that he had come home. Delight turned to confusion when she saw a dark-haired English lady standing on the porch in an aura of light with Mr. Goodman. In her two years as Mr. Goodman's cook and housekeeper, she had never seen another female on the Goodman farm. *Why is this Yankee woman here?* she wondered.

She felt their eyes on her as she slowly crossed the grass toward them, out of habit wiping her hands on her white apron. She watched the English lady's eyes travel over her, from head to toe. She was used to the rude stares of *der Englischer,* and this lady was no different.

Despite the plainness of her unfashionable clothing and the absence of makeup, Hannah had been told often enough that she was pretty and she tried to remember this as she approached them. By Amish standards, she was ripe for marriage, but she had, so far, refused to "go shteady" with any of several Amish boys who sought to court her, much to the not unspoken annoyance of her parents.

At seventeen, Hannah was tall, and she knew that her well-rounded bosom and narrow waist were not hidden despite the coarsely cut dress she wore. Today her dress was bright blue but the same style as all her dresses—a pattern handed down through generations of Amish women, its full skirt the prescribed eighteen inches from the floor. With it she wore a bibbed white apron; long, black stockings and black tie-shoes.

Her long blonde hair was parted in the middle, knotted at the nape of her neck and covered with a white organdy prayer cap. She hoped that the heat of churning had made her fair skin rosy. Irritated by the strange lady's scrutiny, Hannah arched her golden eyebrows and allowed herself an icy stare back into the deep blue eyes of the English lady. Imitating the lady's perusal of her, Hannah deliberately passed her own light blue eyes over the small but beautiful, black-haired lady who so shamelessly placed her hand on Mr. Goodman's tanned, muscular bare arm, holding on with red-nailed fingers, as if she owned him. Hannah tried to deal with the strange resentment that she felt filling her chest.

Yesterday, when Mr. Goodman had asked her to come again today, it had never occurred to her that the guest might be a woman. She had rejoiced at the idea of working on a Saturday, not only because she would escape the preparations for the church meeting at her parents' house the following Sunday, but because it was one more day she could be near Abram Goodman. Hannah felt tricked, for a reason she would not have been able to explain, even to herself. The way that the lady clutched Mr. Goodman annoyed her, but, more, the way he did not seem to mind.

"Hannah," Goodman said pleasantly, beckoning her forward, "I want you to meet Sandra." The lady at his side smiled and said hello, but Hannah stared in stony silence.

"Sandra," Goodman went on, "Hannah is my housekeeper." Turning his attention back to Hannah, he said, "We're going for a walk to the pond. Can you have lunch ready in a half-hour?"

He kept his arm lightly around the shoulders of the petite, dark-haired lady who wore a short, pale blue dress and flesh-colored sandals that exposed most of her naked feet. The nails of her toes were painted to match the red of her finger nails.

Abram Goodman stood tall, tanned, and smiling on the large, ornate porch that encircled his home. Dressed in a light peach, short-sleeved shirt and khaki dress-slacks in honor of his guest, he looked even more handsome to Hannah than he did in his usual jeans, tee shirts, and boots.

"Yes, Mr. Goodman," Hannah said, finally allowing one curt nod in the direction of the woman by his side. Brushing past them as the lady accepted an early, pink rose Goodman had plucked for her from one of the bushes near the porch steps, Hannah hurried into the house.

Pulling back the ruffled white curtain from the kitchen window, Hannah watched the couple strolling hand-in-hand in the direction of the pond. She heard Abram whistle for Laddie, the Sheltie that had become his after his parents died. Laughing, the lady bent to make friends with the grinning, silver-gray dog who bounded out to meet them.

"Even Laddie," Hannah said, blinking back tears that threatened to spill. "Even Laddie forgets who takes care of him."

Turning abruptly from the window, Hannah jerked out of a drawer a yellow, linen tablecloth and tossed it over the kitchen table, ignoring the wrinkles she'd ordinarily have pressed out. Slamming cupboard doors and drawers harder than necessary, she set the table for two.

Unschooled in the art of faking a smile, Hannah placed a crystal bowl heaped with fresh strawberries, blueberries, pale orange melon cubes and chunks of yellow pineapple on the light oak kitchen table where the other woman sat with her hand in Mr. Goodman's.

Next to the fruit bowl, Hannah laid a matching crystal platter with slices of cheese, cold cuts, and red-ripe tomatoes pin-wheeling around curly green lettuce. In a woven basket lined with a white linen cloth were thick slices of her home-made bread. Nearby were two small brown crocks filled with pale yellow butter and creamy mayonnaise.

"This looks wonderful, Hannah," the lady said, clasping her hands as if she were going to pray. "Abram tells me that you baked this beautiful bread yourself!"

Mr. Goodman joined in the praise by saying, "She even makes the butter."

Ignoring their compliments, Hannah spoke, flat-voiced, to Abram only. "Let me know if you need anything, Mr. Goodman. I'll be back to my churnin' in the springhouse."

As Hannah left the kitchen, she let the blue, louvered cafe doors swing savagely behind her, hoping Mr. Goodman and his guest would notice.

The cool air of the springhouse felt good against Hannah's hot, flushed cheeks. It was not only the vigorous churning of the cream that had brought this heat to her face but the anger churning in her breast.

"'She even makes the butter,' indeed!" she spoke aloud to herself, her words resounding in the small, whitewashed cement block building. "His 'housekeeper'!" she said, kicking at one of the stainless steel milk cans that stood in the cold water of the springhouse trough. "I wonder if that fancy lady knows how to churn butter and bake bread."

Tears formed in Hannah's eyes, but, with a haughty toss of her head, she dismissed them and went back to furiously churning, something she had taken upon herself ever since she had discovered Goodman's fondness for her mother's sweet, freshly-made butter on the thick, heavy bread that Hannah baked for him. The warmth of remembrance flooded her as she recalled his words, and more, his kiss of thanks on her forehead.

~ ~ ~

"Sweetheart, you are too good to me," he had said. His lips felt soft and smooth on her brow. "If possible, this butter is even better than your mother's."

Unaccustomed to endearments and weak-kneed by his kiss, Hannah could not find breath to respond. She turned away to the dishes in the sink so that he wouldn't see the effect his words and actions had had on her.

That night, back home in her own rumpled bed, she could still feel the silken brush of his lips on her forehead. Soundlessly, she formed the unfamiliar word—"Sweetheart." In her life, she had never heard it used, let alone been the object of it. She pondered its meaning until sleep finally overcame her, and the pillow she embraced became Abram.

~ ~ ~

As her anger and the vigor of her churning subsided, Hannah considered the why of her feeling of betrayal. She only knew that she loved Abram, but, beyond that, she had not thought. She came to his home, day after day, and every menial task she performed on his behalf—the washing of his clothing smelling of his masculine sweat, the smoothing of the sheets on his sleep-warm bed, the cooking of the foods that he put into his mouth—all were done with a deep but quiet inner joy.

She had not even guessed that his weekends were spent away from their home—she had come to think of it that way—and in the company of a woman, this Yankee woman with the shining, free, black hair and with the lovely, shapely legs wrapped one around the other as she sat, smooth legs exposed for Abram to see.

When the difficulty of moving the churn told her that her job was finished, she eased herself to the damp, springhouse floor and sat with her back against the wall. Stretching her black-stockinged legs in front of her, she eyed them with distaste. She pushed off her clumsy, black shoes without untying them and pulled off each long, black stocking and studied her own long, white legs.

They were pretty legs, too, she decided, but the golden down on them made them the legs of an Amish, not a Yankee, girl. She thought about the buzzing electric razor she had heard Abram using. But what would be the use? Her legs had to remain covered in his presence, even in summer. She picked up her rumpled stockings, put her face in them and wept.

Chapter Three

Abram frowned at the thunk of the kitchen's louvered café doors hitting the walls as Hannah pushed through them. He had half a notion to drag her back to apologize for her rudeness to him and Sandra. His guest's words proved that she had been aware of the housekeeper's snub.

At Hannah's exit, Sandra sat back in her chair and expelled her breath audibly. "Did I just get the cold shoulder or what?" she asked with no question in her voice.

Although Abram planned to give Hannah a piece of his mind later, he tried to make light of it now. "Sorry about that," he said, refilling Sandra's glass with iced-tea, "Hannah's probably feeling a little possessive or something. She's been, more or less, the lady of this house for the past two years, and, for some odd reason, she seemed to be protecting her turf."

"Are you part of her turf?" Sandra asked, with a small smile.

Reaching across the table for her hand, Abram laughed. "No, Ma'am, she has no claim on me."

Leaning forward and resting her breasts on her crossed arms, Sandra changed the subject, dismissing concerns about the housekeeper. "Tell me about your parents, Abram. How long has it been since they died?"

"Almost four years. You'd have liked them, and I know they'd have liked you. They were country folks, through and through, worked hard, and, even though Dad was a smart business man, he never acted like he thought he was anything special." His gaze turned to the green hills outside the large bay window next to the table. "Money never changed them. They lived a quiet life, enjoyed their farm and the neighbors they called friends. That's why the way they died was so hard for me to take, dying in a fiery crash that made headlines. They wouldn't have liked being in the news."

"Both of my parents died in their sleep, but they died young," Sandra said, lowering her eyes as she stroked the slender glass that held her tea. "Mom died in her early forties—a reaction to medication she was taking for strep throat, of all things, and Dad died at fifty—a heart attack. For both of them, it was sudden and made it very hard for my sister Kendra and me."

Abram heard the lingering sadness in her voice and reached for her hand again. "How old were you and Kendra when you lost your mother?"

"Kendra was fifteen; I was eighteen, just starting college. Dad died right after my graduation, so at least he got to see his daughter as the family's first college graduate. I was determined to put Kendra through school, too, and I did." She lifted her head proudly and met his eyes.

"You're close, you and Kendra?" He loved to watch her full, pink lips as she spoke.

Sandra smiled. "Yes, we even shared an apartment together for a while. She just moved in with her boyfriend about a year ago, but we still live in the same city, just on opposite sides of it."

He sighed. "I don't think I told you that I had a brother—a twin, in fact—he died at birth while I lived. It would've been great to have a brother."

He rose, walked to the refrigerator and opened it. "Aha! I knew there had to be dessert somewhere. Vanilla pudding!" He carried two stemmed crystal bowls to the table and set one before Sandra.

"How pretty," she said, "vanilla pudding topped with kiwi!" She scooped into it with her spoon. "Umm, who doesn't like pudding? But finish what you were saying about your brother."

Abram sat and took up his own spoon. "It would've come in handy to have a brother to help me with the farm . . . . He might have wanted to be a farmer, something I never wanted."

He looked up from his dessert and into her blue eyes, noticing that the blue dress she wore made them even bluer. "Hey, this conversation is getting pretty somber. Let's talk about something else."

"It's fine, Abe. I want to know everything about you. Why didn't you just sell the farm instead of coming back here to live?"

He saw the compassion in Sandra's eyes and wanted to tell her all that he had kept to himself. "I couldn't let everything my dad had worked so hard to accomplish just die with him. I had to keep this place going, and there was nobody but me to do it. At first, it was hard." He looked out the window again, remembering. "I liked the engineering firm I worked for. I had my own life, but I had to come back and run the place for Dad."

Reclaiming the present, he dipped into the pudding again. "Don't get me wrong. I always loved the farm, but being a dairy farmer wasn't what I wanted to do with my life. I confess, now I pretty much let the hands take care of the dairy end of things, while I keep track of the accounts and Dad's investments. I guess I should say 'my investments,' but I'm following his lead. He was a smart investor. That's how he made his money."

"You said you had your own life. Can I ask . . . was there someone special in that life, a girlfriend?" Sandra's tone was light, but Abram knew it was a serious question.

Abram sat back, blew out a breath and tried to match her seriousness. "I had some good women friends—who still are my friends—and I dated some of them, but I just wasn't ready for any commitments. I was busy climbing the ladder in my company. I was gunning for head engineer, and I was on the way to getting it . . . until I made the decision to come back here." He hesitated and then asked a question of his own, "What about you? Was there somebody special in your life?"

Sandra said, "For a while I thought so, but he's history since I met you." She rose and kissed Abram before turning to lean against the white kitchen cabinets. "And you live in this big beautiful house all by yourself!" she said, surveying the big, high-ceilinged kitchen wall-papered with quaint flowers in pastels. Iced-tea glass in hand, she strolled to look out white French doors that opened to a flower garden not yet in bloom.

"I have to admit, Abram, this isn't what I pictured when you said you were a farmer. That day you came to my class to speak, I expected some old guy in bib-overalls with cow poop on his shoes!" She kissed his cheek again before taking her seat across from him at the big pine table.

Abram threw back his head and laughed. "Even my dad didn't look like that, and my mom never would have put up with poop on his or anybody else's shoes." He stood and pulled her along. "C'mon, let me show you around. I had let the house turn into a veritable dust museum, but, thanks to the Amish girls—Hannah and her sister Mary—it's spotless now."

As Sandra reached to clear plates and bowls from the table, Abram laid a hand on her outstretched arm, caressing her beneath the sheer fabric of her blouse. "Leave that. Hannah will take care of it before she goes home."

After the death of his parents, Abram Goodman had struggled through his initial year of grief by working seven days a week on the dairy farm until he dropped exhausted and lonely into his unmade bed at night. After the first year, he had hired two more men, doubled the size of the herd and had two more silos built. He moved as a machine, determined not to lose the land and the accounts and investments Ira Goodman had worked hard to acquire.

He soon found that the need to invest perpetuated itself, and he multiplied the wealth that his father had left him, though he had no real joy in accumulating or spending it. His only extravagance was to collect automobiles, which he seldom drove.

At thirty, he was becoming a silent man who only worked, ate, and slept—alone, except for the Sheltie dog who slept at his feet since the death of its masters. Laddie still waited for Ida and Ira Goodman to come home, and it broke Abram's heart.

His energy sapped by grief and overwork, Abram regularly resisted the attempts of his boyhood friend and college roommate, Charlie Cochran, to involve him with his women friends. Yet, it was Charlie who had introduced him to Sandra, the woman whose buoyant personality had brought him back to life.

~ ~ ~

"You have to get out of the sticks, Man. You can't even get a cell phone signal out here," Charlie said, sitting in his little white convertible and grinning up at Abram who stood bare-chested and in jeans on the porch of the Goodman house. "I tried to let you know I was on the road, but no bars."

"What kind of bars were you looking for, you old, red-headed devil? Get in here and drink a cold one." Abram managed a smile for his old friend.

"Nah, grab a change of clothes," Charlie said, exiting the car and stretching, "and let's go back into the city, stay the night and I'll run you back here tomorrow."

Perched on bar stools in the orange glow of neon lights later that night, Charlie admitted he had a favor to ask of Abram. "A woman I teach with needs a high-tech farmer to talk to her classes for her career unit. I told her I'd produce one—you. I told her you'd be there—tomorrow morning. I waited 'til you had a few beers in you to tell you."

"I should've known you had something up your sleeve. You're match-making again, aren't you?" Abram accused, meeting Charlie's eyes in the mirror behind the bar.

"No way, Man," Charlie said, taking a swig of his beer, "this is an old English teacher. An old maid you'd never be interested in . . . but she's in a bind—could get a bad evaluation if she doesn't do something to make her classes more interesting—and I promised her you'd be there for her third period class, ten o'clock tomorrow. It'll only take a half hour out of your exciting life. These city kids think that all farmers are tobacco-chewin' rednecks. Don't you want to prove them wrong?"

"I don't care what they think about farmers," Abram said, returning his attention to the bowl of pistachios on the bar.

"C'mon, Man, you owe me for all the dates I got you back in college."

"I owe you nothing, but I'll do it, since she's expecting me, and you damn well know I'm not the type to be a no-show. I'm giving it exactly thirty minutes, not a minute more."

Scrunched in a school desk two sizes too small for his more than six feet, two-hundred-pounds frame, Abram sat uncomfortably in the back of the classroom waiting for Miss Waters to introduce him. To the pimpled boy on his left, he whispered, "They sure don't make English teachers like they used to."

Sandra Waters' petite, shapely form moved gracefully as she walked on red high heels, distributing papers among the desks, managing to look sexy though she wore a tailored gray suit. Her black hair was knotted up in some way and skewered with a red pick. Abram found himself imagining pulling out that pick . . . . The "old maid English teacher" was a knockout.

He recognized the easy camaraderie she had with the teenagers in the room, as she stopped to ruffle one already ruffled head, to tease another slumped in his chair, to chide another whose wrinkled composition she said looked as though he "had slept with it." A smile was in her strong, clear voice and in her dark-lashed eyes.

She has a way with these kids, he thought, *hard-assed, street-smart cats mesmerized by this little bird.*

Abram couldn't stop looking into her eyes, the violet-blue of a summer sky when a storm is threatening. As she directed the class's attention to him, the blue eyes met his, and he heard her falter in her introduction—"Abram Goodman, dairy farmer."

Weeks later, as they sat in a dimly lit restaurant overlooking the city lights, deaf to the supper crowd around them, he took her small, white manicured hands into his tanned, callused ones. She had just confessed that she had been startled by what she had read in the eyes of the "handsome farmer" that day.

"It was as though you . . . knew me . . . as though I had been waiting for you," she said, blushing at her own candor.

He had sat quietly, listening and watching the flickering light of the candles reflecting in her eyes as she searched his face for understanding.

"I know what you mean," he said, wanting to be completely honest with her. "I had never believed much in destiny, or whatever they call it, but I did then. I suddenly understood what one woman for one man means. I knew I'd found . . . my wife."

That was how he had proposed to her, and she had given her assent simply by nodding slowly, her eyes glistening with tears. From his pocket he took a small, red velvet case. From it, he removed an emerald-cut diamond, of at least two carats.

"Did that nod mean 'yes'? You'll marry me?" She nodded again and he slipped the ring on the third finger of her left hand.

She gasped and found her voice. "Abe, it's beautiful, but . . . can a farmer afford this?"

He said, "You let me worry about that, Sweetheart."

And so they had begun to plan a visit to his home, the place he had avoided taking her, despite her coaxing. He had lied, "The place is a mess. Wait 'til I get it cleaned up."

~ ~ ~

Their footsteps echoing on the hardwood floors, he gave her what he called "the grand tour" of the house. "Don't give me credit for any of this," Abram said. "What you see comes from my dad's hard work and my mother's decorating sense. I haven't changed a thing."

Off the kitchen was a formal dining room with highly polished mahogany furniture and a crystal chandelier. A marble fireplace with a mahogany mantel graced one wall. "We hardly ever used this room," he said. "The kitchen table was more to our liking."

Opening a white door, he said, "The downstairs guest room and bath"; then he guided her through an inviting chintz-and-flowers living room with a white but well-used fireplace, framed by book cases with glass doors; a paneled den with soft brown leather chairs, a massive roll top desk, a handsome red brick fireplace and more bookshelves.

Sandra ran her finger across a set of five leather-bound books on the open shelves. "Wow, this appears to be the complete set of James Fennimore Cooper's *Leather Stocking Tales!*"

"Yeah, my dad was a fan. Both my parents' idea of a good time was to curl up by the fire with a good book—there are six fireplaces altogether—though there's a huge TV screen on the wall behind these doors." He pushed a button and carved cherry-wood panels slid back to reveal a flat screen.

"Like your parents," Sandra said, "reading by the fire appeals to me more than watching television. The only thing I like to watch is football."

Abram feigned a stagger backward with his hand over his heart. "I do believe I have found the perfect woman!"

She put her arms around his neck and pulled his face down to hers. "You never know," she said. "I could be frigid in bed, something you've never bothered to find out."

Even though they had been dating for months, they had never made love. In fact, Abram had told her he wanted to wait until they were married. At first, Sandra had been amused by this quaint notion, sure that she could get him to change his mind; then, when she saw that he meant it, they had argued about it, something he wanted to avoid now.

"I have no doubt that you're as passionate in bed as you are about everything else, Sweetheart. I'm a patient man who loves suspense."

Before she could take up the argument again, he planted a kiss on her mouth and ushered her toward the wide staircase which curved upward to a landing overlooking the foyer.

"This'll take us to three more bedrooms—each with its own fireplace and bath," he said, indicating the staircase, itself a work of art with graceful, white spindles supporting a carved cherry-wood banister.

"This looks like it's out of *Gone with the Wind*," Sandra said as she looked up at the vaulted ceiling of the foyer from which a massive brass chandelier was suspended. "Where on earth did they find an amazing chandelier like this? It looks as though it came from a church!"

"You're exactly right," Abram said. "They got it from a razed cathedral in Rome."

"Abe, this house is magnificent. I had no idea," she said, starting up the staircase. "I can't wait to see the view of the chandelier and the foyer from the landing."

Abram smiled as he followed her up the staircase, her short, filmy blue skirt hugging her shapely bottom before fluttering about her bare thighs. "The view from back here is even better," he said.

"It's all for you," she said, without looking back.

At the top of the stairs, he led her down a long hallway with a red Oriental runner. Lining both sides of the hallway were white doors with decorative panels and moldings. "The house is spotless except for this room, my bedroom," he said, pausing before one of the doors.

"Better not show it to me then, because so far you've given me the impression that you're Mr. Perfection, himself, except for lying about your house being a mess."

"The truth will out," he said, opening the door to his bedroom with a flourish. He had expected to see an unmade bed, clothing draped on a chair and newspapers and books strewn about. "Looks like Hannah's been in here straightening up. She's not normally here on a Saturday, but I guess she peeked in here today and cleaned up after me."

Sandra surveyed the large room with its double bed covered by a red and gray plaid bedspread that matched the drapes. Soft, gray carpeting covered the floor. Books were neatly arranged on shelves next to a gray, stone fireplace with a blackened opening that proved its frequent use. Beside a black leather easy chair with matching ottoman, there was no sign of yesterday's newspaper. She walked to the bureau and took into her hands a silver-framed picture of a smiling, older couple.

"Your parents?" she asked as she studied the picture.

"Yes, taken on their fortieth wedding anniversary."

"You look like your dad. The same gray eyes, the same square jaw, the same smile and a full head of hair, though his is white. He was a handsome man, definitely the father of the hunk with me now." Turning toward Abram, Sandra went up on tiptoe to kiss him, holding the picture between them.

Abram returned her kiss, then placed the picture back on his bureau. "Come here," he said, "and let me kiss you properly." They kissed deeply and lingered in a quiet embrace.

Suddenly, Sandra pulled back and looked up at him. "This can't be the master bedroom. Where is it and why don't you use it?"

Leading her out of his room by the hand, Abram took her to the end of the hallway to a pair of white double doors with shining brass handles. "Enter, Madam, the master suite."

Behind the doors was a spacious room with doors that opened to a balcony overlooking the front of the house. As promised, this bedroom had its own mauve-bricked fireplace, sitting area and a bathroom decorated in white marble and polished brass. The bed was a high four-poster with a velvet patchwork quilt in rich shades of red, blue, green, orange, and gold.

Sandra stroked the luxurious velvet. "Oh, this is gorgeous. It reminds me of autumn. This bed is so high; I'd need a step-stool."

"There are, in fact, step-stools on each side of the bed. Take your pick."

Sandra kicked off her sandals, and, with her hand on one of the spiraling posts, climbed to the bed and lay down, her slim body sinking into it. "Oh, it's down-filled. What luxury!"

Reaching her hand out to Abram, she said, playfully exaggerating a seductive tone, "Come to me, Darling. It's time, don't you think?"

He hesitated a beat too long, and she lost her come-hither smile. "Ah, Sweetheart," he said, "you look altogether too tempting. This was my parents' bed. My father shared it with his wife. I want to wait to share it with mine."

"Abe, that piece of paper won't make us any more committed to one another than we are now," she said, letting her fists drop on either side of her, into the soft coverlet. "If it's the bed you don't want to defile, there are at least three more in this house."

He stood looking down at her. "No, Honey, I'm serious. This or that bed has nothing to do with it. I want to wait. I know you think I'm old-fashioned, but I have my reasons. C'mon there's a lot more house to see." He reached out his hand to her.

She crossed her arms over her body and turned her face away from him. Her voice was hurt and angry when she spoke. "I've heard your reasons." She mimicked him with a sonorous preaching voice. "I want to honor you above other women. I want to set you apart as special, above other women." Suddenly she was crying, her tears wetting the dark hair at her temples as she lay there.

He sat on the bed and pulled her to him. "Yes, those are my reasons, but I doubt if I spoke them in that tone," he said, stroking her hair. "Why are you crying, Sandra?"

"Because I don't feel special. I feel rejected! You've admitted you've had intimate relationships with other women. Why them but not me?" Her tone was bitter.

He let go of her and stood. Moving across the room and turning toward her, he said, "I've explained it to you before, Sandra. I don't feel good about the women I used—there's no other word for it—when I was at the university. Even if they were willing, I knew most of them were hoping for more. I used them with no intention of giving anything more."

"So," she said, sitting cross-legged and waving her hands, "now you've had some big religious conversion. Is that it? Spare me your sanctimony. I am the normal one, here. Not you!"

He moved no closer. "I'm not religious, not in the usual sense of the word, but I'm a man who believes that I have choices . . . ." He ran his hand though his hair and paced as he searched for new words to express what he felt.

"I have a choice to debase or to exalt you . . . above every other woman I've ever met. I want our wedding night to be brand new, special, our gift to one another." He was pleading with her to understand what he couldn't articulate. Sex in college and after had been too available. Cheap. He wanted intimacy with her, his wife, to be redemptive, "a pearl of great price," though he kept this thought to himself, embarrassed at its poetry.

"Let me repeat, Reverend, I don't feel 'exalted.' I feel refused, not good enough for Your Holiness."

He felt her sarcasm like a slap in the face. He turned to look at her for a long moment, swallowing his anger before he spoke quietly and with little emotion.

"Sandra, you're playing the part of a woman scorned when you know it's not true. I cherish you as the best thing that's ever happened to me. We've both said we're tired of the typical dating game. We wanted our relationship to be different. I'm offering you that difference. Having sex is no proof of love. If you don't know how much I love you, want you . . . I'll be downstairs." He walked to the door, lowered his head, and spoke with his back to her.

"Come down after you've decided whether we'll head back to the city . . . or spend the day." He left the door open behind him.

He sat on the top step of the front porch, leaning forward with his elbows on his knees, head down as he fondled Laddie's silken ears. He wondered at his own stubbornness. He truly believed that, too often, the wrong people married each other, mistaking sex for love, wearing that out to the point that the wedding night—the marriage, itself—was ho-hum. He desperately wanted her to understand that. He knew that what she would say could be the end or the beginning of something.

He felt a shadow cross over him and looked up. Hannah stood at the base of the stairs, staring at him. Her face was flushed and sweaty; a tendril of blonde hair had escaped to trail down one side of her neck.

"What's the matter, Mr. Goodman?" Her voice was hesitant, shy.

"Nothing's wrong," he said. "I'm waiting for Sandra . . . to freshen up. Lunch was good. Thanks again. I can clear the table later if you want to start home."

"Oh, no," she said, hurrying up the porch steps, "I'll chust take care of it now."

Her cold "Excuse me" told him that she had encountered Sandra as she passed through the doorway. He heard Sandra's steps behind him. They halted and suddenly she was sitting beside him, timidly touching his hair.

Her voice was soft and tearful. "Abe . . . I love you. You're like no man I've ever met. You honor me so . . . . I'm sorry."

As her voice broke, he took her into his arms. Murmuring her name, he kissed her wet face and eyes, her nose, her mouth; then smiling, he pulled her to her feet.

"Let me show you my cars," he said with enthusiasm.

"Your cars? You mean that little silver Buick you drive isn't the only one?"

He laughed. "I have six—real beauties. I drive the Buick when I don't want to fall prey to gold-diggers, the same reason I didn't want to bring you here right away . . . ."

"What? You thought I was a gold-digger? How dare you . . . ." she said, though she laughed as he dragged her by the hand, off to a six-bay garage across from the house.

Chapter Four

The budding red roses of early summer had replaced the yellow forsythia of spring, and almost two months had passed since Abram brought the English lady to his home. In those two months, Abram, to Hannah's quiet relief, had behaved no less kindly to her. She ignored rumors that young Goodman would marry and the jibes that she heard coming from his hired hands at lunch-time, especially because Abram himself always laughed off their teasing.

"When's the big day?"

"When're you gittin' hitched?"

"When're we gonna see that black-haired gal we heard about?"

"What makes you think I'd want to be tied down like the rest of you?" Abram asked in answer to their questions. Sometimes he told them to mind their own business.

Reassured by Abram's denial of marriage plans, Hannah's shock was supreme when, on one glorious Monday morning in June, arriving to work as usual, she pushed open his bedroom door to make his bed, humming to herself, only to find that it had not been slept in. She stood puzzling for a moment, wondering if Abram hadn't come home after the weekend.

Stepping back into the hallway, she heard laughter coming from the big room with the double doors, the room that Hannah called "the parents' room." Though the soft laughter coming from that room was muffled, Hannah recognized the voice as Abram's; then came the breathy laughter of a woman.

Hannah's breath came short and dizziness nearly overwhelmed her. Placing her hand against the brocade wallpaper of the upstairs hallway, she fought to steady herself and to clear her head. In confusion, she hurried down the staircase and through the front door, letting the screen door bang behind her.

Gasping and nearing hysteria, she ran the shortest route back to her home, through the damp morning woods, caring nothing for briar bushes that tore at her arms, face and dress, like witches' hands grabbing at her. As she stumbled forward, her sobs interrupted the birdsong she no longer heard.

She had made no plan of what she would say as she arrived, tear-streaked and disheveled, at her family's front yard where her mother bent over a wooden washboard that was propped in a big galvanized tub, up to her elbows in sudsy water.

She heard her mother gasp at her appearance and hastily tried to arrange her clothing and her thoughts to answer her mother's questions. "*Was der schinner is letz?* What in the world is wrong? Are you sick, *mei dochder?*"

"*Ja, Mamm, ja.* Something has made my stomach turn sour," Hannah said, slowing her walk toward her mother and trying to hold back the tears that threatened to start again. "May I shtay in bed awhile?"

"Why, *ja,* but how will Mr. Goodman know your whereabouts?" Her mother laid a damp hand on her daughter's sweating brow. "Your father and brother are at work in the fields . . . ."

"Mr. Goodman won't notice . . . . He won't care . . . . He's very busy today," Hannah said, cringing at the truth in her lie.

Feeling abnormally weary, Hannah used the banister to drag herself up the steep stairway leading to her room. Chilled despite the heat, she pulled down the quilted bedspread that she had smoothed out that very morning and crawled beneath it, removing only her shoes.

For hours, she lay with her eyes tightly shut against reality and the harsh afternoon sun that shone on the unadorned, white walls of her stuffy room. It was something she had not done since she had had the measles as a child. Against the red background of her eyelids, she played out the scene that she imagined happening in the parents' room at the Goodman house. She saw Abram holding the English lady in his arms, kissing her and stroking her long, black hair. She saw him naked atop the lady's petite body, his hands cradling the lady's enraptured face.

When she could stand it no more, she opened her eyes and stared at the thin cracks crawling like hideous spiders on the white ceiling of her room. The peculiar, lusty sound of Abram's laughter that morning haunted her, and she pressed her hands over her ears as if to block it. Instinctively, she had recognized in his laughter the primeval pleasure of a man enjoying his woman. She had heard it before, within the walls of her own home, as she giggled with her sisters.

With sudden decision, she cast the rumpled bedding from her, jumped to her feet, and began to strip herself naked, until she stood, shaking slightly despite the heat, before the wash basin on its heavy wooden stand. As she poured water from the pitcher beside it, she could hear her mother calling the men and children to table. It was four o'clock, suppertime.

Having purged herself of the grime of her flight through the woods, Hannah dressed in clean clothing, from the skin out, and descended the narrow, steep stairway to the first floor of the house. She felt a twinge of guilt when she saw her mother and Fannie clearing the debris of the meal, the men already gone again to tend to their barn chores before they would finally rest on the porch at twilight.

"Have you stomach for food?" her mother asked, her hands ready to return food to the table for Hannah.

"*Neh, Mamm,* but I do feel a bit better. I think I'll go to sit with Gabe's mother a while. Gabe told me at singing last night, that she is no better," she said, donning a black bonnet over her prayer cap but leaving the cape hanging on its peg because the day was still warm. Tying the strings of the bonnet into a bow at her neck, she turned to face her mother.

The smile that spread on Mrs. Miller's earnest face revealed the pleasure that Hannah's words had brought her. "Why, *ja,* do so, Hannah. Take with you some peaches," her mother said, turning to fetch a gold-filled quart jar from the canning cupboard. Swiftly, she pulled a square of blue-and-white checked gingham from a drawer, placed it over the seal of the jar and secured it with a metal ring to form a little ruffle around the neck of the jar. "There!" she said, as she handed the jar to Hannah.

Hannah knew that her subtle mention of having talked to Gabe at the Sunday evening "singing" hinted to her mother that she was allowing the young man to court her. She also knew that her mother would ask no questions, in keeping with the Amish custom of pretense of keeping a "secret" when young people were dating. The truth was that Hannah had never given Gabe Yoder a drop of encouragement. Hannah dropped her eyes in guilt and went out the door, carrying the jar of peaches.

Hannah sat dutifully but impatiently in the dimly lit sick room that smelled of a recently used chamber pot and focused her eyes on Mrs. Yoder's thin, withered lips as she recited her droning litany of ailments and her hymn of praise to God who had blessed her with daughters, who, though married, came daily to look after her. Hannah jerked to attention when she realized that Mrs. Yoder had asked her a question:

"Well, will you?" The old woman narrowed her eyes as she waited for an answer.

Hannah felt her face redden as she guessed at the right response. "*Ja,* I will."

"That's good." Mrs. Yoder smoothed down the quilt that covered her chest. "My daughters made this quilt, to keep me warm. Every mother needs to know that her daughters will care for her if she lies stricken as I am. I thank *Gott* for my daughters. Every day, they leave their own houses to bring food for me and their brother, and they look after my house. You can't count on sons."

Hannah nodded her agreement and kept her eyes on the sallow face in the bed, but, at the mention of the brother, her own thoughts returned to her real reason for being there. The sisters had come and gone, but Hannah knew that nineteen-year-old Gabe would be alone in the barn. As the only son of a widowed mother, his work was never done. Gabe was responsible for all the chores that went with tending animals and the land. Hannah felt like defending him to his mother, but one did not challenge her elders.

After an hour had passed slowly, Hannah rose and bade her good-byes to the older woman. "I'd best make my way home, Mrs. Yoder, before it gets dark. I don't want to worry my *mamm.*"

A spark of approval lit the old woman's deep-set brown eyes, as she managed a wrinkle-shrouded smile. "You're a good daughter not to worry your mother. Say '*denki*' for the peaches, to your mother. I'm sorry I can't go to the door with you." From beneath the covers she pulled her blue-veined hand and extended it to Hannah who clasped it, despite the aversion that she felt.

"No need, I can see myself out. I'll pray that you gain back your strength." Satisfied that Gabe's mother would not rise from her bed to watch her go, Hannah strode with purpose across the dirt road that separated the Yoder house from the barn. Entering the lower level of the darkening two-story structure, she stood just inside the door and waited for her eyes to adjust to the light change. When she saw the silhouette of the broad-shouldered but thin boy seated on a milking stool, his forehead pressed tiredly against the side of the cow whose teats were in his hands, she moved toward him.

"Gabe." Hannah spoke only his name and watched him startle at the sound of her voice; then his beardless face flushed with pleasure. He jumped from his hunkered position and wiped his hands on his pants before speaking and stepping toward her.

"Hannah! What brings you to this dirty barn and you so clean and shining?" He addressed her in English and ran a hand through his shaggy hair, as if to make himself presentable.

Though Hannah had learned through her association with *der Englischer* to spurn the odor of perspiration and barn that clung to Amish men even after they had bathed, she mirrored Gabe's approach and directly put her arms around his neck, feeling him startle again, this time at her touch. Undaunted, she moved her hands to the shoulders of the boy whom she'd never allowed to so much as hold her hand.

"I want to mate with you, Gabe," she said in a voice filled with determination, the only passion she could muster.

At her plain words, Gabe leapt away from her, and, in his haste, kicked over the half-full pail of milk he had set aside, spilling its contents on the straw-strewn barn floor, while half-grown cats scampered out of hiding to take advantage of this unexpected boon. With their paws, whiskers and tongues in the thin, blue-white milk, they lapped greedily, nudging one another in their eagerness.

As he stepped around cats and the milk puddle, Gabe's words came out in a stammer. "Why, *ja*, I'll have the deacon speak to your parents soon about a wedding . . . in a good month . . . if you're willing now . . . ."

Hannah pulled him toward her again and renewed her grasp on his neck. Turning her face up to his, she met his eyes and clarified her intent. "Not 'soon,' not 'married'; I mean now, here, right now."

Even in the half-light, she could see the red flush that crossed Gabe's face. He pulled her arms down from his neck and spoke in a voice that revealed his shock. "Hannah, you know as well as I do—*Das Verboten!*"

In spite of his words, Hannah heard both fear and desire in his voice. In her mind, the taboos, the customs, had all become a meaningless blur. She placed a finger on his lips to silence him. She knew Gabe would follow her lead. She stepped away from him and removed her bonnet. Letting it drop to her feet, she began unhooking the bodice of her dress. At first, she modestly turned aside, but then she turned back to face him. She freed her shoulders and arms from her dress and undergarment, and stood, bare to the waist, before him. She watched him drop his eyes to her full, rounded breasts and stand in open-mouthed fascination. She was surprised when she felt her nipples stiffen under his scrutiny. Then she heard him groan in surrender as he reached for her.

There in the dusty barn smelling of dung, on straw that clawed at the tender flesh of her bare back, Hannah laid her maidenhood on the altar of anger, while, Gabe, the clumsy, panting priest took what was offered him.

Lying beneath him, Hannah experienced one sharp, burning pain and considered the intensity of the agony Gabe seemed to be enduring. Within minutes, he rolled away from her and lay panting beside her.

Hannah lay still, too, wondering about the woman's laughter she had heard coming from the newly-marrieds' bedroom that morning. What was there to laugh about? Then, with one hand, she reached down to touch herself and brought a bloodied finger to Gabe's face.

"Look," she commanded him.

He obeyed and rose on one elbow to reassure her. "It's normal, Hannah. Now we must marry."

The second time he took her, she found that by keeping her eyes tightly closed and pretending that he was Abram, she could at least feign passion . . . but not laughter.

Chapter Five

Luxuriating in her comfortable wedding bed, Sandra, two days a wife, lay quietly listening to the spray of the shower coming from the bath nearby, and she thought about the blissful two nights and a day she and Abram had shared as man and wife.

He had been so right, she decided, to insist that they consummate their love on their wedding day. Their love-making had been unbelievably intense, spell-binding, as together they unveiled the mystery of knowing each other intimately, exploring each other with unreserved delight and curiosity, seeing, hearing and touching one another in this way for the first time, awash in an ecstasy that was unjaded.

She cringed to think of how hard she had pressed him to give up his desire to wait. She thought of one day in particular, when Abram had visited her in her city apartment, and she had decided to make seduction her goal for the day.

~ ~ ~

Sandra studied her prey. Abram sat at a small, red-lacquered kitchen table that overlooked, by means of a floor-to-ceiling window, the leafy canopy that shaded the city park on a sunny day.

"I can't get over the athleticism of those skate-boarders," he said. "Let's go sit in the park and watch them."

Barefoot and wearing white shorts and a navy tee-shirt, Sandra lifted a leg to straddle his lap. Cradling his face in her hands, she punctuated her words with kisses. "I have a better idea," she said, "if it's athleticism that impresses you." She pulled her tee shirt over her head and sat before him in a black, lacy bra that she moved to unhook from the front.

He laid his hand over her fingers, preventing the unhooking of the bra. "Honey, you are one lovely lady, and it's taking all I can do to muster the strength to turn down your very appealing offer, but, let me explain it again . . . ."

"Surely, Abe," she said, interrupting the spiel she had heard before, "you don't think we have to wait for a piece of paper to give two consenting adults a green light to intimacy. No one waits these days. Besides, we'll be married in a few months . . . ."

Yet his reasoning enthralled her. "I want our wedding night to be amazing," he said. "Imagine what it will be like to unwrap each other like presents we've been wanting—bad—for a long time. That's what I want to experience with you." He kissed her hands and waited.

Despite the fact that she never really believed that she couldn't get him to change his mind, Sandra found herself imagining what first-time love-making would be like, on their wedding night, no less. Abram kept describing their intimacy as "a gift" they would give one another on their wedding day. It certainly was an old-fashioned and novel notion, an exciting one, too.

She decided she'd play along with the idea until she had had enough of it. "Well, okay, Baby," she said, pushing herself back from his lap in resignation. "But let's move the date up!" Sighing, she put her tee shirt back on and raked her fingers through her hair.

"I want you to see the farm first," he said, standing and pulling her back into his arms. "We need to find out if the city girl can adjust to life as a farmer's wife. Seriously, I want you to be sure. Let's plan a trip to the farm next Saturday. We'll have lunch, and I'll give you a preview of life on a dairy farm."

"It's about time! I've been waiting for you to take me there, Abe. What took you so long?" She noticed his hesitation before he answered.

"I wanted you to want me for myself, not for my . . . farm."

She laughed out loud. "That makes no sense at all," she said. "As you well know, I'm city born and bred. I like bright lights and sky-scrapers, but if I have to live on a farm to get you, so be it."

"You like being cooped up in this little apartment? Speaking of which, let's get out of here and go feed the ducks in the park or something," he said, holding out her sandals.

Sandra took her shoes from him and sat on the floor to strap them to her feet. "Okay, I'll think about life in the country, but, either way, I'm going to keep teaching, even if I have to drive into the city to do it. I might even keep my apartment and just be Mrs. Goodman on the weekends. What would you think of that?" She rose and looked into his face to discern the impact her words had had on him.

"I wouldn't think much of it at all. What's the point of getting married if we aren't going to live together?" She heard the disappointment in his voice.

"Oh, Abe," she said, taking the hand he offered to pull herself to her feet, "I'll try hard to find a teaching position in a school district near the farm. Keeping my job in the city would be a last resort. And, don't forget, I'd be at home on the farm for three months of the summer. I have all my post graduate credentials . . . unless you're saying you don't want a wife who works." She waited, hoping this once-cleared issue didn't have to be revisited.

He smiled and she was relieved to see that his disappointment had lifted. "I've already told you," he said, "I have no problem with my wife working, if that's what she wants to do. Now come on, let's get out in the sunshine." He took her hand and pulled her toward the red-painted door to her apartment. As they walked silently on the swirled gray-and-red of the carpeted hallway that led to the elevator, Sandra heard Abram, walking behind her, mutter something. She turned immediately and demanded to know what he had said.

"What are you muttering about? Don't deny it. What did you just say?"

Laughing, he pushed the down button and stood looking up at the lighted down-arrow above the silver doors of the elevator. The doors of the elevator opened, and she stepped inside and faced him. "Tell me!"

Abram said, "I said, 'Sure, you can work, until I get you—as we country folk say—in the family way!'"

They had already talked about having children, and she had said, yes, she'd try staying at home, but if she didn't like it, a nanny or a day-care would be used. He had agreed. But she knew he didn't really like the idea.

~ ~ ~

Now his wedded and bedded wife, she admitted to herself— again—that he had been right about waiting for the wedding night. She thought of how he had talked her into waiting to go on a honeymoon because he wanted to bring her here, to the Pennsylvania farmhouse that was now their home. She knew it was important to him, to use this very room on their wedding night, and so, she had agreed, though she knew that he could have afforded an exotic honeymoon island or an isolated chalet in the snowy Swiss Alps, both of which they had discussed.

Up the wide staircase he had carried her, to this opulent master bedroom, the room that now belonged to the new Mr. and Mrs. Goodman. Sandra lay looking around the immense, old-fashioned room and thought of the unspoiled farm wife who had created this love sanctuary, a room done in muted shades of brown and gold, a room with quiet dignity.

Despite the sexual desire that she felt trembling within Abram, Sandra was impressed with her new husband's gentleness as he had placed her on the soft autumn colors of the velvet patchwork quilt as though she were precious and fragile.

"Be fruitful and multiply, Wife!" He laughed as he said it, and so had she, but it was, they both knew, a solemn moment, a sacred promise.

She thought of how controlled he had been as he slowly undid the ivory, satin-covered buttons of her wedding suit. "But I'm in no hurry for us to multiply," he had said. "You'll be quite enough for a long while, Mrs. Goodman . . . ."

She had felt the heat of his desire and heard the catching of his breath as he had bared her breasts, seeing for the first time what he had only imagined, stoically allowing himself no more than an occasional caress during their courtship. Unwrapping her like the gift he had described, he explored her body, slowly, deliberately, telling her over and over again that she was beautiful, "beyond beautiful . . . ."

Sandra shivered again as she remembered how slowly he made love to her, savoring every part of her. Now, amazed that her body could begin to respond again, just to the memory of his recent touch, she got out of bed and walked, naked, toward the bathroom and opened the door to the steamy room. Through the misted glass shower door, she could see her husband's shadowy, nude body.

She paused to enjoy the sight of his broad shoulders and tapering back, his lean buttocks. As he turned amid the watery spray, his strong chin was lifted; his eyes, closed. Then he opened them and smiled at her, standing naked on the other side of the shower door. He slid the door open and welcomed her into the cascading water, where they enjoyed, for the first time, the sensation of their smooth, slippery bodies joined in a sensuous baptism.

"What shall we do today?" Sandra asked as she smoothed lotion on her shapely legs and arms.

Already dressed in jeans, tee shirt and Western boots, Abram sniffed the air and said, "Well, first I think we should take advantage of the breakfast smells that are wafting up from the kitchen. Hannah's back, apparently."

They entered the kitchen together, arms around each other. Sandra noticed that Hannah glanced briefly at them and pursed her lips before turning back to the pancakes on the griddle.

"Good morning, Hannah," Abram said. "Sandra and I are married now." Getting no congratulatory response from the hired girl, he went on. "I hope you weren't sick yesterday."

"I was under-the-weather, Mr. Goodman, but I'm all right and ready to work today," she said, with what Sandra saw as a pretense of great concern for her pancakes rather than acknowledge the new lady of the house standing at Abram's side. Sandra felt snubbed, for the second time, by Abram's Amish housekeeper.

This will have to change, she thought. *Or she's out of here. I will not be treated this way!*

But she decided to try to win her over. "Those have to be the fluffiest pancakes I've ever seen, Hannah. They can't be from a mix. Are they a special Amish recipe?"

Hannah ignored her question but gestured for them to sit at the table that had been set for two. Silently, she poured glasses of fresh orange juice for them, from a frosted, crystal pitcher.

"To us!" Abram said, clinking Sandra's glass of sparkling orange juice with his own.

Sandra saw the housekeeper's face flush red just before she turned off her griddle and hurried out of the kitchen.

Chapter Six

Earlier that morning, Hannah, with one black shoe perched on the bottom step of the front porch, had gazed upward with bitter eyes to the half-open window of the parents' room. Ascending to the porch, she felt the soreness between her legs and thought of Gabe whom she would meet again on Saturday night. She wished that Abram could know—know that she had given herself to Gabe. She wanted to believe that his knowing would hurt him the way knowing about the lady hurt her.

Tossing her head regally, she used her key to enter the quiet house, walked to the kitchen and set about preparing breakfast— for Abram—she reminded herself. If he wanted to share it with the Yankee woman, that was his choice.

But I work for him, not her, Hannah made clear to herself.

The smell of vanilla deliciously emanated from the pancakes bubbling on the griddle, and it wasn't long before the newlyweds made their appearance. They laughed as they came through the café doors, arms around each other. Even dressed in jeans like a man, Hannah saw that the lady looked shapely, feminine. The simple, short-sleeved, white blouse she wore was not buttoned to the neck, but a few buttons had been left open, exposing skin and the cleavage of her breasts. At her throat was a thin gold chain with a heart-shaped pendant, encrusted with what looked to Hannah like diamonds. On the lady's hand was another big diamond. The lady's shining, black hair rested on her shoulders, and, even from a distance, she smelled like flowers.

In her coarse, green dress and white apron, Hannah suddenly felt like an ugly oaf. Tears of frustration started in her eyes, and she concentrated mightily on the white circles of batter dotting the steaming, black griddle. Over them she sprinkled bits of fresh apple.

She could think of no response when Mr. Goodman told her that they were married. When he asked her if she had been sick, her discerning ears told her that his voice held no real concern. She turned to the refrigerator and took out the pitcher of fresh orange juice she had squeezed earlier that morning, *for him, chust the way he likes it,* she thought.

"To us!" he had said, turning to the lady and touching his glass to hers.

"To us!" the lady agreed.

Quickly, Hannah turned off the griddle and hurried from the kitchen, leaving them to their breakfast. She climbed the staircase, and at the top, out of habit, she turned to the first room on the right, Mr. Goodman's bedroom, to make his bed and straighten the room. The bed had not been slept in, and everything in the room was in order.

Of course, she thought, *he'll sleep with her in the parents' room now . . . .*

Hannah's stinging eyes fastened on the closed white double doors at the end of the hall. Moving slowly toward them, she stood and looked at their brass handles before summoning the courage to turn them. Stepping inside, she felt the blood rush to her face when she saw the rumpled pale yellow sheets, the beautiful velvet hap crumpled on the floor at the foot of the grand bed she had needed to change once every few months to keep it fresh.

She walked to the side of the high, unmade bed and saw, lying on it, a very sheer black nightgown, trimmed in lace . . . discarded . . . and on the saffron satin pillow were strands of long, black hair. Thrown carelessly over a rust-colored loveseat near the window was an ivory, satin wedding suit. Covering part of it was a man's black tuxedo. Lying askew on the floor was a pair of men's shiny, black patent-leather shoes, mingled intimately with a lady's ivory satin shoes. Nearest the bed were the lady's lacy underpants and a matching bra. Abram's white, cotton briefs appeared to have been flung across the room where they landed on a dresser.

Paralyzed with grief, Hannah could barely summon her leaden limbs to move, but, at last, she began to tug at the satin bed sheets. Touching them awakened the smoldering fury in her breast, and she ripped the sheets viciously from the bed. She was standing, her aproned breast heaving, clutching the sheets to her when the lady walked into the room.

"Oh!" the lady said. "Hannah, thank you, but I'll do that!" Although the lady seemed to flounder with embarrassment for a moment, she reached for the perfumed but well-used sheets, pulling them from Hannah's arms. The lady managed to say, "I'll take care of this room . . . our room . . . from now on. You have plenty to do in the rest of the house."

Hannah let go of the sheets and bowed her head in understanding. The master bedroom had become a love sanctuary off limits to the hired girl. The lady of the house would take care of it herself, she said.

The lady seemed to be waiting for her to speak, but her mind was paralyzed. She could think of nothing to say. But the lady's words gave her a clue. "I know you're used to doing as you wish in this house, Hannah, and that won't change much. But I'm here now and there are bound to be certain changes you'll have to accept. I'll take care of our room and our laundry. I'll rarely request a particular meal, but, if I did, you wouldn't mind, would you?"

Hannah knew there was no getting out of answering. "No, Mrs. Goodman," she said, forcing herself to look into Abram's wife's eyes, "I wouldn't mind."

"And I like to cook, when I feel like it," the lady said laughing lightly and putting her arm companionably around Hannah's shoulders, "so I may be giving you a hand in the kitchen from time to time. You can teach me some Amish recipes, and I can share some of mine with you. Is it a deal?"

Would the lady never stop talking? Would she stop touching her? All Hannah wanted to do was flee. But she knew another response was expected. "Yes, Mrs. Goodman, it's a deal."

Then the hired girl gently but deliberately wrenched herself away from the weight of Mrs. Goodman's arm resting on her shoulders.

Hannah gulped air as she descended the stairs, shocked by her confrontation with Abram Goodman's new wife. The lady's words had been friendly on the surface, she knew, but beneath them she had detected a warning.

She wants me out of here. She wants him all to herself. She probably tried to get him to fire me before . . . before they married. Mr. Goodman wants me here. That's why I'm still here. How am I going to stand her being in our house?

Then she remembered hearing that the new Mrs. Goodman would be teaching at the local high school. School would start in late August, she thought. The lady would be gone every day except on holidays. Brightening at this realization, Hannah went to the kitchen and vigorously cleaned away all remnants of the breakfast Abram had shared with his wife.

Chapter Seven

"She hates me!" At this angry outburst from his wife, Abram opened his eyes. Sandra stood over him with reddened face and blazing blue eyes.

He and Laddie had been enjoying a warm summer evening, snoozing on the veranda as they waited for her to join them. In the two months he and Sandra had been married, it had become their custom to retreat to the rose arbor after their evening meal, for coffee laced with Bailey's Cream. Red and white roses now in full flower scented the air, but he doubted that Sandra would be soothed by their fragrance.

"Now, Sandra," he said, knowing full well that it was Hannah to whom his wife referred, though Hannah had, by now, gone home for the day.

His wife held up a hand to stop his words. Perching on the edge of a cushioned lounge chair opposite him, she began her rant. "Don't 'now Sandra' me. I find myself tip-toeing around in my own house, trying to stay out of her way, just to avoid that sullen, pouting look on her face every time I enter a room. I don't want her here anymore. I can cook and take care of the house until school starts. In the meantime, we can find someone else."

The tone she used welcomed no disagreement, but he was, once again, going to try to persuade her to the notion that she, perhaps, mistook Hannah's shyness for rudeness. "Now why would she hate you, Honey? She may be a little jealous of you, but I don't think 'hate' is the right word." It was his turn to hold up his hand to stop her protest, and Sandra folded her arms and sat back to listen, though her face registered impatience.

"Think of what it's been like for her," he said, sitting up and brushing his hair out of his eyes. "She's a kid who's lived a plain and boring life of hard work. With this job, she was transported to the magical kingdom of fancy things and modern conveniences, and she gets paid for it! Everything was going great for her until I surprised her by bringing home a wife to share her little kingdom."

Sandra was able to spit out one word before he held up his hand again. "But . . . ."

Abram went on, attempting to sooth what he saw as his wife's hurt feelings. "She feels threatened by you, Sandra. She's afraid that now that you're the lady of the house, sooner or later she won't be needed."

Sandra rose and began to pace the patio's blue-gray flagstones that trailed off to become a path leading to the rose arbor. Emphasizing her words with sweeping gestures, she argued with him. "It doesn't make sense, Abe! I've tried to befriend her, complimented her profusely on the cooking, on the cleaning, on everything! And she knows I'll be teaching this fall. Of course I wouldn't replace her if she knew how to be civil . . . not to mention respectful."

Abram rose and stilled Sandra's agitated hands in both of his. "Why don't I point that out to her, Honey? Maybe she needs a few words of reassurance from me."

Pulling her hands out of his, Sandra resumed her pacing and then whirled to face him again. "Listen, Abe. That's not what she wants from you. She's in love with you and I'm the rival!"

This was a first. Abram had not heard this accusation from his wife before. He let his irritation show in his voice. "That's ridiculous, Sandra. She's a seventeen-year-old kid, and I've never treated her like anything but just that—a kid! She calls me 'Mr. Goodman,' for God's sake. I'm thirty years old and in love with my wife. She knows that! Every day she can see for herself how I feel about you."

Sandra's laugh was bitter. She wagged a well-manicured finger in his face. "You better believe she knows that. That's why the jealous wench is so unfriendly to me. She sees me as the enemy of her dream."

Arms akimbo, Abram spoke, controlling his irritation. "What 'dream' would that be, Sandra?"

"Oh, who knows what's going on in that white-capped head of hers?" Sandra sighed and moved close to him to kiss away his frown, saying, "But let's not spoil the evening, Love. You speak with her as you see fit, and we'll see if that changes anything." She enfolded him in her arms and gazed up at him. "Now, can we go upstairs? Suddenly, I feel awfully possessive of you."

"So possess me, Pretty Lady. I'm all yours," he said, his mouth close to her ear. "But why does it have to be 'upstairs'? The cushions on this chaise lounge look pretty comfortable to me. The patio's secluded; the night is warm; the roses, sweet . . . and Laddie won't talk . . . ."

He allowed Sandra to push him down onto the chaise lounge. She strolled a distance away from him and then cat-walked back to him, as she slowly began a strip-tease that captured him completely. His response was immediate, but, just as he reached for her, she turned and strode the opposite way, giving him a delightful view of her curvaceous, bare behind. She paused to pull a red rose from the arbor and sauntered coquettishly back to him, wearing nothing but the red rose she had placed behind one ear.

The next morning, Abram left Sandra, wrapped in satin and sound asleep, to go down to breakfast alone. As he came through the cafe doors alone, he saw that Hannah's face lit up, and her "Good morning!" was cheerful, something it had not been of late.

She hovered near him as he ate bacon and eggs, filling his coffee cup, moving the strawberry preserves just a little closer for him. It was obvious to Abram that Hannah was delighted that this morning was just as mornings used to be—just the two of them in the kitchen. A morning like this had not happened since Sandra had come here as his wife.

"Sit with me, Hannah," he said. From the flush that instantly flooded her face, he saw that his request had genuinely startled her. She had never before sat with him, not even to share a cup of coffee. Cautiously, she wiped her hands with her apron and sat across from him, unnecessarily rearranging the preserves and the butter on the table, rather than look at him.

Abram rose. "I'll get you a cup of coffee," he said. "How do you take it?"

"Oh, no, Mr. Goodman, it's not your place to serve me . . . ." She half-rose from her chair in protest.

"Shush," he said and carried a cup of coffee to the table as well as the cream and sugar.

"Thank you," she said, so quietly that he could barely hear her. Abram waited while she added cream and sugar to her coffee and took a sip.

Leaning back in his chair, Abram crossed his arms over his chest. "Look at me, Hannah," he said firmly. She lifted her eyes and blinked rapidly, and he saw that she was afraid. He softened his tone. "I need to talk to you, Punkin."

She blushed. He realized that he probably had not called her "Punkin" in his wife's presence, not since he had married. He took a deep breath and began. "Sandra thinks you don't like her." Her blush deepened to bright red. "She says you're cold and unfriendly toward her. Now, why would she say that, Punkin?"

He saw that her hands trembled, and she hid them in her lap. She managed to stammer, "I . . . I don't know. I try to do as she asks . . . ."

"Your work is not what she complains about, Hannah. She thinks you're a marvel around here, as far as that goes, but I think she gets a little lonely while I'm at work, so she'd really like another woman to talk to." He knew Sandra would hate him for making her sound pathetic. He knew loneliness wasn't the issue, but he was trying not to accuse Hannah of anything, sensing that she'd be devastated by any criticism.

But Hannah's haughtiness surprised and angered him. She lifted her chin and made eye contact with him. Even the tone of her voice became regal and her English was flawless. "Why would an English lady of the world want to talk to a simple Amish girl like me, Mr. Goodman? I think it best that the lady finds someone like herself to talk to. And I don't want her in my kitchen . . . ."

For the first time in the two years that she had been in his employ, Abram spoke to her sharply as he interrupted her. "It's like this, Hannah," he said, unfolding his arms and leaning toward her. "It is not *your* kitchen any more than this is *your* house. In fact, it's *her* kitchen, *her* house. You start treating my wife with respect, or I'll have to let you go. Do you understand me?"

She flinched as though he had slapped her, and he had to remind himself that he had not. He saw her pale eyes fill with tears and she was breathless and timid as she spoke. "Yes, Mr. Goodman . . . . I'll try to do better . . . ."

A pang of remorse shot through Abram as he saw that he had made her cry. "Look, Punkin," he said hurriedly, gesturing toward the veranda, "why don't you surprise Sandra with some of those roses? Take a nice big bouquet up to the landing for her to wake up to."

She rose unsteadily from her chair and kept her eyes averted, though she seemed to try to smile and to look willing to take his suggestion. "Yes, Mr. Goodman," she said, "I'll do that now. I think you're right. I need to show her that I . . . like her."

He watched her stumble to the kitchen drawer that held the scissors before sliding the doors that opened on the veranda and the rose garden.

He remained at the table, wondering why she hadn't just said, "I quit," if she didn't like the woman he had married. He had expected her to do that. But there she was, out there, dabbing her apron to her eyes and reaching in among the thorns to gather roses for Mrs. Goodman.

Chapter Eight

With her light blue dress and quaint, white prayer cap, the Amish girl moved among bushes of pink roses that matched the flush on her cheeks. The only outward sign of her inward agitation was a tremor in her hands as she reached in to snip roses for the mistress of the house. The man who had spoken sternly to her and ordered her out here to gather roses was an Abram Goodman she didn't recognize.

He would never talk mean to me like that, if she hadn't put him up to it! He had to do it to keep the peace in his house. With those thoughts, Hannah assuaged her hurt feelings as she prepared a bouquet of roses for Mrs. Goodman, at his request, though it felt to Hannah more like a command.

The lady is spoiled, used to being pampered and now I must help him with that. I should chust quit, that's what I should do, chust leave him high and dry. He'd see how fast this house falls apart . . . . Deep within herself, Hannah knew that nothing would make her leave the Goodman farm. Nothing would make her cut Abram Goodman out of her life, even if she was only his hired girl. It was better than nothing.

Keenly aware that she had to change her ways, Hannah greeted Mrs. Goodman each morning, with a small smile, but a smile, nevertheless. She patiently answered Sandra Goodman's questions about life in the Amish community. Hannah thought some of the lady's questions were none of her business, but she did not allow her face or voice to betray her thoughts.

"Do you have a boyfriend?" Sandra asked one day as they— Mrs. Goodman insisted on helping—peeled potatoes for the noon meal to be shared with the hired hands.

"Yes, Mrs. Goodman."

The nosy lady wasn't satisfied with Hannah's brief reply. "What's his name?" Sandra asked, paring the potatoes in peels that were wasteful, much too thick, in Hannah's opinion.

"Gabe—Gabriel," Hannah said, intending to reveal no more than that, but, sensing that this subject was important to the lady, Hannah directed the conversation away from Gabe and elaborated on Amish dating customs.

She spoke of the Sunday evening "singings" that took place every other week, on *Gemesspunndaag,* Church Sunday, in the evening. Here young people gathered to sing the "fast tunes," hymns not so mournful as the "slow tunes" sung a cappella by the congregation on the two Sundays a month that the community assembled at someone's home for church.

"On the other two Sundays, we either spend the day visiting others or just staying home and visitors might come to us," Hannah patiently explained, pronouncing all of her words just right, keeping her eyes on the potato she was peeling. She had hoped to ward off more questions about Gabe, but the curious lady kept probing.

"I hope this doesn't offend you," Mrs. Goodman said, "but do you 'bundle'? I've read about it . . . how dating couples share a bed."

"Bundle? Oh, you must mean *Bie-schlof,* lie together in bed, but fully dressed. In the summer months there is no need to; some do it in the winter to keep warm," Hannah improvised, hiding her amazement at the lady's brash questions.

"With a board between you?" Mrs. Goodman asked.

"No, Mrs. Goodman, there is no board between an Amish *madel* and her *kal.* "

"No kidding? And you behave yourselves?"

Hannah thought Mrs. Goodman was going too far with her questions. She paused to drop a long, brown potato curl from her knife before she answered. Looking with innocent blue eyes directly at her questioner, she said, "Yes, Mrs. Goodman, we Amish behave ourselves."

In truth, Hannah and Gabe were not behaving themselves. On Saturday night, date night for Amish teenagers, Gabe hitched up his rig and traveled the two miles to Hannah's house. He carried with him the customary flashlight to shine on the window of Hannah's bedroom, only after the darkened house told him that her parents and siblings had gone to bed for the night. He waited for Hannah to let him in through the front door. Even if her parents had heard them, they would have pretended not to. Such was the custom.

When Hannah saw the flashlight beam arc across her darkened room, she rose and tip-toed downstairs to open the door for Gabe. She greeted him without a kiss—in fact, she had never kissed him. She turned her mouth away so that his kisses fell on her cheek. Wordlessly, she led him to the bedroom that had been given her when she had reached dating age. Except for Gabe, no suitor had ever been admitted.

It was a spotlessly clean room with a light oak floor and white plastered, totally bare walls. The woodwork and dresser, nightstand and bed headboard were all of a varnished light oak that matched the floor. On the nightstand were a white pitcher and wash basin. The single bed was covered with an orchid-and-white, diamond-patterned quilt, the only colorful decoration in the room, except for a small, multi-colored, oval rug by the side of the bed. There were no signs that this room belonged to a teenage girl—no posters, no mementoes of parties or school, no stuffed animals, no makeup. On the plain white scarf that covered the dresser were a hairbrush and a mirror no bigger than an orange.

"Can we chust talk awhile?" Gabe asked as Hannah made the first move to undress, something she usually did as soon as the bedroom door closed behind them, before they were alone five minutes.

At his question, she paused and sat beside him on the bed. "What do you want to talk about?"

"It's almost autumn," he said, rising to place his hat on her dresser. Instead of sitting beside her again, he remained standing and cleared his throat. She could tell that he had prepared a speech, another effort, she guessed, to assert his masculine rights.

"It's almost wedding season. It's time we had the banns announced in church."

"I'm not ready," was Hannah's quick reply. She knew that Gabe's guilt—and fear—over what they did, at least once a week, sometimes more often if they could find a way, was talking now. He had spoken of their marriage more than once and she had led him to believe that she was considering it. She knew that he feared the Ban of Avoidance, ex-communication, and getting her pregnant. At their second mating, he had withdrawn before spilling his seed and provoked her fury.

~ ~ ~

"You will not do this ever again, or it is over!" she had said, wiping her belly with a towel.

"But, Hannah," he pleaded, "if you get in the family way, everyone will know. We'll be punished."

"Not if we marry," she said, pulling on her slip. "Then everyone will pretend not to know. It has happened before."

Gabe hesitated for a moment before speaking. "If that's the only way I can get you to marry me, so be it."

~ ~ ~

Now Gabe stood awkwardly as she undressed deliberately, methodically, with no hint of teasing. Then she lay back with her full breasts falling slightly apart and her legs spread; as usual, she did not reach for him, would never touch him first. She knew that the sight of her inflamed him instantly, overcoming all of his guilt and fear. But this time was different. He still stood by the bed, looking down at her. She was surprised that he appeared to have more to say. She heard him swallow hard before continuing.

"If you get in the family way," he said, "we'll be found out, Hannah! You know as well as I do that fornication is a sin, whether we intend to get married or not. We'll be put under the Ban of Avoidance. We both accepted baptism into the church last September. We could be ex-communicated. Doesn't that worry you?"

"No," she said, "it doesn't. But don't do anything you don't want to do. You can go now." With this she covered herself with the quilt, rolled away from him and waited to see what he would do. He let out a long sigh, and she heard the crackle of his straw hat as he placed it back on his head.

"I'm done with this carryin' on, Hannah," he said. "I'd marry you any time, if you wanted me to. Why you want to do this," he said, making a sweeping gesture to indicate the bed, "is beyond me. You lay beneath me like a sack of grain. You never say my name or kiss me back."

She knew he was waiting for her to say something. Her tongue felt frozen. She let him go. She lay listening to the sound of his heavy shoes descending the stairs, the opening of the door, and then all was silent until she heard his brief, "Hah!" as he awakened his nag to pull him home.

It doesn't matter, she thought. *I'll give him a few weeks to come to his senses, and then I'll go to singing.*

Chapter Nine

Hannah waited, hidden beneath the long fronds of a weeping willow outside the Stoltzfus house, where church members had gathered earlier in the day. After church, there had been the traditional feast, served by unmarried girls like her and her sister Fannie. More than once, she had felt Gabe's eyes upon her, though she had not returned a glance. After the meal the table was cleared, and the dishes were washed, a huge task handled by the married women, while the younger ones were now free to join in the games.

Hannah had waved away attempts to draw her into games of volley-ball or croquet, saying that she had to mind the baby for her mother. She sat with Baby Aaron on an old quilt and, for his amusement, gave him two church-mice made from cleverly twisted handkerchiefs.

Even as she had kept an eye on her little brother, she watched a ferocious volley-ball game played by teams made up of the older boys. Hatless in the sunshine, Gabe leapt for a volley-ball and spiked it hard across the net. A cheer went up, and she noticed how he blushed at the attention. When he looked over at her, she smiled at him and watched as his blush deepened.

Now, as dusk fell, she had retreated beneath the weeping willow that grew on the edge of the Stoltzfus yard while adults and teens filed back into the house for the evening "singing." The adults were there to chaperone. The teens were there to socialize and to sing the fast hymns, rarely sung in church.

She knew Gabe would look for her, but he would soon discover that she was not inside with the others. Keeping an eye on the doorway to the house, she saw his lanky form emerge. He stepped off the porch and turned his head side to side as he scanned the yard. Hannah parted the hanging willow branches that draped like sage-green curtains on a window and let herself be seen.

He walked to her, as she knew he would, and ducked under the willow branches. Hidden by boughs that touched the earth, she did not resist when he took her hand. She even lifted her face to be kissed, and he hungrily obliged.

"Get your rig," she said, "and let's go for a ride."

The huskiness of his voice told her he had more than missed her over the past few weeks. "It's chust over there," he said. "Give me a minute to hitch up the horse."

They rode in silence, but Hannah slipped her hand into the crook of his elbow as he held the reins. "Where to?" he asked.

"Your barn," she said, knowing he would not refuse.

They rode in silence, sitting closer than they ever had before. He slowed the horse to a walk when he came to his barnyard. "Go quiet, now, Sally," he said to the horse, holding her back from the trot she tried as she sought the sanctuary of the barn and a bucket of feed.

Hannah glanced at the house silhouetted against a fire-streaked sky, dark except for a light in a side window that had to be Gabe's mother's bedroom.

"Do you think she heard the horse?" Hannah asked, with some apprehension.

"I don't think so, but it doesn't matter. She won't come out," Gabe said, offering Hannah his hand to help her out of his uncovered rig.

Gabe laid a brown, quilted horse blanket on the straw. "Not so comfortable as your bed," he said apologetically, "but it's better than nothing." He was breathing hard.

Hannah feigned innocence with her question: "Do you want to talk first, Gabe?"

"No," he said, "I chust want to . . . be with you. I can't do without you, Hannah."

Neither of them heard the agonized creaking of the barn door as they moved together, Gabe's white buttocks rising and falling in the semi-darkness, as he lay between the legs of Hannah Miller. His earthy grunts obliterated the sound of slow, shuffling feet accentuated by the rhythmic stomp of a cane. Even the intruder's first gasp of shock escaped their hearing.

The eruption of a stream of curses in German paralyzed them in their coupling. Though Rachel Yoder's raspy, hysterical voice was weakened by breathlessness, the meaning of the vehement words she hissed at the lovers was clear: Gabe's mother fully intended to bring down upon their heads the wrath of God and the Amish bishop, even if it meant that her own son would suffer.

Ashen-faced and wide-eyed, Gabe Yoder tried to cover his now flaccid organ with straw as he rolled away from the glowing white nakedness of Hannah Miller who lay there in the dimness of the barn, spread-eagled and too petrified to move.

Shaking with fury, old Mrs. Yoder raised her cane as if to strike them. Instead she pointed her stick at Hannah and said to her son, "Take this sinful girl to her family; from there go to get the bishop. Bring him here tonight!"

"Mamm," Gabe tried, now kneeling before his mother despite his nakedness, pleading in German. "Please, listen to me. Hannah and I will marry . . . . We'll have the banns announced."

Hannah slowly dressed in a darkened corner of the barn and knew that Gabe's pleading would do no good. The old woman would not be persuaded. Regally, Hannah walked from the barn without a glance at Gabe's mother and made her way to the buggy and sat waiting.

She watched the hateful crone limp her way back to the house, while her now clothed, weeping son led the horse from the barn. No plea for mercy would stop the summoning of the bishop to the Yoder home that very night. Hannah knew that rapid judgment would soon fall upon their heads.

Throughout the week, the Old Order community buzzed with news that Gabriel Yoder and Hannah Miller had been caught in fornication and, on the coming Sunday, punishment would be meted out by the furious bishop. Word had been sent to the Goodman farm that Hannah would not return to work there.

Some whispered that this is what came of letting your girls work for *der Englischer* whose ways had surely corrupted Hannah Miller. Though it was understood that boys found it nearly impossible to resist the influence of a wayward girl, Gabe Yoder would be held accountable, too.

Without the usual greetings and banter, the people of the Old Order, including the children, silently filed into the bishop's house. Benches had been arranged inside, and they took their places behind the row that held the Yoder and Miller families, sitting with shoulders like rounded tombstones.

With their backs to the congregation, Gabe Yoder and Hannah Miller stood before the scowling bishop. Having been privately terrified by him, the fornicators were now ordered to stand in confession before the congregation.

Hannah stood motionless beside the kneeling boy, her white-capped head unbowed, her fair skin rosy rather than pale. In the stifling heat of the crowded room, she would not move to wipe the perspiration that beaded on her upper lip, lest they think she wept like the boy who sobbed beside her. She felt the weight of the eyes of her parents on her back, silently willing her, beseeching her, to kneel, to confess along with the sobbing Gabe, her sin of fornication. The piercing black eyes of the Amish bishop stared into hers as he waited.

The only other sound in the room besides the quiet weeping of the women was the humming of flies, droning their mourning song high above a long, sticky, hanging trap.

Held fast, the black bodies of those who had not escaped struggled and died. Hannah wanted to lift her eyes and voice to warn the blue-black flies dancing against the sunny, white ceiling, but she could not, would not, let go her stony stare into the sunken black pits that were the eyes of the bishop.

Gradually, the piteous weeping of the women on the benches behind her and to her left, her mother's and sisters' voices among them, became a crescendo of loud wails. Her own eyes were dry, and Hannah wished she could turn to the women to intone, "Weep not for me, daughters of Jerusalem . . . weep for yourselves." The verse repeated over and over in her mind, a monotonous mantra accompanied by the flies. Dimly, she was aware of another sound, too, the stifled sobs of the boy whose shaggy bowed head brushed the fabric of her dark dress as he knelt beside her.

She swayed on her feet, refusing to kneel and confess after Gabe had finished. She had not died under the first scathing rebuke by the bishop. She had survived and still she would not kneel in gratitude. A sound interrupted the mantra in her mind. The bishop was speaking again.

His aged voice quaked with indignation and outrage as he railed against Hannah Miller's unrepentant soul once again. Hannah roused her mind to awareness. From the bishop's spit-flecked, thin lips, moving like a purple worm above his graying beard, would come her fate. He was her uncle, but that would make no difference. He would dispense divine justice with unwavering vengeance.

Her uncle raised his arms as he directed his pronouncement to the congregation, like an avenging angel hovering over a dark sea spread out before him. "Gabriel Yoder, the son of the widow Rachel, will, after a period of one year in which his behavior will be spotless in the sight of God and *der Gemein*—the Church—be restored to it, but, until that time, he will endure excommunication for one year and will be set back from assembly and communion. He shall fellowship with no one outside of his family—mother, sisters and their families. None but they shall benefit from the work of his hands and none will offer a hand to help him in his labors without first seeking God's will in prayer.

Still kneeling, Gabe nodded his head in acceptance of his punishment.

The bishop's voice rose in volume and shook with wrath. "Hannah Miller, in the stiff-necked disobedient spirit with which she now stands before you, I commit to *dem Teufel und allen seinen Englen ubergeben*—to the devil and all his angels. I appoint her to *Ban und Meidung,* as we, the Church, form a bond of agreement under which she will endure excommunication and shunning until such time as she sees fit to confess and repent of her sins against God and the Church.

"I caution all of you, her parents and family, to rigorously shun Hannah Miller; that is, you will receive no favors from her, no work from her hands, hold no conversation except what   is absolutely necessary with her; she will not eat with baptized persons . . . .

"I ask for unanimous accord, the Bond of the Church, in voting for this counsel in keeping with the *Ordnung.* And now *Ich will schweigge*—I will remain silent."

The vote was unanimous. Even Hannah's mother and father dared not support her in her flagrant disobedience, as she understood they could not. Back at home now, she heard her family moving in the kitchen beneath her room. They moved, but the somber mood silenced even the youngest children.

Chilled to the bone, Hannah pulled the quilt on her bed up around herself. She let her eyes roam the room and thought of the times she had sinfully shared more than conversation with Gabe when he had come courting over the past four months. She remembered how he had struggled to make no sound during their mating. She thought of his pathetically bowed head as he had knelt before the bishop and felt, not pity, but loathing for Gabe.

She knew what she must do. Heaping the quilt onto the bed, she knelt beside it as if to pray. Instead, she withdrew from beneath the bed a cardboard box which contained sheets and pillowslips she had made, at her mother's insistence, for "someday when you have your own house" and emptied its contents messily onto the bed beside the quilt.

Rising, she walked to the small oak dresser that her father had made for her recently. It still smelled of varnish. From it she took undergarments and filled the box with as much as it would hold. From her closet, she pulled dresses in four colors from their hangers, folded them and pushed them down into the box as far as they would go. With not so much as a backward glance, she carried the heaping box from the room and descended the creaking, narrow stairway leading to the lower hall.

Pausing at the entrance to the lamp-lit kitchen, Hannah passed her eyes over the stricken faces of her family seated stiffly round the big oak table; they had ceased their praying, praying for her, no doubt, to stare dumbly at her standing in the doorway with the box in her arms. She turned slightly to deposit the box on the bottom stair and reached to take her black cape and bonnet from a peg at the bottom of the stairway. With her family watching silently, she donned the cape and bonnet, leaving its ribbons untied.

Her mother rose to her feet, and, with the lamp's dancing flame casting shadows on her haggard, white face, opened her mouth as if to speak. She closed it after a glance at her sad-faced but stern husband. Hannah looked deeply into her mother's tear-filled eyes before turning away. In them she read the shame and grief she had caused her mother. She bent to retrieve the box, straightened, and moved wordlessly to the door.

Without hesitation, she strode to the porch steps but carefully descended them, peering around one side of the box she carried. At the bottom of the steps, she picked up her pace and stepped onto the dirt road that passed in front of the white farmhouse that had been her home.

Keeping her eyes on the red, bleeding evening sky, young Hannah Miller did not look back even when she heard a sob escape her grieving mother who stood at the screen door watching her go.

Chapter Ten

Darkness had fallen by the time the Bond Woman reached her destination—Abram Goodman's home. Her arms ached from the burden of the cardboard box she had clutched in front of her during her three-mile journey on foot. She stood woodenly before the partially lit, big house which had been both her liberation and her undoing. Through the screen door, she could hear the distant sound of a television somewhere within.

Why had she come here, she wondered, but where else could she have gone? She only knew that she could not remain where she had been. Her mind had been set in stony silence since the night, less than two days ago, when Gabe and she had been caught in the act of sin; yet an eternal gulf seemed fixed between then and now. In fact, from that moment in time, she had not uttered a word, not even under the angry bishop's interrogation, and she had thought very little. If she had been pressed to define the heaviness that weighed against her breast, she would have had to think hard to answer what it was she felt.

Hannah became dimly aware of the scent of a remnant of summer's roses still clinging to the porch, a soothing fragrance to one condemned. She began to hear crickets which must have been singing all the while. Tilting her head back to look up into the cool September night, she realized that in the blue-black sky shone a perfectly round, white moon with blue shadows like bruises on its delicate face. By its soft light, she had made her way here.

How long she had been standing thus, not even resting her cardboard burden on the porch steps, Hannah did not know. Just as she tried to shake her mind from its numbness, to think about what she would do next, Abram's voice reached her.

"Here, Laddie, let's go outside," and in a moment he was holding the screen door ajar for the Sheltie who barked once before recognizing the apparition in the semi-darkness, then tail-wagged his way to Hannah's feet.

Hannah heard the startled catching of Abram's breath as he beheld her unmoving form standing at the base of his porch steps.

"Hannah! What's the matter?" he asked, stepping onto the porch in his stocking feet. He seemed paralyzed, too, as he towered on the top step, staring down at her rooted there with her arms wrapped around a box.

After her long silence, Hannah's own voice sounded hollow and strangled to her, as she tried to unglue her tongue from the roof of a dry mouth. "I . . . am . . . under the *Meidung* . . . under the Bond . . . their agreement to cast me out."

"You're what?" Coming down the steps, Abram took the box from her and relief flooded through her aching arms. "Come inside, Punkin, and tell me what you're talking about." He climbed the porch steps ahead of her and struggled to tuck the box under one arm as he held the door for her to enter his home.

Inside, Hannah asked for water. "I'm so thirsty, may I trouble you . . . ." She rubbed her arms under her cape. Removing the stiff bonnet that had limited her side vision, she remained standing in the foyer where he had left her.   As she took the glass of cold water from his hand, she asked, "Where is the lady . . . Mrs. Goodman?" She let her gaze roam the doorways off the foyer.

"Upstairs taking a bath. Come, sit down, Hannah, and tell me what's going on and why your parents sent word that you wouldn't be working for me anymore."   Placing his arm gently around Hannah's shoulders, he led her into the den where sequin-bedecked women sparkled and sang on the television screen.

Hannah wanted to crumble against him, but she moved forward with him as he led her to the big, soft brown leather chair that still held the warmth of his body. Drawing comfort from it, Hannah let her weary body be enfolded by it and released the tears she had been holding back.

Switching off the television, Abram pulled up a matching leather stool in front of her chair and sat looking up into the Hannah's downcast face, as she silently wept. "Sweetheart," he began, and Hannah could barely breathe at the word and the tenderness in his voice. "They told me you wouldn't be back. Have you run away from home?"

"No, Mr. Goodman," she addressed him by force of habit, trying to speak clear English. She did not meet his eyes. "I walked away from it. I am outcast . . . under the *Meidung* . . . the Ban of Avoidance . . . shunned. I cannot, will not, bear it!" Her weeping increased and she could not stifle the sound of her sobs.

"My God, Hannah, why? What do they say you have done?" He forced her to look at him by taking her face in his hands and using his thumbs to wipe away the tears on her cheeks.

Hannah fought to keep the resentment she felt for Abram out of her voice, resentment toward him who had brought her to this disgrace. "I am a fornicator. I have given myself to Gabe, and they know." Then came a kind of satisfaction that, at last, he knew also. The pain in his gray eyes was what she wanted to see.

Dropping his hands from her face, Abram rose, expelling his held breath. He offered no admonishment. "And what do they want from you now?"

"They want me to repent and to marry Gabe." To her own ears, her voice sounded cold.

"And you won't?"

Repugnance at the thought of it filled her, and she shook her head as she spoke. "I will not!"

They turned at the sound of Sandra's voice as she approached the den. "Abe, who are you talking to?" She entered wearing a loose, white terrycloth bathrobe. Her damp, black hair was tied up with a blue ribbon and her feet were bare.

"Oh, Hannah! What's wrong?" she asked with genuine concern in her voice.

Taking Sandra's hand and holding it to his chest, Abram stood beside her and intervened for Hannah who wanted to collapse with exhaustion. "Honey, Hannah's left home. She'll stay with us until she has had time to think." He stated it as a fact, but Hannah heard the plea in his voice, a plea for his wife's agreement.

Sandra hesitated a moment, and in that moment, she met her husband's eyes. "Certainly," she said, "the downstairs bedroom is ready, but, of course, Hannah knows that." She laughed, seeming to be embarrassed at her statement of the obvious. "Come on, Hannah, let's get you settled. You look exhausted."

As Hannah rose and followed Sandra to the downstairs guest room, just off the den, she thought, *All of the bedrooms are ready, but she doesn't want me upstairs where he is.* Turning to face Sandra, she said only, "Thank you, Mrs. Goodman. Yes, I'm very tired."

Abram briefly entered the room to set Hannah's box on a chair near the door. "Goodnight," he said, "We'll talk in the morning."

Sandra added, "Goodnight, Hannah, sleep well," as she closed the door softly behind her.

As Hannah laid her cape and bonnet on the bed, she heard the clicking off of lights and the sound of Abram talking softly, no doubt telling his wife what he understood of Hannah's story, as they climbed the stairway to their bedroom.

Alone in the downstairs guest room, Hannah looked at the green and white quilt on the queen-size bed and felt hot tears come to her eyes. "The Tree of Life," she said softly, running her hand across the fabric.

She knew the pattern well. It was her mother's design. Dusting this room weekly, Hannah had proudly smoothed the quilt, admiring her mother's artistry. Her mother had made this quilt for Abram's mother. Now, as she touched it fondly, the tears began to fall again. The memory of her mother's stricken face was before her, and she ached to explain what her mother would never understand and what Hannah, herself, barely understood.

Lying fully clothed on the quilt, Hannah buried her face in it and let sorrow wash over her, sorrow for her family, suffering shame because of her. Her weeping went on until the face of her mother began to dissolve into the face of Abram Goodman, and, comforted, Hannah slept.

Chapter Eleven

The sun rose on the new day, a cool but sunny morning with a hint of fall in the air. Abram lay propped on an elbow, looking down at Sandra's sleeping face framed by black hair that spilled on the white satin pillow. She didn't seem to hear the soft strains of music that issued from the clock radio on the night stand. It was 5:30 a.m. Gently, he began to kiss her awake, and she smiled, encouraging his caresses long before she opened her eyes.

When her dark lashes fluttered open, Abram greeted her with the words, "I love you, Sandra . . . ."

Her quiet response was "I know," and she opened her arms to receive him.

Married almost four months now, Abram had developed the habit of letting Hank give the hired hands their orders and preferred to spend the morning hours with his bride. In the summer months, he didn't join his men until nine o'clock, smiling sheepishly at their jibes concerning his "banker's hours." Now that Sandra left for school by 7:30 a.m., his earlier appearance turned their good-natured taunts to "Uh-oh, the honeymoon's over."

The leisurely summer schedule was behind them, but the newlyweds simply awakened earlier to enjoy the ritual of love-making, as a daily gift of affirmation of one another, that could be satisfied no other way. Sandra often felt herself to be the special woman—set apart—the way Abram had wanted her to be.

As they descended the staircase to share a hasty breakfast, they realized that Hannah did not intend to play the role of a guest. The smell of bacon beckoned them, and they entered the kitchen to find a table already laid and waiting for them. Hannah stood guard over the shining Chrome toaster, a ready butter knife in her hand. She looked rested and immaculate in her fresh Amish dress in green, white apron and cap.

"Good morning, Mr. Goodman, Mrs. Goodman." Nodding, she greeted them shyly, perhaps embarrassed to have invaded their home the night before and, more, to have them know that she was not the innocent girl she had seemed.

"This is great, Hannah," Abram said, "but you didn't have to make our breakfast . . . ."

Sandra interrupted him quickly, "But I'm so glad you did! I'm starving." She pulled out a chair, sat at the table, unfolded a yellow napkin and put in in her lap.

Abram, picking up on Sandra's understanding that Hannah needed to be useful, sat, too. "This is sure a big improvement over the cold cereal with milk we've had the last few days."

"Look, she's even picked roses for the table," Sandra said, fingering a slim silver vase that held two pink roses. "What a fantastic way to start the day. Thank you, Hannah."

Hannah blushed at their compliments and brought platters of bacon and eggs to the table. "It's the least I can do," she said, and hurried back with a stack of buttered toast and a white carafe of coffee.

"Sit and eat with us," Abram urged, half-rising and reaching to pull out a chair for the hired girl.

"Oh, no, Mr. Goodman, I've already eaten. I'll see to my regular chores, if you'll excuse me." With a rustle of starched crispness, she was gone to other parts of the house, leaving the newlyweds to themselves.

As the blue cafe doors swung closed behind Hannah, Sandra and Abram looked blankly at one another. "Does she intend to be a live-in maid?" Sandra wondered aloud.

Abram shrugged and dipped his toast into the golden puddle of egg yolk on his plate. "Would that be so bad? But, no, I think she'll want to go home in a few days. Amish families are very close."

Sandra sighed and picked up a knife to add grape jelly to her toast. "I certainly hope so, Abe. I don't want her living with us."

"I get that, Honey, but I think her parents will be over here to pick her up, probably before you're home from school. Maybe I'll drop by and let them know she's here. They're probably worried sick about where she spent the night."

"What's with this shunning thing?" Sandra asked, checking out the time on her wrist watch. "It seems pretty primitive, even for the Amish."

"Yeah, they have a lot of customs that just don't make sense. I've lived around them all my life, but, between you and me, I think the way they live without modern conveniences is ridiculous. As though God gives a hoot about that. And shunning your own daughter? What about the God of love and forgiveness? Where the hell do they expect her to live?" Frowning, Abram revealed opinions about his Amish neighbors that he had never voiced.

"Your mother was friends with Hannah's, right? Would she have liked a woman with the potential to kick her daughter out of the house?" Sandra reached for a second piece of toast and then pulled back her hand. "Gosh, if I eat like this every morning, I'm going to be a cow!"

"Maybe just a little heifer," Abram said, laughing and patting Sandra's cheek. "Both of the Millers—Rebecca and Joe—always seemed like reasonable people to me. Good parents. I can't imagine them holding their daughter's feet to the fire for her sins. Yeah, I think they'll be over to get her soon."

Rising, Sandra brushed crumbs from her navy, straight skirt and white blouse, tied a red silk scarf around her neck, and pulled on a navy jacket that she retrieved from the back of her chair. "I have to get going, Honey. Will you get my car out of the garage while I brush my teeth?"

"Will do," Abram said, taking a final swig of coffee.

As his wife neared the café doors, she turned back to face her husband. "But aren't you surprised that little Miss Goody-two-shoes has been getting it on with her boyfriend?" Leaving the question unanswered, she pushed through the doors and was gone.

Abram sat musing for a minute, a frown on his face. "Yes," he said to no one. "I certainly am."

Chapter Twelve

At the sound of Laddie's frantic barking, Hannah removed her hands from sudsy dishwater and leaned forward to peer through the white-curtained window above the kitchen sink. She was stunned to see a black Amish buggy entering the driveway that circled in front of the Goodman house. The brown mare pulling it shied from the excited dog that ran barking at its side. She knew that this was not her father's buggy, nor his horse.

Hannah's heart thudded in her chest and ears, and her breath came short as panic seized her. Frantically, she looked for a way of escape and headed for the French doors that led to the rear of the house. She froze at the sound of heavy shoes already thudding up the front porch steps. The visitor did not ring the bell but banged loudly on the aluminum screen door.

She eased herself through the French doors to the patio, pressed herself against the side of the house and waited for the banging to cease, for the clopping of the horse's hooves to start again, but the visitor was relentless. She feared that whoever it was would break Mr. Goodman's door. Taking deep breaths to calm herself, she slipped back inside the house and moved slowly toward the rattling front door. Her blood turned to ice at the sight of the bishop's high-crowned hat on the other side of the door. Shading his eyes with a gnarled hand, he peered through the screen into the house. Then he saw her standing at the end of the foyer, as far away from the door as she could get.

"Hannah Miller, you must come home!" he demanded in German. When she did not move, he pulled hard on the latched door.

"Open the door, Girl! Your parents are worried about you."

Trembling, Hannah hurried to the door, fearing that he would break the latch. She took a deep breath before she opened it. She did not invite her uncle to enter; instead, she stepped out to the porch and faced his fury.

"I will not go back," she managed to say even as her voice shook. Though she trembled, she stood tall and faced the bushy-bearded bishop who also trembled, but with rage.

"What? Will you defy me? Will you defy God? You must allow the *Meidung* to work repentance in your proud soul. Hannah, your mother is suffering. Leave this place with me!" Gripping her arm strongly, he pulled her to the edge of the porch. Hannah screamed and resisted, dropping to the floor of the porch. In her uncle's iron grip she was being dragged down the porch steps, with her hip bumping on each wooden stair.

"Abram! Abram!" she screamed his name—the first time she had ever used it—desperately hoping that he could hear her. "Help me!" Her voice pierced the morning stillness.

As the bishop wrestled her toward the buggy, she saw him grip the buggy whip and raise his hand to strike her. Cowering on the ground, she covered her face and waited for the blow to fall. "Don't hit her!" Abram's voice was threatening in tone and it stayed the bishop's arm. With long steps and swinging arms, he was striding purposefully toward the bishop.

When the Amish man loosened his grip on Hannah's arm, she scrambled to stand sobbing behind Abram's broad back.

The bishop dropped the buggy whip and stepped forward, palms outward to halt Goodman's approach. "Mr. Goodman," he said, "you must not interfere. Hannah belongs with her own people. Her parents have sent me for her."

"Did they send you to manhandle her? I know Rebecca and Joe, and I doubt it!" Abram advanced and stood toe-to-toe with the bishop who looked diminutive next to him.

The bishop kept his tone reasonable. "Your English laws do not allow you to give sanctuary to an underage child, and I know you to be a law-abiding man. I wouldn't want to have to go to the authorities about you."

Emboldened by Abram's presence, Hannah stepped forward to contest the black-coated man's words. "I am eighteen! The English law recognizes me as an adult. I am here by my own volition, and you cannot take me against my will!" She shocked herself at the vehemence of her words.

The bishop argued, "You are seventeen. Your own mother will swear that you are seventeen."

Hannah laughed a mirthless laugh. "I have been eighteen for two days. My birthday was Sunday past . . . . My gift was the

Meidung. My mother had forgotten, but, trust me, she will remember." Her voice was bitter.

The bishop seemed to wither under her scathing words. She knew that he believed her.

He stared at her and in a steady, sorrow-laden voice, reverted back to German to ask the question, "And, now, do you renounce your birthright among God's Chose people? Do you . . . go English?"

Hannah straightened and lifted her hands to the white covering on her head, removed it, and, with deft fingers, the pin that constrained her hair. Shining, sun-lit blonde hair tumbled to her shoulders.

Knowing that Abram had not understood the bishop's question, Hannah now turned to face him. By the shocked look on his face, she saw that he had, indeed, understood the profound meaning of her gesture.

Chapter Thirteen

Home at last from a hectic day at the country high school where she now taught English to tenth-graders, Sandra carefully guided her new black Jaguar, a recent gift from her husband, into the garage. At first she had been embarrassed to drive such a luxury car to school, but then, she reasoned, *so I married a rich man. I certainly couldn't have bought it on a teacher's salary. They all know that. And they all seem as surprised as I was that the unassuming Abram Goodman can afford this.* Her colleagues had admired her Jag and she had taken them for rides in it after in-service days.

Briefcase and books in her hands, she walked to the house with Laddie who whirled and danced with joy at her return home. "You missed me, did you?" She laughed at the gleefully barking dog. She thought of how good it was going to feel to kick off her heels and to exchange her tailored navy suit for a sweatshirt and jeans.

As she ascended the porch steps, she was surprised to find Abram sitting in one of the big wicker chairs, a luxury he seldom enjoyed this early in the day. She lost her smile at the troubled look on his face.

"Abe? What's the matter?" She felt afraid as she asked her question.

"Hi, Hon," he said, rising, taking her briefcase and books from her and depositing them on a porch table. "I've been waiting for you. I got lost in my thoughts and didn't even notice that you had pulled in. I wanted to head you off before you went into the house."

"Abe, you're scaring me!" she said, glancing apprehensively at the door to the house.

"No, no, there's no big problem. It's just Hannah."

Relieved, Sandra sank onto the cushioned glider, slinging off her navy and white spectator pumps. "What about Hannah? Has she gone home?" She rubbed one nylon-stockinged foot against the other.

"No," her husband said with a sigh as he settled back into his chair. "She's still here, and she's let her hair down . . . literally."

"What on earth are you talking about?" Sandra felt impatience rising in her. Abram moved over to sit beside her on the glider and lowered his voice to describe the scene between Hannah and the bishop that he had witnessed earlier that day.

"But, Abe! Do we dare let her stay here? And for how long?" Sandra was beginning to feel as though an albatross had come to torment them. She wanted Hannah as a housekeeper, but she did not want her living with them indefinitely.

"I've made it clear, Abe, that I don't want a live-in maid. Our privacy is more important to me than having her as a housekeeper. There's a list of women on the bulletin board in the faculty room, women with families who want day work. I'm not giving in on this!"

Abram ran a hand through his hair. "What can we do, Sandra? Put her out? Where would she go? We're her only connection with the 'Outside', as they say. I can't just tell her to find somewhere else to stay . . . ."

The anxiety in her kind-hearted husband's voice caused Sandra to soften. "I guess you're right, Abe. Let's give her some time to think this over. When we make it clear that she can't live with us, she'll decide to go back." Kissing his cheek, she added, "Now I'm going to see what the cook is making for dinner. Then I shall take a long bawthe . . . ." she said, feigning royal status, as she entered the house. She was greeted by the cinnamon smell of freshly baked apple pies. Determined to take the good with the bad, she stepped jauntily into the kitchen, exclaiming, "I smell apple pie!" as she pushed through the cafe doors.

At the sight of the hired girl, she stopped abruptly. Hannah still wore her usual Amish attire, but her waist-long blonde hair was down, though tied at her neck with a strip of white rag. Her prayer cap was no longer on her head. She was bending before the oven, with oven-mitts on her hands as she lifted out a steaming apple pie. Another had already been placed on a cooling rack atop the kitchen counter.

As though there was no change in her appearance, Hannah placed the pie on another rack, turned toward Sandra and said simply, "I found some apples in the orchard."

But Sandra was not to be put off. After all, she reasoned, Hannah was making her and Abram out to be collaborators in her defection from the Amish community. "Hannah, we have to talk," she said, unconsciously using her school-teacher voice with the girl. She beckoned for Hannah to sit at the table with her. Obediently, the servant girl complied and sat calmly and waited. Only a faint pinking of her cheeks told Sandra that Hannah was nervous.

Trying to keep her voice gentle but firm, Sandra spoke. "What do you intend to do, Hannah?" She sat back in her chair, brushed a strand of dark hair away from her face and pulled off the red scarf that was around her neck.

"I shall go English," was the girl's steady reply. She looked directly into Sandra's eyes, saying the words as if it was not a life-changing statement.

"Don't you think you should talk to your parents about this? This is a huge decision you're making here." She waved the red silk scarf for emphasis.

Hannah unclasped her hands and made a gesture of futility with upturned palms. "If I wanted to talk to them, they wouldn't talk to me, Mrs. Goodman. I am cast out of the church. They have all voted and agreed to avoid me. My family will be shunned if they talk to me. Amish is not the way I want to live anymore! I want to go English. Now that I am eighteen, I am free to do that."

Sandra sighed audibly. "That's up to you, Hannah, but are you just assuming that you can live here, with me and Abram?" Sandra's tone was direct.

The girl blinked several times before she answered with a question. "Are you not satisfied with my work, Mrs. Goodman?"

Infuriated by what she took as Hannah's presumption, Sandra felt heat flood her own face. "Yes, of course, but room and board are not parts of the package."

The quickness of Hannah's response made Sandra realize that the girl had anticipated her objection to her living with them. "I was wondering," she said, "if I could rent the little house, the cottage down the lane. I would go there after my day's work . . . ."

"Rent the cottage?" Things suddenly seemed brighter to Sandra. Hannah did not intend to invade their privacy after all. Pushing herself up from the table, she said with enthusiasm, "Let's see what Abe says! Come on. He's on the porch."

In the early days of their marriage, Abram's parents had lived in a small, white cottage not far from the big house which had been built later, the reward for years of hard work and the senior Goodman's smart acquisition of land which he then sold to a developer at a substantial profit.

"The little house," as it came to be called, had been the first home that Abram had known as a child. It was still in relatively good repair, though it had not been inhabited since, except for occasional "camp-outs" or over-nighters shared by young Abram and his friends.

When Sandra burst onto the porch, pulling Hannah by the hand, she smiled broadly at the alarmed look on her husband's face. She was sure that he had thought she was literally dragging Hannah out of their house, ready to throw her off the porch.

"Hannah has a great idea, Abe!" she said, pushing Hannah forward. "Tell Abram what you thought of."

Hannah's lowered eyes and barely audible words caused Sandra to blurt it out for her. "The little house! She wants to rent the little house your parents used to live in. What do you think, Hon?" Not waiting for an answer she offered, "I think it's a great idea! She'll have her own house but be close at hand. She could even be our nanny when we have a baby!"

"Whoa, whoa," Abram said laughing at his wife's exuberance as she totally overwhelmed the hired girl's feeble attempt to explain. Turning to Hannah, he asked, "Are you sure about this, Hannah? I don't want to go to the trouble of fixing up the little house for you and then have you decide you want to go home. Take some more time to think about it."

Sandra watched the girl for signs of ambivalence. There were none. In fact, Hannah cleared her throat and spoke up emphatically. "I don't need more time, Mr. Goodman. There is no way I can go back home. They won't take me back unless I agree to marry . . . Gabe . . . Gabe Yoder. I don't want him. I will miss my family, yes, but I can't stand the thought of marrying Gabe. Please, may I rent the little house? You don't have to fix it up . . . . It's okay the way it is."

Sandra laid her hand on her husband's arm and spoke to him softly, as if Hannah were not there. "Let her try it, Abe. If she changes her mind, we'll just be out a little bit of paint. She shouldn't be forced to marry somebody she doesn't love . . . ."

Abram expelled his breath and held up his hands in surrender. "Okay, but I'll get the guys to give it a fresh coat of paint, Hannah, and I don't want any rent. The house was just sitting there. I should have been keeping it looking nice anyhow. It's an eye-sore as it is."

Sandra picked up her shoes from the porch. "Let me go in and change out of my school clothes, Hannah, and let's get the key and check out the little house."

She ignored Hannah's words, "But I have chicken and dumplings almost ready . . . ."

"Keep it warm. We'll eat it—and apple pie—after we check the house. I can't wait to see what it needs." The lady of the house had spoken. Hannah returned to the kitchen to turn off the flame under the bubbling chicken stew.

Fumbling momentarily with the key that Abram had given her, Sandra pushed at the white, paint-chipped door that opened into a grimy kitchen. A gray film of dirt coated the once white counters, appliances, wooden table and chairs, and the red-and-white tiled floor. Dirt-streaked windows were bare except for lopsided Venetian blinds and cobweb curtains.

"This place is filthy," Sandra said, stating the obvious.

"I can clean it and have it sparkling in no time," Hannah said, making a finger streak on the dirty countertop.

"Or we can hire a cleaning crew . . . ." Sandra couldn't imagine one person tackling this grime.

Hannah sounded confident, even as a cord on the Venetian blind broke when she pulled it. "No, no, I want to clean it. I don't want you and Mr. Goodman to pay for something I can do."

"It's creepy in here," Sandra said, brushing a cobweb off her arm. Nevertheless, she followed her hired girl into what had to be the living room. It was empty except for flowered linoleum on the floor. Electrical cords sprouted through wall outlets.

Through rounded archways, they entered two bedrooms containing empty bed frames and old dressers with black-spotted mirrors. Between the bedrooms was a rust-stained bathroom with a claw-foot tub encircled by a brittle, plastic shower curtain with faded flowers.

Sandra was overwhelmed by the poor condition of the unused cottage, but one look at Hannah's face told her that the hired girl was undaunted by the task ahead of her. And so it was agreed; Hannah would begin the cleaning of the little house and take up residence as soon as it was ready.

"Abe will have the house painted and check the roof, furnace, hot water heater and appliances. He won't have you living here unless you're safe and comfortable." Sandra's words were received with a humble nod of Hannah's head. Sandra could see from the girls reddening face and rapidly blinking eyes, that she was about to cry.

Walking back to the house, Sandra, with her arm chummily about the girl's shoulders, said, "And now, Hannah, I have an idea to help you get yourself some 'English' clothes, if you're serious about—how do you say it—'going English.'"

"I am very serious, Mrs. Goodman. My church doesn't want me anymore." Hannah spoke matter-of-factly, with resignation. "What is your idea for English clothing? I can alter my dresses."

"First, let's have that scrumptious dinner you've made and then I'll tell you my plan." Sandra gave Hannah's shoulders a friendly squeeze. She realized that she was going to enjoy making over the Amish housekeeper into a modern American girl!

Chapter Fourteen

Hannah's chicken 'n dumplings were a hit, and the lady of the house said that the apple pie was "to die for," an expression Hannah had never before heard. She realized that, although she spoke English well, she would have to get used to the peculiarities of language in the non-Amish community. Mr. and Mrs. Goodman, for example, called each other "Baby," or "Honey" interchangeably, along with a few "Sweethearts" thrown into the mix. Her Amish parents never used endearments like that. They used first names or called one another *"Mamm"* or *"Datt"* as the children did.

Another thing Hannah thought she'd never get used to was the unfeminine way that Mrs. Goodman dressed when she wasn't going to work. At home—or even going out and about—Sandra wore pants or shorts that made Hannah feel embarrassed for her. She had often seen Abram stroking his wife's bare legs or shoulders, even caressing her backside. This, too, was embarrassing, though it introduced her to the sin of envy, a new emotion for the Amish-brought-up girl.

As she washed the dishes after the evening meal—which Hannah had insisted eating in the kitchen while they ate in the dining room—she pondered just what Mrs. Goodman, who wanted to be called "Sandra," meant by saying she had an idea to help Hannah get herself some English clothing, but it wasn't long before Mrs. Goodman—Sandra—burst through the café doors and asked, "Are you finished in here yet? I've got something to show you."

Hannah put away the broom that she'd used to sweep the kitchen floor and followed Sandra upstairs to the third floor attic of the big house. In the stuffy confines of the slanted uppermost room, Sandra pointed to two large black trunks with brass hinges.

"In those trunks, Hannah, is the clothing that belonged to Abram's mother, everything from shoes to underwear. There's more in that wardrobe over there," she added, pointing to a huge upright piece of furniture with two doors. "You may have some altering to do, but I've asked Abe, and he said everything is yours, if you want it . . . until you're able to do some shopping."

Hannah was stunned by Abram's and his wife's generosity, their concern. Tears welled up in her eyes as she watched Sandra struggle to draw one of the trunks into a more accessible position.

"Oh, let me help you . . . ." Hannah said quickly, hoping to convey with her voice the gratitude she was feeling. Getting behind the opposite side of the trunk, Hannah pushed while Sandra pulled on a leather handle, until the large hump-topped black trunk was in the center of the attic. As Sandra opened the brass catch that held it closed, Hannah gasped at the piles of neatly folded skirts, blouses, nightgowns and pants that Sandra called "slacks."

"Everything's probably out of style," Sandra said, "but this may get you by 'til you can buy some things. You can use Mrs. Goodman's sewing machine that's in the den. Lord knows *I'll* never use it! You can take it to the cottage when you move over there."

Hannah laughed. "Oh, Mrs. Goodman—Sandra—I've been wearing styles from the 1600's! Anything in here will definitely be a big step forward." She floundered for more words to convey her excitement and gratitude, but, unaccustomed to displaying emotion, she could only ask, "How can I repay you for this . . . .?"

Sandra dusted off her hands. "Listen, Hannah, this stuff should have been donated to The Salvation Army long ago. We should be paying you for clearing it out of here."

Together the two women tried to lug the heavy trunk down the attic stairs, but, thinking better of it, Sandra said she'd get Abram to do it for them. "After all," she laughed, "what are men for?"

Long after Sandra and Abram had retired to their room for the night, Hannah worked well past midnight laundering items of clothing that she pulled from the two big trunks that Abram had brought to the downstairs guestroom for her. Between loads, she selected a few pieces that she set to altering that very night. Having made up her mind to go English, dressing their way couldn't happen soon enough to suit her. She was glad, though, that Abram's mother had worn housedresses, apparently preferring them to slacks, though she had some of those, too.

In the morning, she, along with the new day, made her debut. Despite her late hours, she had risen early to prepare a breakfast of fruit, hot cinnamon rolls and coffee for her employers who now stood staring at her in shocked silence.

For the first day of what she thought of as her new life, Hannah had chosen a shirt-waist dress made entirely of white eyelet, as though for a christening. The short-sleeved, tailored blouse, open at the throat, was the first buttoned garment Hannah had ever worn. She tucked the blouse into a matching full skirt, feeling a bit self-conscious without the bib that had covered the bosom of her Amish dresses. She had worried about the bit of cleavage that showed just above the first button of the blouse and thought about putting a safety pin there, but she had seen Sandra with much more cleavage showing. She decided that the blouse would not seem immodest to her employers.

Her face was, as usual, devoid of makeup because Amish women did not use it. Her long, straight blonde hair she had tied back with a strip of white eyelet taken from the hem of the dress. Gone were the white cap, apron and black stockings; but on her bare feet were the black oxfords, the last vestige of her Amish upbringing.

Embarrassed by Sandra's and, particularly Abram's, open-mouthed stares, Hannah felt a blush creeping up her neck and into her face. "Your mother's shoes don't fit," she stammered and held out a foot for them to see. "So these are all I have."

Sandra recovered first. "Oh, that's an easy fix, Hannah. I'll take you into the city for shoes, the first Saturday I can." Taking the housekeeper by the hands, Sandra pulled her around to face Abram. "Doesn't she look pretty, Abram?"

Abram seemed uncomfortable at the question, but he said, "Yes, she sure does . . . except for the shoes." They all laughed at his joke.

"Please sit. The cinnamon rolls are best eaten warm," Hannah said, trying to deflect the attention away from herself. As she poured juice and coffee for the Goodmans, she was aware that their eyes kept returning to her again and again as she moved between the kitchen counter and the table.

Neither of the Goodmans was at home later when Hannah hung the white eyelet dress in the closet of the downstairs bedroom. Donning a green plaid blouse and khaki "slacks" salvaged from one of the trunks, she ignored a drizzling rain to march with bucket and broom to the little house across the way and about a five-minute walk down the lane.

Taking the key from the breast pocket of her blouse, Hannah opened the door wide and stepped inside and tried the hot water faucet in the kitchen. As promised, Abram had lit the hot water tank, and hot water sputtered and gushed into the dirty sink. Hannah smiled as she said softly to herself, "I'm going to have indoor plumbing!"

For weeks, she worked tirelessly, cleaning, measuring for curtains, using material she had scrounged from attic boxes and trunks, while two of Abram's hired men power-washed the little house and gave it a fresh coat of white paint, inside and out. In their wake, the impatient girl scrubbed, washed windows, and hung the curtains she had made.

Abram had given Hannah freedom to choose, from the sheet-draped furniture in the attic, the once-cherished possessions of Ida Goodman when she was a bride. Trips to the third floor of the main house were like treasure hunts to Hannah, who could barely hide her excitement as the hired men carried her selections to the cottage for her. Ida Goodman's first furnishings had made their way back home.

By the time October had blazed and died, Hannah Miller was happily settled into the little house on the Goodman farm, just out of sight of the main house.

Sandra, too, had been doing her part to help the hired girl in her transition from her old way of life to the new. For several weekends, Sandra had given up her cherished Saturdays with her husband to drive Hannah into the city for shopping, after the girl had confided to her that she feared a chance meeting with any of the Plain People in the nearby town, which had few stores anyway.

Trying to make the most of Hannah's paychecks, the two women diligently searched for bargains among racks of colorful clothing or shoes and laughed at Hannah's attempts at walking in high heels which they didn't buy.

Sitting in a pink suede chair in a shoe store, Hannah blushed furiously as a young salesman held her nylon-stockinged foot in his bare hand and slipped a red flat onto it. He smiled up at her and said, "We have these in navy and black, too."

From the chair beside her, Sandra spoke up. "Oh, don't show her the black ones! That's what she'll pick!"

"You're right," Hannah said. "I think shoes should be black."

"Really?" said the salesman. "Most pretty young girls like you want red."

Hannah felt Sandra's nudge in her side but maintained her composure. "Well, I guess I could take two pairs—black and red."

As they left the store, laden with two more packages, Sandra said, "He was flirting with you, Hannah."

"Oh, I think he was chust trying to sell me two pairs of shoes instead of one."

"You better get used to men flirting with you. You're a pretty girl, even with no makeup. Speaking of makeup, let's go in here and try out some shades for you . . . ."

Hannah let herself be dragged into a cosmetics boutique where draped women sat on stools with makeup artists at work transforming them with lipsticks, eye shadows and powders, but she refused the full treatment. Instead, she let Sandra choose a pink-toned lipstick she said was perfect for Hannah's fair skin and blonde hair.

"What about some eye makeup, Hannah? Some mascara and liner to bring out those pretty blue eyes of yours.

Hannah held up a hand. "Stop, Sandra. It's too much all at once. As it is, it'll take me years to get up the nerve to try the lipstick . . . ."

"Oh, don't be so Amish," Sandra said, only half kidding.

On one such trip to the city, they returned, giggling like school girls, to surprise Abram with their new hair styles. Hannah's waist-long hair had been cut to shoulder length; the ancient middle part and rigid finger-waves at her temples had been replaced by a side part with soft half-bangs.

While the change in Hannah caused Abram Goodman to say, "Wow, Hannah, is this really you? You look fantastic," Hannah saw that his startled gray eyes were on his wife who seemed to leave him speechless. Her straight black hair had been loosely permed and cut into a chin-length bob. With violet-blue eyes sparkling beneath artfully applied eye shadow and liner, Sandra laughed as she watched her husband's shocked expression evolve into a grin of pleasure.

"Do you like it?" Sandra asked, wiggling her shapely body in its tight fitting red sweater and jeans as she strutted toward Abram. His answer was to bury his hands in her bouncing black curls as he enthusiastically kissed her laughing mouth.

Absorbed in each other, they did not see Hannah's smile fade. While Amish couples, married or single, did not display affection in public, Hannah had seen this and much more on the English television; but she had never seen Sandra and Abram exhibit more than a quick kiss exchanged in a loose embrace. Unable to bear the sight of them now, the hired girl fled from the room and made her way to the little house, shopping bags in her hands.

Throwing her packages on the maroon mohair couch, Hannah didn't take time to admire her newly decorated little house as she usually did. Nor did she pause at the bathroom door to marvel that she actually lived in a house with indoor plumbing. Instead, she allowed herself a long look in her bathroom mirror, something she usually avoided because of the sin of vanity. She opened the little bag she clutched in her hand and took out the lipstick Sandra had encouraged her to buy.

With a shaking hand, she applied color to her full lips and rubbed them together as Sandra had taught her. A sullen, unhappy girl sporting pouting pink lips looked back at her. Hannah felt a rush of disgust, picked up the lipstick again and drew a big "X" over the face of the miserable girl in the mirror.

"This is what you mean to him," she said to the girl behind the "X." "Nothing. You've been crossed out, replaced!"

Chapter Fifteen

"What do you think's eating at Hannah?" Sandra asked as she flung a billowing clean sheet across the mattress so that Abram could help her make up the bed.

"Why do you say that? I haven't noticed anything different. She seems her usual quiet self." Abram bent to tuck the squared off sheet corner under the mattress.

"Typical oblivious man. She's been going around moody and sullen for days now, no longer sewing new clothes or trying non-Amish recipes. Just now when I went downstairs to take the sheets out of the dryer, she barely spoke to me when I asked her if she'd like to go on another shopping trip this weekend."

"Maybe homesickness is starting to settle in. I was afraid of this—that all the big fuss about going English would fade once reality hit her."

"Well, maybe you're right," Sandra said, stuffing a down pillow into a king-sized lavender pillow case. "I'll take her shopping Saturday, since you're going to be off buying a new tractor. I'll try to get her to tell me what's bothering her."

"Maybe I haven't been complimenting her enough on her cooking and all that. I used to do it all the time because I could see how much what I thought mattered to her. I've been pretty negligent in saying thank you lately." Abram helped his wife pull the plush velvet patchwork quilt up over the pillows.

"Yes, my dear, I know she glows at the least bit of attention from you. I still think she has a crush on you, boyfriend or no boyfriend, but who can blame her?" Sandra stepped into her husband's arms and lifted her face to be kissed.

"Don't start that again," Abram said and kissed her thoroughly. "Now that we've made up the bed so nicely," he added, "what say we mess it up again?"

Sandra noticed that Hannah's mood of veiled joy had returned, probably after Abram had spent some time marveling over the waffles that morning. *Oh well,* she thought, *if that's all it takes to keep the wench happy.*

Waving goodbye to Abram from Sandra's black sports car, the two women set off for another day of shopping in the city.

"What a beautiful, summery autumn day! I think it's warm enough to open the sun-roof. Let me know if you get cold," Sandra said, pushing a button on the dashboard of her Jag.

"It's fine. I like the way the wind blows my hair. It feels so different after having it bound up under a cap all my life." Hannah lifted her face to the breeze flowing into the car.

"I'll bet it does! Someday we'll take Abram's red convertible out for a ride, but we'll probably have to wait 'til summer. Today's unusually warm for early November." Turning right out of the gravel lane that led to the farm, Sandra pressed her foot to the accelerator.

Sandra had so far been unable to convince Hannah to buy standard attire for every American girl: jeans and tennis shoes. Persisting in her efforts, she had at last succeeded in bustling the girl into a dressing room to help her struggle into a pair of blue jeans.

"I can see that they're going to be too small. I won't be able to breathe!" Hannah insisted as Sandra held out the jeans for her to try.

"They're made of a stretchy fabric, Hannah. They're supposed to mold to your body. If you've got it, flaunt it. And you, dear girl, have got it." Sandra laughed as she knelt to pull up the zipper that Hannah struggled to close over her belly.

It was then that Sandra saw, with shock, the thickening of Hannah's waist. Standing, she now grasped the meaning of the blue veins showing through the transparent white skin of Hannah's full breasts, cupped by a lacy bra they had just bought.

Sandra lifted her eyes to meet Hannah's. The girl nodded slowly, wordlessly affirming the question in Sandra's eyes. After a long moment, Hannah spoke without emotion. "Gabe," she said.

Sandra's mouth had gone dry but she managed to ask, "How long?"

"Two months, I think." Her voice was toneless and her eyes never left Sandra's.

Sandra steadied herself with a hand on the wall of the dressing room. "You *have* to go back now, Hannah." She held the hired girl's gaze.

"No! I won't go back!" Hannah's panic was evident though she spoke just above an urgent whisper.

Sandra held up her hands, palms out, and closed her eyes. "Okay. Okay. I get that." Opening her eyes, she faltered only slightly when she asked the question: "Have you thought about abortion?"

Hannah seemed ready with her answer. She spoke slowly and deliberately, not letting her eyes waver from Sandra's face. "I will not add sin to sin."

The two women sat side by side in silence during the two-hour ride home, the only sound the monotonous hum of the car's engine. Gripping the leather-wrapped steering wheel, Sandra wondered at the seething resentment she was feeling toward the statue sitting in the passenger seat. Accustomed to self-introspection, she began to sort through the tumultuous thoughts in her mind.

Smug. Hannah seems so damn smug! Who does she think she is, anyway? Sandra silently screamed the question. *She's pregnant, so whose problem is it? Hers! And there she sits waiting to see what Abram and I will do about it. Damn her!"* Her thoughts raced with the streaking black car.

Sandra smashed the accelerator to the floor, causing the engine to roar as the car hugged a curve in the road, not caring that her passenger struggled to lean with the curve, and, righting herself, sat as though hypnotized by the double lines that flashed by, mile after mile.

At last wheeling the car furiously into the rough gravel lane that led to the farm, Sandra knew that she was going too fast, but still she tortured herself and her passenger with the jolting, washboard ride, engulfing them in a billowing cloud of dust. Hannah swayed and bounced beside her, staring straight ahead and uttering not a word of protest.

Abruptly slamming on the brakes, Sandra brought the car to a halt, not in front of the main house, as usual, but in front of the little house where the hired girl now lived. Without a word or a glance at Hannah, Sandra sat fuming, waiting for her to get out of the car.

Sandra felt more than saw Hannah slowly turn her head to look at her; then she quietly gathered her packages and opened the car door. Before getting out, she paused to say in a level voice, "Thank you for taking me." Getting no response, she closed the door and started down the red brick walk that led to the little house.

Sandra plunged the gas pedal to the floor and, two hundred yards away, again slammed on the brakes to bring the car to a lurching stop in the paved driveway that circled in front of the big house. Packages in her arms, she kicked at the door of the Jaguar to close it.

She jerked her head furiously in the direction of her husband's voice as he walked toward her. "Hey, hey, take it easy! That's an expensive machine you're abusing. What's got you so riled?"

"Your little Amish wench is pregnant!" Sandra spat the words at him. They stood staring at each other, a November wind scattering curling, brown leaves at their feet.

Abram reached for the packages in her arms and said quietly, "Let's go inside."

Chapter Sixteen

Later that night, Abram put on a jacket and walked out into the chilly autumn night. He made his way to the little house. Pausing on the small porch where he had played as a child, he glanced back toward the glowing window of the main house where he knew his wife sat waiting.

At his knock, he heard a stirring within, and soon Hannah stood in the lighted doorway. He could not help but think how lovely she looked. She wore a soft, white-and-pink flowered flannel nightgown that had belonged to his mother, and her feet were bare. Her pale hair swung gently as she stepped aside to let him in.

Her face had flamed at the sight of him and he heard a small gasp escape her. Wordlessly, he walked past her and pulled out one of the white wooden kitchen chairs and motioned for her to sit; then he took the one opposite her. Between them on the small white square table was a tiny bunch of yellow mums in a glass of water.

"We have to talk about this, Hannah," he began, as she sat quietly waiting and, no doubt, trying to catch her breath. Looking up from his folded hands propped on the table, Abram met her eyes. "Sandra tells me that you're pregnant." Her blush deepened and she looked away, saying nothing. "Look at me, Hannah," he said, and she obeyed, blinking rapidly. "You know what you have to do now, don't you?" he asked.

When she spoke, she sounded childlike to him. "Yes," she said, "I have to have a baby."

"Well, yes, of course," he said, exasperated by her simplistic answer. "But you also have to go back . . . to marry Gabe."

Suddenly she was on her feet. "No! I don't love Gabe!" she said, her voice uncharacteristically rising in both tone and volume.

"Sit down, Hannah," Abram said, indicating the chair opposite him. "You loved him enough to . . . ." He didn't finish the sentence.

"It wasn't love! It was . . . something else," she said, sitting again, only to rise abruptly and raise her voice again. "If you're saying . . . that the baby means I can't stay here . . . I'll . . . get rid of it!" She trembled visibly, and Abram felt a surge of pity.

Reaching out, he took her hand and drew her back to the chair. "I'd never ask you to do that," he said. She seemed to melt as she lowered herself to sit again. Still holding her hand, he changed the subject. "Tell me, Honey, tell me what's so terrible back . . . there . . . living with the Amish."

"It's the *Meidung.* They have formed a bond against me, to shun me. Even my family may not speak with me. I am useless to them, a disgrace to them . . . ." Tears spilled from her transparent blue eyes, and her wet cheeks glistened in the gleam of the kitchen light above the table.

"What about the baby?" he asked gently. "You have a child to consider. Do you want him to grow up without a father?"

He felt her cold fingers move a little inside his warm hand. "Someday . . . he may have a father. Please just let me stay . . . until . . . ."

"Until what?" Sighing, he let go of her hand.

"Until . . . until I think of something else." She dropped her eyes and tucked her hands into her lap.

"Okay," he said, blowing out a long breath of air. "But it's not me you have to convince. It's Sandra you have to woo."

Her voice sounded almost tender. "I understand. I know that you would never put me out. I thought Sandra liked me now, but, perhaps I was wrong . . . ."

"Don't blame this on her," he said, rising and zipping up his jacket. "She's been super to you and you know it. You're going to have to find a way to explain to her why she would want a housekeeper with a child in tow. Goodnight, Hannah."

Sandra opened the door for him as soon as he stepped on the porch of their home. She, too, was dressed in a nightgown, a lacy black one covered by a sheer, matching peignoir. Her bouncing black curls shone even in the dim light of the foyer sconces. She was beautiful. He couldn't help but notice the contrast between her and the woman he had just left, both beautiful but different.

"Well?" Sandra watched him as he shrugged out of his jacket and threw it across a chair in the foyer.

"Oh, good, you've got a fire going," he said. "I'll mix us a drink and we'll sit by the fire and discuss our . . . growing household."

"There's a pitcher of martinis on the sideboard," she said, sighing, all the earlier anger and frustration gone from her voice.

Handing her a glass, he sat beside her on a loveseat that faced the fireplace. "She won't go back. She won't marry Gabe. She says if we won't let her stay here if there's a baby, she'll 'get rid of it,' and I'm quoting."

"Oh, God, Abe, she's laying the abortion decision on us? She should know *you* well enough to know that you'd never demand that of her. Neither would I, even if she thinks I'm the Wicked Witch of the West. What are we going to do?"

"I guess we just take it one day at a time and hope she changes her mind as her time gets closer." He put his arm around his wife, drew her to him, and kissed her temple.

"What about her medical bills? She won't have an Amish mid-wife to deliver her baby."

"That's the least of my concerns," Abram said, leaning toward the glass coffee table to refill their glasses. "She seems terrified at the prospect of going back there, and I can't bring myself to load her up and drop her off. We took her in, so to speak, Sandra, and now we have to help her through this."

"You are one kind-hearted, dude, Sweetheart," Sandra said, snuggling closer to him. She placed her small palm against his larger one and intertwined her fingers with his. "It's not that I don't like children. I love children. I hope to have children of our own . . . ."

He kissed her hand and said, "Just let me know when you want to start workin' on that, Lady Love. Meanwhile, you can practice on Hannah's."

Chapter Seventeen

Early December brought snow, and each day, when Sandra came home, tiredly proclaiming that her sophomores were crazed by pre-holiday hysteria, Hannah made sure that she was greeted by the welcoming aroma of fresh baked goods and supper cooking. She kept the house spotlessly clean and decorated it a bit here and there, to cheer Sandra and to get her "in the holiday spirit" as the English said.

Despite the wintry cold, Hannah had bundled up in the first Mrs. Goodman's warm coat, hat and mittens, but with new boots on her feet. From the woods surrounding the house, Hannah brought woody branches of orange bittersweet and arranged them on the mantle with thick ropes of silvery-green ground pine. She filled crystal vases with red-berried holly branches she had clipped from bushes that grew near the little house and graced lace-topped tables with them.

Crimson flames danced in the fireplace in the den where the couple customarily spent their evenings after a supper unobtrusively served by Hannah. While the lady of the house voiced her enjoyment of these pleasantries and extra touches, the hired girl had come to understand that what Sandra Goodman valued most was privacy for her and her husband. And so Hannah stole away to the little house as soon as she had cleared the supper dishes, leaving the newlyweds to themselves.

She spent her evenings alone in the home she had made, and, without television or radio, listened only to the ticking of her wind-up clock as she worked on a patchwork quilt she was making from scraps of material gleaned from attic boxes. It was to be her Christmas gift to the Goodmans, a warm throw for them to take with them on the football weekends they loved to spend in the city.

Weekends were lonely for Hannah. Even if she had had transportation into town to visit the ice cream parlor or to see a movie—something she had never done in her life—she had no friend with whom to share these simple pleasures.

One of the younger hired hands, Clay, had shown a keen interest in Hannah's emergence from her cocoon, from Amish to English, from girl to woman; and she had actually considered accepting a date with him, should he ask her. But his attentions abruptly ceased, probably when he noticed the swelling of her waistline.

She spent the daylight hours of her days off making baby clothes for the child who had begun to move within her. Listening to the hollow ticking of the clock, she thought of Abram or of the family she had left behind.

Sometimes she bundled up in the short, white fur jacket she had inherited from Ida Goodman and ventured out into the snow-filled nights wearing her new suede, fur-lined boots. On one such night, she left her usual course around the farm and found herself, instead, walking the now white-blanketed road that wound its way through silent woods. It was the path she had traveled daily from her childhood home to the house of Abram Goodman.

With snow-cushioned steps, she moved onward until she came to the white expanse of Amish fields that lay before her in the moonlight. In the distance she could see, white rising out of whiteness, her Amish home, dark now, except for a faint glow in one tiny window of the second floor. Then, out of the night, she saw a minute black figure moving against the snowy background. Ant-like, it scurried and paused to emit a thin beam of light upward to meet the dim light of the window. Another tiny figure appeared momentarily framed in the glow of the window, then vanished somewhere within the shadowy recesses of the house. Outside, the thread of light was extinguished by its instigator who now moved to the front of the house where the light and the other figure reappeared. Then darkness swallowed them both.

When the rosy glow returned to the upper story window, Hannah realized from its location that it was her old room, the one that had been given to her to entertain her beau. As she stared across the white gulf that lay fixed between her and the home of her parents, revelation crept into her numbed mind: Life in the Amish homestead had gone on without her these past three months. Her room had been given to someone else, to sixteen-year-old Fannie. While her parents slept, no doubt entrusting Fannie to God and the memory of the *Meidung* imposed upon her older sister, a different Amish boy had come out of the chilly night to be warmed by Fannie's presence.

Cast out, Hannah stood shivering in the empty white night, and the child fluttered like a moth within her as if to rouse her. Slowly, she turned to face the woods again and followed homeward her own solo footprints in the snow.

Chapter Eighteen

Three months ago, the black-coated bishop had stood, solemn-faced above his wiry gray beard, just inside the doorway of his sister Rebecca's home. His words had come to Rebecca as through a fog that dulled not only sight but hearing as well.

"Hannah will not return. She has gone to the Outside and is lost to you and to God . . . bound for the Lake of Fire." He pointed at Rebecca and her grim-faced husband, Joseph.

"You have brought this tragedy down upon your own heads, for I warned you that this very thing would happen. Separation from the world must be maintained. Forget Hannah. Turn your attention to your other children . . . lest they, too, go the way of the sinner." Then Hannah's uncle turned and walked away, hunched in grief over the spiritual death of his niece.

As if in sympathy with the weeping mother as she lay in her bed that night, a September rain had begun to fall. Its steady patter on the steel roof above her head kept up throughout the night, and, by evening of the next day, the muddy road in front of Rebecca's house was lined with dripping, black-hooded buggies, like a rosary of shining ebony beads. As if to a wake, the Plain People had come with comfort and covered dishes, as the word of Hannah Miller's defection from the church had spread throughout the Amish community.

Black-garbed men gathered in groups under the roof of the porch. Shaking their heads sadly, they talked in subdued voices and sucked corn cob pipes, their smoke drifting heavenward to appease some god offended. Joseph Miller sat dry-eyed among them and neither talked nor smoked. Despite the dark throng around him, he was alone with his grief. Rebecca knew that she had no words to comfort him, drowning as she was in her own unspeakable sorrow. Inside the house, sobbing women and girls hovered around Rebecca, to "weep with those who weep." She knew they meant well, that their sorrow was real, but she wished she could be alone to wrestle with her pain before God. She would not tell them to go, however. One had been lost from their midst, for a reason worse than death. And so she let her voice join those of her Amish sisters in a symphony of wails pouring out to their men and upward to God.

By morning the rain and the black buggies were gone. Weak rays of sunshine filtering through a hazy sky began the process of drying the oozing mud of the road into hardened ruts. Rebecca Miller was in her kitchen as usual. The last to take a seat at the breakfast table, she sat across from her husband. They spoke no more of Hannah. She had tried a time or two, but Joseph had raised his hand to her and stopped her from saying more.

Now, avoiding each other's eyes, they talked, instead, of the new chores which came with each change of season. There were warm clothes to be sewn, wood to be cut and stacked, and oats to be bagged for the long winter ahead.

Taking their cue from their parents, the children made no mention of their cast-out sister and smiled shyly when their mother asked them if they'd like to take a buggy ride to the harness shop.

"I've been thinking," Rebecca said, "that we ought to investigate the new supply of puzzles that Levi has no doubt got in, knowing that we'll all need something to keep us busy as the days grow shorter and the evenings longer."

"*Ja, Mamm,* we can do that today before the puzzles get picked over," her husband said, not lifting his eyes from his breakfast of soft-boiled eggs and toast.

Chapter Nineteen

"Can't you chust do it for me?" Hannah asked, lapsing into her Pennsylvania German accent brought on by the anxiety she felt about what Sandra was expecting her to do. "I've never touched a computer in my life . . . . It would be so much faster if you chust did it for me, please."

"Okay, but you have to start learning things like computers to get along in the English world, Hannah. I admit that these insurance forms can be confusing, so I'll do it with you sitting beside me giving me your information."

The Goodmans had told Hannah that they would start including her in the health insurance package Abram had for his employees, which would include maternity benefits. There would be a small co-pay for her doctor visits, they said, but they would increase her monthly paycheck by enough to cover that. Hannah knew that some of the Amish had started buying health and other insurances, since disaster could strike even the chosen people of God, so she was not unfamiliar with the concept. In fact, she was grateful. It was the computer that scared her.

The problem of how to get her to her monthly doctor visits had to be solved, too. With Sandra at school, the duty fell to Abram who had passed it along to George, one of his hired hands. Although George was a kind man who was considerate of Hannah's comfort, the girl could barely hide her disappointment that Abram chose not to drive her there himself.

She made up an excuse—although true—for her downcast demeanor. "I'm so afraid that I'll meet the People in town," Hannah confessed to Sandra. Her first appointment would be tomorrow, and she had been gripped by anxiety for days in advance.

"What can they do to you, Hannah? Nothing. But if it'll make you feel better, I'll loan you my hooded cape and you can go incognito," Sandra said, opening the door to the coat closet in the foyer.

"What is 'in…cog…nito?'" Hannah had been making a determined effort to increase her English vocabulary.

"It means 'in disguise, without being recognized'." Sandra pulled a beautiful grayish-blue wool cape from a hanger and handed it to Hannah.

Hannah stroked its softness. "Oh, this is beautiful and looks so varm!" She heard herself replace the "w" with "v" and corrected it. "Warm, I mean."

"I've been noticing that your German accent has been becoming more pronounced since you left home, Hannah. I'd think the opposite would be true."

"It happens when I get nervous," Hannah said, standing with the cape draped over her forearms. "So many dings have been happening."

Sandra laughed. "There you go again—so many 'dings'—but you need to get a grip on your nerves, Hannah. It's not good for your baby. That baby is connected to you and affected by what you feel." She put her arm around the servant girl. "They can't get to you here, Hannah. You're safe here."

"I know that—it's chust—just—that I still have nightmares of when my uncle came here," Hannah admitted, inwardly shuddering at the thought.

The next morning, Hannah pulled the hood of the blue, wool cape over her blonde head before she opened the door of the pickup truck and stepped to the running board. With her head down and her hands tucked into the folds of the full cape, she placed each booted foot carefully on the snow-swept walk and up the stairs that led to the obstetrician's office.

At the receptionist's window, she whispered her name, "Hannah Miller," and winced when the woman behind the glass said loudly, "Okay, Hannah, take a seat and the doctor will be with you soon."

Even though the waiting room was warm, Hannah did not remove the cape, or the hood. Avoiding eye contact with the other women seated on comfortably padded turquoise chairs placed around the room, Hannah picked up a copy of *Family Circle* and pretended great interest in it.

She felt reasonably secure that she would not encounter any Amish women in this doctor's office because they preferred the services of "the baby-catcher"—the midwife—within their own community and sought the English doctor only for difficult pregnancies or anticipated abnormal births. She let herself relax and only startled briefly when her name was called by a smiling nurse who held open the door to the inner rooms.

Her anxiety was replaced with joy as she hurried back to the truck where George sat waiting and listening to a Bluegrass station on the radio. The doctor had confirmed her pregnancy, declared her healthy, everything normal, and she had encountered no Amish women.

"How'd it go, Missy?" George asked as he leaned across the seat to give her a hand up into the truck.

"Just fine, George, just fine!" She said, missing none of her "j's."

A month later, on Hannah's second visit to her doctor, her security and her hidden identity were both in jeopardy. As with her first visit, she had not removed her cape and hood and had not dared to glance around the waiting room to peruse the faces of her pregnant sisters; but, as her downcast gaze traveled to the various pairs of shoes or boots before each chair, her heart froze at the sight of unmistakably Amish black oxfords on the feet of a woman across the room from her.

Not daring to look up, Hannah fought the panic that seized her and stared at the swimming words of the magazine she held before her eyes. A door opened and a crisp voice spoke the name: "Anna

Byler?" The black shoes moved as the woman pushed her heavy body up out of the chair and made her way to the open door. Hannah breathed deeply to calm herself. Anna had not recognized her. Or had she? When Hannah's own name was called, Anna Byler was still somewhere within the maze of examining rooms, and Hannah, deposited safely in another room, did not see the woman leave. Her fear subsided, and she could think clearly now. *What if Anna had recognized me? What of it? She would not have spoken to me, shunned as I am. I am no longer part of that world.* Yet, a worm of anxiety gnawed at Hannah. She set her mind to pondering why.

George's rugged but friendly face greeted her as he stepped out of the driver's side of the red Bronco he had driven this time, saying that he thought the pickup truck might be too high for Hannah to get in and out of. Coming around to the passenger side, he helped her into the vehicle.

"Sorry about last time, Missy. I wasn't thinkin' or I'd have helped you into the pickup last time . . . ."

"It was no problem, George. Think no more about it. I'm not an invalid," Hannah said, settling herself into the passenger seat. Foregoing her usual casual chat with George on the trip home, Hannah sat silently, groping in her mind until she had found the answer to her uneasiness: Anna's discovery, had she made it, would be on the tongue of every Amish woman, and, before the day ended, in the ears of her own mother. This possibility filled

Hannah with a strange admixture of dread and desire. She did not want to cause her mother more pain; yet she longed to share with her the news of a grandchild to come.

Now four months pregnant, Hannah was surprised at the emotions that stirred in her breast each time her baby moved within her. The first time she had "felt life" had been when she was bending to pull hot towels from the clothes dryer. Alone, she had had no one with whom to share that magical moment, and tears sprang to her eyes, even as she smiled.

But on the second occasion of her child making its presence felt, she had been serving lunch to Abram and the four hired men, engaged in the usual light banter into which they unfailingly drew her. Startled by the sudden but delicate movement of her baby, she had stopped mid-sentence; and, as a small gasp escaped her, had placed her hand over the spot where the tiny person fluttered.

Five men looked up from their plates to question her. "Are you all right?" "What's wrong, Missy?"

Laughing at their concern, Hannah put their fears to rest. "My baby—he moved!" Gentle, big men, they began to applaud, their faces reflecting the awe that Hannah felt. Feeling the blush on her face, Hannah was embarrassed but pleased by their attention. She curtsied and shyly met the tender smile in Abram Goodman's gray eyes.

Chapter Twenty

Christmas in Hannah's Amish home had not been cause for much fuss. In most English homes, she knew, weeks of decorating, shopping, cooking and baking went into preparation for Christmas Day. The Goodmans were no exception. Sandra had handed Hannah a red and green cookbook dedicated to the creation of Christmas cookies. Lime green Post-its marked pages with cookie recipes that Hannah was expected to bake and freeze for the party the couple would be hosting in celebration of their first Christmas together.

For their part, the Goodmans had begun to decorate their home with large, fresh green wreaths accented with bright red ribbons. Two of the largest had been placed side by side on the white, double doors; the rest were hung on the front windows of the house, encircling electric candles that glowed with single white lights from inside.

Two weeks before Christmas, Abram and Sandra had scoured the farm for the perfect tree. Hannah was amazed at the size of the huge blue spruce that had to be tightly bound to get it through the front door and into the living room. She swung the double doors open wide for them as two of the hired men pushed and pulled the big tree through the door. A large tree stand had already been attached to its trunk.

Sandra directed traffic. "Put it in front of the bay window . . . center it . . . more to the right . . . no back the other way about six inches."

Upright and unbound, the tree's gracefully swooping boughs touched the ceiling and filled the bay window on one side of the living room. Boxes of ornaments had been hauled down from the attic, and a new decorating ritual began that evening, amid Christmas music created by strings and chimes.

In the kitchen, Hannah wrapped the last of the cookies that had been set out to cool on the counters, deposited them in the freezer, donned her coat for the dark, snowy walk home and bade the Goodmans goodnight.

Passing the lighted end windows of the living room, Hannah paused on tiptoe to watch in wonder as the newlyweds sat before the fire, gingerly fingering sparkling crystal ornaments that had been collected over the years by Ida and Ira Goodman. Hannah could see the gentle movement of Abram's lips as he held up this delicate glass sleigh or that glistening snowman, no doubt recalling for his bride times and places when he and his parents had bought them.

Wearing blue jeans and a soft white turtleneck sweater that clung to his wide shoulders and flat stomach, he sat cross-legged on the floor with Sandra seated in the same fashion, facing him. Standing out in the cold watching them, Hannah longed to be the one opposite him.

In the light of the fire, Sandra's bouncing black curls shone; and, like him, she wore a turtleneck sweater, but of brightest red with form-fitting black jeans. Faint strains of "The First Noel" came to Hannah's ears, and, although she could not hear the words Abram spoke, she knew that some memory had moved him to tears, as he wiped at his eyes. Tears filled her own eyes, and she wished she could comfort him, but it was his wife who rose to her knees to cradle his head against her breast.

She watched Sandra console him, tilting his face upward to cover it with kisses. Hannah could see his hands moving over the red sweater that covered Sandra's back, and soon he became the aggressor, his mouth still on hers as he lowered her to the soft Oriental rug before the fireplace.

The hired girl knew that she should not be spying on her employers, but she could not seem to force her feet to move, even when she saw Abram lift his wife's red sweater, pull aside her lacy, black bra and lower his mouth to her round breast. Hannah gasped. She had never dreamed that men did such things to their wives. She touched her own tingling nipple through her coat.

Hannah's face grew hot in the winter air as the Goodmans' intimacy progressed. Still, she stood frozen in the wintry twilight, mesmerized as desire coursed through her own body. She knew that she should flee, but she could not move, so absorbed was she in watching Abram Goodman undress his wife and then himself.

Weakness overwhelmed Hannah as she swayed rhythmically with them until the three became two, and she became Sandra.

Finally, Abram pulled the fur throw from the loveseat and used it to cover himself and his wife as they lay in each other's arms before the dying embers in the fireplace.

In darkness, Hannah made her way back to her own home, feeling shame and a sense of having betrayed the people who had been so kind to her. She knew that they had not seen her, but God had. She felt afraid and began to pray for forgiveness.

Morning came too soon for Hannah who had struggled through a mostly sleepless night spent trying to shut out the images of Abram and Sandra that continued to play out in her mind, no matter how much she prayed. As her alarm shattered the stillness of the little house, she knew she had no choice but to face her employers this morning. She rose and got ready for the day.

As she walked to the main house, she glanced guiltily at the window where she had stood the night before, and she was glad that a fresh snow had fallen to cover her footprints beneath the window. Opening the back door which led to the kitchen, she was startled to see Abram alone. His words terrified her.

"I've been waiting for you, Hannah."

Her breath came short. Would he say that he knew that she had spied upon them? But he smiled.

"Beautiful morning, isn't it, Punkin? A fresh snowfall, I see," he said, bending to look out the kitchen window. He turned to face her as she removed her coat and hung it on a hook in the mud room off the kitchen; then he spoke again. "Sandra and I were talking last night, and, well, we'd like you to come to our Christmas party—not to serve or anything like that—but as a guest. What do you say, Hannah? Are you ready for a little fun?"

Hannah's shame doubled at the hopeful anticipation on Abram's face. "Oh, I . . . I couldn't do that, Mr. Goodman, but thank you for asking." She couldn't meet his eyes.

"Why not? It's exactly what you need, Hannah, a chance to see how the English half live or at least how they party. I won't take no for an answer. Now, get the coffee perking, and I'll be back for breakfast after I get the men started. Sandra's sleeping in, so I'll eat without her."

As he went into the mud room to pull on his coat and boots, Hannah protested once more. "But, Mr. Goodman, I wouldn't know what to wear . . . ."

"Sandra will help you with that," he said. And then he was gone.

Chapter Twenty-one

Nervously twisting her hands, Hannah watched the colorful parade of vehicles of all shapes and sizes filing into the plowed Goodman driveway.   The voices of high-spirited party-goers echoed in the starry December night. But the servant girl was too afraid to leave her house and join them, though the dress Sandra had helped her select and order from an online store was perfect for the occasion and for Hannah.

Folds of white crepe fell gracefully from an empire waistline to the floor, in their descent, hiding the mound that was Hannah's belly. From her shoulders to her wrists, the same sheer fabric billowed and ended in cuffs covered with white sequins that matched the shimmering bodice of the dress. Wearing it now, Hannah worried because its low, sculptured neckline displayed her rounded breasts in a way they had never before been uncovered . . . except with Gabe . . . . She shrugged the now repugnant thought from her mind and looked, again, into the full-length mirror on her bedroom door. A worldly young woman stared back at her.

Imitating a picture she had seen in one of Sandra's magazines, the girl had anchored her shining blonde hair atop her head with pearl-tipped hairpins she had found in Ida's jewelry box, leaving golden wisps to touch her cheeks and the nape of her slender neck. She had applied medium-brown mascara in the way that Sandra had taught her and added a pink blush to her cheekbones and lips. Finally, Ida Goodman's pearls hooked with a silver clasp and rested at the cleavage of her breasts. On her feet were white, satin pumps she had risked going into town to buy, just for the Goodmans' party.

Sandra had not offered to take her to the city since the day she discovered that Hannah was pregnant. Nor had she offered to drive her to the nearby town. It was George who came to Hannah's rescue when she asked him if he would drive her. She was too proud to ask Sandra even though Sandra was off school for Christmas vacation.

Looking down at her satin-slippered feet now, Hannah wondered how she would keep them from being ruined walking in the snow from her cottage to the house. And how could she wear fur-lined boots with such a dress? Overwhelmed by this dilemma and her anxiety, she moved stiffly from the mirror to a kitchen chair and sat there, like some marble nymph, too paralyzed with fear and indecision to venture any further.

From her window she could see the lights of the big house and the driveway lined with cars. Warm shouts of friends greeting friends rang in the chilly air, and she was reminded of her Amish family and neighbors, hailing one another at barn-raisings, weddings . . . .

In stillness, Hannah sat, long past the time when the voices had subsided; now, the only sound she was aware of was the steady, lonely ticking of her kitchen clock.

Chapter Twenty-two

Inside the big house, Abram had been busily presenting his wife to friends and relatives who nodded approval of the vivacious, dark-haired woman at his side. He beamed at her proudly. The sleeveless, floor-length, red silk sheath she had chosen for their holiday party revealed her dainty, shapely body, and its high neck set off perfectly the diamond pendant and earrings which had been his Christmas gift to her.

Abram wore a tuxedo, not something he felt comfortable in, but Sandra had really wanted their party to be black-tie. The formally-dressed party guests were a combination of their families and friends, and Sandra's red-haired sister, Kendra, was among them. He grinned when he overheard Kendra whisper into Sandra's ear, "My goodness, Sis, you've got it all!"

"No," he said, leaning to whisper into Kendra's ear, "I'm the one who has it all."

A lavish buffet had been spread in the dining room with foods catered or prepared by Hannah. Like life-sized, wind-up dolls dressed in black and white, two serving girls and a bartender moved mechanically, tending to the needs of the guests. A three-piece band played music for dancing on the gleaming, wood floors of the cleared living and family rooms.

Abram and Sandra had spared no expense for their party, even to the point of hiring a limousine which would carry tipsy out-of-towners to hotel rooms rented for them in town.

It was only when one of Abram's elderly aunts commented to him that the pastries were wonderful that he realized that Hannah had not appeared. Seeing that Sandra was encircled by a group of admiring males, he threw on an overcoat and slipped out the back door to make his way toward the single light that shone from the cottage of the hired girl.

Through the window, he saw her sitting there, like a fair goddess in a flowing white gown. He tapped on her door and blew on his hands to warm them. He tapped again, and when there was no response, he tried the door knob. The door opened.

"Hannah?" Even at the gentle nudge of his voice, she did not stir. Abram, too, stood unmoving for a long moment, wondering if she had fallen asleep at her table. Intrigued by the classic beauty of the woman sitting there, he approached her and knelt at her feet to look up into her face. "Hannah?" he asked again. Her eyes were open. She blinked as though awakening from a trance and focused on him.

"May I escort you to the party?"

At last, taking his offered hand, Hannah rose slowly with him and returned his gaze. Her stony stare had softened, but still she did not speak.

Trying to keep his eyes from caressing her full breasts, Abram spoke quietly, interrupting the ticking of the clock. "You're lovely . . . like a bride."

Lowering her eyes shyly, she finally spoke, "Thank you, Mr. Goodman."

"How about you call me Abram tonight," he said. "I should have been here earlier to escort you to the party. I'm sorry."

"It's all right," she said. "I was afraid the snow would ruin my shoes. I couldn't think what to do." She reached for Ida's white fur jacket draped across a chair. Abram took it from her and stepped behind her to wrap it gently around her shoulders.

"Please, Mademoiselle," he said, smiling, "take my arm," and he guided her to the door. The brick walkway from the cottage had been shoveled, and the paved driveway to Abram's house had been plowed; but slushy patches here and there made the going slow. Abram was quick to notice Hannah's concern not just for her shoes but for the hem of her dress. He chided himself for not having brought a car the short distance to her house.

At the point where Hannah slipped and nearly fell, Abram said, "Well, Hannah, there's only one thing to do," and, before she could object, he scooped her up in his arms to carry her to his house.

"No!" Hannah protested, and, struggling, nearly upset the two of them.

Abram laughed, "Now settle down and let's do this without getting wet." He felt her relax in his arms as she wrapped her arms around his neck.

"This is embarrassing," she said.

Carrying his beautiful burden the distance to his house, Abram breathed heavily, making puffs of white in the cold December air.

At the house, he bent his knees so that she could reach the handle to the back door and deposited her inside the warm room. "There we go, milady."

After chivalrously removing her jacket from her shoulders, he tried to guide her immediately into the throng of guests, but Hannah begged, "Please, Mr. Goodman, let me stay in the kitchen for a bit . . . ." Her hand fluttered involuntarily to cover her bosom.

Hesitating before he turned to go, Abram offered, "Hannah, to the people in the other room there is nothing unusual about the way you look." Pausing, he added, "Except that you'll be the most beautiful woman there."

Chapter Twenty-three

As Abram let the kitchen doors swing behind him to rejoin his party guests, he could not have known the profound impact his words had on Hannah. Stunned, she leaned against a kitchen counter and savored the words he had just said to her. *The most beautiful. He said I am the most beautiful. He called me a "woman." Did he mean that he thinks I'm more beautiful than his wife?*

She relived the unprecedented nearness of him as he had carried her to his house. It filled her with sensations she had never before felt in her eighteen years, not even with the father of the child within her. Weakness had flooded her as he carried her, and she wanted to lay her head on his shoulder in absolute surrender.

Hannah was startled out of her reverie when she spied two shockingly blue eyes crinkled in laughter just above the equally blue cafe doors that led to the kitchen. The owner of the eyes pulled the doors suddenly toward him as though opening a surprise package.

"Heyyyy," the man drawled, "what have we here?" as he stepped inside the kitchen.

Hannah moved quickly to put the table between them as the grinning, red-headed man came toward her. Undaunted, he moved forward to occupy the space where she had stood. With a low whistle, he let his eyes travel over her, as she backed away from him like a skittish filly.

"Who, may I ask, are you, Gorgeous, and why in God's name are you hiding in this kitchen?" Only slightly taller than she was, the man stood toe-to-toe with her and caged her with his arms outstretched against the kitchen counter on either side of her.

"Nice," he said, "very, very nice." Deliberately, he dropped his eyes to admire her half-naked breasts.

"Please . . . let me go . . . ." she pleaded, pushing against his chest with both hands, her voice betraying that she was about to cry.

Moving away from her, the man held his hands, palm out, to indicate that he was backing off. "Now wait . . . . I'm sorry, Hon, didn't mean to scare you." Reaching into his back pocket, he withdrew from it a folded, white handkerchief and handed it to her.

Hannah took it and dabbed at the tears that had spilled to her cheeks. "Please, leave me alone!"

"Please, let me start over," he begged, seeming to be genuinely sorry. "I'm Charlie Cochran, an old buddy of Abe's. He can tell you I'm harmless. On second thought, don't believe a word he says about me." He laughed.

Hannah had heard Abram speak of Charlie Cochran. Still clutching his handkerchief, she tried to regain her dignity. "I'm sorry. I'm not . . . used to this. I'm Mr. Goodman's hired girl, his housekeeper."

She saw revelation hit Charlie Cochran's handsome face. "Oh, I really blew it, didn't I? You're the Amish girl!"

"I *used* to be the Amish girl." Hannah corrected him quietly. "I'm no longer . . . that. I gave it up." She faltered and he came to her rescue.

"And it's a good thing you did! It'd be a waste of a beautiful girl to cover you up in old lady dresses like they wear. What's your name? Let me guess . . . . Beulah or something, right?"

Her fear having subsided, Hannah couldn't help but laugh. "Something almost as old-fashioned. It's Hannah." She blotted her cheeks one more time and handed his handkerchief back to him.

"Keep it, Sweetheart. So you're Hannah! So, tell me, Hannah, are you hard-hearted?"

Baffled by his words, she stammered. "I don't know, but my heart beats the same as anybody else's . . . ."

He laughed aloud. "Well, Sugar, you've certainly set *my* heart to beating! How refreshing to meet a woman without guile!"

She had no idea what "guile" was, so she changed the subject. "I'll wash this and get it back to you," she said, indicating the handkerchief that she pushed into the small, white handbag she had brought with her.

"C'mon, Hannah! Let's go dance!" He took her hand and pulled her out of the kitchen with him.

Hannah panicked as she let her eyes take in the colorful throng of dancers bouncing to the music of the band. "But I don't know how . . . to do this kind of dancing." She pulled back toward the kitchen doors.

"Well, you're in luck!" he declared, letting go of her hand and bowing. "Charlie Cochran, also known as Fred Astaire, will teach you."

"Fred, who?" she asked, laughing as she let him drag her into the midst of the dancers.

Chapter Twenty-four

Abram rested his chin atop his wife's perfumed, black hair as they danced. From across the room, he watched Charlie and his partner in dancers' stance but with a space between them as they both looked down to watch the progress of Hannah's white slippered feet. Abram could see the girl's pink lips move as she counted her steps; then she broke into a dimpled smile from time to time at something her dancing instructor had said to her.

Jolted back to reality by the sound of his own partner's voice, Abram realized that the music had stopped.

"They're good, aren't they?" his wife was saying.

"Uh . . . yes . . . she's catching on fast," he said, still watching Charlie with his arm possessively about Hannah's shoulders as he guided her to the bar.

"Who is?" Sandra laughed as he gestured toward Hannah and Charlie. "I meant the band," she said.

"Oh, sure, the band's great," Abram said, laughing at himself. "Did you see Charlie? He's actually set the Amish maiden's feet a-dancin' . . . ."

"Who knows? She might actually get a daddy for that baby yet," Sandra said. "Look at them over there at the bar, close as two peas in a pod."

In three long strides, Abram had left his wife and was heading for Charlie Cochran. "Charlie, I want a word with you." Taking the mixed drink from Hannah's hand, he gave it back to the bartender. "Give her a Shirley Temple. She's underage."

Sandra had followed Abram to the bar and now the two women stood alone as Abram pulled Charlie aside and began to talk to him in a subdued voice.

"Pregnant! How the hell was I supposed to know?" Charlie retorted with a hint of anger in his voice. His eyes on Hannah's elegant profile as she stood talking with Sandra, he regained his sense of humor. "By who?" Charlie asked, with a grin. "Bayouuuuu?"

Abram was not amused at Charlie's joke or his New Orleans imitation. He playfully shoved the incorrigible Charlie and warned, "By her Amish boyfriend, that's who, but don't you be giving her any alcohol. And don't do anything with her but dance."

A lock of red hair bouncing as he took another shove from Abram, Charlie protested, "Aw, Abe, buddy, what damage could I do that's not already been done?"

"I'm dead serious, Charlie. That girl's innocent by anyone's standards, and I'm responsible for her." There was a mild threat in Abram's tone, as he stood next to his first roommate and studied Sandra and Hannah who stood chatting with Sandra's sister Kendra.

"Who's the gorgeous red-head?" Charlie nodded his head toward Kendra who was stunning in a glittering royal blue dress.

"Sandra's sister." Abram was about to suggest to Charlie that Kendra was also unattached and more his age, but, on second thought, he realized that it was Hannah who needed to be included in the party festivities. Kendra, who had come to the party without her boyfriend, had already been sought out by several of the single men.

"Hey," observed Charlie, "those three chicks look like the flag—red, white, and blue. You take the red. I'll take the white *and* the blue! Just like in the good old days."

"Forget it, Buddy. You'll have to get in line to get any attention from Kendra, and my housekeeper's too young for you." Abram wondered at his attempt to dampen Charlie's interest in Hannah. *Charlie's a rogue. She'd never know how to handle him.*

"I promised I'd teach her how to dance, and I intend to do that, Buddy." With those words, Charlie strode back to Hannah.

Whether to annoy Abram or to please himself, Charlie devoted the evening not just to teaching the Goodman's hired girl how to dance but with flirting with her until he had her blushing and smiling as she danced without looking at her feet.

Chapter Twenty-five

Hannah excused herself to go to the powder room off the kitchen. Checking her hair in the mirror, she saw that her lipstick had worn off and, taking a golden tube from her little handbag, she applied more. There was no need to pinch her cheeks, she realized. Her face glowed with the exertion of the dance Charlie had just been teaching her. Something called the jitterbug. Charlie said it was an old-fashioned dance, but Hannah had never heard of it, let alone tried it. Smiling at herself in the mirror, she realized that she was actually having a good time.

She took a deep breath and went back into the living room where the bandleader had just introduced a piece he called a waltz. She sought out Charlie's red head and saw him whirling Sandra in his arms. Standing quietly in a corner, Hannah noted that with a partner whose skill equaled his, Charlie really was a very graceful dancer. Mrs. Goodman seemed to be enjoying herself immensely. Her bright laughter rippled above the music, and her diamonds sparkled as they caught the lights of the chandelier overhead.

A light touch on Hannah's elbow startled her, and she turned at the sound of Abram's voice. "Since I seem to have lost my date temporarily, may I?" He crooked his elbow as he had done in the cottage, but she, unsure of his intention, hesitated. "Dance?" he asked, and her heart leapt.

"N-no, I don't think I'm good enough . . . ." She hated herself for stammering.

"Nonsense! I'm no Fred Astaire, myself . . . ."

Then he was leading her to the dance floor, throwing his head back to laugh when she asked, "Oh, you mean Charlie, his other name?"

Carefully placing her left hand on his shoulder, she wondered if he felt the trembling of her right hand in his. She kept her face averted, hoping that he wouldn't notice the flush that she knew was there.

"Relax. You're stiff as a board," he said. "Just follow my lead the same way you did with Charlie. It's one two three, one two three. One long step and two short ones. There, you've got it!"

He had pulled her closer to him so that he could guide her with his thighs. The touch of him like that turned her knees to liquid, and she was glad that she could cling to him for support. Concentrating mightily on the rhythm of the music, she was surprised to discover that she actually could follow him. Gradually, she allowed herself to melt into him.

Floating with the music, she enjoyed the smell of him and his big, warm hand holding hers. Her stomach touched against him, and, she, feeling the baby move, wondered if he could feel it, too. She found herself hoping that he could.

Just as the music ended, Hannah, wanting to keep him near her if just for a minute longer, lifted her head to ask, "What did you say to Charlie?"

He didn't pretend not to know what she meant. "I told him that you were too young to drink, but, even if you weren't, alcohol could harm your baby."

He had met her eyes and still held her as though they were dancing. Hannah's eyes misted at the tenderness and concern in his tone. Blinking away tears, she smiled as Abram steered her toward Sandra who stood watching them through narrowed eyes.

"Thank you" was all Hannah could think to say in response to Abram.

Chapter Twenty-six

Gabe Yoder tried to swallow the tension that had lumped itself in his throat. Listening to the wet clop of the horse's hooves as he drove his mud-spattered buggy to Abram Goodman's house, he wondered what he would say when he got there.

His best friend, Eli, had risked his own censure by breaking the Ban of Avoidance to whisper to Gabe that he had seen Hannah, heavy with child, in town. Eli had been waiting in the pickup truck of an English neighbor who had gone into the hardware. His attention was caught by a cloaked woman, dressed this way despite the fact that it was a pleasantly warm spring day, as she passed by on the sidewalk. The profile that peeped out of her hood reminded Eli of someone. He watched as the woman gripped the railing on both sides of the short set of stairs that led to the landing of the English doctor's porch, and he had seen the hood slide back during her lumbering ascent. Though her blonde hair had been cut and was worn loosely, and though she had quickly replaced the hood, Eli knew that this obviously pregnant young woman was Hannah Miller. He knew, too, that he had to tell Gabe, Ban or no Ban.

~ ~ ~

Gabe had been surprised at the sound of a human voice addressing him. It had been months since anyone had talked to him. He couldn't hide his delight at the sight of Eli peeking around the house to call out to Gabe who wielded a garden hoe to break up clumps of hard earth.

"Gabe, I have to talk to you," Eli said, pressing himself against the back wall of Gabe's house.

"You're going to get yourself into trouble, Friend, but it sure is good to see you!" Gabe removed his straw hat and lifted his arm to wipe his shirt sleeve across his sweating forehead, as he, too, stuck close to the house to be out of sight.

"I have something to tell you and, by the looks of Hannah, I can't wait six months to tell you." Eli looked nervously around though there were no homes near Gabe's. "I walked so nobody would see a visiting buggy."

"What do you mean 'by the looks of Hannah'? Get to the point before I shake it out of you." Gabe was only half joking.

"She's in the family way and ready to pop soon by the looks of her. I saw her in town. She was goin' into the English doctor's office."

Gabe could barely breathe. "She didn't tell me," he said, "but that baby has to be mine." He started toward the barn to fetch a horse; then he turned back to Eli. "I'll never forget the risk you took to tell me, Brother . . . ."

~ ~ ~

Paradoxically, it was the very Ban which imprisoned Gabe behind walls of silence that now gave him freedom to slip away to see Hannah that very day. Except for an occasional word with his ailing, cantankerous mother or with his disgraced, indignant sisters, Gabe was alone. In accordance with the partial Ban imposed upon him by the Church, no neighbors came to help the fatherless and brotherless boy with spring planting or to ask his assistance with their own. No one would notice his absence from the fields.

Loneliness was all but killing Gabe, and he wondered how he would bear another six months of it. And here he was, risking permanent excommunication by visiting one under the *Meidung* at its most severe, the woman he, along with everyone else, had been commanded to shun, this woman who had been his undoing.

Months ago, he had gotten the dreaded news. Hannah Miller was as one dead. Hannah Miller had left the People of God and gone English. His mother had spat the words at him, her pointed chin quivering with joy, it seemed to Gabe, although he knew that the rest of the Amish community would assemble at the Miller home to grieve for one lost.

Four months ago, his mother had hurled her spiteful words at her son's back just as he was about to cross the threshold on his way to the barn for evening milking. Stumbling, he bore them like daggers as he, a dying man, made his way to the dung-smelling sanctuary of the barn where he mourned Hannah's death until the roosters heralded the dawning of another day.

That day and every day thereafter, Gabe Yoder, a young man grown old, sorrowed for his personal loss of Hannah.

What he expected to see when at last his eyes rested upon her, he had not really considered. Standing awkwardly on the grand porch of the English man's home, the gangly, straw-hatted boy clad in a coarse blue work shirt, suspendered broadfall pants, and clumsy work shoes had not been prepared for the sight he now beheld.

She stood some three or four feet behind the closed screen door, arrested by his presence on the other side of it. Slowly, staring at him all the while, she dried her hands on a familiar white, bibbed apron that did not hide the colossal mound beneath it. Deliberately, she removed the apron, laid it on a small table to her right, and walked to the door.

Through the screen, they silently looked at one another for several seconds. Gabe found his voice first. "Come out." To his amazement, she obliged and wordlessly led the way to the white wicker furniture on the porch. Easing her body into a cushioned chair, she motioned for him to take another across from it.

Gabe watched the spring breeze play with strands of her silky, long hair. He let his eyes caress her face. Her eyes were as blue as he remembered, her lovely mouth the same. The pale pink dress she wore was tied with little bows on her bare shoulders. It hugged her rounded breasts before billowing over the bulging stomach that was the child. Sighing, she settled more deeply into the chair and stretched her sleek, white legs and bare feet out before her. He noticed that her toenails were painted a light pink, as were her fingernails.

Her question was direct. "Why are you here?" she asked levelly, her eyes unafraid to meet his gaze.

Gabe swallowed before he spoke, with his hat in his hands. "I want you to come back."

"Never." Her lips moved with the word, but her face was rigid. She had always been a woman of few words, but her bluntness, her coldness, unnerved him.

"But the child . . . *our* child . . . ." Timidly, he reached as though to touch her belly, his hand hesitating in midair.

"*My* child." Her own hands possessively clutched her rounded body.

"But . . . Hannah . . . it's mine, too. We should be married."

She was struggling to her feet, and he, also rising, extended his hand to help her.

The word she spoke came without emotion. "Go."

He pleaded, "Hannah, don't do this to us . . . and to our child."

The loathing in her voice stunned him. "This will never be your child. I despise the memory of how he was conceived. We do not belong to you. Now, go!" The screen door slammed behind her and the inner door as well.

An upright cadaver, Gabe Yoder sat hunched in his black buggy, staring fixedly at the narrow world that bobbed up and down between his horse's ears as he let the animal carry him back home.

Chapter Twenty-seven

On the day that Hannah's child was born, the Goodmans might have noticed the silence in the kitchen and the lack of aromas issuing from it, but, on this particular day in May, they were resting in an embrace, savoring a last few moments together after early morning love-making.

In fact, while Sandra and Abram had been enjoying a different kind of agony, their hired girl writhed alone in her bed, in the throes of childbirth.

Abram went ahead to the kitchen, leaving Sandra to her hurried toilette, as she tried to recoup the moments lost in her husband's arms. Smiling at the memory of her, Abram pushed the café doors aside and entered an empty kitchen.

Immediately sensing that something was wrong, he hurried back to the foot of the staircase and called up to Sandra. "Honey? Hannah's not in the kitchen. Someone has to go to the little house to check on her."

He was gone before Sandra could finish saying, "Oh! You'll have to go, Abram; I have to get ready for school."

He ran the short distance to the little house and pounded on the entrance. With his ear pressed to the door, he thought he heard the sound of moaning within. Quickly fishing in his pocket for his key-ring, he found the old-fashioned skeleton key that was his key to the cottage. As he fumbled with it, he noticed that his hands were shaking.

His head inside the door, he heard Hannah crying out in pain. He hurried to the bedroom with the open door and hesitated only briefly before stepping inside. She lay amid the tangled white sheets of her bed, rocking her swollen body from side to side in her misery. By the quality of her piteous whimpering he knew that her travail was real.

As he spoke her name, her clenched eyes flew open, and she begged desperately, "Help me!" and, as he fled, "Don't leave me!"

Sprinting to the main house, Abram wondered how he could have been so stupid not to see to it that Hannah had a telephone at her house. With her Amish upbringing, she would not have thought of it either, but he, he cursed himself, should have known better!

He searched the phone book for Dr. Addison's number, grabbed the cell phone he had left behind and punched numbers into it as Sandra came down the stairs strikingly dressed in a fitted yellow dress with a short black jacket. He glanced at her but was already speaking into the phone.

"Tell Dr. Addison that Hannah Miller's baby is coming . . . yes, this is Abram Goodman. She works for me. No, I don't think there's time. Can he come here? She'll never make it to the hospital."

He waited anxiously and stared as his wife's shocked face until Dr. Addison's receptionist came back on the line. "Okay, I'll be outside waiting for you. Hurry!" To Sandra, who stood frozen on the bottom stair, he said, "Call off from school. Tell them there's an emergency. Dr. Addison's coming here. It's Hannah's time!"

Outside the little house, Abram stood waiting as a red-and-white ambulance roared into the driveway followed by the doctor's black sedan. They screeched to a halt to avoid hitting Abram who had jumped out to meet them, frantically waving his arms. At a trot, he led the paramedics, the doctor and his nurse to the laboring girl inside with Sandra, who had known nothing more to do than giving Hannah a hand to clutch.

"She's in there," Abram said, pointing to the bedroom. Dr. Addison and a nurse nodded briskly as they passed by him, carrying boxes of supplies.

To the paramedics, the doctor said, "Stand by with oxygen if we need it."

As Sandra hurried to get out of the way of the doctor and nurse, she offered, "Her pains are only two minutes apart."

Abram felt proud of Sandra for having had the sense to time Hannah's pains. He took her cold hand and led her to the table in the kitchen to wait with him, while the paramedics waited in Hannah's living room.

After a few moments alone with Hannah, Dr. Addison reappeared and spoke to the paramedics. "Bring the oxygen in here. She's capping already. I'll deliver the baby here."

Sandra and Abram sat watching an old-fashioned wind-up clock that sat on a counter in Hannah's kitchen. For the past twenty minutes they had been listening to Hannah alternately panting and bearing down as the doctor coached her.

After one particularly long groan, with the nurse commanding, "Push! Push!" Hannah screamed once; then, after a heartbeat or two, a baby's lusty cry came from the bedroom. Astonished, the Goodmans then heard the baby's mother laugh.

Abram wiped his eyes and handed his handkerchief to Sandra, who seemed as surprised as he was to discover that they had been crying along with the child. They smiled through their tears and clutched one another's hands across the little kitchen table.

A half-hour passed until Dr. Addison emerged from the bathroom, drying his hands on a towel. "Come in," he said, gesturing toward the bedroom. "The new mother has a baby boy to introduce to you."

Propped against pillows, Hannah sat up in bed. Her unkempt blonde hair was wet at the temples from the sweat of her work, but she smiled as she looked down at her red-faced little son who had been cleaned up and put to her breast.

Shifting her gaze to Sandra and Abram, Hannah introduced her baby boy. "His name is Joseph, after my *datt* . . . Joseph Abram . . . if you don't mind." She looked questioningly at Abram.

Abram was speechless for a moment, but, recovering, he said, with embarrassment and delight, "Well, yes . . . I don't mind."

Remembering his wife standing at his side, he asked, too late, "Sandra?"

He saw that Sandra had whitened with shock, but, to her credit, she did not spoil the moment. She nodded her acquiescence. "Joseph . . . Abram. It's a good name." But Abram heard tears in her voice. "Let's go, Abe. Hannah needs her rest," Sandra said.

"You don't mind? You don't mind?" Alone again, at their own house, Sandra vented her fury on her husband. "How could you, Abe!" She ceased her angry pacing to pound on the kitchen table at which the sheepish Abram sat, waiting for her temper to cool. "What about *our* son," she demanded, "the son *we* hope to have?"

He patted the table to ask her to sit with him. "What was I supposed to do, Honey? She caught me off guard. I was in a real spot . . . with the baby not an hour old." He took her hand though she tried to pull away.

Sighing, she dropped into the chair beside him and admitted that this was true. She had been in the same "spot." Now, her anger spent, she wept tears of frustration, covering her face with her hands.

Abram pulled her to him and removed her hands from her face. He kissed her wet cheeks. "Now, wait a minute, Sandra. 'Abram' is my *middle* name. I've still got a *first* name to give our own boy . . . ."

Sitting up straight, his wife blinked away her tears. "What? A first name? You mean 'Abram' isn't your first name? You mean I don't even know my husband's name?"

He laughed at her chagrin. "You should, Sweetheart. Did you ever take a close look at our marriage license?"

"No," she conceded, "but don't keep me in suspense. What is it, this first name you claim to have?"

"My parents wanted to keep the 'I' thing going, you know, with their first names starting with 'I'—Ida and Ira—so . . . ." Teasing her, he hesitated.

"Come out with it!" she ordered, smiling in spite of her tears.

Now he roared with laughter. "Trouble is, you'll hate it. That's why I don't use it. I, my dear, was christened 'Israel Abram Goodman,' and my poor brother, had he lived, would have had to go through life as 'Isaac Matthew!'"

"Israel? Your name is Israel? Sandra smiled widely and wiped away the last of her tears, surprising him. "I love it! A good, strong Bible name for our son!" She rose to her feet in excitement. "And we'll use your brother's name for his middle name!"

"Israel Isaac?" Abram asked, genuinely concerned.

"No, Silly. Israel Matthew! Don't you remember? 'Matthew' was my father's name, too." Her joy at this revelation filled him, too, and, just as he was about to suggest that they take up where they had left off that morning, the sound of the hired men stomping on the porch made him realize that it was lunch time.

Sandra bounded to the kitchen door to greet them like royal guests. "Hannah's had a boy!" she announced. "So I'm the new cook . . . at least for today. I hope you like Campbell's Soup because that's what I'm cooking. And you can make your own sandwiches!"

Chapter Twenty-eight

Abram Goodman employed a private duty nurse to look after Hannah and the child, though Hannah, with Amish frugality, had insisted that it was not necessary.

"I'm not sick, Mr. Goodman. I need a couple of weeks to get back to normal, and then I'll be back to work, taking Joey with me." It was the day after her delivery, and she sat gingerly on her couch with her baby in her arms. "You don't have to pay for a nurse."

Abram zipped up his jacket as he prepared to leave the little house. "I can't leave you here all alone, and Sandra has to work. We're going to do this my way, Hannah. You need rest and someone to look after you and the baby. Mrs. Boyer will be here in an hour. No more arguing." With that, he had turned on his heel and left, closing the door softly behind him.

Hannah's heart was touched by Abram's concern and by his generosity. "Well," she said, to the baby sleeping in her arms, "he wants to take care of us, I guess. If we were at my *mamm's* house, she'd be makin' chicken broth for me and fussin' over you . . . ." Tears filled her eyes, and she knew she had to pull herself out of the melancholy that had plagued her as soon as Joseph was born.

I shouldn't be sad. I have a healthy boy, and Abram is so good to me. It's just that I wish my mam could see you, Joey. I wish I could tell her about you . . . .

After a week, Hannah Miller dismissed the nurse herself. When her baby boy was two weeks old, she swaddled him well and carried him in her arms to the Goodman house, singing an old German lullaby softly as she walked, feeling strong and well.

Using her key to enter quietly by the kitchen door, Hannah paused to listen. All was quiet. *Good. They're not up yet,* she thought. Then she whispered to her baby, "I want to surprise them."

From the laundry room, she took Ida Goodman's wicker clothes basket and lined it with soft white towels. Into it she placed her son and carried the basket, baby and all, back to the kitchen.

Joseph Abram Miller gurgled quietly in his basket in a corner of the kitchen, while his mother, humming contentedly, used a fork to lift crisp strips of bacon out of a big, black skillet and placed them on a plate lined with paper towels. She knew that the smells of coffee and bacon had to be making their way to the noses of her employers. Soon she heard them on the stairs. Cracking eggs into the bacon grease, she was pleased that she had perfectly timed the Goodmans' morning descent.

Hannah had dressed carefully for her first day back to work. She'd even applied just a little bit of lipstick to her mouth, wanting to look pretty for Abram. She wore a waistless dress of pale yellow, covered by her old Amish apron; but, after years of wearing her hair bound and hidden, she loved to brush it and let it swing freely about her face. From time to time, she looked at her baby and smiled, even though he slept.

Her smile broadened as Abram stood, arms akimbo, on the kitchen side of the swinging doors. "Well, to look at you, who would believe what you've just been through?" His own smile was wide.

Hannah felt her face get hot as she realized that he had heard the earthy sounds of her labor, but she said, "What I have just 'been through' is the most natural thing in the world."

Quickly shoveling the eggs out of the bacon grease with a spatula and covering them with a lid, Hannah turned to see Abram hunkered down by the baby asleep in his basket.

"Wow, he is . . . really . . . something!" he said.

Hannah loved the look of awe on Abram's freshly shaven face. Her heart was full when he added, "Something pretty wonderful."

"Thank you," was all that Hannah could think to say. The doors swung and Sandra, looking sharp in a white linen suit, was there with them.

Rising, her husband beckoned her, "Come here, Honey, and look at this."

"Oh, you have him in a clothes basket! Now I know what to get Joseph for a gift—a bassinette—or a cradle!" Sandra said, obviously pleased with her idea.

"Hey, wait . . . what about *my* old cradle up in . . . ." Abram began but was abruptly interrupted by his wife.

"That's for *our* baby . . . someday." Sandra laid a hand on her husband's arm and seemed to falter with embarrassment "Joseph needs a new one."

The hired girl pretended not to notice this exchange as she carried plates from the stove to the table; then, stooping, she lifted basket and all to take with her to other parts of the house.

On an early June afternoon, Hannah sat in the comfortable wicker rocker on the Goodman's front porch, crooning softly to the child sucking at her bulging breast. Bees buzzing around the spring laurel bushes accompanied her song. Rocking contentedly, she tilted her head back to smell the freshly cut grass. Her son was now four weeks old, and she pondered the likelihood that school would end this week, sending Sandra home for the summer. A twinge of irritation at that thought caused her and the baby to squirm slightly. She stared through the woods bordering the yard, as though she could see her Amish home on the other side of it. Her brothers would have been out of school for weeks already and helping with spring planting. A pang of remorse shot through her, and Joseph whimpered.

Kissing his soft head, Hannah said, "But you, you will go to *der Englischer* school someday, and you will learn much more than chust how to write your name and read a little bit."

Her thoughts were interrupted by the distant sound of footsteps on the black-topped driveway. Ducking her head to peer through the bittersweet vines that shaded the porch, she saw Abram jauntily walking toward the house, a large roll of paper in his hand. Although he rarely returned to the house except at lunch time with his men, and sometimes he was gone on business for entire days, his occasional surprise stop-ins at the house were what Hannah lived for. His interest in her newborn child was casual, but he never failed to check on the two of them when he came to the house. Hannah enjoyed the feeling that he was taking care of her and the baby.

She reached to cover her breast with the light blanket that she had flung over her shoulder, but then she let it stay where it was. She lowered her eyes as though absorbed with her baby whose tiny fists pushed against her white breast. Abram Goodman was on the porch, and she looked up, feigning surprise.

"Uh-oh, somebody's hungry," he said, his voice friendly as he looked down at her and the nursing child.

"He's had quite enough, I think," she said. Her eyes demurely downcast, she pulled the swollen, wet nipple from her son's mouth and covered her breast.

"Now, let Mama burp you," she sweetly chided as she balanced the limp baby on her lap, one hand propping up his chin while the other patted his rounded back.

Abram reached down to touch the baby's downy head and laughed. "He looks like a little Buddha sitting like that." He turned and disappeared into the house.

A tiny burp escaped Joseph's moth, and his satisfied mother put away her breast and settled back to rock him, wondering what a "little Buddha" was.

That evening, Hannah's contentment was shattered. As she cleared the table of the supper dishes, Abram and Sandra, who had retired to the den as usual, summoned her to join them before she went home. Hannah thought this very strange since she had learned long ago that Sandra jealously guarded her time with Abram. Even now, the girl was reluctant to impose her presence on them, but she had, after all, been asked to come to the family room when she was through in the kitchen. Thoughtfully, she put away the last of the dishes, hung up her apron, picked up Joseph, and entered the lovers' sanctuary.

They were sprawled on the floor, a large map and many colorful pamphlets strewn in front of them. The hired girl noticed with distaste the way Sandra's buttocks peeped from the hem of the white terry-cloth shorts she wore. She lay on her stomach, legs spread, her upper body propped by her elbows. Her black hair was tousled, and her face was flushed and happy. Abram reclined on his side next to her, and he, too, seemed very enthused about something.

Without altering his position, Abram spoke as he saw Hannah come into the room carrying Joseph. "How would you like two weeks off, Hannah?" Before she could respond, he continued,

"Sandra and I are going to St. John's Island to celebrate our first anniversary."

Sandra sat up with her legs crossed and beamed at Hannah. "And you can have two whole weeks to yourself!"

The hired girl hoped her face did not reveal the sick feeling that had swept over her. "I guess it would be a year, wouldn't it? That would be very . . . nice . . . thank you." She tried to look pleased at the idea of two weeks' "vacation" as they called it.

"Great!" Abram said, rising and giving Sandra a hand up. "This Friday is Sandra's last day of school, so we'll be flying out Sunday. You don't have to bother with lunch for the men either. I'll tell them to go into town to the diner, and Hank will take Laddie to his house."

"But . . . Mr. Goodman, I don't mind fixing lunch. It will give me . . . ." She stopped short of adding, "something to do."

"Nonsense. You need a rest," he said with finality.

Hannah barely felt the warm evening breeze as she, on leaden feet, carried her baby home. Today was Wednesday. He would be gone in three days.

Chapter Twenty-nine

Loneliness descended upon Hannah. From the first day, after she had said goodbye to the Goodmans—gleefully waving from a red convertible with the top down—she felt the burden of loneliness aching in her chest and the pressure of unshed tears behind her eyes. The pit of her stomach felt hollow and she had no desire to eat.

Even her child and his needs could not fill the void that Abram's absence had caused. Automatically, she tended to Joey, or spent hours in the rocking chair the hired hands had rallied to buy for her, rocking and comforting herself as much as the child.

When the morning of the second day came, she awakened to the sounds of the hungry baby fussing beside her in the bed and lay listening to him for several moments before she rolled over to feed him. Some nameless grief, some lurking dread came to her, and she searched her mind to remember. As her memory stirred, the hot tears that had been dammed up let loose. Sobbing, she tried to feed Joseph, but he only screamed and would not suck.

It did not occur to her that she could leave her house and walk with her little son in the sunshine. At noon of the third day, she was startled by a knock on her door. Squinting at the light as she opened it, she stood as though dumbfounded to discover a world on the other side of it.

Hank, Abram's head hired hand, stood on her porch, wearing a red plaid flannel shirt and bib overalls, despite the warmth of the day. His smile changed to a look of concern as Hannah, still in her nightgown, stood in her doorway. "Is everything all right, Miss?"

"Oh, yes, everything's fine," she said with embarrassment, realizing that she looked a mess with her tangled hair and a wrinkled nightgown that she hadn't been out of for the past two days. "The baby kept me up last night, and I . . . slept in."

"I remember when my wife used to have nights like that . . . with our kids. Anyhow, me and the guys are on our way to the diner in town. I wonder if you might want to git out a bit, come along . . . ."

She glanced at the other men waiting in the truck, one in the back seat, and two in the bed of the truck. "Oh, I can't . . . . I'm not dressed . . . . I wouldn't want to keep everybody waiting."

"We'll wait for you, Miss. Nothin' big goin' on around here today anyhow. It'll do you good to git out, nice day and all."

"The baby . . . ." she said, glancing back over her shoulder into her house.

"Take 'im along, Miss Hannah."

At Hank's insistence, Hannah hurriedly showered and brushed her hair. Out of the bottom drawer in her dresser, she pulled the jeans she had never had the nerve to wear and squeezed into them. With them, she wore the white eyelet blouse and pushed her bare feet into loafers. A quick brush of pink on her cheeks and lips, and she was ready. She stepped back from the long mirror to see the overall effect. Suddenly she wished that Abram were here to see how she looked in her jeans.

Getting Joseph ready was simply a matter of changing his diaper, his "onesie," and wrapping him in a light yellow blanket that matched the booties on his feet. While she had neglected herself over the past two days, she had kept her baby scrupulously clean. Looking more like the teenager that she was than a mother, she placed him in the car seat she had bought months before and carried it and Joseph to the silver pickup truck waiting outside.

"Now, that's better!" Hank said with a grin, and the two younger men riding in the truck bed hooted and whistled appreciatively.

Hannah blushed and kept her eyes downcast as she belted the baby and his car seat into the back seat of the truck with George, the hired hand who had always driven her to her doctor's appointments.

"Don't worry, Missy. I'll keep an eye on 'im back here."

As she hoisted herself into the front with Hank, she felt the unaccustomed tightness of the denim jeans covering her rear end; yet she savored the compliments of Clay and Pete who joked and guffawed in the back of the pickup. With the air from the open window blowing her hair, Hannah began to feel better.

In town, she opted for the grocery store because she suddenly felt awkward about sitting with four men at the diner. Besides, she really did need to buy some food for her little house, her cupboards and refrigerator almost bare because she usually ate at the main house.

"I'll pick you up out front of the grocery store in about an hour, Missy," Hank said, as he helped her lift out Joey in his car seat.

Hannah felt grown up and very English as she propped her baby in his seat in the grocery cart, tossed her hair, and re-adjusted her shoulder bag. Passing others on her way to the produce department, she noticed that no one stared. She was just another shopper. She smiled. *It is good to look like everyone else.*

Sorting through piles of apples, pears, and oranges, Hannah realized that she had not eaten since the last plate she had taken alone at the Goodmans' kitchen table. Her stomach grumbled audibly, so she steered her cart in the direction of the cookies and crackers aisle, thinking she'd get something to snack on while she shopped.

Rounding the corner, she stopped abruptly. A black-bonneted woman perused a pyramid of graham cracker boxes at the far end of the aisle. Though the woman's face was shrouded by her bonnet, and though she was dressed like any other Amish woman out shopping, there was something in the woman's stance that caused Hannah's heart to leap.

Was it Wednesday? Hannah groped in her mind to remember what day it was. *Good Lord,* she thought, *it is Wednesday,* shopping day for most of the women of the Plain People who were used to regimented lives, Hannah's mother included. She realized that any horses and buggies would have been tethered at the hitching rail the store kept for its Amish customers at the side of the building. Hannah had entered from the front.

Hannah swallowed hard and pushed her cart forward, toward her mother, even though her heart hammered in her chest. Rebecca Miller did not look up at the cart's approach and merely stepped aside to let it pass.

Impulsively, Hannah said, "*Mamm!*"

The Amish woman froze at the sound. Slowly she turned to look at the fair young English woman who met her gaze. Hannah saw a flicker of joy cross her mother's countenance and fade as she wordlessly let her eyes take in her daughter's face, her hair, her clothing. Then she visibly startled as she saw the child.

Wrapped in a yellow blanket, he slept in the car seat carrier propped in the shopping cart. Hannah watched her mother's face as she stared at the yellow bundle, then raised her eyes to meet hers. Hannah saw the grief and the question in them. Aware that her hands shook, Hannah uncovered the child. "His name is Joseph," she said, "after *Datt.*"

Startled by the sudden rush of cool air, Joseph Abram Miller flailed his arms and kicked, emitting gurgling sounds of protest. Hannah saw a fleeting smile quiver on her mother's pale lips as she permitted herself to study the tiny, squirming form—her first grandson, son of a daughter who had died. Uttering not a word,

Rebecca Miller straightened, met her daughter's eyes again briefly, pushed her own cart around the corner, and was gone.

Hannah did not try to follow her. She stood frozen, clutching the cart to keep from losing her balance. With unseeing eyes, she stared at the boxes on the shelves. Finally, she pulled herself back to focus on a box of graham crackers, opened it, and unwrapped a cracker. Taking a bite, she chewed slowly and made her way to the next aisle.

"That was your *Grossmammi*, Joey," she said with a small smile.

That night, Hannah dreamed that she, dressed in Amish garb, bustled around a big kitchen teeming with people waiting to be fed. Seated at the table were bushy-bearded men chewing and nodding in unison. Serving frantically to satisfy their hunger, she reached to place a gravy boat on the table; and one shaggy man touched her arm with his lips. Slurping and sucking, he would not let go of her arm. The other men seemed oblivious to this and kept to their chewing and nodding. She tried to pull back, but he looked up smiling, and she saw with relief that the eyes above the bushy beard were Abram's. Just as she relaxed to allow him to go on covering her arm with wet kisses, he became the fumbling, groping Gabe.

"*Neh!*" she heard herself scream as she awoke. Beside her in the rumpled bed, little Joseph's slippery mouth searched her arm in vain for a nipple.

Chapter Thirty

Abram Goodman admired his wife's lithe, black-bikini-clad body as she ran towards him, the white ocean foam nipping at her heels. Scattering sand, she dropped to stretch out on the striped beach chaise next to his. Her black hair curled in wet ringlets around the tanned, happy face she turned to him.

Suddenly, he wished the beach were empty, so that he could make love to his wife then and there. He ran a hand up and down her thigh. "Let's go in," he said, knowing she'd understand his intention.

She laughed. "Again?"

"Again," he murmured and pulled her to her feet to return with him to their luxury suite high atop the hotel, overlooking the pounding sea.

Later, they lay naked on white satin sheets in a king-sized bed and let the ocean breezes from the open doors to the balcony wash over them.

"Abe?" Sandra laid her head on Abram's hairy chest.

"Ummm?" He had been almost asleep.

"When do you think we should start trying for a baby?" Her fingers caressed his shoulder.

He didn't answer for a moment. "When you say so, Baby . . . ."

She hesitated before answering. "I'm thirty-one, Abe. I think I should 'say so'." She turned her face up toward him and he saw that she was dead serious. He glanced down into the wide blue eyes looking into his.

Sleepily, he said, "Can you give me an hour, Sweetie?"

She laughed. "I can give you more than that. I have to get off the pill first."

"Deal," he said. She was quiet. He was glad that she seemed occupied with pondering the immensity of the decision they had so casually made. He wanted to sleep.

At dinner later that night, Abram reached across the table for his wife's slender hand. "I have an idea," he said, winking at her. She tilted her head and looked over the edge of her wine glass at him and waited. "I checked with the hotel clerk, and our suite isn't booked for the third week. Would you like to stay?"

Her tanned face erupted into a broad smile. "Do you mean it? Can you be away from the farm that long?"

"Sure, all I have to do is give Hank a call. He'll keep things running, and I don't have any investors' meetings scheduled."

"Oh, Abe, yes, let's stay!" She lifted her wineglass for a toast.

"To another week!" he said, tapping her glass with his. He pushed his chair back from the white linen-covered table. "Be right back."

Chapter Thirty-one

Hannah walked in the sunshine with little Joey, trying out an adjustable stroller she had bought at the second-hand store. She had sewn a new blue liner for it and hung rattles for him to enjoy as they wheeled along on the paved driveway.

"Isn't this fun, Joey?" He smiled up at her. "I knew you'd like a ride in your new stroller."

She was on her way to the barn to ask Hank for the key to the house, since the two weeks "vacation" would end in two days. She wanted to make sure everything in the house was in good condition. As she neared the barn, the smell of hay unexpectedly renewed the homesickness she had been experiencing since the encounter with her mother last week. Deliberately, she conjured up the faces of the bishop and Gabe to rid herself of the feeling.

She walked in the direction of male voices, finally seeing Hank standing just inside the barn door. She called to him, and he turned, grinning as he hooked his thumbs into the straps of his blue denim coveralls.

"Well, Missy, I'm glad t'see y'took my advice and got out in the fresh air some."

"It's not very fresh in here," she said, laughing and wrinkling her nose at the barn smells. She turned the stroller so Hank could get a look at Joey.

"That's a growin' boy y'got there! Fresh air will do 'im good."

"Yes, I wanted to get him out for a walk, but I also need to ask you for the key to the big house. I foolishly locked mine inside the day they left. The Goodmans will be home day after tomorrow, so I thought I'd do a bit of dusting and air the place out." As Joey fussed, she took the pacifier pinned to his clothes and placed it in his mouth.

"I was gonna stop t'tell ya on my way home, Missy. The boss called last night. Said they're plannin' t'stay another week. Be home a week from Sunday, instead of this Sunday."

Hannah struggled to maintain her smile, but she felt suddenly light-headed. She tried to keep her voice casual. "Oh? Well, that's nice . . . for them. I guess I can just wait 'til next week . . . ."

She was deaf to Hank's words as she turned the stroller and hurried away from the barn. Blinking in the bright light, she strode quickly toward the little house, not caring if she hit rough spots in the driveway, jostling her baby until he lost his pacifier and cried. Tears streamed down his mother's face, too.

Friday crept to Sunday. Hannah awoke and stared at the pink-flowered walls of her bedroom. A whole week. Abram would not be home for yet another week. She boosted Joey to her breast and winced at the initial sensation of his mouth pulling at her.

"You are my only companion, Joseph Abram," she said aloud. Yesterday afternoon and into the night she had wept at the news Hank had given her. But by morning, her lonely sorrow had turned to bitterness, bitterness toward Sandra. *I know she talked Abram into this. I'm sure of it. She thinks only of herself. Abram would know that I'm used to having a large family around me and that being alone like this all but kills me. He had no choice but to stay if that's what his selfish wife wanted.*

Even though these empty days had been almost too much for her to bear, Hannah seldom allowed herself to think of her family, but now she found herself wondering what Sunday it was—Church Sunday or Home Sunday. By tradition, the Amish valued fellowship at home as much as the church assembly. Every other Sunday was a day to visit with friends or to just stay at home with family.

Hannah counted on her fingers, trying to sort through the many weeks since she had been placed under the *Meidung.* If she calculated correctly, she decided, this was "home" or "visiting" Sunday, but she wasn't sure. She guessed that the Miller homestead would probably be empty, with her family off to visit someone old or sick.

Suddenly, she needed to know which Sunday it was; she needed to know how to imagine what they—her family—were doing. When she had lived with her parents, she used to lie in bed and try to imagine Abram at work or at rest. Summoning up his face in her mind had been oddly comforting and pleasant. What he was doing now, with his wife, she did not want to know.

Dismissing the Goodmans from her thoughts, she sat up to burp Joseph and felt excited about the day's adventure she was now contemplating. She and Joey would visit her old home! *If no one is home, that is. And what if they are? What would they do if I boldly walked right into their midst? Wouldn't it be impolite to shun an English neighbor?*

Playing out her fantasy, she practiced what she might say to them if they were at home. "It's visiting Sunday, after all," she'd say lightly to them. "My little boy and I came to visit!" Her breath came fast at the prospect of it.

At eleven o'clock on this fine Sunday morning, Hannah and her son, both of them freshly bathed and neatly dressed in the style of *der Englischer,* emerged into the June sunlight. Hannah decided not to use the stroller because of the bumpy dirt road and because she planned to cut through the fields so that her family would not see her coming, should they be at home.

Instead, she tied a wide piece of blue cloth around her neck and fashioned a little hammock in which to carry Joey on their three-mile journey.

Chapter Thirty-two

Swaying in front of his mother's body, little Joseph promptly fell asleep with the rhythm of her steps. Leaving the Goodman property, Hannah entered the coolness of the leaf-canopied dirt road that led to the Amish settlement.

Above her head, the sun shot shafts of light through her cathedral of green trees, just as it used to when she walked to work as Abram Goodman's housekeeper. She smiled to see, on either side of her, bunches of daisies blended together to form delicate hedges of white and yellow. Daisies would be growing in abundance around her father's barn and chicken coop, she remembered. Ever since she had been a little girl, she never could resist picking a bouquet to place in a jelly jar on the big wooden table in the kitchen.

Her mother used to pretend to frown at this worldly adornment, chiding Hannah, "Now you're getting fancy, Girl," but she always left Hannah's daisies there, except at meal time.

Hoisting Joseph in her arms to relieve the weight on her neck, Hannah left the road after about two miles and ventured into the waist-high timothy grass that had been planted by her father, no doubt, in the field that stretched from the road to the Miller house. Bright pink wildflowers swayed on long stems in the rippling grass. Hannah stood still amid the blooms and gazed across the field to the white farmhouse. She could just see its steel roof glinting in the sun. As she moved through the tall grass, she watched the house grow larger. Now she could see the barn, the chicken coop, her father's tool shed, the outhouse and her mother's clothes-line.

She crept cautiously forward. The front porch and yard were now in view, and she unconsciously bent her knees to sink lower into the tall grass. Peering above it, she could see only a few cats asleep on the porch. There were no other signs of life. She wished she could see into the entrance of the barn, to determine if her father's buggies were there. Listening carefully for the sounds of children, she was suddenly startled by a barking dog that came rushing into the timothy toward her.

"Biscuit!" she whispered as the dog began to growl. Biscuit picked up his ears at her voice, then bounded to meet her. Hannah laughed as the tan-coated mongrel joyously licked her face and Joseph's, too. "I see you're not shunnin' me, Boy. Thank you for lovin' me just the same . . . ." She fought tears and trudged on with Biscuit prancing at her feet.

Hannah Miller stood in the dust of the road that lay before her childhood home. She saw the familiar crisscross pattern of buggy tracks stretching before her like a web etched in the dust. She stepped carefully across them to the simple porch and placed her foot on the first stair. Glancing at the long windows on either side of the front door, Hannah saw that no face peeked from behind the plain white, single-panel curtain pulled to one side of each window to advertise that the family included a single woman—Fannie—old enough to be courted.

No one was home. Feelings of relief and disappointment warred in Hannah's pounding heart. Her eyes on the white doorknob, she stepped forward to try it. She was not surprised to find the door unlocked. The Amish did not steal from one another, and their simple lifestyles did not tempt the worldly thief, though the more affluent members of the clan often buried cash in buckets somewhere on their land.

"Stay, Biscuit!" she commanded, as she eased her way into the cool, uncluttered kitchen she knew so well. The hardwood floor shone; the big oak table was bare. On the clean white counters were glass storage jars containing dried noodles, sugar, flour and coffee. The largest jar was full of her mother's molasses cookies, and a white cloth covered what Hannah guessed were fruit pies baked yesterday for a Sunday snack today. A peek under the white cloth confirmed her guess. They looked just like the ones Hannah baked for the Goodmans. *I am my mother's daughter,* she thought.

Joey's hunger cry broke the silence, and Hannah looked down at him struggling in his little hammock, as if she were surprised to find him there. Shushing him, she unbuttoned her blouse and sat at her old place at the kitchen table to nurse him. She looked around her and realized that she felt nothing. It was peaceful here, she admitted to herself, but no great nostalgia filled her. Only when she thought of Abram did she feel any sense of longing.

She sat quietly and listened to the steady ticking of the big wind-up clock in the next room as she nursed her son; then, she gently laid Joseph, satisfied and asleep, in a small crib that had been kept in the kitchen for years. From the hammock she pulled the clean diaper she had tucked in there before starting her journey. Bending over the crib, she deftly changed Joey's diaper, and, without hesitation, opened the drawer where her mother kept plastic and paper bags. She placed the soiled diaper in a plastic one and tied it shut. Then she pumped water to wash her hands and dried them on the hand towel that hung near the sink.

As Hannah considered venturing into the rest of the house, Biscuit's barking terrified her. She stood very still, her heart thumping and her breath coming fast. She listened for the clopping of horses' hooves or the babble of voices. Hearing none, she peeked out the window and saw only Biscuit frantically sniffing in the tall weeds near the barn. Hannah expelled her held breath, quickly tied Joseph's hammock around her neck and once again scooped the drowsy baby into it.

She put the bag with the soiled diaper into the kitchen garbage and pushed her chair in at the table. Taking one last look around her, Hannah opened the door and stood on the porch a moment and took in the familiar yards of the house and barn.

Just as she knew they would, daisies grew profusely around the outbuildings. An idea came to her that made her laugh aloud. Instead of plunging into the timothy field once again, Hannah stooped to pick a bunch of daisies. Holding them proudly before her and admiring their beauty, she took them back to the house. Opening the cupboard above the sink, she selected a jelly jar and pumped water into it. Deftly she arranged the daisies in it and set the jar in the middle of the oak table.

She stepped back to enjoy the effect, turned and was gone, but not before she had taken two of her mother's molasses cookies to eat on the trek home.

Feeling light and free in the sunshine, even though encumbered by the living bundle that swung at her waist, Hannah strolled through the timothy with her head held high. She hummed around mouthfuls of molasses cookie and did not look back at the white house that grew smaller with every step.

Just as she left her father's field and entered the wooded part of her journey, a gadfly's monotonous hum interrupted her own wordless song. Hannah repeatedly batted at the black tormentor, but it returned time after time to buzz around her sweet-smelling hair. She gave up swatting at it, only to have it land and bite the soft flesh of her neck. The harassed girl tried to outrun the persistent insect, but it followed relentlessly.

"If I get out of the woods, it will leave me be," she said aloud to herself. Leaving the wooded road, Hannah veered to the left and picked her way through tangled vines and fallen branches until she reached an open field. She was on Goodman land now, and not far ahead of her was the pond. Just as she had hoped, the tormenting gadfly gave up its pursuit and flew off in search of other prey.

The summer sun was now high overhead, and sweat poured down Hannah's flushed face. Red and itching welts, the marks of the gadfly, had formed on her arms and neck. She walked to the pond and looked with longing at its cool green depths. Although the pond was out in the open, a grove of maple trees shielded it on one side and tall weeds and cattails on the other.

Hannah sat in the shade of a tree with Joseph in her lap and untied the knot at the back of her neck. Being careful not to wake him, she laid her son at the base of the tree with the hammock beneath him. She removed her blouse and gently laid its sheer fabric over him to protect him from insects. Moving behind the tree, Hannah stepped out of her skirt and half-slip, and, after a second thought, took off her bra. She peeked out and listened intently for human sounds. Hearing only the twittering of birds and the bubbling of the spring that fed the pond, she ran, clad only in panties, and lowered herself into the coolness of the pond.

As she lay back on the surface of the pond, her full, white breasts bobbed and peaked on the undulating water, like little sailboats setting out to sea.

Chapter Thirty-three

The third week of Abram's absence passed slowly for his hired girl, despite her daily walks with Joey and evening dips in the pond. When Saturday finally came, she made her way to the barn to talk to Hank again, fearing that he'd say the vacation had again been extended.

"Good morning, Hank. I'd like to have the key to the house, so I can make sure everything is in order for them . . . ." Hannah dreaded what he might say.

To her relief, Hank fished a bunch of keys out of the front pocket of his bibs and searched through it for the house key. "Here y'go, Missy."

Trying to constrain her joy, Hannah casually put the key to the house into her jeans pocket and said, "I'll try to get in there today . . . ."

As she was about to leave the area of the barn, she was hailed by Clay, the youngest of the hired hands, a cowboy type whose job it was to look after Abram's six riding horses, and, with his Western shirt and cowboy boots, he looked the part.

"Hey, Hannah, wait up!" He walked toward her with a certain swagger that Hannah recognized as his. Somewhere in his twenties, his typical apparel consisted of tight-fitting faded jeans, a plaid shirt rolled at the elbows, scuffed boots and a light gray cowboy hat pushed far back on his head of copper-tinged wavy hair.

It wasn't until Hannah had shed her Amish trappings that Clay paid any attention to her. He had flirted with her each time she served lunch to him and the others and hinted that he'd like to take her out to a movie. Because Hannah had never seen a movie, she would have accepted, though he never did ask. She suspected it was because the rumor went around the farm that Hannah was expecting a baby. Although Clay continued to be friendly toward her, Hannah knew that the quality of his attention had changed. Lately, as her figure had come back, she also noticed that his interest in her had returned.

Joey began to fuss in his stroller and Hannah scooped him up and held him up to her shoulder as she watched Clay saunter toward her. His grin was infectious and she smiled back.

"What've you been up to, Girl? I haven't seen you around." He reached out and patted Joey's round bottom.

"Oh, the baby keeps me busy," she lied. Bouncing slightly, she soothed Joey.

"Well, I've been wantin' to ask you if you like to ride—horses, that is." He adjusted his hat as if to shade his eyes.

"I don't know if I like it or not," she answered honestly. "We used to lead one another around on the buggy horses, but I've never actually been in a saddle. In my family, it wouldn't have been appropriate for a girl."

Clay grinned and his white teeth flashed in his tanned face. "Then I'm gonna take you out ridin'! How about tomorrow?"

"But . . . the baby . . . I don't have anybody to tend to him."
She wondered if Clay knew that babies can't be left alone.

"No problem. I already thought of that, so I'll bring my little
sister along. She can babysit the little fella. What's his name?
Joey?" He patted Joseph's cushioned bottom again.

"Oh, I can't ask . . . ."

"Well, I can. I'll see you tomorrow afternoon about two.
Michele, that's my little sister, will be here, too." Abruptly he
turned and went off to do whatever it was he did with horses.

As she watched him stride away, Hannah said to her son, "Well,
Joey, it looks like you're going to have your first baby-sitter and
I'm going to have my first date . . . on the Outside. I wonder what
Abram Goodman will think of that!"

True to his word, the next day at two Clay stood on Hannah's
front porch with his arm affectionately around a teenage girl
standing beside him. "This here is Michele. She babysits for a
livin'."

The girl jabbed him in the ribs. "Oh, I do not. I'm still in high
school and I just babysit in the summers . . . for some spending
money." She laughed and shrugged off her brother's arm.
Michele's honey brown hair was cut very short, and she looked
like a grinning female version of Clay in her tight jeans and pink
plaid blouse.

"Well, hello, Michele, I'm Hannah. Come in and meet Joey." Hannah realized that she was about two years older than Michele. She suddenly felt shy. She wondered what Clay had told his sister about her.

"Just show me where everything is, and we'll be fine. I love babies and Joey is the perfect age—too little to be trouble but big enough not to choke to death or anything." She laughed easily, like her brother, and seemed perfectly comfortable with the idea of babysitting someone as young as Joey. She never asked anything about his father.

"I pumped some milk that you can give him in about fifteen minutes after he's had a chance to look you over. This will knock him right out and he'll probably nap most of the time I'm gone." Hannah went to the refrigerator and showed Michele how to warm the bottle of breast milk in a little pan of water sitting on the stove.

"I know to check to see how warm it is by sprinkling some on my arm and how to burp him. So don't worry or hurry. While Joey's asleep, I've got a good book I want to finish."

"I'm a little bit nervous about leaving him," Hannah said. "I've never left him with anybody else, except the nurse when he was just born, but I was close by . . . ." She turned to Clay and asked, "Can we ride where Michele can yell at us if she needs me?"

"She can call me on my cell phone if she needs us . . . ." Clay said, trying to usher Hannah out the door.

"But I don't have a phone . . . ." She said no more as she saw Michele hold up a cell phone of her own.

As they walked to the stable, Clay walked backwards a few steps and said, "You look real good, Hannah."

Hannah was wearing the tight blue jeans and a pale yellow summer blouse. Clay's admiring glances embarrassed her. "Don't make me self-conscious. I'm still not used to wearing pants like a man."

"Trust me, Honey," he said. "You do not at all wear 'em like a man." He glanced down at her clean white tennis shoes and said, "We'll have to get you some boots and a hat if you take to this."

He slapped her firm behind with his hat and laughed as she reacted. "Don't!"

Breathless and pink-faced, Hannah kicked her horse to urge it on. After being beaten by Clay all afternoon, she was determined that this race would be hers. So far she was in the lead as they streaked across the fields nearest to the main house. Despite the cell phone connection between Clay and his sister, Hannah had insisted that they not stray to the farthest points of the Goodman acres. She wanted to be close by if Michele called.

Knowing that she had won, she laughed and slowed her horse to look back at Clay galloping to catch up. Then she noticed the red convertible parked in front of the main house and her heart leapt.

Movement near the fence line caught her eye and there they were, Abram and Sandra walking toward the fence across from the house. Hannah slowed her horse to a walk and approached them.

She heard Sandra say, "And you were worried that Hannah might be lonely. If that blonde girl on the chestnut is who I think it is, it looks like she made out just fine."

Before Hannah could say a word, Clay yelled out, "She's a natural!" as he caught up to the three of them at the fence. "Of course, I let her have the best horse. Hey, welcome home, you two!" He dismounted, tipped his hat to Sandra and shook Abram's hand.

The three of them stood looking up at Hannah, still astride the horse. "Welcome back," she said, brushing her wind-swept blonde hair out of her eyes. She saw amazement on the tanned faces of her employers as they gazed wordlessly up at her. Conscious of her tight jeans and spread legs, Hannah grasped the saddle horn and tried to swing out of the saddle as Clay had taught her. With her left foot still in the stirrup, her horse began to walk as he dropped his head to graze. Hannah hopped on one foot, yelling, "Whoa! Whoa!"

Abram swung over the fence and took the horse's head, while Clay, enjoying Hannah's plight immensely, grabbed her by the waist to steady her as she tried to get her foot out of the stirrup. Hugging Hannah from behind, he laughed against her ear. Aware of Abram's gray eyes on her and Clay, Hannah looked up to see that he was straight-faced though Sandra was laughing at Clay's antics.

Pleased, the hired girl playfully pulled Clay's hat off his head and put it on her own.

Chapter Thirty-four

On a warm evening in August, Sandra and Abram relaxed in the shade of their front porch. Sandra smiled and squeaked a toy frog at Joey, now almost three-months-old, who sat in her lap.

"I think I'm pregnant," she said mildly.

Abram did not react, absorbed as he was in watching Clay's old green Chevy going round and round in the driveway. Clay had taken it upon himself to teach Hannah to drive. Abram startled at his wife's raised voice.

"Abe! I said I think I'm pregnant . . . this time for sure," Sandra repeated.

He came back to Earth and gave her his attention. "I sure hope so, Honey . . . ." But his eyes were still on the car and its occupants.

"What is it with you and this Clay-Hannah thing, Abram?" He noted the irritation in his wife's voice.

"She's been seeing a lot of him . . . and he's a wild type." He pulled on his lower lip and went back to watching the lurching car.

"So what? I'd think you'd be glad that she has someone to spend time with. She's young, and all she does is work and take care of her baby."

"I just hope Clay doesn't take advantage of her. She's pretty innocent, and he's loved and left a lot of 'em."

Sandra's words were pointed. "It's really none of your business, Abe, and she didn't get this little guy in my lap from under a cabbage leaf."

Abram sighed and leaned forward to chuck Joey under his chubby chin. "You're right, as usual. I guess I just feel kind of responsible. Now what's this about you being pregnant . . . again?" His voice had taken on a teasing tone. Sandra had been sure her two previous menstrual periods would not come.

"For your information," she quipped, "I was due yesterday and still nothing. I'm usually regular as a clock, so there, Daddy."

As Joey squirmed and probed Sandra's breast for nourishment, they both laughed. "Might as well give it up, Fella," Abram advised. "This here is a dry cow, and, besides, those two are mine."

"Cow! You'll live to regret those words, Mister," Sandra said, feigning indignation.

Clay and Hannah had parked the Chevy and were strolling toward them. "Might as well get this girl an Amish buggy. She still refuses to try the open road," Hannah's instructor informed them.

Hannah's face held a pout, but she defended herself. "I've only had my permit a few weeks, and I'm not ready."

Abram was glad to see that she was losing her shyness and had argued against Clay's impatience and teasing.

"You're just in time," Sandra said as she handed Joey to his mother. "Master Joseph wants something I can't give him."

As Hannah carried Joey into the house to nurse him, Clay called after her, "Hey, don't leave on my account. Joey might need some help."

As Abram Goodman scowled, his wife punched his arm and said, "Oh, lighten up!"

Morning light crossed Abram's face. Barely awake, he rolled over and reached for his wife, only to find her side of the bed empty. He heard the flushing of the toilet and waited for her to return to bed. In a few minutes she appeared, wearing a clean nightgown and a look of disappointment.

"What's wrong, Hon?" He caressed her back as she sat on the edge of the bed.

She didn't answer for a moment. "I . . . have my period." Her voice was flat with depression.

"Come here," he said as he pulled her to him. "Don't worry, Sandra. It's only been a couple of months since we started trying."

Sighing, she relaxed in his arms and conceded that she was just being impatient. "I know . . . it's probably still the effect of being on the pill, and maybe all that stuff about trying too hard and needing to relax is true."

"So let's just forget about it, and when it happens, it happens." He hoped his calming words would stop her constant striving about it.

"I'll try. I read in an article that stress and anxiety are fertility killers." Rolling onto her stomach, she said, "I could use a massage, you darling man."

Chapter Thirty-five

Hannah noticed Sandra's uncharacteristic quietness as together they peeled already cooked potatoes and hard-boiled eggs for potato salad. Something was definitely eating at the lady of the house.

"Do you think the men will want to eat on the patio today?" Hannah asked, trying to draw Sandra into conversation. "It's almost ninety now."

"What? Oh, no, I suppose not."

Sandra's sad countenance piqued the hired girl's curiosity. *Are the lovebirds fighting, at last?* Hannah tried again. "Clay wants me to go swimming with him, but I told him I can't."

Sandra didn't take the bait. She remained stubbornly silent, with her lower lip in a pout.

Hannah hated the inept way Sandra peeled eggs, rolling the egg back and forth on the counter to pulverize the shell into hundreds of little pieces to pick off instead of giving it one good crack and splitting the shell into three or four big sections. *I'll be glad when she goes back to school at the end of the month.*

Sighing, Hannah moved to the sink to wash the starch of the potatoes off her hands. "I told him to forget about it. I won't be going swimming."

Finally, Sandra spoke. "You can't swim?" Mrs. Goodman's voice held no real interest in the answer to her question.

"Well, yes, I can swim, but I have no swimming suit." Retrieving jars of mayonnaise and mustard from the refrigerator, she set them on the counter.

"What did you wear when you swam before?" Sandra's mildly sarcastic emphasis on the word "before" did not escape Hannah's notice. Sandra took the shelled eggs to the sink to rinse them in case microscopic pieces of shell might have been missed. "Don't tell me that Amish girls swim in the buff."

Hannah knew the English slang, but she asked, "In 'the buff'?"

"Nude. Naked. Without clothing," Sandra defined the word as though she were reading from a dictionary. Hannah thought of another English slang word but she didn't say it: *Bitchy. Why is she so bitchy?*

"Swimming was really something just for the boys, but my sisters and I used to sneak off to the swimming hole when we could. We wore old dresses. Only our feet were bare." Hannah stared out the window, remembering.

"So buy a swim suit. That's one thing Ida probably never owned." Now Sandra was chopping onions too coarsely for Hannah's liking.

"I don't think I'd have the nerve to wear one, even if I could get to town." Using a little sarcasm of her own, Hannah alluded to the disgraceful bikini that she had seen the other woman wearing when she and Abram strolled off to the pond. She also hinted at the fact that Sandra never invited her to go shopping as she had in the beginning.

"Get the catalog," Sandra advised coldly. "You'll see that there are plenty of styles besides bikinis. You can even order a suit from there."

Hannah thought about coming right out and asking Mrs. Goodman if she was angry with her. She knew something was amiss, but she couldn't figure out what it had to do with her. Just as she entertained the thought of being brave enough to ask, the men entered the air-conditioned house. She was disappointed when Abram went directly to his wife and hugged her for a long moment before kissing her on the forehead.

"Great day for swimmin', Hannah," Clay said, grinning and drying his hands on a paper towel.

"Take me to town to buy a suit, and I'll go swimming with you," the hired girl said with sudden decision.

"What? No skinny-dippin'?" The other men joined in Clay's roguish laughter, but Abram had picked up his plate and followed his wife into the den.

"I like that one," Clay drawled as he pointed to a store mannequin wearing a hot pink bikini and sunglasses.

"You would." Hannah was becoming adept at handling Clay's wisecracks.

"But, Babe, she even *looks* like you! Blonde hair, great body, and hey, look at this . . . ." He pulled off the pink-framed sunglasses to reveal the mannequin's fixed, blue-eyed stare. "She has your eyes!"

"I told you not to call me 'Babe,'" she said, brushing past him to search through rotating racks full of swimwear.

They had made the trip to town precisely to take advantage of the "end of season" swimsuit clearance. As she had seen other women do with their men, Hannah directed Clay to a chair while she selected some of the more modest styles and took them with her to the dressing room. Twenty minutes later, she emerged fully clothed and shaking her blonde head.

"I can't do it," she said.

With his hat pulled down over his eyes as he slouched in a barrel-shaped chair, Clay peered up at Hannah. "Can't do what?"

"I can't wear something like this in public." Frowning, she held out a fistful of garments.

Clay protested, "Hey, Babe, I'm not 'public'! We'll keep it very private . . . the pond is pretty secluded." He stood up and took the suits from her. "Geez, these are old lady one-piece suits anyhow."

Hannah crossed her arms to indicate that the subject was closed. "I don't care. I'll never be *this* English."

"Okay, if that's the way you want it. Sit around fryin' in the sun while the rest of us are swimmin' in the pool next summer." Clay pointed to an exit sign. "There's the way out. No sense wastin' time here."

She stopped shoving the swimsuits back onto their hangers to turn and ask, "What pool? What are you talking about?"

"Haven't you heard?" Clay mimicked a story-book voice. "Sandy said to Abey, 'Oh, let's put in a pool!' Abey said to Sandy, 'Oh, yes, we'll put in a pool!' And they clapped their hands and lived happily ever after."

"Why can't you just talk plain instead of always in riddles, Clay? Now tell me what you're talking about without joking around." Hannah felt like storming away from him, but he was her ride back home.

"I'm serious. I overheard Abe and the missus talkin' about puttin' in a pool next spring. A big underground one, not one of those tacky above-ground things. If I know them, they'll let all of their employees use it, too. We'll all be coolin' off in the pool while prudish Amish girls who won't put on a bathing suit sit and roast!"

Hannah had seen the way Abram looked at Sandra in her bikini.

"Sit down," Hannah said. "I'm not through shopping yet. She stepped over to the blonde mannequin in the hot pink bikini and circled it.

"Help me find this in a medium, Clay."

Chapter Thirty-six

Clay knew enough to keep it low-key when he finally saw Hannah dressed, or undressed, for swimming. "You look better than the dummy," he said casually, when Hannah stepped shyly from behind the stand of trees near the pond.

His inner response was anything but casual. Struggling to keep his breath even, he asked, "How'd your stomach get so flat, so soon after the baby, I mean?"

For once, he had embarrassed even himself, but Hannah surprised him by answering candidly. "It's the nursing that does it."

Wanting those long white legs wrapped around him, those soft white breasts against his chest so much that he could hardly stand it, Clay dived into the pond to hide the evidence.

The once-Amish girl daintily stepped into the water until it was up to her shoulders. Stretching out, she swam gracefully, twice around the pond's perimeter. Clay treaded water and watched her, wondering if she'd swim over to him and let him touch her.

Before he could object, she swam to the bank of the pond and, dripping, stepped out and picked up her towel. "I better get back to the baby. He'll begin to think that Michele is his mother."

"Don't go yet, Hannah, we've only been here ten minutes!" Clay said. He dog-paddled toward her as she wrapped a blue towel around her long, wet hair.

"It was long enough to show you that Amish girls can swim. I believe I've proven that."

Unable to convince her to linger, Clay sighed and climbed out of the water. Ogling her shapely long legs and the firm cheeks of her buttocks, he watched as she retreated into the leafy grove of Maple trees that had been her dressing room.

Clay stood motionless just inside the shaded sanctuary. She was naked, towel-drying her hair, when her eyes met his. He waited for her reaction. There was none. Transfixed, he slowly and deliberately let his eyes explore her full, blue-veined breasts with enlarged brown areolas surrounding her nipples, the cleft of her navel in the slight mound of her belly, and the scant blonde pubic hair beneath it.

Like a Greek statue, she did not move to cover herself from his scrutiny. She stood straight, her arms bent at the elbows as she held a crumpled blue towel to her hair. Unblinking, she returned his stare.

Clay swallowed hard and advanced cautiously, unsure, holding her gaze as he cupped her silken breasts in his hands. Still she remained, with her hands to her head, even when he bent his mouth to her breasts, tasted milk, and was emboldened when he heard her gasp.

Crazed with need, Clay grasped her arms and tried to pull them around him as he crushed her mouth with his own. With one hand, he pulled at his bulging swimming trunks and finally kicked them aside. Backing Hannah against a tree, he bent his knees to thrust upward.

"No!" Hannah awakened from her catatonic-like state and forcefully pushed the dazed man away from her. "Get away from me!"

Staggering backward, Clay almost sobbed. "You've got to be kidding!" He leaned against the tree, his heart pounding with desire and anger and watched Hannah frantically pulling on her clothing. Clutching her shoes, the blue towel and the pink bikini, she ran barefoot out of the grove and in the direction of the little house.

Chapter Thirty-seven

"Where's Clay?" Abram pulled out his chair and noticed Clay's vacant place at the big table when the men came in for lunch.

"Dunno what's eatin' 'im. He says he's not hungry." Hank answered nonchalantly and reached for one of Hannah's home-baked buns.

"That doesn't sound like Clay, him not bein' hungry," Pete said, forking up baked ham to build himself a sandwich. "He must be havin' woman trouble."

Quietly the hired girl removed Clay's plate from the table. She caught Abram and Sandra exchanging glances and then both of them looked at her. She pretended not to notice the question in their eyes.

"Man, these baked beans are good!" George chortled around a mouthful of the sweet and spicy food.

Glad for a diversion from the subject of Clay, Hannah unconsciously lapsed into Amish dialect as she eagerly urged George and the others. "Eat until it's all, there's more back."

By the end of the week, Clay still had not appeared for lunch with the hired hands. Hannah was not sure how she felt about his absence. As she removed his plate from the table each time, she felt both disappointment and relief.

At the end of the work day on Friday, Clay surprised Hannah by knocking at the kitchen door as she scrubbed the pots and pans she had used to prepare the Goodmans' evening meal.

Her face burned, as she remembered all that had passed between them at the pond; but she nodded to him to come in, keeping her hands in the sudsy water.

"Close the door, please," she said. "The air conditioner is on." She heard the soft bump of the door, but, when Clay said nothing, she turned her head to see if he had left. He was still there, his tanned face uncharacteristically solemn.

"Can you let that go for a minute?" he asked, gesturing toward the kitchen sink.

In answer, Hannah dried her hands and took a seat at the table. She had known that a confrontation was inevitable. She sighed and waited.

Clay took off his hat, wiped the sweat from his forehead with the sleeve of his shirt and sat opposite her. "Feels good in here . . . cool," he said lamely.

Hannah looked directly at him. "Yes," she agreed, but she had no inclination to make it easy for him. After avoiding her all week, he had obviously come here to talk. *So talk*, she thought.

After an awkward moment of silence, Clay blurted it out. "Hell, Hannah, I got somethin' to say, somethin' to ask, actually." His agitation was in his voice; the usual tone of teasing was gone. "Why'd you let me go that far? I mean, maybe I shouldn't of . . .

but you had plenty of time to say 'git outta here' or somethin'." He slapped the table with his hand, and she jumped.

She tried to control the tremor that played at her lips. "I don't know," she managed, sounding as though she were ready to cry. She saw his anger instantly fade. He reached across the table for her dishwater-reddened hands.

"Don't cry, Honey. I didn't mean to scare you. Are you mad at me . . . for . . . . "

She spoke hurriedly, not wanting him to say it. She wanted to get this over with. "No, I'm not mad at you, Clay. I'm sorry if I made you think I was . . . ." Groping for a word, she added, "willing."

She heard him swallow hard. "And you're not 'willing'?"

"No." She kept her eyes on her water-swollen hands.

"Not now?"

"Not ever." She brought her gaze level with his and spoke calmly. He sat back as though she had struck him. She paused before explaining. "There's someone else."

He was on his feet. "Who? That goddamn Amish bozo who left you on your own to have a baby?"

The intensity of his reaction surprised her, but she sat with her head bowed and waited for him to finish.

His voice was quieter. "I wouldn't of done that, Hannah."

She heard the door open and close, and he was gone. How could she have explained? How could she have said, "I was curious, curious to know how it feels when Abram touches *her* like that"? In all of Gabe's clumsy pummeling of her breasts, none but her son had ever put his mouth to them, as Clay had done with her, as she had seen Abram Goodman with his wife.

A rainy weekend accentuated Hannah's return to loneliness. Every weekend for the past two months had been spent going places with Clay. Now, to fill up the silence of her little house, she turned on the radio that he had given her after he had discovered that she was without a source of music or a television or, until recently, even a telephone. He had wanted to complain to Abram about it, but she wouldn't let him, insisting that she was used to doing without such things.

So Clay, himself, had seen to the installation of a telephone for her, had given her the radio, and had helped her pass a driver's test. He had been "finaglin'" a way to get her a television . . . and even talked about a car. She stroked the shining, black metal case of the radio and smiled to remember Clay's boyish grin, his teasing . . . and the way he called her son "Little Joe." She had not expected to miss him. On Monday, she decided, she'd seek him out to tell him just that, that she missed him.

On Monday she learned that Clay had, on Saturday past, given Abram two-weeks-notice. His boss, however, had waived the two weeks, giving Clay the opportunity to take another job he had been offered "down South."

Chapter Thirty-eight

Sandra lay on the examining table, her knees bent, her feet in the stirrups. She winced at the pressure of the cold instrument the doctor used. In an effort to relax, she began to count the little black holes in a square of the acoustic tiles above her head.

"How long since you've been off the pill?" Dr. Kipp's voice came to her from between the stirrups.

"About four months," Sandra said, losing her count of the holes in the tile.

"You can sit up now."

Sandra held the pink dressing gown closed and searched Dr. Kipp's face for some look of foreboding, but the pretty lady doctor only smiled and stripped off her latex gloves.

"Get dressed and meet me in the consultation room." She smiled again and disappeared through an opening in the mauve and turquoise curtain that concealed the examining table from the doorway to the room.

Encouraged by Dr. Kipp's smiles, Sandra took a deep breath, tossed the dressing gown into a bin marked "laundry," and got dressed. *Maybe she has something good to tell me.*

"Have a seat, Sandra. Just give me a minute to look through your folder."

Sandra admired the fitted blue sheath that Dr. Kipp, a woman about her own age, wore beneath her open white coat. Sandra was once again impressed with the admixture of femininity and professionalism that was Diedra Kipp. Sandra had been her patient for five years, and she still considered it worth the two-hour drive into the city to see her.

Dr. Kipp brushed a strand of her long brown hair away from her face and met Sandra's eyes. "I can't be sure until I get the lab results, but I think I detect a bit of endometritis, which," she was quick to add, "can usually be treated with medication."

"Endometritis? What exactly is it? Can it lead to cancer?" Sandra heard her own voice quaver slightly.

"It's an inflammation of the lining of the uterus, or the endometrium, usually a reaction to a bacterial attack upon the membrane. Not cancer." The steadiness of Dr. Kipp's voice began to soothe Sandra. "Sometimes," the doctor continued, "it can prevent implantation from occurring."

Tears burned Sandra's eyes, but she held them back. "Will the medication clear it up?"

"It's very likely, Sandra, and when the endometritis is controlled, you'll have an easier time conceiving . . . that is, if your husband checks out. Let me recommend an urologist to run a sperm count on him," she said, reaching for the note pad on her desk.

That evening, Abram leaned against the chaise lounge on the patio. Sandra sat between his legs, her back against his chest.

Cradled in his arms, she felt safe and took assurance from his relaxed tone.

"It's going to be all right, Honey. Make the appointment for me, and we'll get to the bottom of this."

"According to Dr. Kipp, we're not considered infertile until we've had no luck for a year," Sandra said, trying to convey confidence.

"One way or another, we're going to have a baby, Sandra." He hugged her hard. "Even if we adopt."

"No." Her voice was firm. "I don't want to adopt."

He pulled her around to face him. "What? *You* can't love a kid? You who want to bring home every kid at school?"

"This is different," she said, holding her hand to his cheek. "You're the last Goodman. One of the first things you told me is that you want to carry on the Goodman line."

"That was then; this is now," he said, tightening his arms around her and pulling her close against him again. "I'm not hung up on it."

"Well, I am." If he could have seen her face, he would have seen that she was resolute.

"It's getting chilly," he said. "Let's go inside."

BOOK TWO

THE BOND WOMAN
Chapter One

Jostling along the tree-lined country road that was the shortcut to town, Hannah laughed as Joey puckered his lips and tried to whistle "Mares Eat Oats" along with her. She expertly steered her employer's new Land Rover around the deepest ruts in the road and grinned briefly over her shoulder at four-year-old Joey belted into the back seat of the vehicle.

A tow-headed roust-about and the delight of everybody at the Goodman farm, Joey was a happy, uninhibited child who spent as much time with the childless Goodmans as with his mother. In fact, Hannah was glad that today, Saturday, was her and Joey's special day that they spent together, just the two of them. It was August, the time for the annual county fair, the focus of today's outing.

Ahead of them on the shaded road appeared the bright blue shirts of straw-hatted and barefoot Amish boys who stepped aside good-naturedly to let them pass by.

Joey waved and called to them out of the Land Rover's open backseat window, "Hey! We're goin' to the fair!"

Fishing poles propped on the shoulders of the Amish boys left no doubt as to where *they* were going. They smiled and waved.

Hannah's eyes, behind large black sunglasses, watered as she thought of her younger brothers whom she had not seen for almost five years now. Occasionally she had caught a glimpse of her mother and sister Fannie in town during the years since she had been placed under the *Meidung*, but, if they recognized the pretty blonde "English" woman dressed in jeans or shorts, they consistently averted their eyes when hers sought theirs. Hannah knew the seriousness of the law that forbade them to speak to her, but she would have felt blessed by the slightest eye contact or the most fleeting smile if such had ever passed between them. But her Amish kin never offered these small kindnesses.

Lost in her thoughts, she had stopped whistling and it took her a moment to realize that Joey was demanding, "Whistle more, Mom! Whistle more!"

Puckering her lips, she tried, but her mouth was dry, and she emitted only a tuneless rasping sound. "Not now, Joey, my whistler is tired. But look over there." She pointed to the colorful merry-go-round and Ferris wheel which, blinking and spinning, lay ahead of them.

Hannah smiled as she watched her excited little boy run ahead of her to the ticket booth. "Here he is, Mom, here he is, the ticket man! I wanna ride the merry-go-round, and that big white horse, I want him!"

Looking up from digging in her purse for money, Hannah's blue eyes met the unmistakable look of appreciation on the face of the tattooed man in the ticket booth who let his own eyes travel over her well-rounded bosom in the white tank top she wore with denim cutoffs and sandals.

"Two ride passes, please . . . ." she managed to say, hoping that her tanned face hid the blush that she felt on her cheeks.

Hannah had never gotten used to the way that English men responded to her, sometimes making comments about her blonde hair or her figure. The brazen way they stared embarrassed her, and she did nothing to encourage them. In fact, since her brief romance with Clay, she had spurned the attention of the ruggedly handsome young man who had taken his place. Her unspoken reason was simple: No one compared in her mind with Abram Goodman.

For more than six years now, she had loved him from afar, had carefully veiled her face in Sandra's presence and waited, for the rare moments when she could be alone with Abram. Not that he was ever more than friendly with her, but there had been, over the years, precious encounters that Hannah mulled over again and again, deliciously savoring them as she went about her chores or sat rocking on her own porch at twilight.

Closing her eyes, she enjoyed the rhythmic rise and fall of the carrousel, and one of her favorite memories emerged in her mind. It was of the time when she had braved wearing the hot pink bikini in Abram's presence.

~ ~ ~

On a sultry evening when Sandra had not yet returned from a visit to her sister Kendra in the city, Hannah set the table for one, and, after quietly serving Abram, scooped Joey out of the playpen she kept at the main house. She turned to bid Abram a good evening before she left for the day.

"I'll be going home now, Mr. Goodman. Just leave the things on the table, and I'll come back later to clear them."

"Okay," he said around a mouthful of chicken salad, "but it's got to be hot at the little house, so come back for a swim and keep me company. You can look in the bathhouse for extra suits Sandra keeps in there." At her hesitation, he said, "Oh, come on, Hannah, you know you're welcome to use the pool, too."

Hoisting her son on her hip, she said, "Well, all right, but I did buy a suit . . . last summer."

"Last summer? And you've never used it?"

Instinctively, she had sensed that it would not be a good idea to let Sandra see her in the bikini. She could not actually verbalize it in her thoughts, but she knew that competing with Sandra woman-to-woman would spell the end of her employment and the pleasure of seeing Abram, if only in the capacity of his hired girl. It was, she had accepted, the best she could ever hope for.

She would never forget the look in his eyes when she had coyly stepped out of the bathhouse. Had it been desire? Appreciation? Or did he consider her scant attire to be disgraceful? She was too inexperienced to know, but she noted that several seconds had passed before Abram found his voice.

She saw his Adam's apple bob as he swallowed. "I brought the playpen out for Joey."

She bent to put her son in the shaded playpen and surround him with toys. Straightening, she avoided looking at Abram as she delicately dipped a toe into the shimmering blue water before sitting and slipping down into it.

He had disappeared into the bathhouse, and, when he came out wearing tight-fitting black trunks that revealed his slim hips and tight buttocks, Hannah was unprepared for the effect that seeing him this way had on her. She found herself remembering his nakedness when she had secretly watched him and Sandra through the window.

Weakness overwhelmed her, and she clung to the side of the pool and watched his tanned muscles ripple as he bounced twice on the white, shining board. Arching momentarily above the water, his lean body straightened and split the tranquil blue surface. An eternity passed as she watched his wavering form glide toward her under the water.

Suddenly, he was beside her, water dripping from his face and hair, smiling broadly as he said, "You look good, Hannah."

His leg brushed hers accidentally, and she fought to appear as if she hadn't noticed it. He swam away, while she lay back on the water and let its rippling strength hold her. Soon she was aware that his splashing had ceased, and he was floating near her. Side by side, they shared a watery bed which gently surged and ebbed, moving them with it.

~ ~ ~

"Take me down, Mom." Joey's chirpy but demanding voice brought Hannah back from her reverie. The up and down of the merry-go-round had stopped, but she had just sat there, astride a plastic palomino, her cheek resting dreamily on the sleek silver pole that pierced his neck. Opening her eyes, she blinked at the little boy reaching for her from the white horse beside hers.

"What? Oh, yes, wait a minute." She swung off her own steed, feeling embarrassed as though her son had seen her thoughts.

The August sun blazed in the sky, and Hannah coaxed the red-faced boy into the shade of one of the exhibition halls to see the wildlife exhibit while she surveyed the results of the garden harvest competition that had been held the day before. Blue ribbons decked the largest and most perfect fruits and vegetables, almost, she mused, as nice as the ones her father used to grow.

As she made her way through the aisles of the exhibit, rows of canning jars containing golden peaches or grape jellies caught her eye. A wave of homesickness hit her, as she thought that her mother's kitchen counters were probably now lined with similar jars . . . the pungent smell of piccalilli filling the air. The sound of

Joey's laughter an aisle away interrupted her thoughts and moved her in his direction.

"There's some of those funny ladies, Mom." Joey chortled as he pointed at two Amish women in bonnets and long dresses as they inspected the winning patchwork quilts.

Both women turned their heads at the boy's remark, in time to hear Hannah reprimand her son. "Joey! Don't say that. It's not nice . . . ." Straightening from the hunkered-down position she had used to speak to Joey, Hannah brushed a strand of hair from her eyes and looked directly into the faces of Anna Byler and her daughter Abbey.

"I'm sorry," Hannah apologized on behalf of the boy. She watched the polite words Anna had been about to say die unspoken on her pale lips as recognition and shock registered on her and her daughter's faces.

Instead of speaking, Anna turned abruptly and focused her eyes on the quilt display, but Abbey looked boldly back at the Bond Woman, letting her wire-spectacled eyes inspect Hannah from her bare feet in brown leather sandals, all the way up her tanned, smoothly shaven legs, to the crotch of her hip-length denim shorts, to the slight cleavage showing at the neck of her tank-top, to the loose blonde hair that rested on her shoulders. Finally, she stared into Hannah's unblinking blue eyes for a long moment before dropping her disgusted glance to the wriggling child holding his mother's hand.

Under this examination, Hannah had stood stiffly, with a defiant lift to her chin. "I am sorry," she repeated and added pointedly, "for my *child's* rudeness. I can only wonder if you are sorry for yours."

With that, Hannah turned, leaving Abbey to gape at her shapely behind as she strode away. She knew all too well that although the "chosen ones" would not speak to her, they would, without compunction, gladly gossip about her for the rest of the day and for many days to come.

Chapter Two

Something about the solemnity of Sandra's and Abram's faces made Hannah uneasy, as they stood on their front porch and watched her put the Land Rover into its bay.

Joey had bounded ahead and was already babbling excitedly to the Goodmans whom he called "Aunt Sandra and Uncle Abe." Sensing Joey's need for family, and perhaps their own need as well, Hannah was grateful when they had begun to refer to themselves this way, when Joey was just a baby.

Sandra was bending to marvel over some colorful trinket that Joey had brought from the fair, but Abram had descended the porch steps and was slowly moving toward Hannah. His tanned face looked strangely tight, and Hannah felt chills of fear prickle her skin, despite the heat of the August day.

"What's wrong?" She felt afraid without knowing why.

"Come to the porch, Hannah . . . and sit down." He had placed his hand on her back and was already maneuvering her there. As she moved forward dumbly, she could hear Sandra telling Joey that she had something for him in the kitchen.

Obediently, Hannah sank into the soft, flowered cushions of the white wicker chair to which he had led her. Searching his unsmiling face, she asked again, "What's wrong?"

Before he answered, he pulled an identical chair to a position facing Hannah's, and, sitting, reached across the short distance between them. He took her hand and pressed it between both of his own. Hannah's breath came short from his touch as much from fear. The pained look in his gray eyes terrified her. Had she done something wrong?

"I heard something in town today, Hannah, about one of your brothers. They said he was about seven years old . . . Aaron Miller. I'm sorry, Hannah. He drowned in a swimming hole the kids use."

Seven? There was no brother who was seven . . . . Her mind was racing, trying to make sense of the words he was speaking. She could barely hear him because her pounding heart echoed in her ears, as she tried to resist the picture of a rosy-cheeked two-year-old that had begun to form in her mind. From somewhere outside herself, she heard a trembling moan; then she realized that it was her own voice.

"Baby Aaron? Not little Aaron . . . not my baby brother . . . ." She had risen suddenly and the porch floor began to tilt crazily, but Abram was there to catch her before she fell. He carried her to the downstairs bedroom where she sobbed with her face pressed into the quilt created by the dead boy's mother.

She heard Sandra say, "Leave her alone for a while, Abe. Let her cry it out."

Quiet now, Hannah traced the outline of a branch of the Tree of Life and felt in her own heart the pain her mother must be feeling. A longing to go to her mother, to mix her tears with hers, ached and throbbed within her breast. Would her mother blame her for the hand of God that had stricken the Miller household? Would she turn Hannah away? She had to try. She had to try to see her mother.

She found Sandra and Abram sitting quietly on the couch in the den with Joey and a huge children's book between them. Joey loved it when Sandra read to him, but, at the entrance of his mother, he quickly shoved the book aside and ran to her.

"Mommy! Why are you crying, Mommy?"

He had clasped his arms around her hips and was looking up into her red, swollen eyes. The worry in his usually merry blue eyes broke Hannah's heart. How could she explain to him that they had a family they never saw, a family of "the funny people" Joey sometimes stared at in the stores in town? How could she explain the grief that she now shared with them?

"Aunt Sandra said somebody you loved died, Mommy, and that's why you're crying. Who, Mommy?" He clung to her, waiting for her to explain.

Hannah knew she had to tell him something, but grief had numbed her mind. She looked to Sandra for help as she stroked her son's silken hair. Sandra loved Joey, Hannah knew, and Joey loved her. Sandra would know what to tell him.

Sandra acknowledged Hannah's pleading look by rising to take Joey's hand. "Let Mommy freshen up, Joey. You stay here with Uncle Abe and me, and I'll tell you what has happened to make your mommy so sad." To Hannah, she said, "Change your clothes, Hannah, before you go."

Hannah looked into Sandra's moist eyes. She could see that Sandra understood that she had to go to them. Tears of gratitude came to Hannah's eyes.

She would risk their shunning, but she had to go. And, yes, Sandra was right. She should not go dressed as she was.

"Take the Land Rover," Abram said.

"I should walk," the hired girl answered as she turned to go to her little house, there to dress herself conservatively, in the colors of mourning.

Dressed in a long-sleeved white blouse, a black skirt and black flats, her face scrubbed clean of every trace of makeup, Hannah stood on tiptoe to peer over the green rows of corn that lay between the Goodman property and her father's house. She could just catch sight of its steel roof reflecting the red, evening sun. She had not crossed this field since that Sunday, four years ago when she had visited their empty house.

She found herself remembering the bouquet of daisies she had left on her mother's kitchen table, for her to find when she came home. She tried to imagine what her mother's reaction might have been, hoping for some clue as to how she would be treated now. Had her mother tossed them aside, angered by the intrusion of one now a stranger to her? Had she held them to her bosom, weeping for the daughter she had lost?

Chapter Three

On that Sunday long ago, Rebecca Miller had instantly recognized the daisies on her table as her daughter's signature, and her heart had leapt with joy. *My daughter, my Hannah, has come home to work out her repentance!*

Hearing footsteps on the porch, Rebecca quickly laid the sleeping boy, Aaron, in the kitchen crib and, clutching the jar of daisies in her trembling hand, she had met her husband at the door. Stifling a cry of jubilation, she raised the jar of flowers to his eyes.

"Hannah has come home!" she said in a loud whisper. She rejoiced inwardly at the relief that washed across her husband's sun-wrinkled face showing above his unruly beard.

"Where is she?" he asked, mimicking her whisper.

He turned with his wife to look in the living room, and, not finding her there, they had mounted the narrow stairs to her old room. They searched all of the upstairs bedrooms, timidly calling her name because they should not be speaking to her.

"Could she be hiding in the barn? Or the hen house?" Joseph Miller asked as he turned to go downstairs.

They searched both, ignoring the questions of their younger children. Disappointment turned to anger as Rebecca Miller realized that he daughter had played this cruel joke on her. Marching back to her kitchen, she grabbed Hannah's daisies, returned to the porch with them and flung them, jar and all, into the weeds across the road.

Her chest heaving, she stood watching the trickle of water run back toward her, halt, and sink into the dust.

Chapter Four

Hannah saw a thin, short-haired white dog she didn't know making its way toward her down the straight corn row path that she walked. There was no bark or wagging tail, just a low growl that issued from the animal's throat as it approached her. She stopped, wondering if the dog were dangerous. No, she decided, her father would not keep a mean dog on the farm.

Guessing at its name, Hannah crouched and held out her hand, calling softly, "Here Whitey, here Snowball. Come here, Boy. Come here, Girl." The dog slunk closer and cautiously sniffed her hand. Hannah could see the dog's swollen teats and knew that this was a nursing mother. "Nice girl, nice girl," she said soothingly. When she rose, the dog sprang back, startled by Hannah's movement, and ran back to the barnyard. Out of her sight, the dog began to bark, alerting the house's occupants that they had a visitor.

Hannah saw that the dog would go unheeded. There were several black buggies with horses hitched here and there in the Millers' barnyard. Church members would be arriving from time to time to share the burden of grief, and barking dogs would be ignored.

She could see young Samuel, her fifteen-year-old brother sitting on the porch steps. He hung his head and looked the picture of despair. He had lifted his head at the dog's bark. Hannah waved a hand from amid the corn to catch his attention. He stared for a minute, before Hannah saw recognition flood his face. He looked right and left and feigned indifference as he sauntered toward the corn field with the dog at his heels.

Hannah crouched low in the corn and whispered when she saw his pants legs passing her by. "Samuel! I'm here!"

He threw himself into her arms and wept. "It's my fault, Sister. It's my fault that Aaron drowned."

Hannah rocked him in her arms, crying, too, but saying soothing words to him. "No, no, Samuel. It couldn't have been your fault. Why do you say that?'

Samuel scrubbed his face with his shirt sleeve. "Get down, Sparky!" he said to the dog who was trying to lick his face. "Ben and Zach and me were supposed to be watchin' Aaron. I'm the oldest, so it was me who should've been watchin' him. But I was busy showin' off how I could jump from the rope. Aaron must've raised his hand over and over again, and I didn't see him!" A fresh burst of crying rendered Samuel helpless in her arms.

"I don't believe that anybody blames you for this, Samuel. If I know the bishop, he blames me."

Samuel's lack of response told her she had guessed right. "How big you've grown, Sammy. I'm so glad you were out here where I could talk to you . . . ."

He interrupted. "I couldn't take no more of the women in there cryin' and cryin'. I should of gone to the coffin-maker with *Datt.*"

"So *Datt* isn't here? Well, go into the house and whisper to *Mamm* that I'm here. I'll go to the barn and wait for her. Tell her I beg her to see me. Will you do that, Sammy?"

"*Ja,* Sister I will. But don't tell her I talked to you. Tell her you talked to me and I just listened, okay?"

"Yes, Sammy," she said, stroking his hair back from his forehead. "Don't worry. I'll tell her just that. Now go."

In the shadows of the barn, Hannah waited, watching dust particles dancing in the slanting lines of light that filtered through the cracks of the barn wall. Though she stood perfectly still in the semi-light, her thoughts traveled back into the cave of memories where she seldom allowed them to venture.

~ ~ ~

She waved goodbye to her parents in their buggy, off to church on a neighboring farm. Baby Aaron, suffering the sniffles, straddled her hip and waved, too. She was proud of his quick mind. He had been as much hers as her mother's, since she was the eldest daughter at home now, with Mary married and in her own house. He had been a beautiful baby; she thought her own boy looked like him. Aaron had remained a toddler in her memory, a chubby-cheeked cherub with blond curls. Every time she had seen a group of Amish children, over the years, she had searched the faces of each of them, hoping to recognize Aaron's bright eyes and dimpled smile, but she was never sure . . . .

~ ~ ~

The quiet, lilting voices of Amish men droned from the lower level of the barn, which housed the milk cows. Hannah held her breath as she listened to their movements beneath her. She could barely hear what they were saying, but she knew that they were neighbors who had come to take over the milking chores to spare Joseph Miller and his boys the task. Light from their lanterns streamed upward through the floor on which she stood, and Hannah realized that her level of the barn had become dark. She had been waiting a long time. Logic told her that her mother was not coming, but she could not bring herself to move her feet. She waited, waited and remembered.

~ ~ ~

Lying naked on the straw she watched coldly as Gabe struggled out of his work boots and britches. He had said he didn't want to do it again, but she knew he would. Her slow undressing always drove him mad, and he could not tear his frightened eyes away from her. He was skinny and white, except for his tanned face, neck and arms. His veined erection bobbed as he moved toward her. He hesitated before hovering above her, trying to kiss her face while he clumsily kneaded her breasts. But she turned away, saying rudely, "Chust do it."

~ ~ ~

Someone slowly opened the door to the upper level of the barn, and Hannah's mind jerked back to the present. Framed by the dim light outside the barn, a dark figure stood peering into the blackness where Hannah had hidden herself. A small gasp escaped Hannah's mouth, as she saw, not the outline of a woman, but that of a man with a high-crowned hat. Her uncle, the bishop had come instead. *My mother has betrayed me!* She tried to hide deeper in the shadows.

At her small gasp, the bishop's silhouette had turned quickly toward the corner where the Bond Woman trembled. Like a black cat pouncing on a crouching mouse, he was upon her, his claws raking the white flesh of her neck as he grabbed the tail of her hair as she attempted to run. Clutching a mass of blonde strands, he dragged her across the rough barn floor, splinters of wood tearing at her flailing body.

Neither of them had made a sound in their struggle. It wasn't until he dragged her to the grassy mound outside the barn and flung her to the ground that she pierced the night with her screams. Towering over her, the bishop loudly accused her in German, "You came back not to repent but to drag others into the abyss with you, Hannah Miller!"

As she tried to get up, he dealt her a blow across the face with the back of his hand, sending her reeling back to the ground. During this blurred nightmare, Hannah had been dimly aware of the humming of a vehicle off in the distance, and now, in an explosion of light and sound, it bounded forward and stopped abruptly at the base of the grassy incline on which she struggled for freedom from the bishop's hold.

"You lousy son-of-a-bitch!" Abram Goodman roared as he jumped out of the Land Rover. Angrily, the bishop whirled and found himself face-to-face with the fury of Hannah's friend and employer. With one hand, Abram hurled the old man off the mound.

Clambering to his feet, Hannah's uncle reached for his hat and spewed curses of his own, in German. He bellowed, "You have no business here, Goodman; this does not concern you!"

Abram bent to help Hannah to her feet. Straightening up with his arm protectively around her shoulders, he answered the bishop. "The hell it doesn't! I told you once before not to manhandle her!"

Hannah had never seen such rage in Abram. His teeth were clenched and the veins stood out on his neck. She feared that he would kill the bishop.

"Take me home, Abram. Please, let's chust go home."

Abram shook his fist at the bishop who flinched. "Look at you, you cowering bastard. You're not so brave when it's someone besides a helpless girl you're abusing." But he listened to Hannah and walked with her toward his vehicle.

"Go from here!" the bishop shouted. Take the cursed one with you!" Gesturing wildly with his skinny arms, he sounded fearsome, probably for the benefit of several of his flock huddled on the Miller porch and near the lower barn door. From these vantage points, they had witnessed the entire spectacle.

With a glance of disgust, Abram Goodman said to the girl quivering beneath his arm, "Come on, Hannah. Let's leave these . . . holy people . . . to themselves."

Chapter Five

Hannah wept softly against Abram's shoulder on the short drive back to the Goodman farm. He had pulled her to him and drove with one hand, reassuringly patting her shoulder with the other.

Listening to her sobs, he clenched his teeth in anger as his mind played again the scene on the grassy mound, where he, sitting some distance away in his vehicle, had seen Hannah being dragged and struck by the so-called holy man of the local Amish district.

When Hannah had not returned before dark, Abram decided to drive over to the Miller farm to pick her up, concerned for her to walk three miles home at night. Leaving Sandra happily occupied with tucking Joey in for the night, he drove the few miles to the neighboring farm, cutting the engine and coasting down the lane that led to the white farmhouse. Noting a number of Amish buggies lining the lane, he had assumed that Hannah had been welcomed into the house by her family and neighbors, the shunning forgotten at this time of sorrow.

He had sat in his Land Rover as far as he could get from the house but still be able to observe. He watched men come and go from the bottom level of the barn and thought nothing of the lone man who later crossed from the house to the barn. He had been wondering if Hannah had decided to stay with her family for the night, when her screams shattered the stillness and he saw her being roughly handled by a man. The Rover shot forward and he screeched to a halt at the barn.

Now here she sat with him in the vehicle, crying and clearly shatttered by what she had endured at the hands of the bishop. But there was more to it than that. "My mother betrayed me, my own mother!" Hannah wept profusely, and he felt the wetness of her tears seep through the sleeve of his shirt.

"I know, I know, Hannah, don't cry . . . ." Stroking her hair, he wished he knew what to say to comfort her. He felt like cursing those Amish hypocrites, including her mother, but he held his tongue.

Maneuvering the Land Rover into the garage, Abram turned off the engine and tilted Hannah's wet face up to look at him. By the vehicle's interior light, he could see the red welt from the bishop's blow on her cheek and long, bloody scratches on the side of her neck.

"I know, Sweetheart. I see what he did to you. I can see the marks he put on your face and neck, the bastard." She continued to cry quietly, and he pulled her closer. He put his face in her hair and crooned, "Don't cry . . . . He can't get to you. . . . You don't have to think about it."

He felt her relax against him, and she turned her face to him; then he was cupping her face in his hands, covering it with soft kisses, as though to dry her tears with his lips. Then his mouth found hers and she yielded to the pressure of his hand pushing her head forward to meet his open, hungrily moving mouth. She yielded and kissed him with equal fervor.

It was Abram who came to his senses first. As though burned, he dropped his hands from her face and pulled gently back from her embrace. He said nothing for a moment. When he found his voice, he spoke barely above a whisper. "Let's go to the house."

As he stepped out of his side of the vehicle, he turned to take her hand to help her down. He couldn't look at her, couldn't think of a thing to say, but she spoke.

"Joey . . . where's Joey?" She sounded bewildered by what had just happened.

"In the house," he answered, "with . . . Sandra."

They walked wordlessly, side by side, to the house where Sandra waited.

Hannah's voice shook as she unraveled the tale of her encounter with the bishop for Sandra.

"I can't believe that this is what this man sees as Christian behavior! He actually put his hands on you!" Sandra lifted Hannah's hair to see the scratches on her neck and put her hand on the bruise on Hannah's face. "So this is how the Chosen's leader behaves? I'd rather be unchosen than have to follow a cad like your former bishop, Hannah!"

Abram kept his back to them and stood staring into the darkness outside the window. When Hannah began to weep afresh, it was Sandra who drew her into her arms to comfort her.

Chapter Six

Joey spent the night with the Goodmans, and, alone in her house, Hannah lay atop the sheet, letting breezes generated by the fan in her bedroom caress her body, naked except for a pair of panties. The August night was humid, and her sheets were damp with her own perspiration and tears, but it was the tumult in her mind that would not let her sleep. She relived the terrible struggle with her uncle and grieved again for the loss of Aaron.

Yet overpowering both of these was the sweet remembrance of what had transpired between her and Abram as they had embraced and kissed deeply there in the privacy of the garage. She groaned audibly at the memory of his soft lips that had touched her forehead, her eyes, her cheeks and, finally, had sought her mouth in a hungry kiss. Had she dreamed it? No, it was real; it had happened. At long last, it had happened. Had *she* made it happen? Had *he?* Remembering, she knew that he had initiated the kiss. She could hardly believe it, but he had! He had!

Rhythmically repeated words of revelation flowed through her mind and spilled into her body. Half-asleep, she rode a great wave of pleasure, surging and ebbing and surging again until, at last, she slept.

Chapter Seven

Lying awake beside his sleeping wife, Abram Goodman wrestled with his own feelings, reliving the kiss he had shared with the hired girl.

"Damn!" He cursed himself because the arousal he was now experiencing had nothing to do with the woman at his side. He was tempted to waken Sandra, to use her body to relieve his own pent up fury; but he could not bring himself to do that.

How had he allowed it to happen? Concentrating, he forced himself to analyze. He was not unaware of the war he had waged with himself for a long time now. For how long? A year? Maybe more. When was the first time the hired girl had ceased being just that? When had he stopped feeling fatherly toward her? What was the nature of the . . . caring . . . that had replaced it? He hated euphemisms, but "caring" was the one he now used in this heart-to-heart talk with himself. Brutally honest with himself, he finally admitted that his "caring" was heavily laced with lust.

He rolled to his side and half sat up to look at his wife, slumbering contentedly on her side, her shapely body half-covered, curled and facing him. Dark lashes swept downward to meet her finely etched cheekbones; her hair, a dark halo around her head; her innocent mouth, partly open. *She is so beautiful. So loving*, he thought. *So desperate for a baby.*

He stroked the hair at her temple, and she stirred and smiled slightly, even as she slept responding to his touch. His love for her swelled inside him, and he drew her to him, vowing never to betray her again.

Chapter Eight

Entering the door to the kitchen of the main house the next morning, Hannah was surprised to see by cups and crumbs on the counter that someone had already breakfasted, not waiting for her to cook and serve.

She heard Sandra call to her from the patio where she was alone with her newspaper. "Just make something for yourself, Hannah. I'm just having coffee, and Abe and Joey were both up at the break of dawn. They've gone to feed the horses. I think Abe must have fixed toast for Joey and himself." Laughing, she added, "Can't you tell by the mess they left?"

Hannah tried to hide her disappointment at Abram's absence. She had been waiting to look into his eyes, to try to discern what he was feeling. "I'll just clear these things," she said but was interrupted by Sandra who had come into the kitchen through the sliding door that led to the patio and pool.

"And that's *all* you're doing today, young lady. I don't expect you to feel like working. After all, you're grieving, and, on top of that, you've had a shock."

"I'd rather keep busy," Hannah said, but she was again interrupted by Sandra.

"Don't argue with me. Besides, I have an idea I want to talk to you about. I've already discussed it with Abe, and he said it's up to you." She folded her newspaper and laid it aside.

Hannah paused in wiping crumbs from the counter. "What's up to me?"

Sandra met her eyes. "Whether you want to attend your brother's funeral or not."

Sandra's brazen idea both frightened and intrigued Hannah. Tomorrow would be the burial day for her brother, and Sandra had decided that her parents' English neighbors—the Goodmans and their hired girl—would attend; that is, if Hannah wanted to show the bishop that he couldn't keep her away.

"After all," Sandra said with mock innocence, "we're neighbors, aren't we? Hell, I might even take a casserole. Just let that hypocrite bishop try to throw us out. It wouldn't look too good for the non-violent 'chosen ones,' now would it?"

Hannah wore a sleeveless black sheath dress, totally unadorned by jewelry. On her feet were black pumps, and she had twisted her long blonde hair into a knot at the back of her neck, with no attempt to cover the red scratches on her neck.

"That will never do," insisted Sandra. "I don't want you to look dowdy. Didn't you tell me that they say you 'go gay' when you give up the plain life? You don't look very gay. At least let me French braid that hair of yours, if you don't want to wear it loose. And a long strand of Ida's pearls will look good with that dress."

Hannah gave in to the braid but refused the pearls. "I don't want to offend them any more than I already have. They hate me enough."

"Suit yourself, but, as for me, I'm going to look regal in black silk and diamonds. And, with my highest heels, I'll look formidable, a woman not to be messed with!"

Hannah pulled her hair free from the knot at her neck and sat back to let Sandra brush it and weave it into a French braid.

"Sure you won't let me work some pearls into this?" Sandra said, separating Hannah's thick blonde hair into sections.

"No pearls, please. Believe me, the fact that my head will be uncovered and my arms bare will shock them silly." Emotions from grief to fear to nervous excitement warred in Hannah's breast as she sat at Sandra's vanity and looked in the mirror at the determined woman who worked on her hair, but guilt overrode them all. In truth, Hannah had grown to like Sandra over the past four years, in spite of the jealousy she knew she had no right to feel. The gratitude that she felt for what Sandra was doing for her now caused her eyes to fill with tears. Sandra was being protective of her. She recognized that, and she felt ashamed for coveting this woman's husband. *But I loved him before I ever met Sandra,* she thought, partially excusing herself.

Dressed in his Sunday best, Joey bounded into the room. "Uncle Abe shined my shoes! See?" Balancing awkwardly, he held up one gleaming shoe for inspection.

Her boy, Hannah had long ago realized, had become a blessing to the childless couple as well as to his mother. She knew that the Goodmans genuinely loved Joey, and he loved them. They treated her and Joey like family, once they got used to the idea that the excommunicated girl had no one but them.

Hannah, exclaiming the brilliance of Joey's shoes, shyly looked into the face of Abram Goodman who had followed Joey into the room. It was the first time they had been in the same room since the incident two days ago. She was sure that he had been avoiding her.

But now he smiled at her and said, "That's a nice braid you've got there," as if to show that everything was back to normal. Apparently, they would go on from here as if the kiss had never happened.

He turned his attention to his wife to compliment her. "And don't you look like a Hollywood actress, all decked out in diamonds." He kissed her cheek.

She hooked her hand into his arm and smiled at him. "You, Dahling, look marvelous. Whoever chose this smart three-piece suit for you has excellent taste. No one would ever guess that you're a shoeshine boy, divine gray silk tie and all."

"Let's do this, ladies and gentleman," Abram urged with a hint of tension in his voice. "Our Amish neighbors do things early, and it's past eight o'clock now." He led the small procession down the stairs and out the front door.

Abram parked his handsome, white Lexus at the end of a long line of Amish buggies, perched like humped up vultures along the lane that led to the white farmhouse Hannah used to call home. Escorting Sandra, Hannah, and her son along a tree-shaded lane, Abram walked in front as if to shield them from attack. Behind him came his wife followed by Hannah who held Joey's hand.

Buggy horses wearing blinders lifted their heads from grazing the grass at the edge of the lane to listen to the happy babbling of the child who was the only one of the four not silent with apprehension.

"Shhh . . . Joey, be quiet." His mother, her heart pounding, hushed him as they came to the edge of her father's barnyard. The barnyard was already full of black carriages, and she could see a procession of black-garbed Plain People slowly and silently filing into the house. Panic filled her as she saw some of them turn to stare with shock at *Die Ausere*—foreigners—non-Amish people—advancing, themselves dressed in the colors of mourning!

"Let's just stay out here. We can wait out here," Hannah whispered frantically to Sandra's back.

But Sandra merely adjusted her sunglasses, put her nose in the air, and disagreed with Hannah through clenched teeth. "No way. I wouldn't miss this for the world."

His square jaw firmly set, Abram Goodman led on, amid the rush of whispers and gasps that escaped from bespectacled, bonneted women and girls, past the narrowed eyes of bushy-bearded men wearing black "mutzi" frock coats. Miniature clones of their elders, Amish children stared with mouths agape at Joey, silencing the boy. He moved closer to his mother who walked straight as an arrow with her eyes focused on Abram's broad back. A sea of black-coated Amish parted to let *der Englischer* pass and closed behind them as they entered the house.

Inside, moveable wall partitions had been set aside, making the downstairs of the house into one large meeting room filled with benches arranged parallel with the length of the room, just as Hannah had seen on many a *Gemesspunndaag,* when it was her family's turn to host the church meeting. The difference was that today, down the center of the room were arranged fourteen chairs on which sat fourteen high-hatted ministers from neighboring districts. Like grim reapers, they sat silently, each with his stare fixed on the back of the man in front of him.

No coffin was in sight, which Hannah suddenly realized would confuse the Goodmans; however, now was not the time to tell them that her brother's body rested in his bedroom upstairs, in a pine box that would have been placed on a bench against the unadorned wall. On rows of chairs facing the dead boy, his parents and siblings and closest relatives would be sitting, "keeping the vigil." From there the family would be able to hear the loud voices of the ministers who would address the people crowded into the room below and on the porch.

The head usher, whose hat was still on his head, seemed at a loss as to what to do about the strangers among them, but, since no signal or other reaction issued from the line of ministers, he whispered to some teenagers, who promptly gave up their bench to the English and went to stand on the porch with latecomers.

Perhaps one hundred or more adults and children filled the house, while another hundred or more stood outside in absolute silence. In the house, with everyone seated, intense body odor also prevailed. Hannah gave the Goodmans an apologetic look and hoped that Joey would not mention the aroma aloud.

Wind-up clocks were the only sound other than an occasional cough. Time crept by interminably, and, to Hannah who felt eyes on her from all sides, her nervous swallows sounded like thunder in her ears. Amish children had even ceased playing with "church-mice" made from their mothers' handkerchiefs to stare at the ones dressed "chust for show." She noticed that Joey stubbornly stared back at them.

Abram had seated himself between Sandra and Joey, and he reached across the boy to pat Hannah's ice-cold hand. He winked at her and smiled slightly. His gesture was like a benediction, and she bowed her head to receive it. She lifted her head but dared not smile back, though she saw Sandra, with her hand linked in the crook of her husband's arm, smile at Joey.

They waited, listening to the monotonous song of the clocks. Simultaneously, clocks from various parts of the house began to strike nine. At the ninth chime, the minister at the head of the line suddenly removed his hat, and in synchronized motion, the others did the same.

Hannah's Uncle Jacob, bishop of the home district, rose and turned to face the congregation. Diamonds sparkling on a somber sea seemed to catch his attention, and shock registered on his face as he recognized Hannah and Abram Goodman. His seat at the head of the bishops had faced the wall which was now at his back.

Regaining his composure, his small, wrinkle-shrouded eyes darted from Hannah to the child, to Goodman and to the woman who clung to Goodman's arm. Then he shot a glance back at the defiant face of the English man. All witnessing the silent struggle between Bishop Stuckmann and Abram Goodman who had brought the Bond Woman among them again, in direct defiance of the bishop's expulsion of her two nights ago, waited with held breath. Their spiritual leader opened his mouth as if to speak, hesitated and closed it again.

Looking away from the foreigners, he addressed his people in German. "The Holy God has spoken through the death of Aaron Miller. Perhaps, there are those who see only the sins of others being visited upon the child who has died. This is so, but I see in it also a blessing, because, perhaps, Aaron Miller might have grown up to lose his salvation, to disgrace his parents who certainly could not have borne more, and so, God, in His mercy, has taken the child now to spare them . . . ."

Hannah's face burned, but her eyes were dry and unblinking. The bishop did not look at her, nor did any of the others, but all knew that it was she who was being blamed for the untimely death of her brother. Privy to none of this, those who had come to protect her sat unaware of the invective that was meant for her. Though they sat listening to the rise and fall of the bishop's incantations in German and watched the gesturing of his gnarled hands, they could not know that Hannah was being singled out since he neither looked nor pointed at the shunned woman. The Goodmans could not know the punishment that Hannah was now enduring.

A half-hour passed before the floor was yielded to the next bishop in line. He, with his *Biewel* held very close to his hollowed face, read in German from the Scriptures; however, perhaps out of deference to the non-Amish whom he must have noticed among them, his principal address was delivered in sing-song English. He appealed to the audience to forsake the world and to take up righteousness, to remember that the old ways are better, and new ways are evil. No mention was made of the dead boy, nor of his grieving family. Probably because this minister was from another district, no reference was made to Hannah, to her great relief.

After forty-five minutes, he read a very long prayer and sat down. When the third bishop rose, Hannah saw Abram and Sandra exchange looks of disbelief, but their obvious anxiety was appeased when the stoop-shouldered man only asked the audience to rise and a brief benediction was given. The congregation sat again, and an obituary of Aaron Miller was read. Among his sisters, Hannah Miller's name was not mentioned.

Next, those in attendance were asked to leave the house and to form a line for viewing of the body. As they shuffled out with the others, the Goodmans followed Hannah and her son. Outside in the sunshine, Hannah breathed deeply of the fresh air, saw her companions doing the same, and felt embarrassed for her "unworldly" former clan.

Once again subjected to stares and murmurs, the Bond Woman withdrew to stand in a close knot with the Goodmans and Joey under the shade of a large maple tree a good distance from the house.

"Come here, Joe. Let me help you out of that coat. It's too hot for suit coats." Abram removed his and Joey's suit coats and hoisted the boy into his arms. "You're getting to be a load, Big Fella."

"You were such a good boy in there, Joey. I'm so proud of you." Sandra spoke in the tone of a real aunt, or even a mother.

As Hannah watched Abram and Sandra take over with Joey, to free her to grieve for her brother, gratitude for their kindness was mingled with the sorrow in her heart. She stayed close to them, but she let her eyes rove over the people who closely crowded around the front porch, trying to form themselves into a line. She became aware of the slim, black-garbed form of a beardless young man, who, like her and the Goodmans, stood apart from the others. Gabe.

Briefly, Hannah's eyes met his, and the sadness she saw in them added to her already pain-laden heart. His eyes shifted from her face to look at the boy in Abram Goodman's arms. When he turned his eyes back to Hannah's, she looked away.

A line was forming like an undulating, long, black snake as the Plain People prepared to view the deceased. Hannah and those with her did not become a part of it but waited until it had inched its way past the coffin which had been brought to the porch for viewing.

Finally, after three-quarters of an hour, Abram motioned that the tail end of the line was now ascending the steps. "Do you still want to do this, Hannah?"

"Yes." She took her son by the hand and left the security of the tree and the Goodmans.

"We're right behind you," Sandra said.

With her child born of sin by the hand, the Bond Woman moved forward on leaden feet. Hannah's mouth was dry, and her throat ached with emotion. Behind her walked her guardian angels.

The hinged part of the unlined pine coffin was open to reveal the upper torso of a blond boy dressed in white. His innocent face looked startlingly like the boy gripping Hannah's hand, except that it was an unearthly white. No makeup had been used to make him appear to be just sleeping.

Standing in a row behind the coffin were Hannah's mother, father, her sisters Mary and Fannie, her three brothers and Mary's husband holding two small girls by the hand. On their faces were masks of sorrow, but there were no more tears.

Rebecca Miller's downcast eyes had fallen on the English boy. Her sharp intake of breath was evidence that she, too, saw the resemblance to her dead son. Hannah reached her quivering hand across the corpse to her mother who made no move to take it, though, she, like Hannah's father who stood beside her, trembled visibly. A fresh burst of crying came from Hannah's sisters.

Hannah spoke calmly. "*Mamm . . .Datt. . .* forgive me, but I had to come." Tears streamed down her face for the first time today.

Under the watchful eye of the bishop who stood inside the doorway to the house, Hannah understood that her mother was forbidden to speak to her, but Rebecca Miller did not even raise her head to meet her daughter's eyes.

Hannah looked into the brimming eyes of her father. His lips twitched above his beard as he returned her tearful gaze. Visibly teetering on his feet, he spoke to her only with his eyes. In them, Hannah read a plea. Was it a plea to return to them or to go away and leave them in peace? His lips formed two words soundlessly but Hannah read them: *Mei dochder,* my daughter. At the sound of a harsh cough from behind him, her father dropped his eyes.

Hannah's sisters sobbed audibly into hands they held over their faces, their capped heads bowed along with those of Benjamin and Zach. Only Samuel stood erect and looked at her as his father had done. He had been ten when she had died and he remembered her well, for she had spoken with him just two nights ago. Dry-eyed and white-faced, he looked into Hannah's eyes as she spoke to him.

"Ich wunch eucs der Sage Gottes, Samuel." I wish you all the blessings of God, Samuel.

Hannah turned to Abram and Sandra Goodman who waited at the base of the porch. She said, in a voice uncharacteristically loud, loud enough for everyone to hear her. *"Valley hem geh—* Let's go home."

Chapter Nine

Sandra pretended not to see Joey creeping toward her with a green plastic bucket of water as she sat on a chaise lounge by the pool. Carefully, she laid her book aside and covered it with a towel.

When the water hit her sun-warmed skin, she let out the shriek Joey had been waiting for. "Okay, Buster, now you've done it! Prepare to be ducked!" With that she rolled into the water in pursuit of the four-year-old who already swam like a fish.

At the shallow end of the pool they stood splashing one another and laughing until Sandra captured the boy in her arms and set him on the side of the pool. They had spent many summer afternoons together languishing by the pool or playing in the crystal blue water, while Abram and Hannah went about their separate responsibilities.

"You realize, Joey, that we'll be covering the pool soon because the weather is going to turn cold, and I have to go back to work tomorrow."

"But why? Why do you have to go back to work?"

"Well, I'm a teacher, Joey, and my summer vacation is over. You'll be going to pre-school and I'll be going to the big school where I work." She noticed him shivering and said, "Let's get out and wrap up in some towels."

Sandra bundled Joey in her lap and hugged him tightly. It never occurred to her to curb the affection that had grown between her and this tow-headed imp who smiled and splashed and frequently fell asleep in her arms. Not that she would have. Not that she could have.

"Please don't go to work, Aunt Sandra. I'll miss you."

He seemed about to cry, so Sandra said cheerfully, "I think there are some cherry popsicles in the freezer. Would you like one?"

Shrugging off the rainbow-colored towel, he was already running to the patio door.

That night at dinner, Sandra admitted to her husband how attached she had become to Joey. "I love him so much, Abe," she sighed. "I almost feel like resigning my job, just so I can be with him."

Abram poured the last of the wine into their glasses. "He'll be in pre-school half a day this year, and next year he'll be there all day. What'll you do then? Sit here and wait for him?"

Sandra felt the old grief rising to the surface. "I know, I know. I thought we'd have our own baby by now, but I don't think it'll ever happen. You're right—it's best I work. Joey isn't mine." Carrying her glass to the fireplace, Sandra sat in a green, leaf-patterned wingback chair and let out a long sigh.

Abram crossed the room to hunker down in front of her chair. She handed him her empty wine glass and he set it on the fireplace hearth. "Sandra, we've got to talk about adopting. This has gone on long enough." He sat in a chair that was the twin of hers.

Resolute as usual on the subject, she shook her head. "I won't do it. Dr. Kipp says there's still a chance. The endometritis is under control now."

"Well, it should be. You've taken every medication on the market, had two surgeries, but, Sandra, we're thirty-five and thirty-six. Pretty soon adoption will be out of the question."

"It's already out, Abe. I'm not going to pretend I gave you a son by adopting somebody else's. I either do it or I don't." She kicked off her shoes and slumped more deeply into the chair.

"What's to say that it'd be a son anyhow? Ever thought about that?" Abram got up to start a fire, to mark the end of summer.

"It would be. Your father fathered sons. There's a lot of research that shows that you'd be likely to father a son, too." She knew Abram was irritated with her. They had argued over adoption many times. It was the only thing they ever argued about. She watched him lay kindling to start the logs burning. "Besides," she said, screwing up her courage, "there's something I've been trying to get up the nerve to talk to you about." She heard a tinge of fear in her own voice, betraying her lack of confidence in her ability to persuade him to do what she was considering.

He turned to her in surprise. "You have to get up the 'nerve' to talk to me about something? Since when did I become the ogre husband?" He closed the fireplace screen and watched the kindling burst into tiny flames. "What's the topic you're afraid to raise?" He sat and waited.

Licking her lips, she sat up in her chair and turned so she could look at him directly. "Surrogacy. That's the topic I want you to consider."

"Surrogacy," he repeated dumbly, like a child learning to pronounce a new word but not grasping its meaning.

"I conceive, Abe. I just don't 'implant.'" A note of pleading had crept into her voice. She knew what he would say.

"You can't be serious. Rent-a-womb?" She watched his handsome face struggling with astonishment.

She was on her feet now, needing to pace while she made her case. "It's like an incubator, a place for our baby to grow. They take an ovum from me, fertilize it with your sperm, place it into the uterus of a surrogate . . . ." Her voice was racing now, growing more animated, until she saw revulsion at the idea of it cross his face.

"It's just not . . . normal." He rose and pulled her to him as if to protect her from the impact of his next words. "It's playing God," he said.

She shrugged off his arms. "Okay. I knew you'd come off with something like that. Just forget I ever mentioned it." She turned to go and he started to follow. She stuck out an arm and brought it against his rib cage, a warning that he should not follow her.

They slept without touching that night.

The next day, as she dressed for the first day of school, he tried to broach the subject but she ignored him. Suited in cream-colored linen, she adjusted the collar of her black blouse and stepped back as though she hadn't heard him ask, "Can we talk about this?"

She studied her teacher-image in the full length mirror that hung on the back of their bedroom door and said nothing.

"Well?" he tried again, sitting on the edge of the bed.

"Just forget I brought it up. I'm late for school."

Chapter Ten

All that day, even as he worked, joked with his workmen, or did business over the phone, Abram felt her coldness coming to him across the distance, like a chilling wind that made the sun-warmed grain shudder in the fields. It blew into his very soul and created in him an emptiness that he had not felt since Sandra had come into his life.

Surrounded by people and activity, he felt alone. He couldn't wait for the day to end . . . to stop this thing between them. Through the chinking of dishes and rumble of his workmen's voices at lunch, he felt distracted. He chewed his tasteless food and pretended to be there.

"Okay, let's get back to work," Hank, the foreman said to the others. Abram usually worked in the den, making phone calls or doing paper work. But today he wanted to be outside. He couldn't concentrate on paperwork and investments.

As the room emptied, Hannah suddenly stepped between him and the door. Drying her hands on the Amish apron she still wore in the kitchen, she asked with real concern in her voice, "What's the matter?"

"It's nothing," he said, "Sandra and I just had a little . . . disagreement and I'm anxious for her to get home so we can settle it." Forcing a brief smile, he donned his cap and stepped around her. Taking long strides, he caught up with the others on their way to the mowers.

He stood at the garage door, waiting as Sandra pulled her car into its bay. Even as she was turning off the engine, he opened the car door, searching her eyes for forgiveness. He took the briefcase from her hand. "I missed you," he said. Then she was in his arms. She felt small and perfect as he held her, and he wanted to protect her in every way. They spoke, not with words, but with kisses, healing the wound between them.

In the sunshine of the autumn afternoon, they made their way to their home, arm in arm, leaning affectionately on one another as they walked.

As they undressed, Sandra said, "Hannah will have dinner ready in about an hour."

"So we have an hour, but I intend to take whatever time we want," he said, standing naked beside her and lowering her to their bed.

Suppertime had come and gone. "I'm starved," Abram Goodman finally said, as he gently bit the shoulder of his wife curved against him. "Nothin' like makin' love to work up an appetite."

"Making love twice," she added, laughing and snuggling closer to him.

"Hannah's probably furious, her supper waiting and all," he said, unconcerned. Sandra sat up and raised her arms above her head to stretch. Abram bent to kiss the small of her back, nibbling his way upward as he reached around her to cup her breasts in his hands.

"Abe, Love, we can't start this again," she chided and put her hands on top of his to stop their pursuit.

"I can if you can," he teased.

"You've impressed me enough for one day; now let's jump in the shower and then go get something to eat."

Of dried-up baked macaroni, wilted salad and cold meatloaf the lovers age voraciously, then retired to the den to finally talk.

"If you want to try surrogacy, okay," he said, with his arm around her.

"No, Abe, I know you're willing to do it for me, but you don't really like the idea," she said, shaking her head but with no trace of anger now.

He insisted. "I *will* like the idea, if it's what will make you happy . . . ."

"No, we both have to want a surrogate mother for our child or it'll be a disaster. They won't even consider us." She laid a hand over his mouth as he was about to protest again.

"We'll just keep hoping that I can carry our baby, that one of them will 'stick.' That's what I would prefer, after all."

He sighed. "Hoping and praying."

"Yes," she said, "and praying."

The sleeplessness began some time that fall and lingered into the approaching winter. Abram would awake to find his wife's side of the bed empty and cold. Sometimes he found her in the window seat, her face pale and wide-eyed as she looked out at the moon. Or he would hear the faint creak of his mother's rocking chair on the carpeted floor of their bedroom, as Sandra rocked the great misery inside her.

This morning he found her, asleep at last, atop the Tree of Life quilt in the downstairs bedroom. Unwilling to wake her, Abram softly closed the door of the room where she lay. He padded on bare feet to the telephone in the foyer and called the school.

"This is Mrs. Goodman's husband. Mrs. Goodman is ill and won't be in today. Yes, thank you." Soundlessly replacing the phone on its cradle, Abram moved to the front porch to head off Hannah and Joey who were walking amid swirling brown leaves, up the driveway to the main house. Shirtless and shoeless in the chilly November air, Abram shivered and ran with a hopping gait toward them.

Hannah paused and waited, but Joey galloped toward Abram who swooped him up, warming himself against the child as he carried him back to his mother. "Don't come in to make breakfast, Hannah," he said. "Sandra's had another bout of insomnia. She's asleep now."

"She isn't going to school again?" the hired girl asked. "I've seen those dark circles under her eyes and wondered . . . ."

"She's exhausted. Finally fell asleep downstairs. I'd appreciate it if you and Joe would wait 'til later . . . ."

"Fine, I have things to do at home anyway."

"But Mom, you promised me pancakes." Joey slid down out of Abram's arms.

"Yes, and you'll get them. I can make pancakes at our house, you know . . . before I take you to school."

Chapter Eleven

Seated in Diedra Kipp's office with her husband in a navy blue leather armchair beside hers, Sandra stared sullenly at the name on the little white card Dr. Kipp had handed her across the desk.

"Sleep therapist. This is just another way of saying 'psychiatrist,' isn't it?" Sandra was irritated but didn't want to take it out on Dr. Kipp.

"Well, yes, a psychiatrist with a laboratory staff specially trained to monitor sleep patterns or dysfunctions." Dr. Kipp's voice was patient.

Before Sandra could object, Abram spoke up. "Will your office make the appointment, or should we?"

"Sandra?" Dr. Kipp was waiting for Sandra's response.

"I know what they're going to tell me, so why bother?" Sandra's voice was just above a mutter.

"What are they going to tell you?" Dr. Kipp's patience was infuriating her, and she heard Abram's irritated shift in his chair.

"Depression. Insomnia related to depression. I can read, too, you know." Sandra was tired as she continued to stare at the neat black letters on the white card still in her hand. "And we all know the source of the depression," she added bitterly. "So what's the use?"

"The 'use' is," the doctor answered, "they can help you accept your infertility."

"Or make up your mind to adopt." Abram's interruption came with a hint of his own bitterness at his wife's stubbornness.

"Tell him!" Sandra demanded of Dr. Kipp. "Tell him that there's still a chance, or is this just something you tell *me* to string me along?" She had never before shown hostility to Dr. Kipp, but, now, she was past caring.

Rising slowly to perch on the corner of her desk, Dr. Kipp chose her words carefully. It was obvious that she was trying to keep Sandra under control. "Yes, we have determined that you do conceive, but because of the chronic inflammation of the uterine wall, the fertilized egg fails to implant . . . which does not mean that it will never happen. But you, Sandra, are not dealing well with the wait or with the possibility that it may never happen, so we should pursue a different course. Your stress level is so high, it doesn't surprise me that the inflammation persists." Turning her attention to Abram, she added, "It isn't all that easy to adopt in this country anymore, by the way," and turning back to his wife, "but why not try? Why not begin the adoption procedure? If pregnancy occurs in the meantime, or even afterward, so be it. At least you'd be proactive in your attempt to bring a child into your life."

"Sounds good to me," Abram said, reaching for Sandra's hand.

"I had another idea . . . ." Sandra's voice was almost inaudible. She looked up and saw that Dr. Kipp and Abram were exchanging glances, knowing that the word she was about to say was "surrogacy." They had been over this before, too.

In the short silence, Abram spoke. "Will you leave us for a few minutes, Dr. Kipp?"

As the door closed behind Dr. Kipp, Abram pulled his chair around to face her, and Sandra waited, still sitting with her head down, the sleep therapist's card held limply between two fingers of one hand. She felt him stroking her hair, and his voice was as soft as his touch.

"Are you absolutely sure that this is what you want, Sandra? This 'surrogacy' thing? You could accept another woman carrying our child? I already told you we'd pursue this if you wanted us to, but you said no. Now you want to do it?"

"I can accept it because I have no other recourse, but the point is that the baby would be ours, part of you, part of me." She knew the script by heart and so did he.

But it was Abram who changed the next line. "Okay," he said. "Okay. You're right. We'll do it."

She sat up straight. "Why? Why are you saying this now?'

"I've said it before, that's why. You're the one who said, 'No, let's wait.'"

"But you don't really like the idea?" She wanted it all out in the open.

"I've read more about it. We get to screen candidates carefully. I don't want just anybody carrying our baby, you know. And, Sandra, I love you. I want you to be happy."

"You're sure?"

"Yes, I'm sure." She let him pull her out of her chair and into his lap. He cradled her like a baby as she wept.

"It's not all that simple," Dr. Kipp explained. "Pennsylvania, at this time, has no laws on the books concerning surrogate parenting; it's up to you to contact an attorney who will help you contact various agencies who screen surrogates. Louisville, Kentucky, is a good place to start. They have responsibly handled many cases, and I've read that psychological evaluation of all the parties involved is an important part of their program . . . which I highly recommend."

Sandra clung to Dr. Kipp's every word and clutched Abram's hand like a life-line.

Driving home, she said, "I'm sleepy. Do you mind?" And she laid her head on his shoulder as he drove. She slept soundly during the drive. And that night, and for many nights after.

Chapter Twelve

By Christmas vacation, Abram and Sandra Goodman had contacted an attorney who put them in touch with a Louisville, Kentucky, agency. He would also draw up a contract between them and the surrogate mother for their child, once she was selected. Louisville asked the Goodmans to write up a list of requirements that they had for a potential surrogate.

"I feel so racist," Sandra said when, at the top of their list, she wrote the word "Caucasian."

"I know what you mean, but should that even matter? After all, the embryo would genetically belong to two Caucasians. Whatever her own race, the surrogate would be giving birth to a white child."

"So let's take 'Caucasian' off the list.

Abram agreed as he watched Sandra draw a line through the word. "I'm more concerned with what kind of a life she has lived and what illnesses her blood might transmit to our baby," he said.

"Like HIV? Oh, I'm sure the Louisville Agency would have already screened for that."

"Yes, but also sexual promiscuity and drug use in general," Abram said. "And smoking. I don't want a woman who smokes to carry our child. And rare alcohol use." He ticked his requirements off on his fingers.

Sandra threw down her pencil. "So you want a person who has lived a pristine life. I agree about the smoking, drinking and drug use, but if the person is HIV free, what do you consider 'promiscuous'?"

"I'd like her to have had no more than one sexual relationship and possibly to be married, committed to a monogamous relationship."

"You're going to have a hard time finding a woman who has had only one sex partner in this day and age. I am more concerned about how well educated she is. Educated people tend to eat more nutritiously and to exercise. I want a healthy surrogate, more than anything. A good physical exam would do it for me." Sandra wrote "healthy" and "educated" on the list.

"I think you're going to find that most of these women will be women who need money. They aren't going to put themselves through this without money being a consideration." Abram got to the bottom line.

Sandra crossed out "educated." "Okay, but will you at least drop the 'only one sexual relationship standard'?"

"No. If you want me to go along with this Sandra, then you're going to have to at least try for that." He folded his arms and she thought he looked stubborn, set in his ways.

Sandra sighed. "How on earth would somebody prove that?"

"There are private investigators."

"You'd go that far?" She said, incredulous.

"Yes," he said, "I would."

She sighed. "So here is our list: healthy, no prior recreational drug use, no smoking, no alcohol use during the pregnancy, eating a balanced diet during the pregnancy, exercise as suited for a pregnant woman, and, not having been sexually promiscuous, meaning, no more than one sexual relationship. Can't we add 'prior to marriage', if she's married? I had a sexual relationship before I married you. Does that make *me* unfit?"

"You should have been a lawyer, you know." Abram sighed. "Okay, no more than two sexual relationships. All I'm saying is I want somebody who hasn't slept around. And I'm prepared to pay well for it."

Dr. Kipp had done her part by putting the Goodmans in touch with a reproductive endocrinologist, a dark-haired man with a pencil-thin mustache. Sandra thought he looked like 1930's actor, Clark Gable. She chortled openly when she learned that his name was Dr. Clark.

"Oh, I'm sorry," she said, breathlessly. "I'm laughing because I'm so excited and happy that something is finally happening." She couldn't meet Abram's eyes.

"Well," Dr. Clark began, "I'm glad that you're optimistic, but I'd be remiss if I didn't tell you that in vitro fertilization has only about a twenty percent success rate, so I'll be putting you on a hormone to increase the rate of success. This will give us more eggs to work with, with hope that one or two will take hold."

"One or two!" Abram sounded taken aback. "You mean we could possibly have twins?"

"Or even triplets?" Sandra asked, barely able to contain her excitement.

"Well, we might not ask a surrogate to carry triplets," Dr. Clark said seriously. "Maybe one of them would have to be aborted."

"I don't like the sounds of that at all," Abram said, adopting his folded arms stance.

"We'll cross that bridge if and when we come to it. For now, we're just hoping that one fertilized egg will attach to the uterus of a surrogate. Don't go down any 'what if' paths for now." Dr. Clark explained that once Sandra began to produce multiple eggs, the eggs would be retrieved by needle aspiration and then be fertilized by Abram's sperm in laboratory dishes.

"This is the easy part," he said. "The trick, once a suitable surrogate is found, will be to synchronize the maturing of Sandra's eggs with the ovulation period of the surrogate herself, the time when her womb is most receptive to implantation. We hope to implant at least eight embryos, to better insure our chances that one or two will take hold."

"There's that 'one or two' again," Abram said with concern.

"Two would be okay with me, Abe. After all, we practically have a live-in nanny with Hannah." They were back their room at the Hampton Inn in Louisville.

"Okay, one or two we can handle, but let's hope we don't get a litter!"

Sandra literally bounced on the king-sized bed of the hotel room where they were staying overnight. Her imagination was soaring with delight. "I read somewhere where a couple using in vitro fertilization had quadruplets! Oh, Abe wouldn't that be wonderful?"

"No, it would not be wonderful. I can't imagine a surrogate wanting to lug around four babies," her husband said, holding out his arms in case she bounced all the way off the bed.

She stopped bouncing. "Oh, well, in the case I read about, there was no surrogate. The eggs had been implanted in the wife's own womb." A trace of sadness crept into her voice. "I wish I could do that . . . have the experience of carrying a baby in my womb."

"Well," Abram said, pulling her down beside him on the bed, "we're doing the next best thing."

Chapter Thirteen

Accustomed to observing and guessing what was going on with the Goodmans, Hannah had noticed the almost instantaneous return of Sandra's zest for life and the sense of an exciting secret that was unfolding in their lives.

Hannah stuffed towels into the washer and pondered what might be going on. *I wonder if she's finally in the family way. What else could make her so happy?* Ambivalence warred in the hired girl's heart at the prospect of this speculation being true.

Hannah had grown fond of Sandra Goodman. She could not have done otherwise considering the kindness Sandra had lavished on Hannah and her illegitimate son over the years since Joey's birth. Because of this, Hannah had learned to stem the tide of jealousy that threatened to sweep away reason from time to time, not jealousy over the bond between her son and Sandra; rather, it was Sandra's bond with Abram from which the murky green waters of envy threatened to flow.

Abram's resolve to ignore the kiss they had one time shared in the garage had dulled Hannah's once vivid imagination where he was concerned. She had ceased to nurture the fantasies that had kept alive her once flaming hope that Abram returned her love for him. Hope only smoldered now.

Part of her wanted Sandra to have a child of her own. Part of her rebuked the idea because of him who would share that joy, not with Hannah, but with his lawful wife. Hannah thought of the tight jeans that Sandra still wore around the house. *How is it that her stomach is just as flat as ever? But she's been taking off more sick days from school, even though whatever ailed her so much that she couldn't sleep has apparently been cured. Or has it?*

Through eavesdropping, Hannah had learned that Sandra's sick days were being used for overnight trips to some doctor in Kentucky. Her confusion increased when she was informed by Sandra that she would not be returning to school for the mid-January start of the second semester. Sandra said she had asked for and been granted a medical leave.

Hannah's curiosity peaked one snowy February day when Sandra, after glancing through the mail piled on the kitchen table, grabbed a card and ran shrieking to the den where Abram sat at a computer. "Registered mail at the post office!" Sandra yelled.

Her outburst was followed by Abram's own. "Great! Let's go before it closes!"

Amazed, Hannah paused in kneading bread to watch them literally run out of the kitchen door, pulling on coats as they went. She watched them out the window, laughing and slipping in the slushy snow on their way to the garage. They seemed to Hannah like people gone mad.

She had made it a practice to ask no questions of the Goodmans concerning the what and wherefore of their life together, but she could not help herself when they returned from the post office with Sandra clutching a large, bulky envelope to her breast.

"I hope nothing's wrong . . . ." the hired girl began but stopped, embarrassed at the stupidity of her words, since the Goodmans were obviously overjoyed about something.

"No, nothing's wrong." It was Abram who took time to speak to her, just before they disappeared into the den, shutting the door firmly behind them.

Hannah punched the risen bread down, waited an hour for it to rise again and then panned it into six loaves; yet the Goodmans still remained sequestered in the den.

She let the loaves rise, preheated the oven, brushed the loaves with an egg-wash and sprinkled them with sesame seeds. Once in a while she could hear Sandra's voice raised in excitement from behind the closed door to the den. She didn't have the nerve to press her ear against the door, so she had no choice but to wait. Even then there was no guarantee that they would tell her what was going on.

When six golden brown loaves sat cooling atop the counter, Hannah covered them with a clean white cloth, collected Joey from the downstairs bedroom where he had been watching cartoons, and went home bundled up against a February snow that had started to fall again.

I hope one of them has the sense to put the bread in the freezer, she thought irritably.

Chapter Fourteen

With shaking fingers, Sandra withdrew from the package a letter and three blue folders. She handed the letter to Abram and sat very still as she watched his eyes scan the words on the page.

"'Three possible candidates'," he quoted from the letter, his face breaking into an enormous smile.

"Three!" Relief washed through Sandra and eased the pounding of her heart. She spread the three precious folders into a fan before her eyes. They contained the names and biographies of three possible surrogate mothers for their child.

Sitting side by side on the couch, Sandra and Abram carefully perused each folder. They started with a woman named Karen. Karen was the thirty-two-year-old mother of three children. She wanted to have more, but her husband had been out of work for almost two years. They needed the money she'd be paid, and it would also satisfy her hunger to carry another child. Her report listed that she was in excellent health, had never smoked, and had never abused alcohol or drugs. Her husband had been her only sexual liaison.

Twenty-nine-year-old Audra, however, admitted that she had once been addicted to cocaine. She had gone through rehab and was now clean, healthy, and she needed money to get her life moving again. She had never married, but she had had one pregnancy and given the child up for adoption. She said that she liked the thought of having enriched someone's life with a child.

She sometimes drank socially and had an occasional cigarette, but she was well aware that she must refrain from both while carrying a child. She said she would not call herself "promiscuous."

Number three was Barbara. Twenty-five, she had been married briefly and given her ex-husband full custody of their child. "I just didn't think I'd make a good mother," she said. Although she had had "a few" intimate relationships, since her divorce, she did not consider herself promiscuous.

She had never smoked or used drugs, but she did drink wine occasionally. It would be "no problem" for her to give up wine during the pregnancy. She had been a full-time waitress ever since her graduation from high school. The fee she was requesting was double the usual one—enough to pay her way through college.

"Let's meet Karen," Abram said, glancing over her file one more time.

"Yes, but what about Barbara? I agree that Audra is probably out, but Barbara sounds all right. The money wouldn't be a problem, would it?" She hoped Abram would agree to interview two women, not just one.

"No, I don't care what it costs, but Karen seems the most stable of the three."

"You're probably right, Abe, but there is one thing that bothers me about Karen. She wanted another baby. Will she be able to give this one up even though it is not genetically hers?"

"She'll have to. She'll sign a contract."

"I'd hate to see her broken-hearted."

"Better her than you. You're the one whose broken heart would concern me." Abram spoke matter-of-factly, and Sandra was surprised at how . . . uncompassionate . . . he sounded.

Three days later, the Goodmans sat in the waiting room of the Louisville clinic. Sandra studied gargoyle faces in the wood grain of a door which bore a brass plate on which black letters spelled out the words "K. Kenebec, MD." The door opened suddenly, and a tall, sandy-haired man strode toward them.

"I'm Kevin Kenebec, Mr. and Mrs. Goodman," he said, extending his hand to each of them. "I'm terribly sorry, but I got word when your flight was already en route, and I had no way to reach you."

Sandra lost her smile. "Reach us about what?" She clutched Abram's hand.

Kenebec sat and pulled a chair into a triangle with theirs. "Karen backed out. Her husband has begun to reject the whole idea. I can't tell you how sorry I am that she waited so late to call me, and you've made this trip for nothing."

"She won't be here to meet us?" Sandra was having trouble grasping what he was saying. She felt Abram's pressure on her hand.

"No, Honey, that's what he said. Karen has backed out. Her husband changed his mind, so it's for the best that it happened now." Abram put his arm around Sandra.

"I take it that you had objections to the other two?" Kenebec asked, raising sand-colored eyebrows that matched his hair.

Abram spoke up quickly. "Yes. Histories of drugs and promiscuity are a worry. How long will it take to find other candidates?" Sandra could tell he was trying to over-ride any suggestion that she might make to meet Barbara.

Kenebec answered Abram's question. "It could be weeks. It could be months. Not everyone who wants to be a surrogate is accepted into the program. We have basic requirements, and we test them thoroughly, in an attempt to rule out any potential problems. It usually takes about six weeks."

"What about Barbara?" Sandra asked, looking not at her husband but at Kenebec.

Before the doctor could respond, Abram interrupted. "Sandra, I gave you my reasons for rejecting Barbara. She could test positive for an STD at some time down the road, with her track record."

"But she doesn't test positive now. Isn't that right, Dr. Kenebec?" Sandra felt her face flush with anger.

"No, she didn't," Kenebec said, "But both of you should be satisfied with your choice of a surrogate."

Sandra turned her head to address Abram. "Can't we just meet her, now that we're here? I believe that she's from this area. Even if we have to stay an extra day."

Abram Goodman let out a long sigh. "Okay, okay. Please arrange it if you can, Dr. Kenebec, and call us at our hotel." He handed Kenebec a card with his cell phone number.

Barbara was a tall, thin girl with short brown hair. Huge earrings swung as she grinned and looked from Sandra to Abram and back again.

"I'm soooooooooo pleased to meet you!" She smiled broadly, flashing cosmetically whitened teeth in an unseasonably tanned face.

Sandra was impatient to begin. "Why did you decide on this way to finance your education, Barbara? Isn't this a lot tougher than taking out a loan?"

"It's also a lot shorter. Nine months, and I'm debt-free." She dusted her hands together to indicate a clean slate.

"That's your only reason for wanting to be a surrogate?" Abram asked and Sandra could tell that already he did not like Barbara.

"Look, Mr. and Mrs. Goodman, I'm not going to, like, give you any bull about wanting to, like, do some good in the world. This would be strictly a business deal. I've already given birth once, so I do know what I'm getting into. I'll do my very best to deliver a healthy baby for you. I, myself, am very healthy, and I have no rich daddy to put me through school. If I can, like, get what I want and help you guys out at the same time, why not?" She threw her well-manicured, red-nailed hands out in a wide "v" at the words "Why not?"

"How many serious relationships have you had?" Sandra asked, knowing that this was the question on her husband's mind.

Barbara laughed. "'Serious'? Well, since my divorce, I haven't really been 'serious' about any of them."

"Okay, let me be frank," Abram said brusquely. "How many intimate—and by that I mean sexual—relationships have you had?"

Barbara narrowed her brown eyes and stared off into the past. "Oh, I don't know . . . maybe half a dozen? And there's the guy I live with now. Hey, I'm not a slut if that's what you're getting at." She sat up straighter, indignant.

Sandra knew there was no point of going on with Barbara. She had seen Abram's clenched jaw. Looking for a way to end the interview, she asked, "Is there anything you'd like to ask *us?*"

"Yes. Can you guys afford what I want plus medical and legal costs? And could we make that amount flexible-like? I don't know what school I'll get into yet, and I don't exactly know what it will cost . . . ."

There was no use blaming Abram, Sandra admitted to herself. She didn't like this young woman either, not for Abram's puritanical reasons, but because she just didn't like her. Also, the blank check was out of the question. Sandra couldn't see herself bonding with this woman for nine months, not for any reason.

Chapter Fifteen

Returning from her morning walk, Sandra paused at the base of the porch steps and used the toe of her boot to brush April snow off the purple crocuses that were blooming nearby.

As she brushed icy crystals from the delicate petals of the little iris, a half-idea that had been meandering through her thoughts as she walked now came exploding into her mind like a crashing waterfall. Its impact left her breathless as though she had been doused with icy water.

Amazed at her thoughts, she could only say, "My God . . . ."

She walked around to the kitchen door at the rear of the house and stood for a few minutes, watching their hired girl efficiently going about her chores, unaware that Sandra was there.

Accustomed now to shirts and jeans, Hannah wore them most of the time, with the big Amish apron when she was cooking. Smiling, she paused at the kitchen table to admire the crayon drawing that Joey handed her. When Hannah took it to hang it on the refrigerator, Sandra could see that it was a drawing of a stick-boy on a brown horse. As the hired girl turned away from the refrigerator, she startled. She had seen Sandra, clad in jacket and boots, standing and staring in from the snow-covered deck.

"Sandra?' Hannah asked, sliding back the glass door.

Distracted, Sandra stumbled inside and still she stood, forgetting the mat, and letting her wet boots make little puddles on Hannah's clean kitchen floor.

"I'll take your coat . . . ." Hannah offered, but Sandra made no attempt to remove it, so preoccupied was she with the immense idea that thundered and roared in her head. Joey tugging at her hand brought her back.

"What? Oh, oh it's . . . very nice . . . Joey . . . ." She tried to focus on the picture of a toothy black spider that the boy had hastily drawn. Pulled to a kitchen chair by Joey, she sat there, her eyes on Hannah who moved uneasily under her unhidden scrutiny.

"It's pretty warm in here; don't you want to take off your coat?" Hannah tried again.

"Uh . . . no . . . I'm not staying. I mean, I'm going upstairs," she said, as she proceeded to leave the room still wearing her wet boots. Suddenly she turned and added, "I want to talk to you about . . . something . . . after you take Joey to school."

Seeing Hannah's concerned expression, Sandra tried to alleviate any worry. "Don't worry. It's nothing . . . bad."

While Hannah was gone, Sandra took a hot shower to stop shivering. She blew her hair dry and dressed for comfort in a soft white sweater and jeans. With fluffy white slipper-socks on her feet, she descended the staircase to see if Hannah had come back.

The hired girl was on her knees wiping up snow puddles in the kitchen, left there, probably, by Sandra's boots. "I'm sorry for tracking up the kitchen floor, Hannah. I should have taken my boots off."

"Oh, it's all right. You wouldn't be the first one." Hannah rose to her feet and looked anxiously at Sandra.

"Let's go into the den, Hannah," she said, leading the way.

Hannah removed the red cardigan sweater that had covered her white, short-sleeved blouse, folded it and put it over the arm of the green, wing back chair where she sat waiting.

Sandra tucked her feet under herself on one end of the soft leather couch and waited until several seconds passed before she spoke. "You know, I'm sure, that I, that Abe and I, have wanted a baby for some time now; years, in fact."

"Yes." The younger woman nodded and mouthed the word just above a whisper.

"I can't have a baby. I have a condition that keeps me from being able to carry one." Sandra's tone was one of resignation, if not acceptance.

"I know, I mean, I thought so . . . . I'm sorry, Sandra." Hannah leaned slightly forward as she spoke words that sounded very sincere.

"Oh, there's still a remote chance, so they tell me, but, in the meantime, I'm not getting any younger." She untucked her feet and put them on the floor. Leaning forward, with her elbows on her knees, she clasped her hands as if she were about to pray.

Hannah's voice rose with her desire to console. "You're not old. And you have Joey . . . ."

Sandra cut her off. "No, I don't really have Joey. I love him, but he's yours, not mine. I want a child of my own, our own, Abe's and mine."

"Well, could you adopt?"

"I, we, want our own. It wouldn't be the same." She sighed deeply and went on. "Besides, adoption could take years. Anyhow, we've tried everything. We're even considering a surrogate, you know, a woman to have the baby for us."

"You mean like Baby M? I heard about Baby M on television one time . . . in the Sears store."

"No, in the Baby M case, the surrogate mother supplied the egg. The baby was half hers, biologically." Sandra rose to her feet, walked to the mantel and picked up a framed picture of herself and Abram. "I want to give a surrogate my own egg, fertilized by my husband's sperm." She turned with her back to the fireplace and faced Hannah. "They do it in a laboratory, then transfer the egg to the surrogate's womb. The baby wouldn't be any part of her, genetically, except she'd carry it and have it for us. And we'd pay her."

Hannah leaned forward expectantly. "And who is she?"

Sandra sighed and walked back to the couch to sit down. "That's the problem. She *isn't*. I mean, we haven't found a woman who is . . . right for us. They all smoke, or drink, or something. You know old straight-laced Abe . . . ." She saw understanding cross Hannah's face.

Hannah got up from the wingback chair and moved to the couch where she sat beside Sandra and took her hand. "*I* don't smoke or drink or . . . anything," she offered simply.

Chapter Sixteen

"Let's drive into the city for the weekend," Sandra suggested to her husband later that evening. She sat with her head on his shoulder, oblivious to the pictures and sounds of the television, as she reviewed in her mind her conversation with Hannah earlier that day. "Can we get away?"

She had been trying to get up the courage to broach the subject—of using Hannah as the surrogate mother for their child—but her nerve failed her. She was not afraid of Abram, but she *was* afraid of her own reaction should he reject this idea that she saw as the last hope to solve their problem—their *only* problem—the specter which haunted them day and night.

"Is there something you want to see?" he asked, referring to the plays that might be in town.

"No, I just need a change of scene." She tried to sound nonchalant.

She knew that her request to go to the city for the weekend surprised him. She had stayed close to home for weeks, checking every day for word from Louisville that they had another candidate for their consideration.

"Well, then, sure, I can get away. What time do you want to leave tomorrow?" He kissed her temple and got up to call Hank.

On Saturday morning, as they approached the little house in their Lexus, they saw Hannah on her knees helping Joey scoop up slushy April snow, probably to make one last snowman in the yard. She looked up at the sound of the car slowing down in front of her house.

Sandra lowered the window and called to Joey. "Come here and give me a goodbye kiss, Little Man."

Hannah pulled off soggy mittens and walked toward them, bending down to look over at Abram who was saying, "We'll be back late tomorrow night, probably. We'll call if it's going to be any different."

Sandra looked meaningfully into Hannah's eyes and crossed her fingers. Hannah nodded slightly. "Goodbye, have a good time."

Sandra turned off the radio and leaned against the passenger door to study her husband's profile as he drove onto the highway.

"Okay, what's on your mind?" he asked without looking at her.

Sandra laughed. "Who says there's anything on my mind?"

"Don't give me that . . . I can almost hear those wheels turning in there. You've been distracted about something since I walked in the door last night."

She sighed and decided to be blunt, though she had planned on waiting until they were in their hotel room in the city. "I've found us a surrogate."

He didn't speak for a few seconds. "You've found us a surrogate," he echoed.

"Yes." Sandra took a few deep breaths to calm herself.

"Where?" His eyes never left the road.

"Not through Louisville. It's somebody we know."

He slowed the car so much that she thought he was going to pull over. Speeding up, he asked, "Somebody we know? Who?"

"Promise you'll hear me out. Just don't say anything until you hear everything I have to say. Will you do that, please?" She looked at his profile.

"You've found us a reformed hooker, right?" he teased.

"No, I've found us someone squeaky clean, but will you just listen?" She felt frustration that he wasn't taking her seriously.

"Okay. Shoot." He settled himself to listen, his hands relaxed on the steering wheel.

"This is a farm girl from a very religious family. No smoking, no drinking, no sleeping around . . . at least not lately."

"What's that supposed to mean?"

Sandra took a deep breath. There was no turning back. "She's had one child—a pregnancy with no problems—and she is a good mother."

"Where's her husband?"

"She doesn't have one. She chose not to marry the father, but he is the only man she's ever been with."

She heard uneasiness creep into his voice. "How old?"

"Going on twenty-five."

There was silence, except for the low hum of the big car's engine. Sandra waited, watching him, seeing his Adam's apple move as he swallowed hard. "Abe?"

"No. Absolutely not."

She tried to curb the instant anger that flared in her. "Why not?"

"It just isn't a good idea."

Before he could elaborate, she set her anger free. "Goddamn it, why isn't it a good idea?"

He glanced at her once and looked back at the road. "She practically *lives* with us, for God's sake!"

"She has her own house! She works for us! We see her every day, and that's a plus as far as I'm concerned." She was losing it, and she knew it.

"Oh, sure, a plus. That's ridiculous! I'd feel like I had two wives or something!"

"Now, who's being ridiculous?" Sandra was crying now, her words tremulous but clear. "Just shut up and listen, Abe. We'd get to watch our baby grow. We'd get to feel our baby move. It would be the closest thing to being pregnant myself . . . ."

Sobbing, she could not go on. She leaned her head back and let the tears pour out the unquenchable sorrow that was inside her, her voice reduced to the guttural sounds of grief.

He pulled the car to the side of the road and took her into his arms. Together they sobbed out their mutual despair over this desire they could not fulfill for one another . . . to make a child.

Chapter Seventeen

Hannah was surprised to see him standing at her door. She had heard their car returning a few hours earlier, but she thought he would wait until morning. She was also intrigued that he had come alone.

"Where's Sandra?" she asked, aware that he had never come to her house alone, not since the stolen kiss in the garage.

"I told her I wanted to talk to you alone." He wore a brown leather jacket that went well with his hair and eyes, she thought. His handsome face was solemn.

Wordlessly, she led the way to her dimly lit living room. He had been no farther than the kitchen door since Joey's birth, five years ago, and after the kiss, he had not even stood on her porch.

"I feel at home," he said. "You've arranged the furniture the same way my mother did. And this used to be my father's favorite chair. He sat in an over-stuffed arm chair covered in maroon mohair, a match to the couch.

"Well, a room this small doesn't lend itself to many possibilities. I'm glad, though, that it makes you feel at home." She was peaceful in his presence since she had long ago learned to lock away in some secret room of her soul her yearning for him. They sat comfortably without speaking for a minute, the quiet of her home uniting them like the unspoken bond Hannah believed they shared.

"You really want to do this?" he asked finally, without elaboration.

"Yes." Unblinking, she met his eyes.

"Why?" His handsome face held no sign that he suspected her of any secret motive. "Why do you want to endure childbirth again and not even have the baby be yours in the end?"

"Because I can . . . and because you have done so much for me. Both of you have."

"What do you want in return?"

"Nothing. You've already given me more than I can ever repay. But this is something I can do . . . for you." She felt tears come to her eyes. One blink and they'd fall.

"You work for your money, Hannah."

"You know what I mean. You gave me a refuge when I was . . . cast out." The tears spilled to her cheeks, but she held his gaze.

He cleared his throat. "It'll still have to be legal. I have to give you remuneration—money—for it. I'd *want* to . . . ."

"You decide, then; I know nothing about such things." She pulled a napkin out of the holder on the table and wiped away her tears.

"All right then." He rose and walked to the door.

"Abram." She rarely used his name and he stopped in his tracks and turned to her, waiting for what would follow.

"Don't be afraid," she said. "I promise to give you . . . ." She paused to emphasize, "*And* Sandra, a strong, healthy baby. I will not interfere once it is born. In fact, if you want me to . . . go, I will, after the baby is born."

He looked long into her eyes, and she met his gaze searchingly, wondering what he was thinking. She wanted to read something akin to love in them, perhaps gratitude, but she saw only worry.

It was she who finally broke the gaze, feeling the heat of pink blooms on her face as he kissed her cheek, saying, "Thank you, Hannah. We both thank you."

She moved to a window where she watched him walking with his head down and his hands tucked into his pockets. Illuminated by driveway lights, he looked the picture of sadness, not hope.

Realization smote her heart. *He loves her this much. He will give her what she wants because he can't stand to see her suffer. Even though he . . . fears . . . me.*

Chapter Eighteen

"Don't you worry about a thing. Joe and I have plans. I'm going to teach him to play checkers." Sandra's sister Kendra had taken off work to come to the farm to stay with Joey. The Goodmans and Hannah were bound for Louisville to fulfill the evaluation protocol requested by their attorney.

Hannah bent and held Joey close to her. "You be a good boy, Joey. I know you will."

It was the first time she had ever been apart from her son and the first time she had flown. She was apprehensive about both, but she felt perfectly at ease about the unusual "job" she was about to undertake for her employers. She wished she could impart that ease to Abram, but he seemed uptight, filled with dread. As for Sandra, she was clearly exhilarated.

"You can call Joey tonight," Sandra said reassuringly to Hannah.

"If I'm still alive tonight," Hannah muttered under her breath, thinking of the airplane.

On takeoff and landing, Hannah willingly grasped the hand offered by Sandra. She sat next to the window, with her eyes squeezed tightly shut, refusing to look.

At the Louisville clinic, she endured, with Amish stoicism, the drawing of blood and the probing of the most private parts of her body as she spent the day being examined, tested, and interviewed by this or that doctor.

With her feet in stirrups, she conjured up and focused on a new fantasy, the image of Abram's face, his eyes caressing her with gratitude—and love—as she handed him his first-born. Sandra remained somewhere behind him in the blue shadows of Hannah's daydream, but, she, too, exuded thanks for the unspeakable worth of the gift in her husband's arms. She would say, "We never want you to leave us, Hannah. You can stay with us forever." Abram would smile and echo "Forever."

Waiting for her beyond the metallic doors at the end of a hallway were Sandra and Abram. She saw them before they saw her. They had said they'd be browsing the shops along the streets of the city, until they were paged. Now they nervously paced the corridor.

"Hello," she called to them and they ran toward her as though she were somebody important.

"I hope the tests weren't too uncomfortable for you," Abram said, still looking grave.

Sandra beamed. "Don't be silly, Abram. Hannah's been through all of this before."

"Except for all those questions," Hannah laughed. "About the way I was raised and about what I'm thinking . . . ." She laughed again. "I had to think hard to tell them what I was thinking!"

"Did you remember to bring the dress?" Sandra asked, referring to a long-sleeved black velvet sheath that she had encouraged Hannah to pack in Ida Goodman's luggage.

"Yes, but now will you tell me why I needed such a fancy dress for these meetings with the doctors?" Hannah had obeyed Sandra's request, but she had been perplexed.

"Tomorrow the three of us will meet with the resident psychiatrist, but, this evening, my dear, we are going to take you out to dine at the best restaurant in town. That's why I wanted you to bring the dress." Sandra put her arms around Hannah and Abram as the three of them walked to their rental car.

Every meal that Hannah had ever eaten had been prepared by Amish hands: her mother's, the Amish church ladies', or her own. Clay had taken her out for hamburgers or pizza, but there had been nothing to compare with the opulence of décor and the exotic foods artfully presented to her now.

As for Hannah, herself, Sandra said she looked "regal—like you belong in this setting." She wore her blonde hair pulled severely away from her face into a twist at the nape of her neck. She had stood mesmerized at her image in the long mirror in her hotel suite. In it she saw a tall, shapely woman wearing a close-fitting black-velvet dress with a scooped neckline and long tapering sleeves. She wore no embellishment except for pearl earrings which dropped from her ears. On her feet were black shoes with just a small heel. She felt that she could walk gracefully in them without teetering on higher heels Sandra had once insisted she buy. She applied lipstick and mascara, and just a touch of blush.

At the table, the only sign that she felt ill at ease among the rich was the warmth that she could feel from her probably pink cheeks. She hoped they would think it was just makeup.

As Abram ordered for them, easily pronouncing the French words on the menu, Sandra smiled brightly, her eyes the same color as the teal silk dress she wore with her diamonds. She had let her hair grow long again, and it was sleek and shining even in the subdued light of the room. Observing the couple, both of them stylishly dressed and perfectly comfortable in this grand room, Hannah glimpsed the way they lived when they were away from home, as they often were, on trips abroad, cruises, ski or golf weekends, while the hired hands and Hannah stayed at home to work. She saw how preoccupied they were with one another, smiling and touching often as they perused a huge menu they held between them.

Hannah felt like a spectator, not really part of them. Sipping the white wine that had been poured for her, she felt her cheeks flush again, with embarrassment as she remembered how, earlier that day, she had characterized for the interviewer her relationship with the Goodmans as "like family." Keenly, she became aware that she was not really considered family, just part of the hired help, here to do just another job for them. She felt foolish and promised herself that she would not make that mistake again.

At their request, she raised her glass to theirs to toast their success "on this venture," as Abram put it. But she knew her place. She would be nothing more than an incubator, paid for her services and dismissed.

"Having talked to each of you individually and to the three of you together, I can see that there does exist a special bond among you, probably intensified by your common love for Hannah's son, Joseph; yet you have, to a certain degree, maintained the employer-employee relationship that brought you together in the first place." The rotund psychiatrist adjusted his glasses and smiled.

"Sandra and Abram, you are motivated in this endeavor by your desire to have a child. Hannah, you seem to be motivated to take on this extremely significant . . . task . . . as repayment for the psychological as well as physical support you have received from Mr. and Mrs. Goodman." Dr. Millington shifted his bulk in his chair to turn slightly toward Hannah.

"But let's get back to Joseph, or Joey, as you refer to him. How will his mother's pregnancy, if embryo placement is successful, be explained to him?" Dr. Millington directed the question to Hannah. "Ms. Miller?"

Hannah paused to choose her words carefully. "I'll chust tell him the truth," she answered, unaware that hints of Amish dialect still clung to her speech.

"You think you can explain in-vitro fertilization and embryo placement to a five-year-old?" The doctor's tone was not unkind, not sarcastic.

"I read last night, in the pamphlets that you gave me, that most surrogates have other children. They chust tell them the truth in words that a child can understand—that the other couple's baby was planted in their bellies just like a seed is planted in a garden, so that it can grow." Hannah spoke simply but confidently.

"Do you think jealousy will be a factor? He won't be the only baby in the house anymore; he'll have to share Aunt Sandra and Uncle Abram . . . and his mother, to some extent."

"My heavens, Doctor," Hannah said, "I know of families that deal with that easily, as baby after baby comes. I have already taught my son that jealousy is a sin."

Sandra interjected with a touch of impatience in her voice, "Joey's a very sweet child and very smart, too."

"Abram?" the doctor said, urging the would-be father out of his silence.

"Joe can handle it," Abram answered, shifting slightly in his chair.

"There's another aspect to consider, Hannah," the doctor went on, "perhaps the most important one. Will you be able to relinquish emotional attachment, as the 'mother' who bore the child? Will you be able to see this child and remember that he belongs to Sandra and Abram Goodman, not to you?" The doctor waited as a silence followed his words.

Hannah turned her gaze toward Sandra and Abram who sat holding hands. She studied them before she answered. "Yes," she said slowly. "I understand that this is their child, and I am only an incubator. But I'll love their child the same way they love mine. I'll know it is theirs just the way they know Joey is mine." She swallowed hard, determined that it would be so.

Abram finally spoke. "I want to make it clear that Hannah and I have already discussed that the contract we are about to draw up will stipulate that after the birth of our child Hannah and Joey will live elsewhere. That she will leave our employ. In fact, Hannah was the first to suggest it, when I first discussed the idea of surrogacy with her. Isn't that right, Hannah?"

Hannah looked at Abram and remembered that night. She had said it. Now she was being asked to affirm it. "Yes, that was my suggestion. I will leave the farm . . . if you wish it."

Instinctively, she knew that they would wish it. The contract would contain this stipulation. The Bond Woman and her son would eventually have to leave.

Abram's voice softened. "You can rest assured, Hannah, that you will not only be well paid for . . . your part in this . . . but a trust fund will be set up for you and Joey when you leave our employ. You won't have to work again, unless you want to."

Hannah nodded and said, "That's fine. Thank you." She sought Abram's eyes to see if it was definite. But he would not look at her. Turning her eyes to Sandra's, she was amazed that the other woman actually winked at her. What, Hannah wondered, did this wink mean?

Chapter Nineteen

Sandra paid her second visit to Dr. Clark, the reproductive endocrinologist who sat at his desk writing out a prescription.

"Okay, Sandra, everything looks to be in order with you. You are having regular periods, but this is a prescription for the follicle-stimulating hormone shots I told you about. It will cause you to produce multiple eggs, and I want you to watch for a rise in your temperature and, if you think ovulation is occurring, test with litmus paper. That's the time your eggs are most ripe for fertilization. We've already got your husband's sperm in the lab, just waiting to meet up with them. Your ovulation period can last from a few hours to three days, so the very minute you see the litmus indication that you're ovulating, give me a call and we'll get you in here for aspiration. Any questions?"

Sandra's palms felt sweaty. "Will aspiration hurt?"

"A bit," he said, "but not as much as childbirth. You can do this. Don't worry about it. Now let's get your surrogate in here . . . . what's her name . . . . Hannah? I want to teach her how to monitor her own ovulation period by daily temperature taking and litmus testing. Her ovulation doesn't necessarily have to coincide with yours, but we want the lining of her uterus to be hormonally ready."

"She's right outside. Shall I send her in?"

"Fine, don't forget your prescription."

It was difficult for Sandra to keep herself busy at home. After all, Hannah did everything there, but Sandra prepared the nursery and shopped for color-neutral baby clothes. She let Abram beg off because she knew he was not one for shopping. Instead, she met her sister Kendra in the city and the two made several days of it.

"I'm shocked that the Amish girl agreed to do this for you, Sandra." Kendra held back her long red hair as she leaned over to sip from a straw in her lemonade. "Aren't you afraid that you'll get too close to her?"

"Why would I be 'too close' to her? We've already spent time together in the summers when I was off school. Not socially, so this is just an extension of having her work for us. I'll like the fact that I can watch the baby grow, feel it move. She'll be close by, but we're not emotionally close, if that's what you mean."

"Okay, Sis, I hope everything works out perfectly." Sandra watched her sister take a breath and steeled herself for the doubts that she knew were coming. "My concern," Kendra added, moving her lemonade to the side, "is that she'll ask you if she can stay after the baby's born, contract or no contract. Who else does she know besides you and Abram? Do you think there's any possibility that she might go back to being Amish?"

Sandra waited to respond because the waitress had arrived with their lunches. As Kendra dug into her curried chicken salad, Sandra said, "She won't ask to stay. And we won't want her to stay. It would be entirely too awkward. If she wants to live in the

English way, she'll have to do ordinary stuff to meet people—join PTA, go to church, take Yoga. We can't keep watching over her as we have for the past five years."

"She knows how to drive, right? And she'll probably have enough money to buy her own car. This salad is absolutely delicious. How is your wedding soup?"

The next time Sandra saw the specialist was for the aspiration of the ova the litmus test had revealed were ready to be harvested.

"Do you want me in there with you?" Abram asked, holding her cold, clammy hand as they waited for her to be called in.

"You bet. I'm going to dig my nails into you if this hurts. You can't get off scot-free with just a little sperm donation."

"Okay, Sandra, here we go." Dr. Clark spoke from behind a mask with only his dark eyes showing. He was in scrubs with his hair covered, too. "The ultra-sound indicates that your ovaries have been busy. I think I counted eight ova on the film. We'll soon find out."

The eight ova were aspirated through a hollow suctioning needle at considerable pain on Sandra's part. She held Abram's hand and scrunched her face tightly, only whimpering a little as she remembered that Hannah's part would be more painful.

Immediately, the ova were taken to the lab and placed in a dish along with Abram's sperm. "Now we just wait to see if those little prospects like each other," Dr. Clark said. "We should know in twenty-four hours."

Abram left the surgical room while Sandra dressed. She was sore from the procedure but otherwise in good spirits. "Waiting twenty-four hours is going to kill me!" she said, tucking her hand into his arm on the way to the car.

Two days later, the phone rang and Sandra froze. Abram was at the barn, so she had no choice but to answer it. A matter-of-fact voice reported the staggering news that four of Sandra's eggs had been fertilized by her husband's sperm.

Sandra's reaction was anything but matter-of-fact. She grabbed Hannah's floured hands and spun her around in a gleeful dance before running to the barns in search of her husband.

Five days later, Hannah, draped in a white sheet and with her feet in stirrups, held Sandra's hand as she waited for the transfer of the embryos to her uterus.

"I'm so glad Mr. Goodman agreed to wait outside," she nervously said to Sandra.

"I'd have liked him in here, but not if you'd be embarrassed." Sandra squeezed Hannah's hand. "I've been thinking, if this takes, we might have a Christmas baby!" Her eyes sparkled above the green mask she wore.

Ten days later, when Hannah began to menstruate, Hannah, the bearer of the bad news, stood solemnly by as Sandra cried out her disappointment in her husband's arms.

"I'm sorry," Hannah said. "We can try again, can't we?"

Chapter Twenty

Summer came and went and they had tried four times. Weariness and gloom hung over the three of them, as it became apparent that they had not beaten the odds. Sandra's fertilized eggs, in embryonic stage, simply would not implant in Hannah's uterus.

"Is she coming down for breakfast?" Hannah asked. "Or do you want to take a tray up to her?" She had been serving him alone at the table for two weeks now.

"I'll take a tray up, but keep it very simple. Just toast and coffee. I'm having trouble getting her to eat. I just don't know what to do. She won't eat, she won't take the anti-depressants. All she wants to do is sleep now."

"Did she show any interest in your idea of having a Christmas party?"

Abram's laugh was bitter. "Are you kidding? I can't even interest her in breakfast." He realized he had snapped at Hannah and apologized. "I'm sorry. This is not your fault."

She stopped wiping the counter to say, "It feels like it *is* my fault. I can't think why my uterus won't accept her eggs. They say I'm perfectly healthy."

"Don't do this to yourself. You tried. We tried. The doctors tried. Now I'm going upstairs and drag her out of bed. Close your ears. There may be screaming." He took the tray Hannah had prepared and carried it up the staircase. Sandra lay buried under two quilts. She had been sleeping for twelve hours. He was determined to get her up. He opened the blinds and pulled the covers from her as she whined in complaint.

"Time to rise and shine, Beautiful. I have your breakfast here. Let's get some food into you. I don't like skinny women." His jovial tone was forced, but he hoped it would work.

She rolled over and looked at him. "You're so annoying, Abram. Just let me sleep."

"No, I don't care if I have to douse you with ice water. You're getting up. Now sit up here and eat." She must have believed him because she groggily sat up.

"Okay. I'll try. Just pour me some coffee. That's all I want."

"No, Mam, you're having a piece of toast, too, made from Hannah's home-made wheat bread, very nutritious." He sat and fed her bites of toast in between her sips of coffee.

"You're treating me like a baby, Abram, and I hate it."

"Well, stop acting like one and get yourself out of bed, and stop feeling sorry for yourself. This has disappointed me, too, but life has to go on." It was the first time he had shown even mild anger at her refusal to get out of bed and do something with her days.

"You're 'disappointed'? Just 'disappointed'? Well, I've got news for you. I am way beyond 'disappointed.' I'm devastated. So go back downstairs and leave me alone."

He slammed the door and left her chewing a last bite of toast.

In less than a minute, he was back. He went into the bathroom and turned on the shower. He called out to her. "What do you want? Cold water or hot? If you come in here of your own accord, you'll have a hot shower. If I have to come out there and get you, it's going to be cold."

She came to the bathroom doorway. Sullenly, she stripped off her nightgown and got into the shower. He asked, "Do you want me to join you? Remember how you used to love it when I'd wash your hair?"

"No. I do not want you to join me." She pulled the shower door closed.

He sat on the vanity chair in the bathroom and watched her bathing lethargically behind the shadowy glass. At least she was moving. Every night he had tried to make love to her and she had refused. This was just one more attempted refusal. She refused to apply for adoption, too. Her stubbornness was making him damn sick.

She stepped out of the shower and wrapped a towel around her hair. "You can go do whatever it is you have planned today, Abe. I will get dressed and come downstairs. You don't have to sit here and wait. Just go."

"Okay," he said. "I'll make a fire in the fireplace. I'll work in the den and you come sit with me. You don't have to talk. Just be with me, please." Timidly, he ran a finger up and down her bare arm. Then he left her to dress herself.

He knew that she had done it to appease his frustration, but it was something. She came down dressed in jeans and a big red sweater, as if to cheer him. Her fluffy slippers were on her feet, but that was fine. She sat listlessly in the rocking chair and watched the flames of the fireplace. But at least she was with him.

The next day she refused to get out of bed, refused breakfast and Abram knew he had to do something.

Chapter Twenty-one

Abram sat looking out through the frosted filigree of the bay window next to the breakfast table as he lingered where he had, again, eaten alone. As Hannah refilled his coffee cup, he asked her to sit with him. She had seen him trying out words in his mind, and so she was not surprised.

Filling a white coffee mug for herself, she took off her apron and sat across from him waiting for his words to come.

"I've got to do something," he began. "I can't just let her . . . die on the vine like this." He ran his hand through his hair in frustration.

"Maybe she'll try to adopt now." Hannah wanted to comfort him but had nothing more than this to offer. She studied the icy lace on the window, too.

"No," he said, leaning back in his chair, "I've given up on that. Besides it could take years, and then we'd end up getting rejected because we're too old."

Hannah searched her mind for something hopeful to say. "Maybe they'll find another surrogate . . . ."

"We've waited months. I think it'd be too exhausting for her to start all over again with that, but there is . . . something else . . . if you're willing . . . I wanted to talk to you about it before I mention it to Sandra." He seemed to have come to some conclusion.

Something that counted more with her than with Sandra? Hannah was startled by the very possibility. She watched the words form on his lips. "Surrogacy plus egg donation—your egg, my sperm," he said carefully, with his eyes on hers. He paused and waited.

She gasped for breath and widened her eyes, unable to believe that she had heard him right. "You and I?" she asked, her voice a whisper.

He nodded slowly. "You and I."

Still speaking in a whisper, she asked, "But . . . how?"

"You would donate the egg—to be fertilized with my sperm. Sandra would adopt." His voice was calm, but she fought to get words out, needing to understand.

"In a 'dish'?" She referred to the petri dishes in the lab.

"Yes." He maintained a steady gaze at her, and she did not waver under it.

She swallowed and carefully wet her lips before asking, "Why?"

He seemed baffled by her question. "Why? Because your uterus won't accept Sandra's fertilized eggs. This is the next best option, and Sandra would still have her 'Goodman line'."

She blinked rapidly. "No, I meant . . ." and then she said the words quickly, before she could stop herself. "Why in a dish? Mate with me." She used the Amish expression for love-making. Dizzy with shock at what she had uttered, she felt warmth wash over her face, her neck. But the words were out. She could not call them back, and, as the truth of her intention settled between them in the silence that followed, she grew calm, resigned that she had said it. She knew that her words had stunned him, and she hurried to say the rest. "It would only be one time . . . I know how to take my temperature and use the litmus paper now . . . and I'd tell you . . . and Sandra would think that the implantation had finally worked . . . . Wouldn't she be happier, thinking the baby was hers . . . and yours?" Her words and her breath coming fast, she desperately hoped that he believed that she wanted this for Sandra.

"Hannah, don't!" he said, holding up both hands as if to stop the torrent of her words.

Humiliation brought tears to her eyes, and she rose to run away, but he grabbed her hand to stop her. She stood in front of him with her head bowed under his gaze. She felt his thumb rotating in the palm of her hand as he held on to it.

His voice was husky as he said, "We can't, Hannah. We just can't."

She lifted her face to him, and asked the word again, "Why?"

Tiredly, he sighed and drew her to him, and she felt she would melt with weakness. With his lips against her hair, he whispered his reason, and she understood clearly the words and the confession behind them. "Because it wouldn't be 'just one time'."

With the light of a white, winter moon washing over her as she lay sleepless in her bed that night, Hannah relived over and over again, those moments in time and the words that had passed between her and Abram Goodman. Her candor with him astounded her now. She wanted to die every time she remembered her own stammering voice, her eager suggestion that they lie together. But, more, she wanted to die at the thought that they never would.

Over the past few years, since she had "gone English," she had felt his eyes on her many times and knew that he was drawn to her, perhaps even wanted her; but she also knew that he was not a man who would commit adultery. Ironically, she also knew that he truly loved his wife.

She wondered how he would make the suggestion to Sandra, that the surrogate also contribute the egg, fertilized by his sperm—in the laboratory dish. She sighed. "Chust so I can have a little of you, Abram, growing inside me . . . ." she said aloud to the cold moon.

Chapter Twenty-two

Sandra slept deeply these days, the dreamless sleep of depression. Abram sat beside her on the bed, watching her and wondering what her reaction would be if he broached the subject of Hannah as egg-donor. Silently, he rose, went to the window and leaned the heels of his hands on the sill. Against a clear, blue-black sky a white moon shone, and he found, as he gazed at it, that he had begun to pray.

In a little while, he undressed, and, as he lay beside his wife, he gathered her limp body into his arms and cradled her as though she were the child she so desperately wanted. His throat ached with sobs that wanted to be set free. He began to think of Hannah's words, of her admission, for both of them—that they had wanted one another for a long time now. *What kind of man am I?* he wondered. *What kind of man can love two women? Sandra . . . my wife . . . I love you so much.* He kissed her forehead. *Hannah, what are you to me? Sandra. Hannah. God forgive me. God help me. God, help us all.* His prayer spiraled up and away from him, and soon he, too, slept.

It was still and dark when he awoke. Sandra slept in his arms, with her back curved into him. He began to kiss her shoulders to awaken her. She did not stir. He gently nudged her body with his own and made room for her as she rolled onto her back. Slowly her eyes opened, and she strove to focus on the face of her husband hovering above her.

"Good morning, Hon," he said. "You've been sleeping for fifteen hours; let's get up and plan something we can do together today."

"Let me sleep, Abe. I'm so tired . . . ." She whimpered when he sat up and pulled the warm covers from her body.

"Nope. You are getting up, and you and I are driving into the city to shop and take in the Christmas decorations, just like we used to."

"Oh, Abe," she said, rubbing her eyes. "I really don't feel like it . . . and the roads are probably bad . . . ."

"No excuses. We'll take the four-wheel drive. C'mon, you can have the shower. I'll use the one downstairs." Pulling on a pair of jeans, he ignored her sleepy protests and headed for the door. "Get up, Sandra. I'll give you half an hour or it will be the cold shower."

Downstairs, he turned on the kitchen light and started toward the shower in the bathroom off the guest room. He heard pounding on the kitchen door and wondered why Hannah wasn't using her key.

Grinning, Joey stood at the door. "Hi, Uncle Abe! Mom is way back there. She's walking too slow."

"Listen, Joe," he said. "Tell your mom not to bother making breakfast for me and Aunt Sandra. We're leaving in about a half hour. Run back and tell her."

But Hannah had arrived. Rather than face her, he went to take his shower. He heard her reprimanding Joey. "Joey, you're getting snow everywhere. Get over here on this carpet and take your boots off. And don't you pound on the door like that. You wait for me."

He could hear the boy's thin voice delivering his message. "Uncle Abe said to tell you not to make breakfast for him and Aunt Sandra. They're going somewhere. Can I have waffles?"

"Let's go to our favorite bagel shop for breakfast." He had been trying to draw his wife into conversation, but she sat muffled in a red scarf and gray parka, despite the comfortable temperature in the Land Rover. Her eyes were closed.

In response to the bagel suggestion, she murmured an indifferent, "Okay."

Abram felt impatience rising in him. "You know, Sandra, you could try to be a little better company. You refuse to be helped by medication, so that must mean you think you can pull out of this on your own. I suggest you start making some effort."

Ordinarily, his spirited wife would have lashed back at him. Now she just shrugged. "I told you I didn't feel like going anywhere. This is your idea."

He took a long breath and figured this was as good a time as any. "Well, it's not the only idea I have. I wanted you awake and listening before I asked you. What would you say to this," he said, trying to sound casual. "What if a surrogate donated the egg as well as her womb? What if her egg were fertilized with my sperm and implanted?"

When she didn't respond, he went on. "You'd have your precious Goodman line, and you could become the baby's adoptive mother."

Her tired words came tinged with bitterness. "Why is this a new idea, Abe? I suggested using an egg donor to you two years ago."

Baffled, he slowed down to glance at her. "You did?"

"Yes, when we first started talking about using a surrogate, when we learned that the odds are against implantation of one woman's egg into another woman's uterus."

She could not hide her irritation with him, but he was glad for her show of emotion, any emotion. "Okay . . . okay . . . I remember now. I was against it . . . ."

She interrupted with venom. "Because it wasn't 'normal'," she said, finishing the sentence for him, her voice sarcastic as she used her fingers to quote him.

He sighed deeply and settled back into his seat behind the wheel. "Yeah, I've changed a lot. I had no idea it would be so hard to have a baby."

"It's my fault," she said coldly. "Nobody ever blamed you."

He tried to keep his eyes on the road, but she had hurt him deeply. "And have I ever blamed *you?* Don't you for one minute think or say that. We're in this together, Sandra."

Silence lay between them for several minutes until he spoke again, in a quiet voice. "So what do you say, do we give it a try? Would it bother you if the baby wasn't genetically yours?"

She sat up straighter and looked at him. "Well, of course, it would bother me, but nothing bothers me like having no children. But do you think Hannah would do it? Donate the egg and then give up the baby?"

"I'm not sure Hannah's a good idea." It was a conclusion he had come to suddenly. "It'd be better to use someone from the files of a new clinic. Some clinic that doesn't make you jump through all the hoops that Louisville does."

"If Hannah was a good idea before, why not now?" He could hear hope stirring in her, but he had to give his objections.

"How could we ask her not to think of the baby as her own? How could she humanly do it, living there, practically with us, *with* the baby?" He spoke honestly, from the heart.

She slid down into her seat again. "You're right, I guess, but I liked the idea of being near the person carrying our child, and you liked the idea of using somebody whose habits you knew . . . ."

Just when he thought she was going to cry, she sat upright again and her voice became animated, for the first time in months. "Abe, let's ask her. Let's just ask her to tell us how she would feel, leaving a part of herself with us. By that, I mean, we'd have to make it clear that she and Joey would have to leave, as soon as the baby is born. That's the way the other contract is written anyway. She agreed to it. We'd remind her that she wouldn't have to work again, unless she wanted to. Why, she could even get a GED and then go on to college!"

"Well," he said slowly, "don't be surprised if she isn't crazy about that idea. She turned pasty white when I said she'd have to leave when we talked about the contract during the interviews. I think she's scared to death of the world without us in it." He gripped the steering wheel and tried to imagine how it would be for Hannah, "cast out" again.

"She can always say no, but, I don't think she will, Abe. She has a great debt of gratitude to us . . . . We never required that, but she has said as much. Let's turn around right now and go ask her."

"No you don't, Mrs. Bulldozer. We're going to go into the city as we planned and let this sink in for a while." He reached for her hand and she did not pull away.

"Okay," she said. "Okay. What're a few more hours?"

They spent the day in the city, enjoying the glittering window displays on the main streets of "downtown." Snow flakes and the sound of chimes in the brisk air made them relegate the malls to havens for cowards. Bundled against the cold, they strolled arm-in-arm from shop to shop, exclaiming the beauty and the deliciousness of the season as they sampled Christmas delicacies at various stores.

Abram's rejoiced because his wife was renewed and with him again.

It was dark when they arrived home later that day, but Sandra urged Abram to stop at the hired girl's cottage. "Why wait?" she argued. "We've lost so much time. Let's talk to her now."

Chapter Twenty-three

Hannah heard the hum of the vehicle stopping at the end of the walkway she had just shoveled, in anticipation of them. Pulling aside the sheer curtain that covered the door window, she was not surprised to see the Goodmans approaching her house lit by the porch light she had left on for them. She opened the door before they could knock.

The change in Sandra's countenance was proof enough that her husband had made his suggestion to her and that she was in favor of the idea. It occurred to Hannah that she had a power she had never had before. With her refusal, Sandra would wilt like a flower hit by frost. With her consent, the couple would have the child, and Hannah would have a link to Abram Goodman—forever.

"Is it too late for visitors?" Sandra asked, stamping her feet on the little mat outside Hannah's front door.

"No, it's all right. I've just been baking cookies. Joey needs them for a bake sale at school tomorrow. He's asleep, but he won't hear you. He sleeps like a log."

She invited them to help themselves to the cookies that dotted white paper towels like big brown buttons on a white shirt. Munching cookies, she and the Goodmans pretended for a while that their visit was casual, but Sandra's impatience broke through.

"Well, Hannah, Abe told me that he mentioned to you the possibility of you donating the ovum . . . the egg . . . as well as carrying the child. What do you think?" The look of anticipation on Sandra's face told Hannah that Sandra fully expected a "yes."

As for Abram, his face held the usual look of worry where Hannah's involvement was concerned. Hannah noticed that his wife had not mentioned *his* part in the creation of this child.

Keenly aware that this child would be part of her and part of Abram, even if it were conceived in a laboratory dish, Hannah lied, "I think it's not much different from what we tried to do before."

"There's a big difference, Hannah," Abram said pointedly, as usual getting to the bottom line. "You would be giving up a baby that is biologically yours." After a long paused, he asked, "Could you do that?"

Hannah licked her lips and studied their faces before answering. "Yes," she said, "I really want to help you. You've both been so kind to me and Joey." She laid a hand on each of theirs, an unusual gesture for one as reserved as the once-Amish girl.

"But I want you to understand, Hannah," Sandra said, squeezing Hannah's hand for emphasis, "that you would most definitely have to live and work elsewhere after the baby came, because, it would be just too difficult for you . . . and for us, too. The money would be more, of course, but that item about your moving away would be engraved in stone." Sandra's face softened. "It doesn't mean that you could *never* see the child; after all, we are friends. But we can't let you . . . bond with the baby."

Hannah's eyes moved to Abram's face. She sought confirmation of Sandra's frank words. He nodded.

Finally, she removed her hands from theirs, sat up straighter, and said, "I understand perfectly. I am entirely too dependent on you anyway. Joey and I will be fine."

As the Bond Woman closed the door behind them, she also understood perfectly that if she refused them, her going would be inevitable anyway. And so she resigned herself to giving herself to Abram in the only way she could.

Chapter Twenty-four

"Depositing the semen directly into the uterus has a better chance of success and is a less complicated procedure than fertilization of the ovum outside the uterus with replacement following," explained Dr. Clark. "Abram can leave a fresh deposit with us, and Ms. Miller should resume daily monitoring of her temperature, as well as litmus testing. A call to us to let us know when she is on her way is all that is necessary."

Sandra was surprised at the simplicity of it. "That sounds easy, doesn't it Abe?" Her husband's face was red, and he refused to look at the two women who sat in the room with him and Dr. Clark.

"Okay," he said. "Are we done here, Dr. Clark? All the paperwork is in order."

Sandra wondered at her husband's embarrassment. After all they'd been through, for some reason, his donating a "fresh sample" now set his face afire. *Poor Baby,* she thought.

A week later, a blushing Hannah Miller informed Sandra that the thermometer and the calendar were in agreement that she was probably ovulating. She refused to let Sandra into the bathroom with her for litmus testing. Sandra ran to seek her husband who worked at his computer in the den.

"This is it, Abe! I'll call Dr. Clark." Sandra could barely contain her excitement. "Get ready to go, Hannah," she ordered, with her hand on the kitchen phone. Why are you two standing there looking at each other? Get moving!" The petite drill sergeant was in charge.

Sandra voiced her disappointment that Abram had opted out of going with them for the insemination procedure. "I can't get over Abram not coming with us. I thought he'd want to be there to witness the beginning of his child." She turned the car toward the clinic in the city where the insemination would take place.

"Maybe he would be embarrassed to be there," Hannah suggested. "I know *I* would be . . . to have him there."

Sandra's voice was contrite. "I never thought of that, that you'd be embarrassed, Hannah. I'm sorry. I have to start looking at things through your eyes instead of just my own." She hesitated and added, "But I do hope you won't mind if Abram is there for the delivery. I want us both there."

"Oh dear," Hannah said quietly, "but I have some time to get used to the idea, I suppose."

Her eyes glistening with tears above the blue mask that she wore, Sandra Goodman reached for the hand of Hannah who lay draped in a white sheet with her feet in stirrups, her knees drawn up and her hips elevated.

Hannah accepted Sandra's hand, but her own eyes were dry. She closed them at the sound of Dr. Clark's voice.

"Just let your knees fall to the side, Hannah . . . ."

"Oh, my goodness," said Sandra. "That thing looks like a turkey baster!"

Less than three hours later, the two women rode silently homeward, each lost in her own thoughts. Lightly falling snow sparkled in the headlights of the car as it traveled into the winter evening and into the shadows of the future.

Christmas filled the days ahead, a fitting distraction for Sandra Goodman. She channeled her renewed energies into helping Hannah shop for Joey, baking cookies and decorating the big house for the holidays.

"We'll invite a few neighbors in, and Kendra, but I don't want to have to think about a big party. I've got other things on my mind," she said. "How does this look?" She had arranged ground moss and bittersweet on the mantle, with small white lights.

"It looks nice, *chust* the same as it did last year," the hired girl said with little emotion.

Sandra knew Abram was trying to curb her hopes when he said, "Settle down, Hon. You know it's not likely that it'll happen the first time."

"But why not?" she said, her enthusiasm undaunted. "Hannah has a very regular cycle, and she says she's never missed a period, except when she became pregnant with Joey, and, get this, her period's due on Christmas Day! We'll know in five days!"

Sandra's zest for life spilled over into the bedroom, too. They made love voraciously in the evenings, making up for lost time. As they lay quietly in one another's arms, Sandra had a thought. "Wouldn't it be something," she mused, "if I got pregnant now, with Hannah pregnant, too?"

"Oh, yeah," he said dryly, "that'd be 'something' all right . . . something called a nightmare."

Chapter Twenty-five

Hannah sat before the little wood-burning fireplace in her cozy home, rocking and humming as she knitted. White lights on a small tree near the window twinkled, and Joey fingered gaily wrapped presents under the tree.

"This one's for you, Mommy," he said happily. "I made it in art class and Mrs. Tupin helped me wrap it! I hid it under my bed for a long time. Do you want me to open it for you, Mommy?"

"No, Joey, I want to wait 'til Christmas, but you can help me wrap the gifts we have for Aunt Sandra and Uncle Abram. But first I want to finish this little sweater I'm making for them, too. Come take a look at it, Joey."

"Boy, it's really little. It won't fit either one of them." Joey looked worried as he examined the delicate white yarn which his mother deftly handled.

"That's because it's only part of the *real* present we're going to give them, Joey . . . ."

Trying to ride the rocking chair with his mother, Joey asked, "What's the real present, Mommy? Tell me!"

Hannah laid aside her knitting and drew the boy onto her lap. "Do you remember how Aunt Sandra was so sad sometimes, and what I told you when you asked me why?"

"Yes," he said, putting his small hand up against his mother's to measure the difference in size. "You said she wanted a baby, but one wouldn't grow in her tummy, like I grew in yours."

"Well, that's what the present for Aunt Sandra and Uncle Abe is going to be . . .   a baby of their own, and this little sweater is for their baby."

"But where will we buy a baby for them, Mom?" He twisted in her lap to look at his mother's calm face.

"I let a doctor plant a seed in my tummy, Joey, and it will grow into a baby, and you and I will give *that* baby to them. What do you think of that idea?"

Joey jumped off his mother's lap. "That's a good idea! And I can help them take care of the baby." He laid his hand on his mother's flat stomach and asked, "Can you grow a baby by Christmas?"

"No," Hannah laughed, "but we can tell them we have one ordered." She pulled him to stand in front of her. "Now, listen, Joey, you are to keep this a secret. Don't tell anybody at school our secret."

"But can I tell Aunt Sandra and Uncle Abe?"

"When it's time to tell them, we'll tell them together, okay?"

"Okay! But when will it be time?"

"Oh, after I can feel him or her kicking. Then I'll know for sure there's a baby in there."

"Let's give them a baby boy. I think girls are a bunch of trouble."

"Well, we don't get to pick that. God does. If a girl comes out, I know they'll be just as happy as if a boy comes out."

After she had tucked her son in for the night, Hannah walked into her bedroom and stood before Ida Goodman's antique mirror as she slowly unbuttoned her blouse. Dropping it to the floor, she pulled an arm through each strap of her bra, slid the fastener around to the front of her waist and unhooked it. Placing her cool hands at the sides of her sore, swollen breasts, she gently lifted them and smiled at herself in the mirror.

Chapter Twenty-six

Hannah sat in the shade and watched Abram's wet, muscled chest glisten in the sunshine of late June. Straddling his neck were the lean brown thighs of her son who held a yellow plastic pail to his own thin shoulder. The man and the boy moved stealthily through the wavering blue water of the pool, toward the unsuspecting Sandra who lay stomach down on a rubber raft. When the cold water hit her warm back, she shrieked, and the water battle was on.

More than six months pregnant, Hannah shifted her gaze from the frolicking trio in the pool to a bed of multi-colored zinnias on which orange butterflies lit. On one of the tallest flowers, not one, not two, but three of the delicate insects had lighted, balancing precariously on the large red blossom. As she bent to watch them vying for space, she felt the child stir within her.

She had gotten used to Sandra's hands searching her rounded abdomen to feel the vigor of the child, whom they already knew would be a son. Abram, on the other hand, had so far only touched her twice; once, at Sandra's insistence and on a rare occasion when they were alone.

Even before Hannah's pregnancy had been confirmed by Dr. Clark, Sandra had written her resignation to the superintendent of schools and had not returned for the January semester. During the winter months Hannah had to put up with Sandra's constant presence. Together the two women shopped, visited the doctor, or shared in the cooking. Sandra was not satisfied. "Why don't we just move you into the guest room, Hannah, and Joey can have Abe's old room upstairs. That way if anything . . . happens during the night we'll be right there for you."

The thought of no privacy at all made Hannah cringe. "No, I don't want to do that, Sandra. I really love my quiet time at my house." She tried to keep her voice free of the irritation she had felt at Sandra's suggestion.

Sandra sighed in surrender. "Okay, I guess you do need your privacy." Hesitating, she asked, with a crease of worry between her deep blue eyes, "Have I been overbearing?"

Here was Hannah's chance to tell the truth, but she couldn't bring herself to do it. "No, I understand your excitement about your baby. It's chust that I'm used to quiet time for prayer and meditation and I like to do that at my house, while Joey is down for the night."

"Whatever it takes to keep you calm, Hannah. I do understand. Abe and I are going shopping for the baby's layette and nursery. Do you want to come along?"

Cagily, Hannah knew that she had to keep assuring them that she was not emotionally attached to this baby. "That," she said, "is for you and your husband to do together." Nor would Hannah let Sandra tell her the name that the couple had chosen for their child.

The "business arrangement" that she strove to emphasize by her words and actions when she was around Sandra was becoming more difficult to maintain, but she practiced referring to the child-on-the-way as "your baby." "Your baby is active today," she would say, or "When your baby is born . . . ."

But there were moments that Hannah coveted, moments when she and Abram exchanged a glance or a smile. One day, she had been standing at the kitchen sink, washing dishes, when she uttered a small, "Oh!" as the child gave her a substantial kick. Abram, who had been leaning over the kitchen table with blueprints of a new barn spread out before him, looked in her direction at the sound.

"Put your hand here," she had said, as she moved toward him.

Hesitant, he touched the spot on her apron that she had indicated. "I don't feel anything," he said, trying to pull his hand back. But Hannah placed her own hand on his and pressed it to her body.

Her eyes misted as she watched the look of awe on his face as he felt the life within her. For a long moment, she stood still beside him, her hand on his, his on the place where the child moved. Neither of them said a word, but their eyes were locked in silent communication which broke at the sound of Sandra's shoes clattering on the wooden floor as she made her way to the kitchen.

A month later, Hannah's eyes left the ultrasound screen to watch the amazement on Abram's face as he said, "Look, there's his heart . . . ."

He held his wife's hand as he stared at the squirming life on the monitor, but, as his gaze settled on Hannah, his smile was for her.

She tried not to think of the time when she would have to leave. She could not imagine herself and Joey living out in the English world without Abram's protection. While she keenly sensed Abram's attempt to detach himself from her emotionally, she believed it was impossible; they had known each other too long, and now there was his child growing within her.

She stared into the future and tried to imagine the day she would have to say goodbye. *Perhaps.* It was a solitary word written on the blank page of her mind. Beyond that single word, she had no idea how it could happen, but she retained the vague hope that, *perhaps,* she would not have to say goodbye to Abram Goodman forever.

She sat in her rocking chair and sang to the child within her, a lilting German lullaby that she used to sing to her littlest brother and to Joey.

As the summer days grew shorter with the approach of her due date, Hannah realized that she had better start looking for somewhere to live, probably in the nearby town. She spread the classified section of the newspaper on the kitchen table and began to circle potential rentals.

Sandra came into the kitchen and looked over Hannah's shoulder. "What are you looking for?"

"Oh, a place to rent after your baby is born . . . ." Hannah did not lift her eyes, but she hoped her words gave Sandra a pang of guilt. If they did, she gave no sign of it. Instead, she informed the surrogate that it was time for her daily exercise.

Hannah sighed as she folded the newspaper and pushed herself to her feet. It would be no use arguing with Sandra, whom Hannah knew had put herself in charge of Hannah's well-being. She had taken over the job of waiting on the hired girl instead of the other way around.

"Don't move. I'll take care of it," was the frequent command she gave Hannah no choice but to obey.

Hannah had pleaded, "Sandra, I'm not an invalid just because I'm pregnant. You know the doctor said I need exercise . . . ."

"That's exactly why you and I walk the farm for an hour every day. But I don't want you lumbering up and down the stairs or lifting heavy things."

As the two women walked the farm, with Sandra slowing her strides to match those of her very pregnant companion, Hannah asked a question. "I wonder what the workmen think. I see them watching us when we go by. They know I'm not married. Do they think that I'm once again having a baby out of wedlock?"

"Don't worry. Abram took care of it. He overheard some speculation about your condition, and he asked Hank to have a talk with them."

Chapter Twenty-seven

At the sound of Abram Goodman's voice, Hank looked up from fixing a milking machine. He watched the tall man he'd known since Abram was a boy walk toward him with a wrinkle of concern between his eyes.

"Hank, I need a word with you."

"No problem, Boss," Hank said, wiping his hands on a rag. "What can I do for ya?"

"I want you to have a talk with the men about Hannah's . . . condition. They'll be noticing that she's pregnant again, but this time it's different . . . ."

"You don't owe me no explanations, Boss," Hank had insisted, waving his hand dismissively.

"You're going to get one anyhow," Abram said, taking a seat on a nail keg. He launched into an explanation of surrogacy and their agreement with Hannah, since Sandra was incapable of carrying a child herself. "I just don't want anyone to think that Hannah . . . . Look, just explain everything to the others for me, Hank, okay?"

Hank watched Abram walk away. *Still as tight-assed as ever. Most bosses wouldn't give a damn what the men or anybody else thinks.*

Hank's approach had been simple. "You're gonna be noticin' that the housekeeper is in the family way, but it ain't whatcha think. The Boss's wife can't have a kid, so the other one is carryin' for her . . . ."

"Ha!" Bill said. "I was wonderin' how long ol' Goodman'd keep his hands off that good lookin' blonde. Can't say I blame 'im."

"Man, how'd he talk his old lady into *that?* " Pete was clearly shocked.

"You two are ignorant fools," Hank interrupted. "They got a new thing called 'surr-gacy.' There ain't no sex involved. They just do it in the doctor's office . . ."

"They did . . . it . . . in a doctor's office?" Pete asked, his shock escalating.

"No, Moron, I told you there was no sex involved in a doctor's office or anywhere else either. This is a case of makin' a baby in a lab and puttin' it in one woman to carry for the other who's got a medical condition that makes it so she *can't* carry it . . . ." Hank spoke impatiently, realizing that he was confusing even himself.

"Well, I'll be!" was Pete's astonished reply.

Young Bill wasn't convinced. Around the toothpick in his mouth, he made the mistake of saying, "Even if the boss ain't doin' the blonde chick, I'll bet he sure as hell wants to."

Before Bill knew it, Hank had him by the front of the shirt. "You listen to me, Cowboy. You ain't good enough to lick Abram Goodman's boots. I oughta can you for sayin' a thing like that." He pushed Bill and said, "Git outta here before I do just that."

Chapter Twenty-eight

Abram's heart pounded as he struggled to get his bearings. He had been startled out of a sound sleep by the trilling of the telephone on the nightstand next to his side of the bed. He fumbled for the phone, as his wife clutched his arm.

Clearing his throat, he tried to get out the word, "Hello?"

"It's time," the surrogate said.

"What time is it?" he asked, feeling confused.

"It's a little after two a.m.," she said, "and it's time to go to the hospital."

His confusion cleared and he tried to keep panic out of his voice. "Are you . . . all right?"

Sandra had come to stand by him. As she reached for the phone, he held her at bay.

"Yes, I'm all right, but you'd better call the ambulance. My water broke, and we have a long drive . . . . My suitcase is packed."

"I'm on it, Hannah. Just sit tight. We'll be right there as soon as I make the call."

With the receiver still in his hand, he pushed the off-button and turned to Sandra who was flapping her hands in impatience to know what was happening. "We have to call the ambulance . . . . Hannah's water broke."

"You should have let me talk to her!" She grabbed the phone from his hand and punched in the numbers.

"We should be calling the ambulance, not Hannah again," he said, clearly frustrated with his wife's need to be in charge.

"Hannah, what time did the pains start? No pains yet? Well, okay, I think you're right, since your water broke. We'll call the ambulance to be on the safe side. Yes, Joey can ride with Abe in the car, and he'll drop him off at Hank's. I'll ride in the ambulance with you. Oh, God, I'm so excited!"

As Sandra hung up the bedroom phone, she could hear Abram on his cell phone, asking 911 to send the pre-ordered ambulance to the address of the little house. Weeks before, they had decided that Hannah would deliver the baby in the city hospital with which Dr. Clark was affiliated. The plan had been to book rooms in the city a week prior to Hannah's due date, but Nature was having her own way. The unlikely back-up plan had been to go by ambulance since it was a two-hour drive to the city hospital. If Hannah's labor should go faster than expected, medics would be there to deliver the baby.

"Well," Sandra said, as Abram finished his call, "so much for the 'best laid plans of mice and men'. . . ."

Chapter Twenty-nine

Hannah chose to walk around the halls of the obstetrics wing, rather than lie in the birthing room with Sandra timing contractions. Her back ached, but she insisted on staying on her feet for as long as possible, as her mother had, instinctively knowing that gravity would work to shorten her labor.

Almost oblivious to the couple who walked one on either side of her, she focused on the past and remembered how Rebecca Miller, big with Aaron, had started the family's laundry after the first pains had begun.

~ ~ ~

"Let me do it for you, Mamm," Hannah had begged as her mother insisted on bending and straightening, bending and straightening, as she pinned shirts and dresses on the clothesline to dry.

Even as she winced with pain, Rebecca refused help. "Chust keep moving the basket down the line for me, Hannah. I need to do this. I want to stay on my feet and let Nature pull the baby down."

Hannah and Fannie had wrung their hands in anguish as they watched their mother's travail. Finally, Rebecca placed her hands on each of their shoulders and let out a long groan as the pressure of the baby's head became too much for her to bear.

"Get me back to the house and send Samuel to fetch the baby-catcher. Tell him to hurry. I may have waited a bit too long . . . ."

Datt spoke up. "By now Samuel will already be on his way back with her, Rebecca. I sent him an hour ago, because I wasn't about to catch this baby myself." Then he picked up his wife and carried her to her bedroom, as Rebecca laid her head on his shoulder in surrender.

~ ~ ~

An intense pain gripped Hannah, and she held on to Sandra's arm for support. "Let's go to the birthing room now," she said, evenly, after the wave of pain had subsided.

Sandra had attended natural childbirth classes with Hannah and sat, gowned, beside the laboring woman, helping her to establish a rhythm of breathing to work with the pain assailing her body.

Opening her eyes between pains, Hannah saw that even the surgical mask he wore could not hide Abram Goodman's white face. He seemed helpless, without something to do, so she asked him to feed her teaspoons of crushed ice as she requested. As he held the teaspoon to her lips, his eyes met hers, and she saw how distressed he was.

"I shouldn't have agreed to natural childbirth," he said. "I should have insisted that you take the epidural. I asked a little bit ago, but now, they said it's too late."

"No, don't think that. I did it this way with Joey . . . it's only natural . . . ." and Hannah anchored her eyes to his as she bore down with the pain, knowing that it was almost over.

Finally, Sandra asked the attending nurse with excitement, "Is that the head? Is that our baby's head?" Abram refused to look.

The nurse told them to step away from the bed and took a look herself. "I'll page Dr. Clark," she said.

Hannah rode a great wave of pain. Then she heard herself uttering the long, primeval cry of giving birth as she pushed Abram Goodman's son into the world. Out of love for him, for this man she could never have, she had done this.

"He's a big boy; eight pounds, three ounces," announced Dr. Clark, as he looked at the scale on which the nurse had placed the crying baby.

The nurse cleaned Baby Goodman, wrapped a white blanket around him, and handed him to his adoptive mother, who tearfully cooed, "Welcome, Israel Matthew Goodman . . . ."

Hannah asked Abram to have Hank pick her up at the hospital, the day after the birth of the baby, Hank and Joey who had been staying with him. "You and Sandra should be alone when you take him home," she said, keeping her back to him as she folded things and put them in her suitcase. She did not want him to see her quivering mouth.

"You can ride with us, Hannah," he protested as he placed his hand on her shoulder to turn her to face him.

"No," she said, without looking at him. She concentrated on keeping her lips from trembling. "It's better this way."

"Hannah . . ." he persisted, but she held up her hand, palm out, as if to stop his words.

"Don't, Abram. Please don't. I have only one last favor to ask."

When she was sure she was under control, she allowed herself to meet his eyes.

"Anything," he said, and she saw the tenderness in his eyes. Or was it only gratitude?

"May I stay at the little house for a few more months . . . I haven't had much time to . . . ."

"Of course. You don't have to leave . . . yet."

"Thank you . . . just until I get my strength back . . . ."

Drawing her into his arms in a loose embrace, he said, "No, it's you we have to thank, Hannah. We can never thank you enough."

Stepping back, she added, "I won't come near the main house. Joey may want to, though."

"Of course, Joey can come to the house any time. I'll see that Hank gets here by your discharge time." And he was gone, to collect his wife and son.

Hannah leaned against the wall and hugged herself as she slid to the floor, her wet face twisted in the agony of soundless crying.

Chapter Thirty

Abram Goodman held his son in his arms and fed him. He sat on the edge of the bed, and Sandra lay behind him contentedly caressing his back as she enjoyed watching his handsome profile, silhouetted by the light coming from the window, his head bent over the tiny child.

It was early morning, and Israel had awakened his parents with the small, shuddering cry of a newborn. He had been asleep in a cradle that was once his father's, kept near his mother's side of the bed.

As Sandra changed Israel's diaper, Abram surprised her by saying, "Let me feed him this time." In the two weeks since they had brought their son home, Abram had been afraid to handle him. Now he cradled the small downy head in one arm as though he had done it a thousand times.

"Do you like him?" Sandra teased.

"Like him? I can't get over what this little fella means to me, already." He held one of Israel's delicate hands. "He's so helpless . . . . I'm ready to protect him with my life if I have to." He tapped the rubber nipple gently against Israel's small mouth to start him sucking.

"It's amazing, isn't it? This bond of love that's intact already. I love him so much. I've never been so happy." She laid her head against her husband's back.

"That's all I ever wanted, to make you happy, but I can't get over how I'm taking to this fatherhood thing. I had no clue . . . ."

"You're a natural," Sandra said, kissing his back. She sat up, leaned her back against the pillows and reached for her baby. Easily, she shifted the warm bundle to her left shoulder to burp him.

Watching her, Abram said, "You're a natural, too, Sandra."

"I am, aren't I? Even if I didn't get to carry him, I really do feel that he is mine . . . ." She chose not to comment on the fine blond down on her baby's head.

"He *is* yours. Don't ever doubt that, Honey. No one has invested more in his birth than you have. No one has been so unselfish." He leaned in to kiss her.

Meeting his kiss, she added, "He's ours."

As Joey watched Sandra fussing over her two-months-old son, the boy asked, "Don't you like *me* anymore, Aunt Sandra?"

"Oh, Joey," she said, setting Israel in the infant seat she kept on the kitchen table and drawing Joey to her, "Of course I do. You'll always be my little buddy."

"Do you like me better than Israel?"

"Joey, I love you in a different way than I love Israel . . . because, you know, you've got a mommy who loves you very much, and I'm Israel's mommy."

"You mean you love Israel just a teensy bit more than you love me?" Joey held up his thumb and forefinger with just a tiny space between them.

"The way *you* love your mommy just a teensy bit more than you love me," Sandra said, mimicking his gesture.

"Okay," Joey said, happily. "'cause that's a really teensy bit."

Sandra's eyes filled with tears as she kissed Joey's cheek. "Thank you, Joey. I love you, too. Now, would you like to help me give Israel a bath?"

Later that day, Sandra left Israel with his father and walked the short distance to the little house. Bits of snow danced in the chilly November air, and she wished she had worn a coat. She folded her arms and hugged her bright yellow sweater closer to herself.

That morning she had explained to Abram, "This is getting ridiculous. Hannah lives a stone's throw away, and I haven't seen her for two months. I appreciate the fact that she's giving us our space and keeping her end of the bargain, but I never intended to make a . . . stranger . . . of her. I just think we need to talk."

She ignored the "But . . . ." she heard from her husband. "You're in charge. I'm going for a walk."

As Hannah opened the door, Sandra saw immediately that the girl was panicked. *She probably thinks I've come to throw her out.* Sandra smiled warmly to dispel Hannah's fears. Direct as usual, though, she said, "Put the tea kettle on, Hannah. We need to talk."

Hannah meekly obeyed as though she were still in Sandra's employ.

Sandra sat at the kitchen table and looked across at Joey's artwork displayed on the refrigerator. "Joey's really growing up. I remember how he struggled to print his name and look at how neat his printing is now!"

"Yes, he's very proud of his new accomplishment," Hannah said. Then she surprised Sandra by coming directly to the point. "If you've come to ask when I'll be leaving, you'll be happy to hear that I've been hired at the bakery in town, and I'm going to see some rentals this weekend."

Sandra accepted the mug of tea Hannah placed before her, fixed just the way Sandra liked it, with sugar and a squeeze of lemon. "That *is* good to hear. I admit I was taken aback when Abram said he had given you a couple of months to gain your strength back. Even I know that it doesn't take two months for a woman to get back on her feet after childbirth, especially a natural one." She saw Hannah stiffen and blush at her words. Removing her teabag from the mug, she wrapped its string around the bag to squeeze it. "But, otherwise, you've really kept to your part of the bargain, I mean, by not letting yourself get attached to Israel. You've never seen him since the day he was born . . . ." Sandra tried to be matter-of-fact, without getting emotional.

Hannah poured her own tea and waited for it to steep. "Oh, but I *have* seen you pushing him around in a carriage . . . ."

"That wouldn't even give you a glimpse of him. You've never even held him." Sandra put down her mug and looked Hannah in the eye. "Tell me the truth, Hannah; does that hurt you?" Sandra watched Hannah's face as she sat, stirring sugar into her tea, choosing her words carefully.

"Well, yes, in a way, it hurts me. In the same way *you'd* probably be hurt if you couldn't see Joey, but I understand that it has to be this way. I agreed. About the other thing—me wanting to stay here for a couple of months—I admit that the thought of living on the Outside, I mean in the English world, with no friends, scares me. I wanted time to adjust to it, to get Joey ready for it, too. I think I'm ready now. I chust needed that time when I wasn't working, wasn't pregnant . . . . ."

Sandra looked at Hannah's always full cookie jar. "Can I have one of those?"

Hannah quickly rose and laid cookies on a plate between them. "I'm sorry. I wasn't thinking."

Sandra dunked a snickerdoodle and let the sweet, cinnamon cookie dissolve in her mouth. "I guess I can understand how it might be for you. Off the farm is the *real* 'Outside' to you. I never thought of that. Well, you're going to have to do it eventually. You agreed to give up any claim to the baby, your job as our housekeeper and to find another residence. But do you think it's really necessary to agree to *never* seeing the baby, or us, for that matter, again? I mean, we can't allow you and Israel to bond. I'm sure you can understand why. It would be so hard for you not to think of him as yours. But I don't think *seeing* him, even visiting us once or twice a year would do any harm . . . ." Sandra knew she should have been discussing this with Abram first, but . . . surely he would agree.

Blushing furiously, Hannah laid a hand on her own breast. "Really? You'd let me . . . see the baby? Would Mr. Goodman be okay with that, too?"

Sandra sat back in her chair and spoke from her heart. "Hannah, you and I and Abe have been together for a long time, and you've made it possible for us to have a baby. I find that I miss having you around, actually." She smiled. "I don't think it would hurt anybody if you dropped in . . . well, as I said, maybe one or two times a year . . . just so you can keep your . . . perspective about Israel." She paused and looked levelly at Hannah. "Can you do that?"

Hannah's initial flush at Sandra's words had disappeared. "Well, I knew he wasn't mine to keep during the nine months I carried him. I knew I was paying a debt I owed you and Abram." At Sandra's attempt to interrupt, Hannah held up her hand. "No, it was a debt I owed in my mind even if you didn't feel that way. But, fond as I am of you and Mr. Goodman, I doubt if I wouldn't become fond of your son as well . . . . So perhaps it's best if we leave things as they are . . . ."

It was Sandra's turn to interrupt. "I'd think you were a monster if you didn't become 'fond' of our dear little son, Hannah. I mean, can you forget that . . . ." She swallowed hard before she said the words that she seldom allowed herself to think. "Can you look at Israel and forget that he is biologically part of you?"

Hannah's eyes were downcast, her blonde head slightly bowed over the white mug she held. Just when Sandra thought she was not going to answer, she lifted her eyes to meet Sandra's. "The best I can promise you is that if my feelings for Israel begin to become what they should not, I will stay away. For good."

Sandra blurted out the niggling idea she had had all morning. "Then I'd like to invite you to be our guests for Thanksgiving dinner, you and Joey." Trying to downplay the immensity of what she had just said, she added, "I'm turning out to be a pretty decent cook. We'll celebrate your new job." She rose from the table.

Hannah stayed seated. "Wait. Don't you think you should ask Mr. Goodman first?"

"Yes, you're probably right. I'll do that and call you later." With her hand on the doorknob, Sandra turned and gave Hannah a smile. "And thanks for the tea . . . and especially for the snickerdoodles!"

Abram's face was pensive as he considered Sandra's suggestion. As she waited for his response, she held both of

Israel's little feet in one hand and slid a clean diaper under him with the other.

"I don't know what you're so worried about, Abe," she said. " I don't feel a bit threatened by Hannah, and we're certainly secure legally."

He stepped back from his diapering lesson to sit in the rocking chair. "You've had no reason to feel threatened up 'til now. She hasn't even laid eyes on the baby since the nurse handed him to you."

Deftly, she shimmied Israel into his jammies. "And what's she going to do? Come in and say, 'I want my baby'? Come on, Abe, we've known her for a long time. She did this for us. She felt she owed us, and, you know, she *did* owe us. Besides, Hannah is like a rock emotionally. Who else could have given up her family, her religion, *everything,* just because she didn't want to marry some boy?" She bent to lay Israel in his crib and wind up his butterfly mobile.

Pushing himself up out of the rocking chair, Abram expelled his breath and said, "As I've said before, you'd have made a good lawyer. You win every argument. Try it if you want to. I just hope you know what you're doing."

"Clearly," she said, placing her arms around his neck and pulling his worried face down for a kiss, "I've missed my calling."

Chapter Thirty-one

On Thanksgiving Day, Hannah and her son Joseph, each of them carrying a pumpkin pie, walked the short distance to the Goodman house. Hannah breathed deeply of the crisp air, in an effort to calm herself. Except to glimpse Abram passing her house in this or that vehicle, she had not seen him for weeks. She wondered if he ever thought of her when he looked at Israel.

Joey turned into the walkway that led to the kitchen door, but his mother called him back. "No, Joey, I think we should go in by the front door."

Suddenly Abram Goodman stood before her, opening the door to let in Hannah and her son. He wore a soft, green plaid shirt tucked into jeans, and he was in his stocking feet. She noted that he focused his attention on Joey and the pumpkin pies. Unobserved, she drank in the sight of him.

"Hey, Joey, my man! What's that you've got there? Pumpkin pie! Well, let's get these to the kitchen. You can hang up your coats in there, Hannah. Well, I guess you already know where the coat closet is."

She could hear nervousness and embarrassment in his voice, though he said, cheerfully enough, "Come in, come in! The cook is in the kitchen . . . ."

From somewhere within the house, Hannah could hear the plaintive cries of a hungry baby. In the kitchen they found Sandra holding a crying Israel up to her shoulder as she stirred gravy. As though no time had passed since Hannah had last been in her kitchen, she said, "Hi, Hannah, would you get Israel a bottle out of the fridge and run some hot water over it for me, please, and, Abe, feed him while I finish this." She handed Israel off to his father who took over the bouncing ritual while Hannah warmed the bottle.

Sandra put an arm around Joey. "Come and see this big turkey I stuffed for us." Opening the oven door, she pulled the tin foil off the bird that had been set there to keep warm.

"How soon do we eat? I'm really hungry," Joey said, straightening up from his peek into the oven.

"Soon, Buddy, soon. How about you take these napkins and put one to the left of every plate, folded like this. Can you do that?"

Hannah tested the warmth of Israel's bottle on her wrist and handed it to Abram who propped his son in his left arm to feed him. "Hold on, hold on, little guy," he said. "Dinner's on the way."

Incredibly, Hannah heard Sandra say, "On second thought, let Hannah feed Israel and come lift this turkey out of the oven for me. Do you want to carve now or at the table?"

Abram Goodman's mouth was a tight line as he placed the baby in Hannah's arms.

Hannah sat quietly in the family room, looking back into the eyes of the baby who studied this new face as he sucked. His eyes were blue, as was often the case with small babies, she reminded herself, but there was no mistaking the soft blond hair that covered his head. Above the cap of the bottle which covered his mouth, she recognized the features of his father.

"Isn't he beautiful?" Sandra had come to stand beside her.

"Yes, he's beautiful," Hannah said, keeping her eyes on Israel. "He looks like his father."

"I think so, too. You should see Abram's baby pictures. He looks just like Israel, blond hair and all." At the sound of the doorbell, she bounded away, saying, "That has to be Israel's Aunt Kendra!"

Hannah remained, holding Baby Israel Matthew Goodman in her arms, as she listened to the shrill greetings exchanged by Sandra and her sister in the foyer. Though she had no milk, her breasts began to ache as she watched Israel suck on his bottle. Hoisting him to her shoulder, she patted his back and waited for his enthusiastic burp, which made her smile. She enjoyed the smell of him and the way he nuzzled her shoulder. She thought of how he had lived within her.

She knew Abram had entered the room. She could see his reflection in the mirror above the mantel, but she kept still, waiting to see what he would do. He stood for a long moment, looking at them, before he spoke.

"Dinner's ready, Hannah. Here, let me take Israel off your hands. It looks like you've lulled him to sleep."

She followed him out of the room and went into the powder room to wash her hands. From within, she heard Kendra's whispered exclamation of disbelief.

"You've invited her to dinner today? She's in there feeding your baby? I hate to say this, Sister, but you need to have your head examined."

"Shhhh. She'll hear you. I'm sure it's fine. She's not the emotional type."

At the table, Abram Goodman thanked God for the food, for their guests, and for Israel who lay sleeping peacefully in a nearby cradle.

"Amen," Hannah said with the others. Silently, she uttered her own prayer of thanksgiving. *I am thankful that I was able to give Abram a son. I am thankful that I have been invited here today, to see him and his baby. I am thankful that the only attachment I feel is to him, and not to his beautiful boy. I promised him. And I will keep my promise. Help me, God, to let go of my love for Abram. Help me to make my way in this world without him.*

Chapter Thirty-two

A freezing rain began to fall, and Sandra gripped the steering wheel of the Lexus more tightly. She had taken the heavy car because the cloudy January sky threatened snow, but the weather forecast had not promised the icy sleet that now pelted her windshield and made the mountain highway glitter.

She shrugged her shoulders to ease the tension that made them ache and drove slowly, gearing down and staying off her brakes.

It was her first full day away from Israel who was now four months old. A telephone call from Amber, her oldest and dearest friend, had prompted her to bring Mrs. Gregory in to baby sit.

Abram, tied up with gas company executives today, had encouraged her to go. "You're turning into a recluse, and Israel should get used to staying with other people."

Sandra smiled to think of Israel's ready smile. He had been asleep when she left. *What will he think when a stranger comes to take him out of his crib? Well, not exactly a stranger. We've had her over to spend time with Israel while we're home . . . but he'll be looking for Mommy.* A twinge of worry crossed her mind, but she knew Abram was right. She adored being a mother, but she needed an outing.

A brown flash, the doe bounded off the bank to her right, and, instinctively, she hit the brakes, sending the big car into a wild spin. Screaming, Sandra tried to fling herself toward the passenger seat at the sight of the massive tree in her path. The noise of shattering glass and crumpling metal was deafening.

She felt the intense stares of the men as she walked through the doors of the diner. A worried-looking waitress approached her and asked, "Can I help you?"

"The bathroom, please. I need to use the bathroom."

The woman who looked back at her from the mirror above the sink had cheeks red with cold, and her long, dark hair was matted with ice crystals. The blue eyes that met hers registered a look of confusion. The white wool coat she wore was dirty on the sleeves and down the front. She made feeble attempts to clean it with a wet paper towel, but it only smeared and looked worse. She placed her freezing hands under the warm water of the tap and tried to remember. She knew she had wrecked her car, but everything before that was blankness.

She left the bathroom and slid into an orange leather booth across from the counter and sat staring at the diamond rings on her left hand. Startled by the waitress who suddenly appeared beside her, she wasn't sure what the woman had said to her. Hearing her own voice tremble, she guessed that she had been asked for an order.

"Just something hot, coffee . . . yes, coffee."

She saw the waitress whisper to the man behind the cash register. They glanced at her as she sat warming her hands on the heavy tan mug that the waitress had filled for her. As the man from the cash register approached her, she suddenly pushed the cup away from herself. "Oh, I don't know if I have any money to pay for this . . . ."

Searching her pockets frantically, she produced only some tissues and a key that she didn't recognize. It was a single key attached by a small chain to a red ceramic apple bearing the initial "S."

"It's okay. It's on the house. Mind if I sit here?" Without waiting for her answer, the rotund, bald man squeezed himself into the booth, to sit across from her.

She sipped her coffee and wondered if she knew him. She couldn't remember.

He smiled. "Bad roads out there. Are you driving far?"

"Driving? I don't think I'm driving . . . . I'm walking . . . ." She brought her hand to her forehead in confusion and her fingers touched on a painful swollen spot.

"That's a nasty bruise you've got there. It's turning blue. How'd you get that? You look like you've been through something. What happened?"

She brushed her hair out of her eyes with a shaking hand, but she couldn't think of anything to say.

"Are you all right, Ma'am?" he asked kindly.

"No, I don't think I am. I'm so cold . . . . My head hurts . . . ." She felt like crying but held it together.

"Where are you walkin' to? This is a busy highway."

"I . . . don't . . . know."

"Well, if you're lost, maybe I can help you. Where are you from?"

Terror pulsed through her at the answer she knew she had to give. "I . . . don't know that either . . . . I think I may have crashed my car . . . somewhere . . . . I think I remember that."

Chapter Thirty-three

Abram stomped his snowy boots on the porch mat outside the kitchen door. As soon as he stepped inside, he heard the hearty sound of Israel's laughter. *Sounds like he's getting along well with Mrs. Gregory.*

He hung his wet coat in the mud room and slipped out of his boots. He padded in stocking feet toward the family room, in the direction of the ruckus. There sat Israel in his wind-up canvas swing, and each time his bootied feet hit Mrs. Gregory's waiting hands, she said, "Ouch!" eliciting a great chuckle from his son.

"It sounds like somebody's having fun," he said, smiling broadly.

Turning her head toward him, Mrs. Gregory confirmed his words. "Oh, we've been having a great time. He studied me for a long time when I took him out of his crib, kept up the scrutiny when I fed him, but never cried a bit. He's such a happy boy."

"Have you heard from Sandra?" Abram lifted his boy out of the swing.

"Oh, I almost forgot. There was a call from a lady named Amber, about two hours ago. She said your wife hadn't arrived yet . . . ."

Her words were interrupted by the ringing of the telephone, and Abram handed Israel to Mrs. Gregory and strode quickly toward it, his concern turning to fear.

The State Police had found a white Lexus with the driver's side crumpled against a tree on Route 422. The driver was not there, but a woman's purse left on the floor held the identification of Sandra Goodman. In a small pocket on the outside of the purse was a cell phone.

Abram leaned against the wall to steady himself. The roar in his head drowned out the laughter of his son. Mrs. Gregory's worried voice brought him back.

"Is something the matter, Mr. Goodman? Has something happened to Mrs. Goodman?"

He tried to keep his voice steady but failed. "Her wrecked car was found without her in it. I hope you can stay with Israel. I need to meet the police at the scene of the accident. It's about forty-five minutes from here."

"Yes, I'll just call my husband and let him know. Don't you worry about a thing. I'll give Israel his supper and a bath and put him to bed. Oh, I do hope your wife is all right."

Abram frantically searched for footprints that led away from the abandoned car. With him were three policemen, Hank, and Pete. From indentations in the snow beside the open passenger door, it looked as though someone had crawled up the bank that led back to the highway; but, from there, the footprints had been beaten into obscurity by traffic.

"Let's search the woods. It shouldn't be too difficult with no leaves on the trees," the younger of the policemen suggested.

"I don't see much point in it," his partner said. "You can see that she scrambled up that bank. There are no footprints leading into the woods. But let's have a look, just in case."

"If she had enough strength to climb a bank, why didn't she call me? Why would she leave her cell phone behind, unused?" In the grip of fear, Abram's voice shook. "Do you suppose she wrestled the wheel away from someone who had abducted her? Could someone have dragged her out of here?"

"Don't let your imagination drive you crazy, Mr. Goodman. There's one set of footprints and two sets of skid marks—probably from a pair of knees—going up that bank." The policeman pointed as he spoke.

"But maybe the footprints aren't hers. Maybe somebody carried her or dragged her off to God knows where." Unaccustomed to hysteria, Abram now felt that he was on the brink.

He had called Mrs. Gregory several times, for possible news of his wife, but there was none. He knew that if Sandra had been able to call him, she would have. And if she had *not* been able, she should be here, in the car or nearby. The possibilities overwhelmed Abram, and he found that he was trembling with fear.

Hank and Pete walked the road, looking down into the ravine that hedged the highway. They didn't say why, but Abram knew. They were looking to see if Sandra's body had been thrown down the bank, or if she had been hit by a car if she had tried to walk away.

Full darkness had descended, and the beams from large flashlights carried by the searchers crisscrossed the shadows of bare trees that striped the snow-filled woods. The men were silent as they searched, listening intently for the smallest sound of a woman's voice.

Only Abram paused and called periodically, "Sandra? Sandra? Can you hear me, Sandra?" The timbre of his voice was changed by terror that she could not answer him.

Another male voice broke the silence, not calling for Sandra, but for Abram. "Mr. Goodman! Mr. Goodman!" An out-of-breath trooper ran towards him. "The station just radioed and said they've got a woman who could be your wife."

Abram did not feel the branches that whipped his face as he ran, following the officer to the police car. A voice crackled on the radio. "A guy from a diner brought her in. She's got a nasty contusion on her forehead and seems to be disoriented. We've called emergency to let them know we're bringing her over."

"What hospital? Tell them I'll meet them there." Relief flooded Abram as he ran to his vehicle. *Thank God. Thank God. She's alive!*

She had been sitting up in bed, trying to comb her shoulder-length hair with a little black comb that had been given her by a nurse.

"Here, I brought some things from your vanity," he said. "You'll have an easier time with your own hairbrush. I brought your makeup bag, too, just in case you feel like . . . and some clean clothes, if they say you can come home today." As if it were an after-thought, he placed a vase of pink roses on her nightstand. "And these. I brought you these. I know how much you like pink roses . . . . They're hard to find this time of year."

She took the silver hair brush and knew that he wanted her to say something. "Thank you, it's very nice of you . . . ."

Then he said the name he had used with her last night. "Sandra. How are you feeling, Honey? How did you sleep?" He leaned in to kiss her forehead.

"I . . . I'm sorry . . . I feel . . . tired . . . ." She tried not to cringe at the touch of his lips and of his warm hand on hers. "The roses. They're beautiful." She wanted to offer him something, and those were the words she found.

He removed his jacket and threw it on a chair. He wet his lips, and she saw that he struggled with some emotion she could not name. "I brought something else for you," he said. He picked up his jacket and withdrew an object from a pocket. It was a picture in a silver frame. He offered it to her.

Holding it in her hands, she saw that it was a picture of a man and a woman who smiled brightly. In the woman's arms was a baby. She looked at it blankly at first; then she laid a finger on the man in the photo. "This is you," she said, keeping her eyes on the picture.

"And this is you," he said, pointing to the woman beside the man in the picture. "And you're holding our son, Israel."

She raised her eyes to look at the man's face again. His gaze was tender, expectant. "I'm sorry," she said. "I didn't know you had a son."

Chapter Thirty-five

"Look at the woman in these pictures. Now look at yourself in the mirror. What do you see?" Virginia Gradwell, neuro-psychologist, sat calmly, waiting for Sandra to respond.

The patient sighed impatiently. "We've been going over these pictures for days now. People I'm supposed to know have been paraded into my room at the clinic. They all seem like nice people, but I just don't know them."

"Answer my question. What do you see, looking at the woman in this picture and the woman in the mirror."

"I see a woman who looks like me, only she's better looking than I am."

"And who is this good looking woman?"

"I've been told her name is Sandra Goodman."

"Why do you think she's better looking than you?"

"Well, for one, she's smiling. For two, she doesn't have dark circles under her eyes like I do."

"Who are you, if not Sandra Goodman?"

"I don't know. Sometimes I look at her picture and think of her as someone I used to know, someone I haven't seen for a long time. But why can't I remember?"

"You know why. Tell me why you can't remember."

"Oh, for God's sake, are you going to make me say it again?" Sandra shifted irritably in her chair.

"The people who love you say that you're beginning to sound like yourself again instead of some terrified rabbit."

The therapist smiled and annoyingly tapped a pen on her desk pad. "How does a rabbit sound?" Sandra's voice dripped with sarcasm.

Dr. Gradwell laughed aloud. "You've got me there. Okay, that was a dumb comparison. How about instead of some scared nervous-Nelly?"

"Okay, okay, so what did you want me to recite again? Oh, right, why I can't remember. Here goes: I had a head injury, in an accident. I drove a big white car. I lost control of it on icy roads and crashed it down an embankment and into a tree. I was very cold. That's the last thing I remember. The end."

"Sandra, that's your name, you *are* going to remember. It will just take more and more irritating sessions like this to help you develop the brain patterns that are there but traumatized. I'm going to send you home. You can't live at this clinic forever."

"Oh, my God. You're going to send me home with that man who says he's my husband? Why can't I go with the woman who says she's my sister? I'd feel more comfortable with her."

"Because you haven't been living with her for years. She is not your reality. Yes, she's your sister, but you have a husband and a son. That's your reality. I want you to be immersed in it. I'm going to call your husband in now. Ready?"

"Ready as I'll ever be, I guess. I'm not afraid of him, you know."

"That's progress. At first you were." Dr. Gradwell rose to open the door.

Abram and Sandra sat side by side just like a couple. Dr. Gradwell adjusted her blue-framed glasses and spoke mostly to Abram, the patient noticed.

"There's no brain damage beyond the concussion, which will heal itself, in time, with rest. Maybe we've been working her too hard, over-stimulating when the brain needs rest."

"I'm right here, you know. You don't have to talk about me as though I'm not here." The patient's feisty words evoked smiles from the therapist and her supposed-husband.

"You're right, Sandra. I apologize. Let me start again. Familiar surroundings will work to stimulate your memory, Sandra. At least that's my hope. And you, Mr. Goodman, need to be patient with the patient. I think she senses your anxiety and it rubs off on her. Is that right, Sandra?"

"I wish you'd stop with the 'Sandra, Sandra, Sandra.' But, yes, he pushes and pushes and when I can't remember he gets angry." She glared at the therapist as she spoke.

"Now you're talking about *me* as though I'm not here. Say it to me, if you have something to say. Look at me and say it." It was the first time Abram had said anything even mildly confrontational to her. "And I do not get 'angry.' I get . . . frustrated."

Undaunted, she turned her head to face him. "Okay, Abram. You give me a headache when you start pushing things and people at me and demanding that I remember them. I want you to stop that. I'll go home with you, but I want it understood that you are to leave me alone—in every way—just let me observe, just give me a space to relax and see if it all comes back to me."

"Deal," he said and reached out to shake her hand. After the shake, he held on to it. "When can I take her home, Doctor Gradwell?"

"Tomorrow."

"Tomorrow and tomorrow and tomorrow creeps in this petty pace day by day . . . ." The patient said, finishing it off with, "William Shakespeare, Macbeth, Act V, scene V."

Both the therapist and her supposed husband applauded, embarrassing her.

"What's the big deal?" Sandra Goodman asked. "So I like Shakespeare."

Chapter Thirty-six

Abram tapped "end call" on his I-phone. "Now what am I supposed to do?" he asked aloud, though no one was with him in his hotel room near the clinic.

He sat on the edge of the bed and rubbed his hands over his face and through his hair. Again, he spoke aloud. "I really don't want to do this, but I don't see that I have a choice." He punched Hannah's landline number into the phone, wondering if she'd be home or working at the bakery where she'd taken a job a couple of months ago.

After two rings, she picked up. She seemed startled that it was he who had called. "What's wrong? How is Sandra?" He could hear genuine concern in her voice.

"Well, she's less agitated, that's for sure, but she . . . still can't remember. I hope I'm not interrupting anything."

"No, I was just ironing my ugly pink uniform . . . for the bakery, you know."

"Look, that's what I need to talk to you about. They're letting Sandra go home tomorrow, in hope that a familiar setting will help revive her memory."

"That's good, isn't it?"

Abram squeezed his eyes shut at the thought of what he was about to ask. "Well, there's a problem. I just got off the phone with Mrs. Gregory. She says she can't commit to taking care of Israel indefinitely."

"Oh. What are you going to do?"

"I thought about putting him in daycare, but it breaks my heart to do that, and, how is Sandra going to remember him if she hardly sees him?" His question needed no answer. In the silence that followed, he guessed that she knew what was coming. "I know it's asking a lot since you've started a new job, but would you consider coming . . . coming back . . . temporarily? I don't want to introduce anyone new into the scene and confuse Sandra." He heard the sharp intake of her breath and held his own. "It wouldn't be forever," he was quick to add. "Just until Sandra . . . ." Despite his best efforts, his voice broke and he couldn't go on.

"Don't worry," Hannah said. "I'll help you. I don't like the bakery anyhow."

Chapter Thirty-seven

As they circled to a stop in front of the handsome house he said was their home, Sandra gazed at it and felt nothing. He came around and opened the car door for her and took her small bag from the back. Out of nowhere a handsome, silver Sheltie was at their feet, barking and jumping for attention. Without hesitation, Sandra went down on one knee to put her arms around the neck of the dog that was so obviously glad to see her.

The words were out of Sandra's mouth before she could register a thought. "Hey, sweet boy! How's my sweet boy?" She stroked the dog's luxurious fur and looked into his gold-flecked black eyes. She rose and gave Abram the first genuine smile she had given him since before the accident.

"The welcome home committee," he said, grinning broadly and kissing her cheek.

Embarrassed, she said, "I like animals."

"No, not particularly, but you like *this* animal." He spoke with confidence, as though he knew her better than she knew herself. It annoyed her.

"Down, Laddie," he said. The dog obeyed and walked calmly up the porch steps and into the house with them.

He took her coat gently from her shoulders and laid it on a chair in the foyer. She let her eyes travel up the chain of an ornate chandelier to the vaulted ceiling above the staircase balcony. "It's very beautiful," she said, as though she were a guest seeing it for the first time.

The boy she remembered from clinic visits burst through a pair of blue, louvered café doors. He held out a large red valentine heart he said he had made for her.

"You're Joey?" she asked, and her question seemed to silence the boy. He backed away in confusion to stand beside his mother, the pretty blonde woman who had also visited her at the clinic.

Only the blue-merle Sheltie dared to touch her, rubbing against her legs in an affectionate way that seemed familiar to her.

"You remember Hannah?" the man asked. "She's been our housekeeper since we were married." She looked at the blushing blonde woman standing shyly beside the boy. Something about the plain white apron she wore stirred in Sandra's memory. She stared at it.

"Hello, Sandra. It's good to have you home," the housekeeper was saying. "Israel's in his swing."

They moved to a homey kitchen filled with good smells, and Sandra meekly followed them. She recognized the baby who kicked excitedly when she bent over him to say, "Hello, Israel." He was the baby they had brought to the clinic, several times, the baby whose pictures had been shown to her over and over again. They said she was his mother.

He reached for her, repeating, "Mum, Mum, Mum." Sandra felt her throat constrict with a need to cry, but she couldn't make herself pick up the child. The man bent, took the child from the swing and offered him to her. Obediently, she held him. She felt nothing except his little hands tugging at her hair. After several awkward minutes, with the man and the housekeeper expectantly watching her, she handed him to the housekeeper.

The man couldn't hide his disappointment, but he tried to sound cheerful as he said, "I'll show you around the rest of the house."

Everywhere she looked she saw comfortable opulence. *My "husband" must be rich.* "Do I have to share a bed with you?" she asked as he took her into what he said was "our room." She folded her arms and waited for an answer.

"I thought about sleeping in my old room," he said, "but the therapist said it would be best to go back to what you were used to . . . before . . . when . . . . Don't worry. I won't force myself on you. It's a king-size bed. You won't have to touch me . . . unless you want to."

She believed him. For some reason, she knew he could be trusted. He was a gentle man. She nodded her assent. *He's very good looking. I could do worse.*

After a pot roast dinner served by the housekeeper who left them alone and retreated to the kitchen to feed Israel in his high chair, Abram asked her if she wanted to watch television or go through picture albums in the family room.

"Honestly," she said, pushing her hair back from her face, "I'd really just like to have a shower and go to bed. I can find my way . . . . You don't have to . . . ."

He was on his feet. "I'm bushed, too. I'll read for a while. That's what we used to do, read in bed for a while. I'll show you the book you were reading . . . . Oh, wait, you're not supposed to read 'til they give you the go-ahead."

Sandra took a soft white nightgown from the drawer that he showed her. He disappeared into the bathroom, and she looked blankly at the high bed with a beautiful, velvet patchwork quilt that he had turned down. Her eyes moved to a wedding picture on the bureau. In it Abram Goodman wore a tuxedo and smiled into the face of his bride who wore a sleek, ivory satin suit. The woman in the picture tilted her head upward to return the man's smile. Their lips were just inches apart, the beginning of a kiss. She felt a twinge of envy of that woman.

He was back. He wore a pair of pajama bottoms, but his chest was bare. She still stood clutching the nightgown in her hands. "Would you like to undress in the bathroom?" he asked, his voice very gentle. "Your hair brush and the creams you use are all in there on the vanity . . . . Your toothbrush is the pink one. Everything on the left side of the room, towels and stuff, are yours. Mine are on the right . . . and your robe is behind the door."

She disappeared into the bathroom, passing him shyly. *Oh, my God, how am I going to get through this night, sleeping beside a virtual stranger?*

Chapter Thirty-eight

Abram stood with his arms bracing his body as he leaned over the bathroom sink. He lifted his head and looked into his own gray eyes in the mirror. He had lied to her. The therapist had said to let her sleep apart from him if she wished, so as not to frighten her. He desperately wanted Sandra to remember the nights they had shared in one another's arms. Yet, he had to admit his own sense of unfamiliarity with the woman in the other room.

Normally, he slept in his underwear, but now he pulled on a pair of pajama bottoms. He took a deep breath as he prepared to enter the bedroom.

A wave of pity washed over him as he saw her standing where he had left her. She looked small and afraid as she clutched the nightgown in her hands. She had not undressed. Laddie lay at her feet, protectively, seeming to understand that his mistress was not well.

When he spoke to ask her if she'd prefer to undress in the bathroom, she seemed startled at the sound of his voice. "Yes, thank you," she said and walked past him into the bathroom.

He lay on his side of the bed and listened to the sound of the shower. He tried to believe that when the door opened, she would emerge as Sandra, his wife, wearing her fluffy white terry robe and with her black hair tied up in a blue ribbon. She'd take off that robe and either be wearing nothing or a barely-there negligee. He smiled at the memory of her.

Just when he thought she had decided to spend the night in the bathroom, the door opened, and she hesitated before stepping out. She looked exactly like his wife. Her smooth black hair had been brushed 'til it shone. Her feet beneath the long white gown were bare, the toe nails painted a delicate pink. Timidly, she approached his side of the bed instead of walking around to the empty side.

"Do you . . . mind . . . may I use one of the other bedrooms? I feel so strange getting into bed with you . . . even if I'm supposed to be your wife . . . ." Her voice was just above a whisper.

He reached for her hand and drew her closer to the bed. "Please sleep here," he said. "I promise I won't ask anything but to lie beside you. I won't even touch you. If you awake confused or afraid, I'll be here."

She withdrew her hand from his and walked soundlessly to the other side of the bed. He held the covers up in a welcoming fashion, and she climbed in to lie beside him, with a generous space between them.

Laddie jumped up on the bed and lay at her feet, just as he always had.

"Laddie always slept at your feet. Do you mind?"

"No . . . it's comforting to know that this dog has a bond with me. Even if I don't remember it, we must have been close."

"So were we, Darling. So were we." He handed her *The Husband's Secret.* This is the book you were reading, but do you want me to download an audio-version of it on your Kindle until they say you can read again?"

"Thank you," she said, "but shouldn't I go to another bedroom to listen so I won't be keeping you awake? Or are there headphones?"

She sounded hopeful, but he wasn't buying it. "That's okay. Why don't I just read to you?   You said it was really good, and I want to read it anyway."

She sighed. "Okay. I'd have to start at the beginning anyway."

Chapter Thirty-nine

March winds whipped strands of Hannah's long blonde hair across her eyes, but the scent of spring was in the air. She felt utterly contented walking silently beside Abram Goodman. They had left Israel in Sandra's care as they went for a walk. It was an experiment that Dr. Gradwell wanted to try, for an hour a day.

"What if she just sits there, ignoring the baby?" Abram worried.

"She won't. She understands that she's in charge."

"I don't know why you're so confident about that," he said, outpacing her so that she had to take longer strides to keep up. "In the month since Sandra's been home, she sits passively most of the time, just petting Laddie. She seems perfectly okay with letting you take care of Israel as well as the house."

"Oh, she offered to fold towels the other day and she pared potatoes for dinner last night."

"What about Israel? I haven't seen her pay much attention to him, have you?"

Hannah had hoped to avoid that question. "Sometimes she comes and stands by me when I'm bathing him, changing his diaper, or feeding him. I always ask her if she'd like to give him his bath. She says, 'Oh, no, I've never bathed a baby.' I came right out and told her 'You've been taking care of this baby since he was a newborn.'"

"So you don't see total indifference to Israel? She shows some interest in him?"

"Yes, I'd say she is more interested in him than she lets on." Hannah wondered why she was pretending that this was true. She sighed and thought about it. *I want Abram to be happy, and if this little white lie makes him feel better, that's what's important to me.*

"Well, bully for Israel," Abram said, smirking. "He's getting better treatment than I am. Should we go back now?"

"We've only been gone for ten minutes. Let's walk over to see if the ice is off the pond. And, speaking of Israel, he does the cutest things . . . ."

She noticed that Abram laughed in spite of himself as she filled his mind with pictures of his son's mounting accomplishments.

They opened the kitchen door to find Sandra standing at the kitchen sink letting warm water flow over the bottle she was preparing for Israel who sat in his high chair scattering dry Cheerios as he fussed, impatient for his bottle. She stood as though mesmerized by the stream of water that hit her hand.

She turned her head to Abram and said, "Waters. Is my name Waters?"

Joy lit Abram's face as he took the bottle from her and handed it to Hannah. "Yes, Honey, your maiden name was Waters . . . Sandra Waters!" He embraced her, burying his face in her hair, and she did not push him away. She put her own arms around his waist and stayed in his arms.

Hannah Miller said nothing. She turned her attention to Israel whose whining had turned to crying. "Oh, come here, hungry little one . . . ." She, too, felt like crying.

Chapter Forty

Occasionally they awakened in one another's arms, entwining themselves as they slept. Abram kissed the top of Sandra's head as she lay with her cheek against his chest. Asleep, she snuggled against him with one of her legs thrown over his thigh.

He had not attempted to make love to her, sensing that this would drive her away from him. Obediently, she had slept by his side during the weeks since he had been home, at first lying rigidly on her side of the bed; but eventually she had relaxed and touched him as she slept.

Abram lay quietly, unwilling to ruin the pleasure of having her nestled against him. He thought of the break-through the day before, with her remembering her maiden name. She had seemed just as happy about it as he was. He had embraced her and she had not resisted. She had even returned the embrace. He sighed audibly, wanting her now. He had never stopped wanting her, but he feared doing anything that would make her afraid of him. She trusted him, and he didn't want to lose that.

She stirred in his arms and moved her hand to touch him. He barely breathed, as he felt her small hand slipping inside his pajamas, her fingers intimately stroking him. As she shifted her head, her face was now upturned, her eyes closed. He bent his head and kissed her lips. He moaned with pleasure as she returned his kiss.

Suddenly, her eyes flew open, and she pulled away from him, sat up and swung her legs to her side of the bed. He lay very still, his heart throbbing with need. When he could speak, he said, impulsively, "You started it."

She sat with her back to him, seeming to consider his words. "I . . . guess I did. I'm sorry. I was dreaming."

"Don't be sorry on my account. I was thoroughly enjoying . . . hey, wait a minute! Did you say you were *dreaming?*" He sat up and put his hand on her shoulder, turning her to face him. "Sandra, do you know what this means? Dr. Gradwell said dreaming would be sign that your memory is returning! Tell me, Hon, what did you dream?"

"Isn't it pretty obvious?" she asked, and her shyness touched him, though the Sandra he knew and loved had not been at all shy about sex.

He risked pulling her into position to rest against him again. "Well, just so it was *me* you were dreaming about."

She said nothing. He felt sure that if it had been otherwise, she would have told him.

Chapter Forty-one

Sandra sat on the front porch, despite the chilliness of the day. Her eyes traveled over the wicker porch furniture, the circular driveway, and to the white garage and barns in the distance. Winter hills were brown canvases streaked with brush strokes of the gold-green grass of early spring. Framing it all was the white fencing that surrounded the horses and cattle grazing there. The air was fresh and cool. Pulling the yellow cashmere cardigan she had found in Sandra Goodman's closet more closely around her, she breathed deeply and tried to remember a time when all of this had been hers.

Fragments of memories had been flashing in and out of her mind for several days now, and she tried to conjure them up and piece them together. Abstract images of young people sitting in rows had crossed her mind from time to time, and, when she confided this to Dr. Gradwell, whom she saw every two weeks, she had been reminded that she had been a teacher, a profession she had given up for motherhood.

She knew she was supposed to be the adoptive mother of the baby within the house, and she wondered if she had not had time to bond with him before the accident.

"Where'd he get a name like Israel?" she had asked Abram.

"It was your idea, and it's my first name. My real name is Israel Abram."

Beyond thinking that Israel was cute, she felt little else toward him, except the anxiety that she should be feeling love for him. When her babysitting hour ended each day, she was relieved that she could give him back to Hannah, who was obviously very fond of Israel. Hannah. What was it about that apron that she sometimes wore? It intrigued her, but she didn't know why. She had been told that Hannah had been her housekeeper and, until very recently, had lived with her son Joey in the small cottage a short distance from the main house. She knew that Hannah had no husband, despite the fact that she had a son. As she watched Hannah tend Baby Israel, at times a vague image of Hannah-with-child came to her mind.

~ ~ ~

One day she had asked Hannah, "Did I know you when you were pregnant with Joey?"

"Yes" had been the housekeeper's brief reply as she sprayed something on a white cloth and used it to dust the mantel in the family room.

"Where did you get that big white apron you wear when you're cooking?"

"It was my mother's. I miss her, and it makes me feel close to her to wear it."

"Did your mother die?"

"No. But she didn't want to see me any more when I refused to marry Joey's father." Silently, Hannah replaced each item she had removed from the mantel.

"I'm sorry to hear that. I miss my mother, too. She died when I was . . . very young."

Hannah paused in her dusting and looked at her for a long moment. "Is that something you remember or did they tell you that?"

Confused, Sandra said, "I'm not sure . . . . No, I think I remember that. And I remember a young red-headed girl crying in my arms."

"You know who that would be, don't you?"

"I guess that would be a memory of Kendra!" Sandra said with enthusiasm.

Hannah just kept dusting, seeming unimpressed by Sandra's memory break-through.

~ ~ ~

Recalling that conversation with Hannah, Sandra pondered whether her relationship with the housekeeper had been friendly. *Sometimes . . . I feel that she didn't like Sandra . . . me. I wonder why.*

She turned her thoughts to "the man," the way she referred to him in her thoughts. Abram. His tenderness and his patience touched her deeply. She wished she could remember being his wife. He had, from time to time, tried to tell her all that they had meant to one another, frustrated, trying to remember for her.

She always begged him to say no more, even as she knew her saying it hurt him. His gray eyes could hide no emotion. *If I ever fell in love, it would be with a man like Abram.*

She blushed to remember her near intimacy with him that morning. *What would I have done if he had insisted? After all, there is the proof of the wedding picture on the bureau. I am his wife . . . whether I remember it or not.*

Yet she knew he would never insist. "He is a gentle man," she said aloud to no one but herself. "A very dear, very gentle man."

At dinner that evening she felt his eyes upon her, and she looked up from her plate to meet his gaze. She felt her cheeks grow warm as he smiled a slow, knowing smile at her. She bent her head to hide her face behind the curtain of her dark hair. She knew he was remembering that morning. She was remembering it, too.

The housekeeper's lilting voice interrupted the moment that had passed between them. "Oh, Daddy, you should have seen Israel today. He is trying to crawl! He gets up on all fours and sways as though he knows he can do it, if only he could figure out how."

As Abram turned his attention from her to the housekeeper, Sandra thought, *I'm glad he isn't thinking about this morning now . . . or am I feeling a bit . . . left out? That's supposed to be my baby they're talking about . . . why didn't she tell me instead of Abram?* Sandra sawed ruthlessly through the steak on her plate.

Chapter Forty-two

She awoke during the night to the touch of his hands caressing her body beneath her nightgown. Her breath came fast, and she did not want him to stop. Her body burned with need as she returned his kisses. She knew he had been asleep when he had begun but he was awake now.

He said the name of his wife. "Sandra, Sandra, please let me make love to you."

He waited for her response, searching her face in the semi-darkness of the room, until she whispered, "Yes."

Only then did he pause to strip the pajama bottoms from his body, pull her nightgown over her head and cast it aside. She abandoned herself to his touches, and when she moaned her pleasure and her impatience, he stretched his body over hers. She let him carry her to the pinnacle of pleasure that made her heart thunder in her ears.

Dimly, she heard his rhythmic voice saying again and again, "Tell me you remember . . . . Tell me you remember . . . ."

With the dawn of day, she lay quietly beside him, listening to the evenness of his breathing. His pent-up fury spent, he slept deeply, and she wondered if she should wake him, wondered if he had meetings to attend . . . .

For a moment, she felt a rush of panic. *Oh, my God, we didn't use any . . . protection!* Then she remembered that Sandra

Goodman had adopted her baby. They had told her that, but she had never asked why. She resolved to ask Dr. Gradwell the next time she saw her. Slipping out of bed, she stood naked and looked at the nightgown crumpled at her feet. She stepped over it and walked to the bathroom.

She bathed in silver streams of water with her eyes closed, remembering the controlled passion in his touch. *Sandra Goodman is a lucky woman, with a man like that. I wonder what he and I will say to one another now, now that this has happened.* . . .

As she dried her body with a soft white towel, she suddenly became aware of his nude form standing in the doorway. She jumped to cover her own nakedness, as though her body had not been his throughout the night. Embarrassed, she looked away from him.

He casually reached for a towel and wrapped it around himself. Then he moved to kiss her. "Good morning," he said.

"Good morning . . . I . . . I'm through with the bathroom . . . if you want it." She heard the nervousness in her own voice. Stepping delicately past him, she hurried into the bedroom to dress.

She opened a drawer and took out underwear, a bra, and jeans, all of which fit her perfectly. From the closet she selected a white silk blouse and covered it with the yellow cashmere cardigan she favored. She shoved her bare feet into brown leather loafers and sat at the bedroom vanity. The woman in the mirror looked . . .

relaxed. Even a bit happy. She brushed her hair and pulled it up into a pony tail. On her lips she applied a raspberry lip gloss. Putting down the blush and powder she had been about to use, she realized that her face already glowed with . . . some emotion she dared not name.

Abram came into the room, leaned down to kiss her cheek as she sat at the vanity, and locked eyes with her in the mirror. He said, "You're beautiful" before going to stand before an armoire to select clothing for the day. She noted he had chosen a black turtleneck, slacks and a gray sports coat instead of his usual casual attire.

"My, you look nice," she said shyly. "Do you have somewhere important to be today?"

"Yes, I have a meeting over lunch in the city. But I have time to have breakfast with you . . . if you'll join me?" He alluded to the fact that she seldom accompanied him for breakfast these days, keeping to herself.

But today would be different, she decided. "Yes, I'm ravenous," she said, blushing at what her words implied. He only smiled.

The housekeeper seemed rattled when she appeared in the kitchen with Abram. "Oh," Hannah said, sounding annoyed. "When I heard the shower, I only made one omelet . . . I didn't know . . . . Just give me a minute."

"No problem," Abram said. "We're a bit late this morning . . . but we're in no hurry." Turning his attention to his son, he hesitated, and Sandra saw that the boy's hands and face were sticky. His father patted his head instead of picking him up. "You're a pretty messy boy, Son, so you're going to stay right where you are. What's that you say? 'Goo-goo wa-wa'? I agree totally."

He pulled a chair out for Sandra and brought the coffee carafe to the table. Pouring coffee for both of them, he ignored Hannah's frustrated scurrying about and talked about the sunny morning and the coming of spring.

Warming to the topic of spring, Sandra commented on the hyacinths that bordered the porch. "And I see tulips starting. Who planted those? Who's the flower gardener around here?"

"Those were planted by my mother. Remember, I told you that this used to be my parents' house. My mom put in hundreds of bulbs. I should be digging them up each year and separating them, but . . . ." He shrugged as though to indicate his own irresponsibility.

"Well, they seem to be doing splendidly, just as they are," she said. "But maybe I'll add some annuals to the beds . . . if you don't mind."

She saw that her words pleased him. It was the first time she'd indicated that there might be some permanence to her stay.

"You do as you like," he said, digging into the fresh omelet Hannah had placed before him. "This is your house, and the flower beds are your domain. Or you can hire somebody to take care of them."

Sandra noticed that Hannah had given her the slightly dried-up, only slightly warm omelet that had been made earlier. She said nothing and pretended not to notice the slight.

"This is delicious, Hannah," she said, and the housekeeper blushed furiously, before saying that she was going to take Israel upstairs to dress him for the day.

As soon as Hannah had left the kitchen, Abram took Sandra's hand. "Tell me," he said, "who did you make love with during the night?"

His bluntness surprised her. "You," she said simply.

"But did you remember . . . the way we were . . . or was it new?"

"New," she said. At the look of disappointment on his face, she hastened to add, "New but very nice."

He dropped her hand and gave her an imploring look. "God, Sandra, please don't tell me that I was just . . . some guy. That you were just enjoying . . . the act." The mounting desperation in his voice moved her.

Now she reached for the hand he had withdrawn. "Listen to me, Abram. I can't lie to you and say that I remember what we were, but I *can* tell you that I've grown very fond of you; you've been so kind and patient . . . ."

"Fond? You're 'fond' of me so you had sex with me? You've told me you're 'fond' of Dr. Gradwell. Are you going to have sex with her, too?"

He left her sitting there alone. She used her napkin to mop the tears that flowed from her eyes as she felt the effect of his angry words. This was a first.

Chapter Forty-three

Dr. Gradwell listened to the uncontrolled sobs of Sandra Goodman and made a note: "Passivity replaced by strong emotion." After a while, she asked, "How do you explain this sorrow, this grief? Why are you grieving, Sandra?" She sat back, entwined her fingers over the waistline of her white coat and waited.

Sandra reached for more tissues from the pink-flowered box on Dr. Gradwell's desk. "Because I can't bring Sandra back to life. He wants her so badly, but he doesn't want . . . *me!*" Her tears began afresh.

"Oh? And who are you, if not Sandra?"

"I'm a stranger to myself. I'm lost. I'm a woman with a head full of puzzle pieces that won't come together."

"Tell me about the 'pieces,' not what you've been told, but what you actually remember, even if they are disjointed."

Obediently, Sandra took a long shuddering breath, squared her shoulders and recited the few pieces of memory that she had: the rows of students, the name "Waters," the white apron, a pregnant Hannah, the white car, the accident . . . ."

"Can you put these memories into chronological order for me, Sandra?"

Sandra paused to consider; then she said, "I think I already have."

"Wouldn't your maiden name come before the rows of students?"

"No, because I see it, 'Waters,' written on a green chalkboard."

"Very good. And now describe for me your life, as it is now. Include any emotions you may be willing to share."

"Well, I live in a big white house, a beautiful house, in the country. I live with Abram Goodman, his son Israel, the housekeeper Hannah, and her son Joey. I've met the workmen who come in for lunch on weekdays. I tend the baby for Hannah one hour a day. The rest of the time I sit on the porch and read or go for short walks with Laddie; that's the dog. Lately, now that the weather has turned nice, Abram asks me to go for walks with him. I enjoy that time with him. He tells me how he came to take over the farm, what he's changed, what he's left the same. He tells me about his investments. Twice he has taken me to the theater, along with Kendra, the red-headed woman who says she is my sister. I'm very comfortable around her. I like her a lot."

"And Abram? How have your feelings changed toward him?"

"At first, I felt nothing except that I thought he was a good looking man, a very well-mannered man. He seems to get it now that his constant pressure to remember this or that drove a wedge between us. He stopped that and I began to enjoy his company. He's very attractive. At first, when he wanted me to sleep in the same bed with him, I really didn't want to. Then I realized that if I woke up afraid, in a strange place, he'd be right there. He told me

I could trust him, and I have. He's never forced himself on me, but
. . . ." She paused and couldn't suppress a smile.

"But . . . are you now intimate with him, or considering it?"

"Not until two days ago. I mean, we were intimate, two days
ago."

"Oh? Would you like to say more about that?"

"He was . . . wonderful . . . . but now I think I've hurt him."
Her voice trembled again, and she stopped speaking to gain
control.

"How so? How have you hurt him?"

"Because I admitted to him that it wasn't 'my husband' I made
love with."

"Who was it?"

"The man I've known for about two months."

Dr. Gradwell was silent for a long moment, as she let Sandra
collect her thoughts. "Tell me about that man. I don't mean how
he was in bed, of course not, but how you feel about him. Dig
deep. What does he mean to you? Would you be happy if you
never saw him again?"

Sandra's eyes filled with tears again. "Oh, God, I think about
him all the time. I think I'm in love with him. I wish we could
just go on from here, start anew, and forget about this past that I
can't remember anyhow. Do you think that's possible?"

"Israel is part of the package, too, you know. How do you feel
about *him?*"

"That's the sticking point," Sandra Goodman said. "I feel as though he is Abram's son, but not mine."

"Can you love him?"

"I don't know. He's a perfectly adorable baby. I just don't know why, when I look at him, I feel nothing maternal. I'm just a babysitter and, well, Hannah is his mother."

Dr. Gradwell maintained the silence she had promised Abram Goodman, against her better instincts. He had not wanted Sandra to know that the housekeeper was the surrogate mother of Israel Goodman. Dr. Gradwell had reluctantly agreed, but now she pursed her lips and thought while she watched Sandra dab at her eyes with a tissue. *Soon, I must have a talk with this woman's husband. It was a completely dumb idea to bring Hannah back into his house, but he couldn't be persuaded otherwise. Now this is a mess he will have to explain, and she will have to accept if they are to have a future.*

"That's enough for today, Sandra. I must say that I feel that you are on the verge of something. You are almost ready to remember. Now we have to deal with whatever it is that is blocking that. At this point, it is not a physical block."

"You think it's psychological? Something holding me back from taking up my life again?" Sandra looked confused.

"Yes, that's what I think. But don't worry, Sandra. We'll get to the bottom of it. You're making great progress."

Chapter Forty-four

On a rare night when Abram had to be away from home on business, Sandra slid apart the hangers that held the blouses, dresses and suits that hung in "her" closet. She observed their colors and textures, in an effort to glimpse the woman she once was. She tried to imagine the roles the woman had played.

When she pulled stylish suits from the closet, she conjured up the high school English teacher who had worn them. Though tailored, they were unmistakably feminine, with short fitted skirts that would have shown off her figure and legs.

When she and Abram had gone to the theater recently, Sandra had sorted through all of the dressy evening clothing, jewelry, even furs that were hers to wear. On his arm, dressed in a sexy, form-fitting long dress of black sequins, she had felt like the wife of an affluent, educated gentleman-farmer; but she felt like an imposter, too.

Daily, she wore jeans, sweaters, and blouses around the house. They were casual clothes but of the finest quality. Even the clothing she wore when she and Abram went horseback riding made her feel like royalty, the leather boots on her feet, supple and slightly worn.

Running her hands over cashmere sweaters in every hue, woolen blazers, and sheer blouses, she concluded that Sandra Goodman liked colorful and expensive clothing, and, from the rows of shoes lining the sides of her walk-in closet, she had loved shoes, lots of shoes, expensive shoes with purses to match.

She opened the jewelry box that sat atop the bureau. It held designer costume jewelry, but Abram had shown her diamond pendants, bracelets and earrings that were kept downstairs in a vault hidden behind a moveable panel in the family room.

"All of it is yours," he had said, holding the little door open for her. "Some of it came from my mother, but the rest are pieces that I bought for you. You look spectacular in diamonds, by the way."

She had already investigated the bureau drawers, especially the one that held swirls of sheer and lacy lingerie. Returning to it now, she ran her hands through piles of soft pastels and bold colors, concluding that Sandra Goodman had been sexy, a woman of many moods.

One drawer in particular had been dedicated to silken mounds of scanty intimate apparel obviously for entertaining her lover. Sandra Goodman, she understood, was confident about her body. Lingering over a sheer black lace nightgown, she somehow just knew that Sandra had worn this on her wedding night.

Her hand came upon an object hidden among the airy folds of the garments, and she withdrew a book with a silver and blue brocade cover. It appeared to be Sandra Goodman's diary. She closed the drawer, taking the diary with her. Sitting in the rocking chair, she settled back to read. *After all, it's my diary.*

"I have met the most interesting man . . . ." were the first words written in the flowery script that she recognized as her own.

Hours later, Sandra sat rocking soundlessly on the soft white carpet of the master bedroom, her head against the pillows of the comfortable chair. Her eyes were closed, but she still held the diary in her hand.

Now she understood. Hannah Miller was the biological mother of Abram's son. Israel was his, but he was also Hannah Miller's. *Why wasn't I told this? What did Abram have to gain by keeping it from me?*

Some objection gnawed at her mind, something not right about the whole situation in this house. Her head ached from reading, so she gave up trying to put her objection into words.

The next day, he was home in time for dinner. With new perspective, Sandra watched the two of them throughout the meal. They laughed at Israel and smiled fondly at one another as they took turns giving him bites of food from their own plates. Israel, Sandra observed, looked like his father, but the blonde hair on his head was like the housekeeper's.

As Abram helped Hannah clear the table, Sandra could hear their comfortable chatter coming from the kitchen. Later, she saw their hands touch as they passed the child between them.

Sandra withdrew to the family room and sat quietly, pondering the feelings that warred within her. She had felt left out, ignored. As the baby's adoptive mother, she was not really part of their threesome. *I must have agreed to this. The diary said having her as surrogate was my idea. I must have been out of my mind.* Now, she laughed bitterly at the irony of her last thought. *But Hannah was supposed to go. Why is she still here? What happened to that provision of the contract described in the diary? Did I change my mind? Somehow I can't imagine myself being that naïve.*

Her thoughts were interrupted when Abram sat down next to her on the couch and attempted to put his arm around her. He apparently sensed her renewed reserve and withdrew his arm.

"What's wrong?" he ventured.

"Nothing." She was unwilling to confront him with questions yet. She needed time to think.

"Are you afraid that I'll expect you to . . . have sex with me again?" he asked, folding his arms to let her know he wasn't going to try to touch her.

Her voice was icy. "No. You made it perfectly clear that you regretted it."

"Oh, so that's what's eating at you. I didn't say I regretted it. I loved it. I am just disappointed that . . . ."

"Please," she said, rising. "My head is throbbing. I'm going up to bed. I'd like some time alone. Could I ask that you sleep in another room?"

"Forever?" he asked, his coldness matching hers.

She didn't like the sound of "forever," so she gave herself some space. "No, just until I have some time to think things over."

"Okay. Goodnight, Sandra."

She did not reply.

Sandra Goodman woke up. Stretching, she opened her eyes to watch the morning sun dance off the tiny green and mauve flowers of the wallpaper Abram's mother had chosen for the master bedroom. She had thought many times of getting rid of the wallpaper in the house, but old-fashioned décor seemed so much a part of the memory of the woman whose house this used to be that she couldn't bring herself to do it.

She slid her arm across cool sheets as she reached for her husband. Apparently he had gone off to work, leaving her asleep, a realization that troubled her because she had awakened with a keen sense of longing for him. She had dreamed that she had gone on a journey, and as she saw him standing in fog, waiting for her plane to safely land, she couldn't wait to be with him again.

"Oh well," she said as she yawned and turned to look at the clock on her night stand. Nine o'clock. She bolted upright. "My God, what day is it? Am I late for work?" Then she realized with shock that she had not heard Israel. The monitor that should have been on her night stand wasn't there! That's why she hadn't heard her baby's morning cry. She jumped to her feet and ran toward the nursery.

Opening the door to a room decorated with Winnie the Pooh, she startled to find that Israel was not in his crib. Panic gripped her; then she heard the sounds of a woman's lilting voice accompanied by splashing water and a child's giggles. It came from the bathroom across the hall from the nursery. She made her way there, not sure why she was tip-toeing.

The door was partly open. Hannah Miller bent over the tub washing Israel's hair. She laughed and made shampoo mountains on his little head. "I think I've washed all the apple sauce from you hair, you silly boy."

Sandra stared. Why was Hannah here? And Israel was sitting up! She opened her mouth to speak but closed it again, as she sensed an inexplicable need for caution as some revelation was trying to break through the confusion in her mind. Unnoticed, she quietly eased her way back to her bedroom.

She sat on her bed while memories exploded in her mind like flashes of light in a darkened room. She felt her forehead for a lump and remembered the icy night when she had been driving alone—to visit her friend Amber.

She rose to look out the window and was shocked to see that it was no longer winter. The frozen landscape had been transformed by green grass and trees budding with the early leaves of spring. Picking up the small calendar she kept on her desk, she was stunned to see the pages turned to March. *I have lost two months of my life! I can't remember the last two months!* Shakily, she moved to sit on the edge of the bed again, trying to fathom the lost interim between her accident and the present.

She was startled by a light tap on her bedroom door, but, taking a deep breath, she said, "Come in."

Hannah, holding a freshly scrubbed Israel wrapped in a fluffy yellow towel, stood in the doorway. "You'd better get dressed, Sandra," the housekeeper said with some authority. "Don't forget that you have an appointment with Dr. Gradwell today, and Abram will be back about eleven o'clock to drive you . . . ."

Sandra tore her eyes away from the curly blond hair on Israel's head. His hair had grown! *He* had grown! She wanted to rush to him, to tear him out of Hannah's arms, but she could not move. Instead she felt a need to pretend . . . pretend that everything appeared normal to her.

She licked her lips. "Dr. Gradwell? Oh, all right. I'll . . . be ready." As she watched the door close behind Hannah, she wondered at her own instinctive wariness.

"Who is Dr. Gradwell?" she whispered quietly. "But, more importantly, why is Hannah Miller back in my house?"

Chapter Forty-five

Abram mounted the stairs, two at a time. "Sorry I'm late, Sandra. I'll be down in a minute; just let me change my clothes. Make me a sandwich, please, Hannah, and I'll eat it in the car."

He had rushed past Sandra with barely a glance. Like one whose homecoming has been ignored, Sandra felt hurt. Then she realized that he didn't know that she was "back." From the foyer, she relished the sight of him coming down the stairs, not looking at her as he rolled up his shirt sleeves; yet, she felt vaguely unsettled, as though she should be angry with him, but she didn't know why. Something haunted her mind, something that kept her from blurting out that she was back from wherever she had been. Something made her want to wait, to wait and to watch.

She studied his profile as he drove and wondered why he didn't reach over to touch her hand or to caress her knee occasionally, as he usually did. Probably sensing her eyes upon him, he turned his head and smiled as he turned up the music, but he didn't talk to her. She needed to hear his voice.

"What do you think of Dr. Gradwell?" she asked, hoping to get some clue as to what she should expect.

With his eyes on the road, he answered. "What do I think of Dr. Gradwell? What about her?" So Dr. Gradwell was a she.

"Do you think she's . . . competent?" Grasping for information, she tried not to give herself away.

He puffed out his cheeks and exhaled slowly as he contemplated her question. "Well, she has all the right credentials, but so far there hasn't been much of a change. But this is about you, not me. I thought you liked her."

"Oh . . . I . . . do. I just wondered what you thought."

Shrugging his shoulders, he put the car on cruise and settled back in his seat. "To be honest, Sandra, I don't know what to think anymore. Sometimes I think we're getting somewhere, and then . . . nothing really happens." He spoke as though she were not there. She heard the mixture of frustration and resignation in his voice.

"I'm sorry, Abe," she said genuinely. Whatever he had been through the past two months had taken its toll.

He looked at her abruptly, almost long enough to rear end the car ahead of them. "Did you just call me 'Abe'?" He sounded incredulous. "It was what you usually called me!"

"I guess I did," she answered cautiously, wondering what was so earthshaking about that.

"Well, I'd call *that* a breakthrough! Be sure to tell Dr. Gradwell about it." Now he reached across and patted her knee.

What on earth is he talking about? Break through? I wonder if I'm going to see a shrink.

Sandra eyed the tall, salt-and-pepper-haired woman in the white coat suspiciously. Her oversized blue-framed glasses looked ridiculous. If not for the white coat, Sandra would have taken her for . . . an eccentric school teacher, perhaps.

"And how have you been, Sandra?" The doctor relaxed in her chair as though they were two old friends getting reacquainted.

"Fine." It seemed like a safe answer.

"Just 'fine'? Are there any more pieces to the puzzle?"

Sandra knew she was in trouble now. "The . . . puzzle?"

Dr. Gradwell looked hard at Sandra who squirmed under her scrutiny. "Sandra, do you know who I am?"

"Dr. Gradwell."

"And why do you come to see me?"

Sandra licked her lips. "Because you're a fertility expert?"

"Now why would you make *that* guess? And it is a guess, isn't it?" When Sandra didn't answer, Dr. Gradwell added, "Are you remembering something?"

Sandra felt like a student who hadn't studied for the oral test. "I . . . used to see a lot of fertility doctors."

The doctor beamed as though Sandra had said something right. "Very good! I see we do have another piece to the puzzle! Anything else?"

Sandra took a very deep breath, in an effort to relax. With that breath, revelation impacted her. She had lost her memory after the accident. She had not known Abram or Israel or . . . *anybody!* This doctor had to be about that—a memory disorder specialist! Her shock must have been reflected on her face, because the doctor leaned forward expectantly. Sandra knew she had to give her something, but she was not ready to give her the truth.

"I . . . I called my husband 'Abe' today . . . ."

On the way home, they stopped at a restaurant, one of Sandra's favorites, for dinner. Without thinking, she ordered her usual. "Chicken Saltimbocca, please. Bleu cheese dressing, thank you."

She became aware of Abram studying her, so much so that he didn't hear the waitress asking him what *he* wanted. "Uh . . . I'll have a steak, medium rare, baked potato, and the house salad with . . . let's see . . . honey mustard dressing." Turning his attention back to Sandra, he asked, "Do you remember this place?"

"No," she lied.

He let out a sigh. "I was hoping you did, because you ordered your favorite here."

She laughed. "And you ordered yours." Too late, she realized she had tipped her hand.

He was delighted. "You may not remember the restaurant, but you're certainly remembering *us!* This is just great, Honey. I do believe you're coming back to me." He reached across the table and squeezed her hand.

Before bed, she showered, applied lotion and perfume to her body, tied her hair up with a blue ribbon and wrapped her fluffy terry cloth robe around her body.

"Your turn!" she said brightly to Abram who stood bare-chested, throwing dirty clothes down the chute.

He looked at her for a long moment and said, "I haven't seen your blue ribbon for a long time."

"Oh, I just like to keep damp hair off my neck until it dries." She wondered why he had mentioned her ribbon.

She heard the shower running and took this opportunity to sneak next door to the nursery. Opening the room to the dimly lit room, she stepped inside and looked down at her little son sleeping in his crib, lying on his back with his arms bent at the elbows, his open hands above his head. She bent to cover him with the blue blanket he'd kicked off. She felt that her heart would explode with love for him. On a small chest of drawers, a baby monitor blinked. Sandra realized the other half of it had to be downstairs, in the housekeeper's room. *I should have that monitor. Not her. I have lost two months of my baby's life.* Grief threatened to overwhelm her, and she backed silently out of the room.

The shower had stopped, but Abram was not yet in the room. Quickly, Sandra threw off her robe, opened her lingerie drawer, and picked up the topmost item, one of her sexiest nightgowns, the black lace one that was his favorite. She pulled it over her naked body and sat on her vanity stool and pretended to be filing her nails.

He stopped toweling his hair to stare at her again. "It's good to see you've given up that granny nightgown you've been wearing. This one is a big improvement. It was always my favorite."

She stopped herself from saying, "I know," and said, "It's getting too warm for the granny nightgown now."

He turned down the covers, got in bed and picked up his book from the nightstand.

She tried to think of a way to ask him the question that had been plaguing her since she had "come home." "Abe," she said, "how long did Hannah work at the bakery?"

She had tried to sound casual, but he behaved as though she had announced the coming of Christ. He laid down his book and looked at her in astonishment.

"You remember that? You remember that?"

"No, I mean, Hannah told me she used to work at a bakery. I was just wondering . . . ."

"Oh," he said, sounding disappointed. "She worked there just a few weeks. Then I asked her to come back here to take care of Israel . . . and you."

She turned away so he could not see the heat that had flooded her chest and her face. Returning to her vanity stool, she bent her head and brushed her hair furiously to hide the anger that she knew he'd see on her face.

In bed, she turned on her side with her back to him and stared into the darkness. He made no move to touch her. And she was glad. *He brought her back. The idiot brought her back and now . . . she's Israel's mother . . . in every way.* Hot tears wet her pillow, but she wouldn't reach for a tissue until his even breathing told her he was asleep.

Chapter Forty-six

Sandra paused on the stairs to watch Hannah slip a little blue hooded-sweatshirt over Israel's curly head and strap him into a stroller.

"We're going bye-bye, Israel, off to see Daddy at the barn. Won't that be nice? Daddy will let you pet the horses and the moo-cows, too . . . ." Hannah spoke in a sugary tone, unaware of the silent observer standing on the landing above the stairs.

She waited until Hannah had wheeled the stroller through the kitchen and out the kitchen door; then she went to the front porch to watch the housekeeper jauntily pushing the stroller in the driveway, toward the barn. Hannah's loose blonde hair blew in the breeze, and the pale yellow turtleneck she wore with tight jeans revealed every shapely curve of her body.

Moving to the end of the porch where she could see past the budding bittersweet vines that clung to it, Sandra stood behind them, to see but not be seen. She saw Abram pause on his way to the garage. He waited, smiling as he watched the approach of Hannah and the baby.

Rage and grief filled Sandra as she saw the intimate way they both bent over the child holding up his arms to Abram, who took him and carried him to the barn with Hannah tagging behind, pushing the empty stroller. *Time to pet the horses and the moo-cows, no doubt,* Sandra thought, wishing she could be part of it.

In the early afternoon, Hannah surprised Sandra by saying that she would be "going out for a while" and leaving Israel with her. She spoke as though this were a usual occurrence. Sandra was thrilled for a chance to have Israel to herself.

Alone with her little boy, Sandra picked him up from his playpen and hugged him to her body as she let her tears freely flow. Kissing him over and over again, she tried to smile even as she cried, not wanting to frighten him.

She carried him into the family room where most of his toys were kept and lay on the floor beside him, touching and talking to him. He returned her touches, patting her face and tugging on her hair.

"You've gotten so big, Sweetie. And do you remember your mommy, Israel? Mommy loves you so much . . . ."

After a while, she began to weep again, and she saw the trembling of his lower lip as he searched her face with troubled eyes. In an attempt to distract him from the tears she couldn't seem to stop, she said, "Oh, let's go get a cookie. Wouldn't you like a cookie?"

In his highchair, Israel gummed the elongated baby biscuit his mother had given him, smearing his face and babbling contentedly. Sandra had no idea when Hannah would return, and, knowing that she had to compose herself before that time, she disappeared momentarily into the nearby powder room to wash her face.

As she patted dry her reddened eyes, she became aware that Israel's baby sounds had turned to something else. He was choking! She flew to the kitchen and saw his face contorted in a soundless cry as he gagged.

Frantically, she pounded his back, trying not to hurt him, and, when that didn't work, stuck her finger into his mouth in an attempt to remove the piece of cookie lodged in his throat. When she saw his eyes roll back, she screamed, even as she pulled the boy from his highchair to get him into position for the Heimlich maneuver. But her screams were now accompanied by other screams and the frenzied barking of Laddie.

Suddenly Hannah pushed Sandra aside, pulled Israel away from her, bent him over her lap, and tried to press his stomach with her knee as she pushed on his back with her hands.

"What's all the screaming . . . ." Entering the kitchen, Abram didn't finish his question. Hannah shoved the limp child toward him, shrieking, "He's turning blue! He's choking! Help him! Save him!"

His father allowed himself no emotion as he quickly draped Israel over his arm and delivered five quick blows between his shoulder blades. "Hold his head!" he ordered Hannah, as he turned him over and applied five more thrusts just below Israel's ribcage. The chunk of cookie flew out of Israel's mouth, hitting Abram's chest, but Israel's little body crumpled lifelessly against Hannah.

"He's not breathing!" she sobbed. "Abram, our baby, he's not breathing!"

Abram searched Israel's mouth to make sure the air passage was clear; then he placed his own mouth over the child's mouth and nose. He blew, once, twice, three times, and finally Israel gasped and began to cry.

Huddled in a corner, Sandra Goodman watched her husband and Hannah hovering over Israel, crying as they held him and each other. He stroked Hannah's hair as she sobbed against his shoulder . . . and the child was between them, crying, too.

It seemed to Sandra that they looked at her accusingly when they finally noticed her. "I . . . gave him one of his cookies. . . ." she faltered, her voice shaking.

She waited alone, pacing and rubbing her arms to warm herself from the chill that had overtaken her. They had gone with Israel to the emergency room to have him checked, with no thought of asking his mother to go with them. Anger and grief warred within her. Hannah Miller had taken over her house, her child, and her husband in her "absence." And he had allowed it. And he had held her. "Our baby," she had said, and he had held her.

She took the stairs to the master bedroom, two at a time. From the hall closet she pulled suitcases and dragged them across the hall to "their" room. She opened them and began throwing clothing into them, not stopping to fold anything.

Abram stumbled over two suitcases as he came into the bedroom two hours later. Sandra was filling a third one with shoes as it lay wide open on the bed. "What're you doing, Sandra?"

She gave him one furious look but said nothing as she went back to throwing shoes into the suitcase.

"Where do you think you're going? Answer me!" He spoke angrily, and Sandra just as angrily shrugged off the hand he laid on her arm.

"What does it look like? I'm leaving!"

"Look, Sandra, it wasn't your fault that Israel choked. Nobody's blaming you. He gnaws on those biscuits all the time. He's fine, no harm done."

She glared at him. "You're damn right this isn't my fault. This is *your* fault! You're the one who brought your Amish girlfriend back into my house; you're the one who gave her *my* child!" On these words, her voice broke, and her breath came short.

He seemed stunned by her words, but realization flooded his face. "Sandra? It's you, isn't it! You remember!"

Her chest heaving with fury, she spat words at him, close, and in his face. "Yes, I remember. I remember how she was supposed to be gone from our life after she gave birth, well paid, I might add, for her services. But you couldn't wait to bring her back. You let her come in here and bond with Israel, essentially taking my child away from me, not to mention my husband!"

"That's not true. As for bringing her here to take care of Israel, what choice did I have? I did what I thought was best—for you! They said you needed familiarity . . . ." He held his arms out, palms up, pleading with her to understand.

Her anger spent, Sandra sobbed out the question. "Didn't you realize what you were risking? That she'd become Israel's mother in every way? And now she has him, and *you,* too!"

"No," he protested, trying to touch her, even as she slapped his hands down. "It's not that way."

"Save it, Abram. I saw the way you are together. I saw the way you two coo and fuss over your baby. It must have been tough to sleep with her and me, too, in same the house, in or out of my mind, but now you can have it all . . . the baby . . . her . . . all of it!"

"Stop it, Sandra! This is insane! I . . . I've never loved anyone but you . . . . There's nothing between Hannah and me!"

She stepped forward and slapped his face with all the force she could muster. "Liar! Bastard! This has all been very convenient for you. Well, I'll make it *real* convenient for you. I want a divorce."

Chapter Forty-seven

Hannah waited quietly in the dimness of the nursery, lit only by daylight that filtered through the closed curtains. After the trip to the emergency room, where Israel had checked out fine, she had laid the exhausted baby boy down for his nap when the shouting started.

Sandra's voice raised in anger carried beyond the closed door of the master bedroom. Abram's intermittent words were muffled, but their imploring tone was clear.

After a while, she heard the slamming of the door across the hall and the heavy sound of Abram's feet hammering down the stairs. Another slam told her that he had left the house.

Hannah settled herself into the rocking chair and sat quietly, without rocking, absent-mindedly twirling a strand of her hair around her finger. She hoped Sandra would not open the door to confront her. After an hour had passed without the sound of voices, she carefully opened the nursery door. Leaving it slightly ajar, she tiptoed soundlessly down the stairs to the kitchen.

She was surprised to see Hank's weathered face peering in through the kitchen door. Stepping inside, he nodded briefly to Hannah as he walked through the kitchen. "I'll be gettin' the missus's bags," he said.

She could hear his murmured exchanges with Sandra as he made three trips up and down the stairs, no doubt, carrying her luggage. From the foyer, she heard Hank say sadly, "Ready when you are, Mrs. Goodman . . . ."

A tearful voice responded. "I'm ready, Hank. I just need to get a few things from the coat closet."

When the sounds of the vehicles died away, Hannah made her way to the downstairs bedroom to listen to the baby monitor. She heard Israel talking to himself. She smiled and glanced at the clock on the bureau.   It was almost time for Joey's school bus. She had just enough time to get Israel and walk to the end of the driveway where it would drop Joey off.

I'm glad Israel's awake, she thought, as she climbed the stairs to the nursery. *He loves to see the big yellow bus.*

Pushing Israel in his stroller, she summed it up in her mind. *It was not my idea to come back here, so she better not blame me. I have only done what was asked of me and no more. I have taken care of all of them. Including her. My conscience is clear.*

She switched her thoughts to thinking about the supper she would prepare—for Abram and her sons.

Chapter Forty-eight

"I'm afraid she's adamant, Abram, even after the month-long cooling-off period. She wants the divorce." Attorney Lucas Porter was a slim, attractive man who wore his expensive suit with ease. He had first met his friend Abram Goodman's wife at their Christmas party five years ago. He now represented both of them in a divorce uncontested by Abram.

What Abram liked about Lucas was that talking to him was like talking to a regular guy. There was no stuffed-shirt, unfeeling lawyer sitting across the big desk from him. "Can you tell me where she is, so I can at least try to talk to her?"

"No, I'm not at liberty to tell you that. Frankly, I feel caught in the middle here. I hate handling divorces, especially for nice people like you and Sandra. I thought you two had the proverbial marriage made in heaven. She won't see you, Abram. Lucky for you, she doesn't want half of everything you've built up over the years."

Hope died in Abram. "So be it then," he said in a voice tinged with bitterness. "She can have all the cash and cars she wants, but the farm is mine. And Israel is mine. Does she even want visitation rights?"

"She wants only the monthly sum agreed upon and the gifts you've given her, most notably her diamonds and the Jag. And . . . this surprised me . . . she does not dispute that the boy is yours. I told her you were willing to give her visiting rights, but she has relinquished them."

Hurt for Israel smothered Abram, and he found it hard to speak. "If she's that cold, she's not the woman I thought she was. Just finalize it. I'm done with this."

Chapter Forty-nine

For the past month, Hannah had kept Abram Goodman's house and cooked his meals, which he seldom ate. She was reminded of the days after the deaths of his parents when she had first come to work for him, with two great exceptions, of course—the two children who were also in her care. Notable, too, was the fact that she also lived in the main house now, occupying the downstairs guest room.

Because of his always sullen mood, she kept out of his way when he was home, which was infrequent. She was surprised now, to find him sitting at the kitchen table, his head in his hands. Without comment, she set Israel in his playpen and stood behind his father, waiting for him to say something.

She looked at his bent head, then, before she could talk herself out of it, she placed her hands on his shoulders and began to massage them gently. He remained still, and the only sounds in the room were Israel's contented baby words.

Soon she felt Abram's taut muscles relaxing under her moving hands. Without lifting his head, he spoke.

"It's over, Hannah. I give up."

"You tried. I know how hard you tried." She let her hands move from his shoulders to his neck and massaged the muscles there, too. Never, in all the years they had known each other had she ever touched him like this. He had kissed her once long ago. He had carried her to his house. He had asked her to dance. All of it seemed a thousand years ago. Besides once placing his hand on her apron so that he could feel the movement of his child, she had never initiated any physical contact between them. Even though she loved him, she felt innocent of any wrong-doing when it came to the dissolution of this marriage.

He brought his hands to hers to stop them. Standing, he turned to face her. "Will you stay?"

Never for a moment had she expected him to say that she had to go now. "Yes," she said, without hesitation. "I'll stay. As long as you need me, I'll stay."

As he left the kitchen, she said softly, "After all, I was here first."

Chapter Fifty

She knew that he could see her naked body silhouetted in the dim light from the hallway as she stood just inside the doorway. She wore only a thin cotton nightgown, lifted by the dark areolas of her breasts. He lay very still in his bed, watching her. She met his gaze in the semi-darkness of the room. Then she moved toward him. He neither spoke nor moved as he watched her slow approach.

Standing beside his bed, she reached for his hand which lay motionless atop the covers and placed it on her full breast. Only then did he move, his fingers gently caressing her breast while his eyes searched her heated face. She kept her eyes on his as she reached her hand toward the night stand beside his bed and snapped on the small lamp that was there. Illuminated by it, she lifted her arms and pulled her nightgown over her head.

Deliberately, she stepped back far enough that he could see her naked body, all of it at once. Feeling his eyes like a caress, she watched them travel over her full breasts, the slight curve of her stomach, the blonde cleft above her thighs, and her smooth, long legs. She waited for him to tell her what to do next.

"Turn around," he said, his voice husky. She obeyed. With her back to him, she lifted her blonde hair off her shoulders and held it piled to her head, inviting him to kiss her neck, her shoulders, all of her his for the taking. She heard the movement of the bed and felt his hot breath on her shoulders. She bent her head to let him kiss the back of her neck as he reached around to hold her. A gasp escaped her when he pulled her closer to him, letting her feel the hardness of his body against hers.

Keeping her back to him, he lowered her to the floor, kneeling behind her and pulling her downward to his lap, wordlessly letting his intention be known.

At last, at last, she cried silently as he took her, rocking her, soaring upward and upward together until they fell to the soft carpet and lay, collapsed, satiated.

Hannah awakened and felt the delicate brush of his warm breath as he slept with his mouth against her neck. Still on the plush carpet of the master bedroom, they lay covered by a blanket he had pulled from the bed. She smiled. It had not been a dream.

She could hear Baby Israel's sweet voice coming from his crib across the hall. Gently, she extricated herself from Abram's arms, found her discarded nightgown and tiptoed out of the room. She looked in on Joey, sound asleep in Abram's old room. Then she turned to the nursery, ready to tend her younger son.

When he entered the kitchen she was dressed and sitting at the table spooning cereal into Israel's eager mouth. Joey, dressed for school, had already finished his breakfast and was heading to the porch to listen for his bus.

"Hey, Uncle Abe! Look what I'm takin' for Show 'n Tell." He held up his favorite matchbox tractor with black rubber wheels. "It looks just like your tractor."

"Good choice, Joey." Abram handed the toy back to Joey and returned the hug the boy offered him. "Have a great day, Buddy."

Hannah felt her face redden, and she didn't look at him until he said, "Good morning," lightly touching her hair as he spoke.

"Good morning," she said, shyly meeting his eyes. "If you'll take over with Israel, I'll fix your breakfast."

"Sure thing," he said, as though it were any other morning. "And I know exactly what I want for breakfast." He kissed Israel's curly head. "How's my big boy? Ready for another bite of this wonderful looking goop?"

She turned away from the refrigerator where she had been reaching for eggs to make him an omelet. "Oh, what do you want?"

His face was serious but his eyes burned into hers. "You," he said, and he tilted Israel's bowl to scrape the last of the cereal up with the spoon.

She stood frozen with two eggs in her hand, feeling the flooding warmth his single word had caused in her. Realizing that the refrigerator door was ajar, she moved to replace the eggs and close it. Unused to banter, she had no idea how to respond, how to tease him back or whether he was serious or not.

Her face burned as she watched him rinse a clean cloth at the sink and use it to wipe Israel's hands and face. "What time does Israel go down for his morning nap?" he asked, concentrating on cleaning the mess between Israel's fingers.

"Uh, in about two hours," she said, baffled by his intentions. "I usually take him for a morning walk . . . ."

Holding Israel, he turned to her. "Too long," he said. "Will he play in his playpen for a while?"

Grasping his meaning, she said, "For a little while . . . he'll play . . . for a little while."

"Well," he said, leaning in to kiss her cheek, "a little while is better than waiting for two hours." He carried Israel to the net playpen in the family room and set him among his toys.

"Now," he said with just the hint of a smile, "help me clear the table." With his face inches from hers, he reached behind her to untie her apron and lifted its loop over her head. "I've always wanted to do this . . . ."

Her body throbbing, she felt dizzy as she understood his intention. When he began to unbutton her blouse, she said, "Joey," and arrested his hand with her own.

As if at his command, there was the distant hissing sound of the bus's brakes followed by Joey's call, "Bye, Mom!"

Standing face-to-face with their eyes locked, they waited and listened to the grinding gears of the bus and its diminishing sound as it pulled away. He undid the first button of her blouse . . . .

In the bright morning light of the kitchen, to the jangle of Israel's toy tambourine, he took her for the second time, and she found she could withhold nothing from him.

Chapter Fifty-one

Sandra Waters Goodman leaned over the toilet, retching until her stomach ached. She had been sick most of the time since she had moved into a spacious apartment in a city high-rise. At first, she thought it was food poisoning or the flu, but now she was convinced that it was her nerves, perhaps an ulcer. The divorce had taken more out of her than she wanted to admit.

She leaned wearily against the bathtub and groaned at the ringing of her cell phone in the living room. "That would be Kendra," she said to herself.

Relentless about stopping Sandra from wallowing in depression, her sister had insisted on lunch and a day of shopping. At the thought of food, a new wave of nausea washed over Sandra.

"Hello?" She tried to sound normal.

"Hi, Sis, are you ready for a day on the town?" Kendra was an energetic morning person.

"I'm not feeling so hot, Kendra; it's the nausea again."

"You better see a doctor, Sandra. This has been going on too long. Maybe you need a scope of your stomach, to see if you have an ulcer. After all you've been through, I wouldn't be surprised. Let me make an appointment with my GP, Dr. Samuels. He'll take you on as a new patient if I ask him. Okay?"

Sandra was too weak to argue. Besides, it was nice to have someone care as much as Kendra did. "Okay," she said, "it's probably just stress, but I'll get checked out." She felt a surge of nausea and said, "I have to go."

"Yeah, well, I'll make an appointment for you, Sis."

Sandra knelt before the commode and dry-heaved until she thought she had turned herself inside out. She sat back against the tub with her knees drawn up and rested her throbbing head on her arms. She had slept little in the weeks since she had left Abram. Night after night, she struggled to push thoughts of him and Israel out of her mind. Israel. Her sobs echoed in the sun-filled bathroom, sounds of grief incongruent with the bright sunlight that poured through sky lights, glistening off white walls.

Finally, she pushed herself to her feet, went to the refrigerator and took a sip of Gator Aid. *I'm probably dehydrated. That's what the doctor will tell me. It's a vicious cycle . . . .*

Sandra Goodman was in shock. Dr. Kevin Samuels, general practitioner, had just completed a pelvic exam, which he thought was in order after probing her stomach.

"Well, Mrs. Goodman," he said calmly, "this explains your nausea. You appear to be pregnant. About two months, I'd say." He removed latex gloves and asked, "Is this good news?"

The acoustical tile of the examining room began to spin, and Dr. Samuels' voice came to her as through an echo chamber. "I'm going to be sick," Sandra said.

"Help me get her up," he said to his nurse. "Bend your head to your knees, Mrs. Goodman. Let's get some blood to your head."

She took deep breaths and accepted a sip of something sweet the nurse handed to her. The doctor repeated his question. "Is this pregnancy good news?"

"Not really," she said. "I'm recently divorced . . . ."

Dr. Samuels removed his gloves and offered Sandra a helping hand to sit up on the edge of the table. "Well," he said, "if, after you've had some time to think about this, you need to . . . seek other avenues, we can refer you to someone."

Sandra walked on wobbly legs toward Kendra who thumbed through a magazine in the waiting room. She must have looked like death because Kendra, oblivious to curious onlookers, blurted out, "Oh, my God, Sandra, what is it?"

Sandra spoke softly to her sister. "Let's go to the car."

"Oh, my God! Oh, my God!" Kendra couldn't seem to stop saying it as they sat in her Honda in the dimness of the parking garage. "Pregnant! Oh, my God!" Then a look of horror crossed Kendra's face as she asked, "It's surely Abram's, isn't it?"

Sandra didn't know whether to laugh or cry. After all the years of trying to carry a child, here she was, pregnant and without a husband. Kendra's question shook her. "It has to be his! Where have I been but with him? We must have made love . . . when I had amnesia!" Suddenly she burst into uncontrollable laughter, tears streaming from her eyes.

Kendra leaned over to shake her. "Sandra, get a hold of yourself. You're hysterical."

Sandra wiped her eyes with a bundle of tissues she pulled out of her purse and laughed so hard she could barely speak.

"This is not funny!" her sister said.

"Of course it is. Don't you see? I tried to get pregnant for years, and when I did, I wasn't even there. What a devil is Abram Goodman! He took advantage of a crazy woman, a woman out of her mind." She shrieked again with hysterical laughter.

Kendra wasn't laughing. "Listen to me Sandra! How would you even know if somebody *else* didn't take advantage of you? There are other men on that farm. Oh, my God, Sandra, you wouldn't even remember, would you?"

Sandra's laughter turned to icy silence. She turned horror-filled eyes on her sister. "Oh, God," she whispered, "please don't say that . . . ."

"Would Abram have let you out of his sight? Would there be anyone on the farm who would . . . take advantage of you?"

Sandra thought of old Hank and Pete. They would never hurt her. Only Bill was a possibility, but Sandra knew he'd never get past Hank or Pete . . . and she couldn't imagine over-protective Abram letting her roam the farm without him . . . .

Kendra said. "Don't let my imagination drive you crazy. Regardless of who the father is, what are you going to do? Would you consider . . . abortion?"

"I . . . don't know. I guess I'll just . . . wait."

"Wait for what?"

Sandra sighed. "With my luck, I'll probably abort it naturally."

Kendra was silent for a moment. "You sound as if you want this baby, Sandra, no matter whose it is."

"After all those years of trying to carry a child, it's hard to think any other way."

"But you don't even have a husband anymore."

Sandra turned to look at her sister. "Since when does a woman need a husband to raise a child? The divorce settlement gives me a generous income. I wouldn't have to work . . . ."

"But shouldn't you tell Abram, if you think it's his? He wanted a baby as much as you did."

"He has a baby."

"Not with you, he doesn't. And let's face it. That was what you both wanted, to create a child together."

"Too late for that, Kendra. But I *would* like to know if he and I were intimate during my amnesia. We did sleep in the same bed."

"Would you have to wait 'til the baby is born and get him to agree to a DNA test?"

"I don't know, but I could just ask him."

"Ask him if the baby is his?"

"No, ask him if we had sex two months ago."

Chapter Fifty-two

An April rain pattered on the roof of the porch where Hannah sat, folding towels she pulled from a wicker basket. They were still warm from the dryer. Israel was down for his afternoon nap, and Joey was still at school.

Her mind was full of Abram and last night's love-making. It had been three weeks since she had first visited him upstairs, and he had slept with her in the downstairs bedroom every night since. It did not escape her notice that he had never taken her to the bed he had shared with Sandra. Even on the first night, they had made love and slept on the floor of the master bedroom. She tried not to ponder the why of this, but contented herself with the knowledge that he wanted her, and often.

He sought her at any time of the day or night and seemed to court discovery. Though he knew that the men routinely came to the house on weekdays, he had appeared a half hour early one day, and, without a kiss or a word of endearment, taken what he wanted, pulling her into the family room just off the kitchen where lunch waited. *Not that I would ever refuse him,* she admitted to herself.

She had had to scurry into the bathroom at the sound of male voices approaching the house. When she came into the kitchen again, he sat with the men and ate his lunch silently and did not meet her eyes. She was vaguely troubled by this and by the way he had taken her—roughly. There was also the fact that he never said he loved her; yet she was sure he must, wanting her as he did. Surely this was a different Abram. Surely he was more . . . she struggled for a word . . . lusty . . . than he had been . . . with Sandra.

Oh well, it doesn't matter, she thought. She felt as if she were discovering sex for the first time. She had never enjoyed it with Gabe. How different it was with Abram whom she had loved for so long . . . so terribly long.

He had told her that her own forwardness had surprised him. "I'd have expected you to be shy," he said. The truth was she willingly submitted to anything he suggested and felt no shame. She never tried to hide the pleasure that he gave her, freely emitting the earthy sounds that he said added to his own pleasure.

Through the early leaves of the bittersweet vine that covered one end of the porch, she saw him striding toward the house. Her heart beat faster. In a minute, he stood before her.

"Forget the towels," he said simply, and she knew what he intended.

"Joey will be home soon," she said, looking up at him.

"Not for a half hour," he said. Her breath came fast as she watched him dropping the canvas awnings of the porch.

"Here?" she asked as he pulled her to her feet and lifted her tee shirt. "What if one of the men comes to the house?"

"No one will," he said, as he threw soft chair pillows on the porch floor.

"But Joey . . . it's almost time for Joey's bus . . . ." She tried to rise, but he was insistent.

"Relax. This won't take long."

Afraid of discovery, she didn't enjoy intimacy with him when he was like this—rough and urgent—with no patience for kisses or caresses.

The faint hiss of bus brakes froze her with terror. "Stop!" she said, "Joey's bus has turned into the driveway!"

He didn't stop, even when she tried to pull away from him. "It's a long driveway," he said, his voice husky.

As she fled into the house, clutching her jeans and underwear, she heard him speaking calmly to her son who stomped up the porch steps. "Hi, Joe, how was school today?"

Chapter Fifty-three

Sitting in the passenger seat of Abram's pickup, Hank watched the speedometer climb to seventy-five. He slid a glance at the scowling face of the driver and wondered when he had last seen Abram smile. The man he loved as a son had become sullen and abrupt, even with him. The other men now seemed afraid of the boss they would have at one time described as good-natured. Unlike them, Hank didn't fear Abram; rather, he was worried about him.

"Where's the fire?" he asked, in reference to Abram's driving.

Abram ignored Hank's question but dropped the speed back to seventy.

With sudden decision, Hank said, "Do you wanna talk about this Abe?" After all, he reasoned, who else did Abram Goodman have to talk to?

"About what? My driving?" Abram kept his eyes on the road and held it at seventy, still too fast for Hank's liking.

"You know full well what I mean. Do you wanna talk about what's eatin' you?"

"It's no secret."

"So why don't you try to get her back?" Hank swayed with a curve Abram took too fast.

"I don't want her back."

"Seems mighty strange, then, that you're mad at the world. You're rid of her, so you oughta be in a better mood."

"There's nothing wrong with my mood."

"Bull," Hank said with a tone of finality.

"Okay, you asked for it," Abram Goodman said. "If you want to hear my confession, I'll oblige, but only because you're the closest thing to a father I have."

"I can listen but I don't have no absolution to give. But go ahead."

Abram let out a long sigh and slowed down to sixty. "I've always lived by a moral code, you know? If I treated people right, it'd come back to me. I treated Sandra like a queen. I gave her everything she wanted—except a baby that was from both of us— but she knew it wasn't my fault that she couldn't carry to term. I gave in to everything she wanted: Surrogacy. Even using Hannah as a surrogate. Letting Hannah donate the egg. Everything I was against, I went ahead and did, just trying to make Sandra happy."

"I didn't know about Hannah donatin' the egg, too. I wonder if that was a good idea." Hank ran his fingers on the creases of his pants, as he contemplated this. "So your boy isn't from you and Sandra? He's from you and the housekeeper?"

"You got it. It's what Sandra wanted. And I'll let you in on a secret. When I talked to Hannah about donating the egg, because Sandra had already mentioned that possibility, Hannah came right out and asked why we couldn't just sleep together when she was fertile, and Sandra would be none the wiser. Sandra would think her own egg had finally implanted."

Hank whistled. "What'd you say to *that?*"

"I said no. I said I wouldn't lie to Sandra, wouldn't cheat on her, even if she'd think using her own egg had finally worked. But what did I get for that? As soon as Sandra got her memory back, she blamed me for bringing Hannah into the house and, on top of that, accused me of sleeping with her."

Hank could hear the bitterness in Abram's tone and now understood his seething anger. "You always were a decent, truthful man, Abe. Sandra was wrong to doubt you."

"Don't give me too much credit, Hank. I *am* sleeping with Hannah now. Not until the divorce was final, but I am now." Silence filled the space between the two men.

"With them boys in the house, you're sleepin' with the housekeeper?" Hank was shocked.

"I know. That bothers me, too. But they don't know anything. Joey sleeps upstairs and we sleep in the downstairs guest room."

"Are you gonna marry the housekeeper? Or just use her to get back at your ex-wife?" Hank knew his words were harsh, but he didn't care. He was disappointed in Abram Goodman.

"Let me remind you, Hank, that Hannah wanted this long before I did. I'm not a blind man. She's a good looking woman, and I battled attraction to her for years. Mostly to her body, I admit, though there *is* something appealing about a submissive woman. So, if she wants it, and I'm going to be accused anyhow, why not?"

"Because that ain't like you, Abe. That's why not. And I bet that Amish girl thinks you're gonna marry her. I can't see her just wantin' sex without bein' in love with you, too."

"Hank, I've promised her nothing. She seems to like her role as my live-in mistress. And I plan to oblige her."

"What if you get her pregnant? Then you'll be in a fine kettle of fish."

"I made sure she got on the pill. Took her to the doctor myself." He sighed. "I have to trust she's taking it."

"You're still takin' advantage of her, Abe. She was a kid when she came here, and she's been sweet on you for years. Even I could see that . . . ."

"I didn't ask for your approval or your absolution, Hank. You said I could confide in you. Well, I did and now I'm done, except for this: Who can figure women? I might be able to understand Sandra leaving *me,* but *Israel?* After years of crying and moaning about wanting a baby, she left the baby she willingly adopted. Just walked away without a fight."

Abram slammed his foot on the accelerator once again, and Hank did not hide his irritation. "If you want to kill yourself, fine, go right ahead. But don't be takin' *me* with you!"

"Sorry, Hank," Abram said as he slowed the vehicle to the speed limit.

Chapter Fifty-four

Hannah recognized the voice on the phone. She swallowed hard before answering. "Yes, he's here." Handing the phone to Abram, she added, "It's for you." She watched his face register shock as he heard Sandra's voice on the other end.

"Just a minute. I'll take this in the den. Hang it up for me, will you, Hannah?" She knew he was struggling to sound casual. He paused after picking up the phone in the other room; then he said, "Okay, I have it."

Hannah did not hang up the phone. She stood with her heart beating so wildly that she feared they could hear her listening in. "So *she's* still there," Sandra said with a tone of ridicule.

"I have a son to raise, you know," Abram said with only slightly veiled hostility.

"How is Israel?'

"Do you care?"

"Of course I care. I miss him terribly, but you made it clear that you considered him *yours,* not mine."

"You made that clear, Sandra, not me."

"There's no point in arguing about it. I just called to see if we could meet. I need to ask you some questions . . . about when I had amnesia. Can we suspend the hostilities long enough to get together for lunch?"

Abram paused so long that Hannah thought he was not going to answer. She hoped he would say no.

"When?" he asked finally, and Hannah felt like crying

"Is tomorrow okay? Would you mind driving into the city? We could meet at The Old Maid's Sorrow. It's the Irish pub on Second Street."

Hannah quietly pushed the off-button on the phone and replaced it in its cradle before hurrying to sit at the kitchen table. She spoke to Joey when she heard Abram enter the room.

"Are you finished? Eat those carrots and you can have some chocolate pudding for dessert. Look at how Israel loves his carrots."

She spooned crushed carrots into Israel's orange-colored mouth and avoided looking at Abram. He sat across from her and toyed with his half-eaten meal before shoving his chair back and leaving the three of them to finish alone.

Hannah heard the sound of his truck pulling away and tried not to cry in front of the children.

It was well past midnight when he returned. Hannah held her breath as she lay in bed, hoping that he would come to her. He had entered the adjoining bathroom from the hallway, and she heard the shower running. She waited.

The shower stopped and soon the door to her room opened, letting in a glimmer of light from the nightlight in the bathroom. The bed shifted with his weight as he got in beside her, and the smell of alcohol was on his breath. He lay on his back, not touching her, and she knew that he was staring into the darkness, too.

"What did she want?" she asked with no emotion.

"To meet me for lunch tomorrow. To talk. She has questions. About when she had amnesia. She's probably seeing a new doctor who wants history she can't supply."

"Are you going to go?"

"Yes."

"I don't want you to go."

"I'll be back."

They lay silently without touching, until Hannah heard Abram's breathing become rhythmic, a gentle snore. She edged closer to him, but she lay with eyes wide open long into the night.

Chapter Fifty-five

She saw him before he noticed her sitting in the red leather corner booth that she had chosen, in a restaurant where they had never been together. He had lost weight, and his handsome face was rigidly set. She admired the breadth of his shoulders in the white cotton sweater he wore with casual slacks in an olive color. As he turned his head in the direction where she sat, she raised an arm to help him find her in the lunch-time crowd.

His eyes flicked toward her, and he nodded. There was no smile, but she hadn't really expected one. She heard him muttering polite "Excuse me's" as he threaded his way through the crowded tables to get to her booth.

She extended her hand to him, and realized, from the warmth of his, how cold hers had been. He let go of her hand and slid into the opposite booth seat.

"It's good to see you, Abram," she said, meaning it from her heart.

"Is it?"

She sighed at his abruptness. "We don't have to be enemies, do we?" She tried a smile but felt intimidated by the cold look on his face.

"We don't have to be friends either." He took a sip from the water glass at his place setting.

A tinge of anger crept into her voice. "You're determined to be difficult, aren't you? Can't you just decide to be civil, since you agreed to meet me?"

"Sorry. I'm not a very good actor. What was it you wanted to talk about?"

She picked up the large laminated menus from the back edge of the table and handed him one. "Let's order first. This place is known for its Cajun chicken breast sandwich. There's a delicious horseradish sauce that comes with it. I think you might like it."

"Okay," he said and repeated that to the waitress who had come to stand beside them. "No fries. Just the sandwich."

Sandra should have been over her early morning nausea by now, but she felt sick, nevertheless. "I'll have the wedding soup," she said, "and some crackers."

He glanced at her as the waitress picked up their menus and went away. "That's ironic, isn't it? Ordering wedding soup. I wonder if they have a divorce soup."

"Rest assured, I wasn't thinking of anything but wanting a non-creamy soup . . . just something easy on the stomach." She could have kicked herself for saying that.

"Are you sick? You do look pale. You look like you've lost weight. You're all eyes." His tone had softened, and she detected a hint of concern in his voice.

"I thought the same about you," she said. "You look as though you've lost weight, too."

"That has to be from spring exercise. Believe me, Hannah is feeding me well."

Sandra felt a surge of real anger now. "I'm sure she's taking good care of you."

"She is, and of Israel and Joey, too." The sarcasm was back in his voice.

Sandra tried to keep the conversation neutral until their lunches arrived. "Have you bought any new cars lately?" She had always teased him about his obsession. He laughed and admitted that he had . . . .

He took a bite of his sandwich. "This was a good suggestion."

She took a tentative taste of her soup, and it tasted bitter. She sat uncomfortably in the silence that followed and took a bite of a cracker. The silence ticked on.

"It's not easy to make small talk, is it?" he said, wiping his mouth with a linen napkin.

"No, it isn't, so I'll get to the point. I *have* been having some health problems, and it might be helpful if you'd answer some questions for me . . . about . . . the time when I couldn't . . . when I couldn't remember anything."

"I'm sorry to hear you've been having problems. Nothing serious I hope." He sat waiting for her to elaborate.

"No, well, probably nothing serious, but the doctor thinks it might be related to the accident, headaches and so forth, you know.

Did I complain of many headaches before I regained my memory?" She reined in her impatience, wanting to blurt out the real question.

"Not that you ever mentioned to me . . . . You could contact Dr. Gradwell . . . ."

"I've thought of that, but I wanted to ask you . . . uh . . . did I socialize with anybody, besides you, I mean?"

He took a long breath, and she watched his eyes look into the past. "Socialize? I wouldn't call it that. You never willingly left the house, except to see Dr. Gradwell. At first, you were confused and afraid . . . mostly of me. And you didn't show much interest in Israel."

"Did that change?" Feeling frustrated, she wondered how on earth she'd bring this conversation around to the question of intimacy.

"Yes, I think so. I thought we were making progress and then you clammed up again."

"Clammed up?"

"You didn't talk much for a long time, and then you started to loosen up . . . even to the point . . . ." His hesitation hid something. She just knew it.

"Even to the point of . . . what?"

"Even to the point of being willing to make love with me." A storm brewed in his gray eyes, and his voice was cold when he added, "And then you started acting pissed at me. I think you did that to put a barrier between us again, so we wouldn't have sex again."

"I know we slept together," she said, trying to speak evenly though her heart hammered at what he had just told her. "But I don't remember any . . . intimacy."

"Yes, we slept in the same bed, but I never touched you until you wanted me to. You were just as . . . enthusiastic . . . about it as I was." He threw down his napkin. "And then you went right back to being an iceberg again."

She realized how much she had put him through. "I'm sorry. I mean, it must have been difficult for you." She reached for his hand, but he picked up his napkin again to avoid her.

"Yeah, I won't lie to you. It was hell. I never knew whether to show affection or not. You were pretty skittish."

"If I let you . . . make love to me . . . I mustn't have been all *that* unaffectionate."

"It wasn't one-sided. We 'made love' to each other. You even made the first move, not that I minded. But what's that line? 'One swallow doesn't make a summer'?"

"One? It only happened one time?"

"Just once, about two weeks before you left for good. And that's what *I* want to talk about, if you're through asking me what you wanted to know. Except for right after your concussion, you never complained of any headaches, if that's what's going on with you now."

Sandra's mind quickly calculated the weeks that had passed since she'd walked out. Two weeks before she left, he had said, and she had been gone about six weeks more. Two months. She was two months pregnant. His voice brought her back.

"Sandra?"

She fought the impulse to tell him that she was, at long last, successfully carrying his child—so far. Would it be a reason to get back together? Would he even want to? He seemed so angry with her, although he had been trying to subdue it.

"Okay, your turn," she said, fighting to keep emotion out of her voice. "What do you want to talk about?" She tried hard to focus on him and to subdue the tumultuous thoughts in her mind.

"I want to make something clear," he began, his voice firm and unwavering. "I brought Hannah Miller back into the house for one reason. I had a sick wife who couldn't take care of the baby. I was told that everything should be the same as before the accident, as much as possible. I tried to get Mrs. Gregory, but she wouldn't do it. I thought someone new would confuse you even more, so there was no choice but to get Hannah to do it. I've said it over and over again, and I want you to know that it is the truth."

Sandra knew he was telling the truth, but she also knew that it was a bad decision. "Surely you can see how attached she is to Israel now. Didn't you worry about that? Weren't you afraid that she'd try to claim him as her own?"

"Of course I thought about it, but I didn't worry about it. It would take some astute legal maneuvering for her to try to break our contract with her. She's still Amish at heart, very unsophisticated. She wouldn't know how to begin, but I also think she'd never do that to us . . . certainly not to me."

"Are you finally admitting that she resented me, as though I had taken her place? I know she would . . . do anything . . . for you." Sandra bit her lip to keep from crying. She feared what he was about to say.

"I know that. But I never took advantage of that fact. Not until . . . the divorce was final." His cold gaze did not waver.

Though she had guessed it, Sandra felt as though he had slapped her. Had she understood him correctly? Had he just told her that he was now sleeping with Hannah? She tried to keep reaction out of her voice. "You're . . . sleeping with her . . . now?"

He looked at her without remorse. "Yes, but not until I knew it was hopeless between us, not until the divorce papers were signed, sealed and delivered. Let me remind you, Sandra, you wanted the divorce, not me. It shouldn't matter to you who I sleep with."

"Are you," she fought the nausea that threatened to overwhelm her, "planning to marry her? You were pretty sanctimonious about not wanting to sleep with *me* before we married."

He dropped his eyes. "I don't know."

She refused to cry and refused to let it go. She had to know. "It's what *she* will want, Abram. You've always . . . protected her. Surely, you don't intend to just . . . use . . . her and never marry her. That doesn't sound like the upstanding Abram Goodman that I used to know." She knew that he would notice the sarcasm in her words, but she didn't care.

He sighed and looked her in the eye. "I've changed. Life has a way of knocking you around and making a realist out of you. Besides, I'm not 'using' her. It's mutual; in fact, she . . . came to me first . . . . At first I just wanted to get back at you . . . for destroying us."

"And now? No, don't answer that. It's none of my business." Threatening tears burned her eyes and nostrils. She knew she had to get out of there. Quickly, she picked up her handbag as she said, "I didn't realize that the fault is all mine, that I am responsible for what happened to me after the accident. Look, Abram, I appreciate you meeting me, but I really have to get going. Let me get the check." She reached for it and he closed his hand over hers, a tender touch.

"No, I'll take care of it." He was standing because she had risen. "Can I walk you to your car?"

"No, no thank you, I'm just across the street." Impulsively, she went up on tiptoe and kissed his cheek. "Goodbye, Abe. Take good care of Israel."

Chapter Fifty-six

Abram stood numbly for a moment after she had disappeared from view. He fought the impulse to run after her. Dropping heavily onto the red leather cushions of the booth where they had been sitting across from one another, he stared into the now vacant space she had occupied. He touched the spot on his cheek that she had kissed. He remembered the feel of her slim hand in his.

Suddenly he couldn't stand himself. *Why did I have to act like such an ass? She was trying to be friendly . . . I could have sworn there was something more than the reason she gave for wanting to meet me. What wasn't she saying . . . .?*

He thought of her pale but beautiful face, framed by her shining black hair. Her eyes had seemed enormous and even bluer as they picked up the color of the light blue sweater she wore. Her hand had been cold. He had wanted to keep holding it, to warm it.

Why did I have to tell her about Hannah and me? What did I gain from that? I saw the pain in her eyes when I admitted that. Is that what I wanted, to cause her pain?

She had tried to hide it, the pain she felt, but he knew that look well. He had seen it every time she miscarried; he had seen it with every surrogate that didn't work out. His throat constricted with the memory of her face; then he realized that he had been staring at the lipstick on her cup.

He put a fifty into the leather cover that held the check. It was much more than was needed to cover the cost of their lunch, but he was in a hurry. He hoped he hadn't waited too long.

Outside, he looked up and down the street, saw a parking garage across the way and ran to it, dodging street traffic. He decided to stand by the exit and wait to see if her black Jag would emerge.

He waited for almost an hour, though he knew it was pointless. She had gone.

Back in his car, he pondered Sandra's unanswered question: "And now?" Abram knew it was time to answer it. But all he had was another question, for himself. What had he done to Hannah? For the first time, he felt shame, and tears poured down his face as he drove back to his home.

Chapter Fifty-seven

Kendra sat with her head in hands, the strands of her long, red hair spilling through her fingers. She had been listening to the sobbing of her sister for the past two hours. She had tried everything, but Sandra was inconsolable and had been thus for days.

"Call him, Sandra. Tell him the truth. If you didn't love him you wouldn't be hurting like this," she begged.

"He's not in love with me anymore. What am I supposed to do? Throw the Amish slut out of my house?"

"Damn right," said Kendra, viciously attacking the thick skin of an orange with her fingernails.

Sandra sat up and blinked away her tears. "Are you serious? You'd really do that? If you were in my position, you'd do that?"

"That's what the feisty sister I used to know would do."

"Technically, it's not my house anymore. Besides, what if he's in love with her? What if he doesn't want her to go?"

"Then he'll throw *you* out. At least you won't be wondering what might have been for the rest of your life."

"No," Sandra said, her tears beginning again. "I know Abram Goodman. He would not have slept with her if he wasn't in love with her. Damn him! I think he's always been in love with her."

Kendra threw an orange peel at Sandra. "That's not true and you know it. He even told you so at that miserable lunch you had with him."

"Well, he showed no signs of having any feelings for me, except maybe contempt." Sandra threw the orange peel back at Kendra.

"So what are you going to do? About the baby?" Kendra divided the orange into sections, and handed some to Sandra. "Eat this. Please. You have the baby to think about."

"You're right. I have the baby to think about. I have to stop agonizing. This stress can't be doing either of us any good, the baby or me, I mean." She sat up straight, mopped her face with tissues and put a juicy piece of orange in her mouth.

"Well, this is a start. You sound as though you've made up your mind to have this baby. Then what?"

Pausing before she answered, Sandra laid her hands protectively on her stomach. "Yes, I'm going to have my baby . . . and I'm going to keep my baby. Many women raise children without men in their lives. I'm going to be one of them—with a major difference from most cases—I don't have to worry about money, thanks to Old Money Bags Goodman! He insisted on giving me more than I asked for."

"See what I mean? Does that sound like a man who doesn't love you?"

"No, but jumping into bed with his Amish housekeeper does!"

Chapter Fifty-eight

Hannah caressed Abram's shirts as she ironed them, and her thoughts were full of him. She missed him dreadfully and had failed to tantalize him with her warm, willing body. His daytime rendezvous with her had stopped, and, though he still lay with her at night, he excused himself from intimacy, saying that he was "out of it."

She feared she knew the reason why. A sense of foreboding had loomed in her mind since the day that he had gone to meet with Sandra. True, he had come back, as he said he would, but he was not really back with her in the same way.

She had asked him, since he had not commented on what had transpired between him and Sandra, "Is she coming back?"

"No," he had said and that was the end of it.

She wanted to ask, "And are you coming back to me?" But she was afraid of what he might say. Hannah Miller had long ago learned patience. She would be here when he wanted her again.

"See 'ight!" proclaimed Israel Goodman as he pointed a chubby finger at the single candle on his birthday cake. It was a three-tiered marvel which Hannah had baked herself and decorated with blue and white icing.

"When can I give Israel his present?" Joey asked, fingering the gaily wrapped gift.

"Wait 'til I get the camera," Abram said. "I want to get a picture of him ripping open his presents."

His words brought to Hannah's mind the Amish taboo against creating "graven images" of oneself by picture-taking. She wished she could send a picture of her sons to her mother, but she knew it would be an unwelcome idol from the Outside. And how would Hannah ever explain where she had gotten the second son?

Abram took pictures of Israel alone, Israel with Joey, Israel with Hannah and both boys with Hannah. "Here, Joe," he said, "Now you take one of me and Israel. Remember to keep us framed and hold the camera still, the way I showed you."

"Okay, now one of you and Mom and Israel," Joey suggested.

Hannah looked at Abram, waiting to see his reaction before she moved to do Joe's bidding. Abram did not meet her eyes, but he said, "Okay" and moved to stand behind Israel's highchair. Hannah stood beside him. She hoped he would put an arm around her shoulder, and when he did not, she felt his rejection keenly.

"Now let's cut that cake!" Abram said jovially, as soon as the picture was snapped.

It had been a difficult summer for Hannah. Abram had taken to sleeping in his old room again, not the one he had shared with Sandra but the room he had used when he was a bachelor. Broken-hearted, Hannah slept alone in the guest room and moved Joey to the sofa-bed in the den to keep him near her.

Abram had never given her any warning, never any explanation. He just stopped coming to her room. She finally asked him why.

"It doesn't look good in front of the boy. Joey's not a baby anymore." He barely lifted his eyes from the papers on his desk.

"It never bothered you before," she ventured. "Besides, Joey sleeps like a stone."

"Well, it bothers me now." His tone was final. There was no room for her to differ.

She wanted to believe him, that this was the only reason. "You're probably right," she said. But she knew better. She would just have to wait until the lunch with Sandra wore off and he was hungry again.

One day in mid-August, she was overjoyed when Joey received an invitation to spend the night at his friend Michael's house. She gave her permission and made sure to mention it to Abram.

"Joey's been invited to a sleep-over at Michael's tonight. I said it was fine. He's very excited about it . . . ."

That night, she lay in her bed, hoping that Abram would come to her. He had been away for the evening and came home late. Her heart fell as she heard him enter the house and climb the stairs to his old room.

"Maybe he forgot," she whispered into the darkness. Unable to bear any longer her need of him, she wondered if he just needed a little reminder of what they had shared. *I have to try,* she reasoned, putting aside any shred of pride she might have had.

She climbed the stairs to his room. He had left the door open, and he was sitting up in bed, reading.

"May I come in?" she asked, her voice low.

He looked at her and laid his book aside. She wished he would give some sign that she was welcome.

"Joey is spending the night at Michael's . . . ." She was suddenly embarrassed at her own forwardness and how pathetic she sounded.

"I know," he said.

Humiliated, she turned to leave, but then he said her name. "Hannah." She stopped with her back to him and waited for more.

"Would you like to sleep here?" he asked softly.

She turned to look at him. "Do you want me here?"

He sighed and nodded slowly, as he pulled aside the covers of the bed for her. She lay quietly with her head against his shoulder, her left hand stroking the soft hair of his chest.

"Will you . . . ." she hesitated, unaccustomed to using the *Englische* words for what she wanted, "make love to me?"

He expelled a long breath. "I know I've been out of it lately, Hannah, and I'm sorry. You're going to have to . . . get me going again . . . ."

His suggestion that there would be an "again," a future, brought tears to Hannah's eyes. "That's why I'm here," she said, "to get you going again."

Then she sat up to strip herself of her nightgown and him of his pajamas. Naked, she straddled his hips as he lay beneath her, and she bent to kiss him again and again, wetting his face with her tears. "I love you, Abram Goodman," she said for the first time. "No matter if you send me away, Abram Goodman, I love you." Even as she cried, she smiled to feel his manhood rising up to meet her, and she impaled herself upon him.

Chapter Fifty-nine

Indian summer sunshine made the concrete of the city sparkle, but Sandra longed for the country. She knew the trees would be a patchwork quilt of color now, against a background of clear blue sky.

From the balcony of her sixth floor apartment, she stood drinking her morning coffee and surveying the city stretched out before her. Spires pierced the blue sky, and a flash of autumn gold and orange could be seen in city parks tucked among the buildings.

She caught herself thinking of the farm. *The foliage will be breathtaking now . . .* but she refused to allow her mind to paint the full picture. All she had to do was to conjure up a picture of Abram and Hannah to crush fond memories of her life with Abram.

She thought about driving out of the city to enjoy the warm autumn day, but she hated to go alone. Kendra was at work, and Sandra had not bothered to socialize with her neighbors in the high-rise where she lived. In her seventh month of pregnancy, she was entirely absorbed with the child who moved within her and spent her days converting one of her extra bedrooms into a nursery done in white with blue accents.

She had wept with joy when amniocentesis revealed that the child she carried was a healthy boy. Knowing that she would bear a son only partly assuaged the pain she still felt when she thought of Israel. She tried not to think of him and his father, though it was a battle that she lost daily. Despite Kendra's insistence that she should tell Abram that she needed his cooperation for a DNA test, Sandra had refused. She knew within her heart that she would not have been intimate with anyone but Abram, not just because of lack of opportunity, but because of her conversation with him more than five months ago. She believed him when he had told her that they had made love once, during the time when she still had not regained her memory. She knew that he would not have forced himself upon her. She had to have been willing.

She had wept for weeks but then, realizing that all of the emotional upheaval could affect her baby, she set her mind on the future and raising her son alone. The divorce settlement was generous, and she had no need to work, though she missed teaching. *Maybe someday when Isaac is in school.* She had not told anybody that Isaac would be his name, not even Kendra.

Though she had not gone to church for years, she knew that, in the Bible, Isaac was called "the child of promise," the gift of God, the child given to Abraham and Sarah in their old age, after years of Sarah's barrenness. *How fitting,* she thought. And Abram would approve of keeping up the "I" names of his deceased parents, Ida and Ira Goodman, by using the "I" name given to his twin brother who had died at birth. Now Israel would have a brother. She wished Abram could know, but immediately dismissed it from her mind. He had been as cold as ice during their luncheon. And he and Hannah lived as man and wife. Maybe he had even married her by now.

She tried to switch from the negative feelings those thoughts generated. Brushing her long hair, she concentrated on how she could fill her day with sunshine and autumn color; but she found herself remembering that October had been her and Abram's favorite month of the year, a time for long walks on the farm and picnics overlooking a panorama of reds, yellows, and oranges. With sudden decision, she shook Abram's face from her mind and tied a rust-colored cardigan around the shoulders of the yellow tunic she wore with maternity jeans. *I'll spend this bright autumn afternoon outside, reading in the park!*

Chapter Sixty

Abram Goodman impatiently drummed his fingers on the steering wheel of a new white Corvette as he sat in traffic. He preferred to drive his pickup or the Land Rover, but today he had taken his new sports car into the city. He knew he had to look the part of an investor to the gas tycoons with whom he had met that morning.

He tugged off his tie, undid the top button of his white shirt and rolled up the sleeves as he sat waiting for the green arrow to signal a left turn. As he watched people who jostled one another on the sidewalk, he thought aloud, not for the first time, "God, how can these people live like this?" He couldn't wait to get back to his farm, forgetting that he had once loved living in the city.

At the sound of the bell, scowling pedestrians streamed into the crosswalk in front of his car. Shining black hair and a flash of yellow caught his eyes. His mouth went dry. Sandra. What was it about her that his mind was trying to take in?

He shot a glance into his rearview mirror at the rude sound of a horn behind him. The light had changed. He tried to follow her with his eyes, even as he made the left turn, but she had disappeared into the crowd of people on the sidewalk. He didn't consciously decide to circle the block to find a place to pull over, nor did he consciously admit what he had seen.

He took two rights to get back to the place where he had seen her. Frustrated that there was no sign of her and nowhere on the street to park, he made his way to a parking garage. Urgently, he grabbed the ticket and cursed as he circled from level to level, looking for a place to park.

Slamming his car door and clicking the lock icon on the fob, he headed for the stairway to the ground floor, his leather shoes echoing on the concrete. Like a running-back, he dodged people on the street and was nearly hit by a bus as he jaywalked. He scanned the heads that bobbed the length of the sidewalk where he had seen her. She was gone.

Which store would she have gone into? He knew it would be futile to guess, but he lingered on the corner where he had a vantage point of a number of doorways. He paced a bit but carefully watched for her to emerge from one of them. An hour later, she still had not appeared.

His shoulders sagged as he conceded that he had lost her. He retraced his steps to the parking garage, but then decided he could not go home. Not until he was sure of what he thought he had seen. He tried the White Pages app on his phone, half-heartedly, already knowing from their attorney that Sandra had an unlisted number. He did find Kendra's name and punched in her home number, determined to get her to give him her sister's address; he planned to be there waiting when Sandra returned home.

No answer and he didn't know Kendra's cell phone number. He tried an operator, with the unlikely hope that he could get her to tell him Sandra's address.

In response to the nasal voice of the operator, he said, "Do you have a listing for a Sandra Goodman?"

"No, Sir, no listing for Sandra Goodman."

"How about Sandra Waters?"

No, but I do have an S. Waters-Goodman."

"Great, can you give me that number or dial it for me?"

"That's a private number, Sir."

"Could you at least give me her address?"

"No, Sir. That information is also private."

Pushing the off-button on that operator, he immediately tried a new one. "Could you please give me the address listed for S. Waters-Goodman?"

"No, Sir. That is a private listing."

He tried to get chummy with the operator. "I understand, but let me explain my situation. That's my wife—the 'S' stands for Sandra—she's my wife and I arrived home unexpectedly, from Afghanistan, and I want to surprise her by showing up at her door." Suddenly he knew how preposterous that sounded. He was not a good liar.

The operator was not impressed. "Why wouldn't you know your wife's address, Sir? I'm sorry, but I'm not at liberty to give out private information." The operator disconnected before he could make up any more lies.

"Damn!" he said aloud as he clipped his phone back into its holder on his belt.

Again, he searched the streets. Annoying people, he swiveled with his arms akimbo, glancing around him and trying to decide what to do. Then his eyes fell on a small tree planted in a square of dirt beside the concrete sidewalk in front of a diner. Its red leaves were on fire in the October sunshine, and suddenly Abram Goodman knew where Sandra would be.

"Is there a park around here?" he asked the curmudgeon behind the cash register inside the diner.

Jerking his thumb in a direction across the street, the man muttered around a cigarette that hung from a churlish lip. "T'ree blocks down Shady."

Following the green-tinted cement walkway that wound its way among trees and grass that had been spared the encroachment of the city, Abram' eyes searched the cedar benches that had been placed here and there in the manicured refuge for squirrels and the city-dwellers who came to feed them.

And then he saw her. She sat on a bench with her eyes closed, her face lifted to the sun, while the breeze played with strands of her black hair that hung over the back of the bench. Her denim-clad legs were stretched out in front of her and crossed at the ankle. On her feet he recognized her favorite loafers. Her arms cradled the yellow-draped mound that rested on her lap. On the bench beside her lay a discarded sweater and a book, face-down.

Drinking in the sight of her, Abram moved quietly until he stood before her. His eyes caressed her serene face. As his shadow crossed between her and the sun, she opened her eyes. She blinked several times, sat up straight and looked up into his eyes. Then she smiled.

Abram was so relieved by that smile that he knelt at her feet and laid his hands on her belly. Wordlessly, they continued to speak to one another with mutually tear-filled eyes. It was she who found her voice first.

"This time, it only took one swallow to make our summer," she said gently, and her hands were soft on his face as she said it.

Still kneeling, he began to kiss her face, letting his own tears mingle with hers until he found her sweetly welcoming mouth.

"Come home, Sandra," he said, "to me and Israel . . ."

She pulled his hands to the child within her again. "And with Isaac," she said. "His name is Isaac. I'll let you pick his middle name."

"God, how I love you," he said. "I've been so miserable without you . . . ." He pulled her to him and rejoiced in his heart.

Chapter Sixty-one

The Bond Woman clothed herself in a coarse, light blue dress she had pulled from the back of the closet in the little house. Over the dress she tied a black apron. Her legs were covered by black stockings and her feet, by black oxfords. She parted her hair in the middle, knotted it at the base of her neck and hid it beneath a white prayer cap.

She looked at her pale face in the mirror. Scrubbed clean of make-up, it shone in the dim morning light that was reflected in the mirror. As though she were a spectator, she watched the woman in the mirror wrap a black cape around herself and place a black bonnet over the prayer cap.

In the silence of the night, Hannah had washed and ironed these garments for herself and had sorted through her son's clothing until she found a blue shirt and dark jeans. He would not be dressed exactly like the other boys they would encounter, but it was the closest she could come. It would have to do.

Wearing them now, Joseph Abram Miller sat on his mother's bed and regarded her as she transformed herself from the mother he knew to this stranger, one of the funny people he saw from time to time in town or riding in horse-drawn buggies on the country roads.

His mother's silence and the stoniness of her face frightened him. He thought of the words she had spoken to him yesterday after she had motioned for him to come, not to the main house as usual, but to the little house where they used to live.

~ ~ ~

"Come, Joey, we're staying here, but only for tonight," she had said.

"Why? Then are we going back to Uncle Abe's?" He hefted his book bag to his back and started up the walk to the little house with her.

"No. Come inside and I'll tell you where we're going."

Vaguely, he remembered the funeral of the little boy who had drowned and the strange people who were crowded into a big white house. His mother reminded him of that now.

"That little boy who died was my little brother, Joey, and I used to live in that white house with the family that lives there. They are your grandparents, but you've never met them. I left them to live here before you were born."

"Why? Didn't you like them?" He drank from the glass of milk she had poured for him.

"No, I mean, I loved them, but I had to leave because they wanted me to marry someone I didn't want to marry."

"Who did they want you to marry?"

"Your father."

He ignored the plate with two cookies she pushed toward him. "But . . . you said he didn't want us . . . ."

"I'm sorry I didn't tell you the truth, Joey. He did want us. It was me who didn't want him. Your father lives in the Amish settlement. He is one of them. I was . . . am . . . one of them, too, but I didn't love him. I didn't want to marry him." She stared past him and out a window as if she could see all the way to the Amish farms . . . and his father.

"Are we going to live with him now?"

His mother sighed. "I don't know. First we'll go to your grandparents' house. We'll ask them if they will let us stay with them for a while. The whole community . . . all the Amish people . . . and the bishop . . . will have to decide."

Joey began to cry. "But what about my school? And my friends?"

His mother hugged him to her. "If they let us stay, you'll go to a new school, Joey, and you'll make lots of new friends."

Joey put his head on his arms and sobbed. "I want to stay here."

She placed her fingers under his chin, lifted his face and kissed his cheeks. "We can't stay, Joey. It is time for us to go."

"But Uncle Abe . . . *he* won't want us to go. Aunt Sandra was glad to see me. She won't want me to go either. And Israel will miss me . . . ."

"No, Joey, Uncle Abe *does* want us to go. Now that Aunt Sandra is back, he wants to live with just her . . . and Israel . . . ." Joey heard her voice tremble, and he thought she would cry, too, and change her mind about going. But she didn't. She said, "They want to live alone as a family now, and we have to let them do that. They have been very good to us."

~ ~ ~

He cried again when his mother told him he could choose only one toy to take with him, something small that would fit in his pocket. Wiping his tears with the back of his hand, he finally selected his favorite Matchbox toy, the bright red tractor with black rubber tires, the one that looked just like the one Uncle Abe, holding him on his lap, had let him steer.

"Wear your hiking boots, Joey. Your Nikes will have to be left behind," his mother said, holding out the boots Uncle Abe called "clod-hoppers."

He didn't ask why. He understood that she was trying to make him look like the kids he saw walking along the road. In the summer they were always barefoot, but soon it would be too cold for that.

He held his Matchbox tractor tightly in his hand as he waited for his mother who took nothing with her except the funny costume that she wore. He saw her lay her car keys on the kitchen table. She said that they would go on foot.

Holding hands, they paused on the small porch of the little house, and neither of them spoke as they looked at the big white house which was silent in the early morning grayness.